Weeper

GREG MORGAN

ISBN: 978-1-7349657-0-4 (paperback)

www.greg-morgan.com

For Jeanne,
who has lovingly and tirelessly
supported all my artistic endeavors,
especially the writer's life of solitude

"You been my momma, my sista, my friend, alls.
You been it alls. You're my kin. I love ya…"

PROLOGUE
1848
Allegheny Mountains, Pennsylvania
Augustus

Life is eternal and love is immortal,
and death is only a horizon,
and a horizon is nothing save the limit of our sight.

He knew her as "The Weeper," a paid mourner. She was sitting away from the others, her face cloistered under a darkened veil. He couldn't stop himself from approaching her, until a huge, black man almost three times his height stepped in front of him, blocking his path. The giant of a man moved away, waved off with the slightest, most graceful gesture of her left hand. Standing before her, the only parts of his body that could move were his eyes as they examined the veiled creature intently. Without the fear that would typically overwhelm him, his arms moved up. His small, six-year-old fingers slowly lifted her veil, and his bright eyes peeked under. Puffy eyes. Red nose. Tears streaming down smooth cheeks. He was mesmerized by her slate-gray eyes as they looked tenderly into his own. "Hello, sweet boy," her lips whispered with slight hoarseness from crying. Her voice was also calm and gentle, like a good storyteller reading a bedtime tale. The corners of her mouth raised to a small smile, a contrast to the tears falling down her cheeks. Her emotions moved him. So beautiful, but so sad. *Is the remembrance for somebody she loved?*

A tear formed and rolled down his cheek. She wiped it away with her thumb.

"They that sow in tears shall reap in joy." The small smile rose again, brightening her face. "I remember well the day of your birth, Augustus."

"You do?" Augustus asked.

It was then that his brother, Jefferson, pulled him away from her, and her veil fell like a curtain. Although Augustus didn't know it yet, these were the first words he had ever spoken to his birth mother, and he would not uncover this secret for another eighteen years.

CHAPTER I
Seven Years Earlier
1841
Mr. True

One short sleep past, we wake eternally,
And death shall be no more

HE RODE ON a brown horse stained black. His business demanded a black horse, but he also thought the black went better with his clothes; a black stovepipe hat and its long, black, crape streamers that flowed behind it. He complemented his look with a black overcoat that he'd wear even on sweltering days, along with black slacks and boots. He was tall and slim with dark, straight hair, although it could barely be seen under the hat he always wore. His eyes were big, round, and brown under dark eyebrows. And, as always, he was clean-shaven and smelled of pine sap. He took pride in his appearance, and his black-stained horse added to it.

Mr. True believed it to be *her* wagon ahead of him, and his horse's pace was catching up slowly. Yes, it indeed was "The Missus." He thought of slowing down so as not to pass her—passing her would be rude. But he didn't slow down. Micah, the Fenn family slave, or so Mr. True thought, walked in front, leading the buggy's mule. As he heard the hoofbeats behind him, Micah turned and peered around the mule to see who it was. Upon seeing Mr. True's familiar face, he smiled, nodded, and returned his attention to the road.

They called her "The Missus" for no other reason than that's simply what her mother and her mother's mother were called before her. "The Missus" was the name laid upon all of the women in the Fenn family because none of the local folk knew their real names. They usually didn't even know if one of the Fenns passed on or if a child was born. The title "The Missus" seemed to come from a place of respect: all the women born into the Fenn family were weepers. Weepers were given the respect of a preacher or a nun, and if it weren't for that respect, the Fenns would not have any. They were a good distance closer to poor than rich, and aside from selling a few pigs or some extra vegetables now and then, weeper's income was the only income they had.

Mr. True and The Missus knew each other but had never been formally introduced. Mr. True was in a similar line of business to The Missus; he was a warner. Like a funeral director, a warner attended to almost every aspect of a loved one's burial. Mr. True's father and grandfather had also been in that profession. It was probably due to this professional proximity that he and The Missus had never officially met; they just assumed each knew who the other was. As for Mr. True, he didn't know if the current Missus was the daughter, mother, grandmother, or granddaughter. She was always veiled and always, like him, wore black. He assumed she was the woman his father had always dealt with.

Weeping had always been the main trade for the Fenn family. If an outside man married a Fenn, he should expect her to continue her trade and keep the Fenn surname—that would always be discussed before the wedding was arranged. The only thing that would stop a weeper from weeping was pregnancy. A pregnant woman was a bad omen at funerals, not just for the family of the deceased, but the pregnant woman herself.

Although the weepers didn't believe this myth themselves, it was a common notion, and the weepers abided by it. If there were pregnancy or sickness, a sister, mother, or any of the other previous weepers would come out of retirement to take over the duty.

Mr. True rode alongside her and kept pace. "Mornin'," he said to The Missus.

"Good morning, Mr. True," came a youthful voice from under the veil. It wasn't the older, raspy one he had been used to. The soft sunlight filtered through the canopy of trees covering the dirt road. One soft beam of light came through her veil and just touched her chin, but that was all he could make out.

"Fine morning," he said. It was all he could think of saying. He was curious. He wanted to see more, hear more. Mr. True looked over to Micah as he led their mule. Micah was as dark as he was big, so dark it would be hard to see his expression in the dim, light-filtered road. His salt and pepper hair had a two-inch bald patch in the center. He turned to Mr. True as if he felt his eyes on him. Mr. True sharply turned away. Micah was very protective of The Missus, and the Missus was very protective of Micah.

"Fine day for a remembrance," The Missus replied. Mr. True was a little nervous, but he wanted the conversation to continue.

"You must be the daughter of the last Missus."

"We're all daughters of the last Missus," she replied with an unseen grin.

Mr. True also smiled. "Suppose that's true." He again tried to see through her veil, wanting at least a glimpse of what was beneath. "It was your voice that gave you away," he said. "I musta been workin' with your ma before this."

"I've been with you at the last two remembrances. This is my third after taking over from my momma."

All weepers learned the trade starting at age four. Fenn girls practiced with dead birds or squirrels, burying them as well. Sixteen would be the earliest a daughter could take over for their mother, but Charlotte was not as enthusiastic as her predecessors at that age. She wasn't that enthusiastic now.

"I took over for my pa about ten years ago now. I spoke to the last weeper a few times…"

"My momma."

"Suppose. No one really knows which one of ya it was."

She giggled. "I've heard whispers of how we never die and that I'm a hundred and eighty years old."

Mr. True let out a small laugh. "Yep. Heard that many times."

"I don't know why. It's tiring. You'd think they'd know; they see us at market or in town on occasion."

"But y'all are never at church."

"You know we go to the same church y'all do every Sunday. Preacher Dunn. Yep, we just don't use the same church service y'all do. We come later in the afternoon."

"Why's that?" asked Mr. True.

"Preacher Dunn likes it that way 'cause of the foolish

rumor of us all being black widows and all. I was told it used to cause a big commotion when we would show up."

"Yep. I heard that too."

"And might you be thinking it too?"

"Oh, me? No."

"Well, my Pa and my Grandpa passed on before I was born but died same as any other fella. No different. And my uncles and brother? They all moved on. When Fenn boys marry, they tend to move on with their wife's family."

"I remember a couple of your uncles moving on down to Johnstown."

"All the Fenn boys do. Who would want to be living with a gaggle of weepers?"

"I would," said Micah.

The Missus rolled her eyes, facing the back of Micah's head. "Anyway, it's all them rumors. You know what folk say about us, Mr. True. That ain't no secret. If it were up to me, I'd be in church with y'all, but it ain't up to me. I guess it's the way it's always been done."

Mr. True nodded and adjusted his hat. "Better be gettin' on. Nice talking to ya. Good day."

"Good day, Mr. True."

It was the most he'd ever spoken to any Missus. But this one intrigued him, and the desire to see beneath her veil grew with every step his horse took away from her.

CHAPTER 2

The Missus

Your love will light our way

IT HAD BEEN two weeks and a day since The Missus had seen Mr. True last. It was eight in the morning, and Mr. True was already at work in the home of Mrs. Josephine Tait, a mother of six and grandmother of fourteen. Mrs. Josephine was the one in the casket, and this was her wake. She had died not so unexpectedly at the age of eighty-eight.

Mr. True was at the front door with Mrs. Tait's grandson, Able. They were standing in front of a carved oak side panel to the left of the door.

"Now, pulling the pin right here and from the bottom will open this panel," said Mr. True as he swung it open, making the doorway half again as large. "Now a large casket and all the pallbearers can easily make it through."

"How'd ya know that, Mr. True?" asked Able.

"Don't ya remember your grandpa's funeral? We did it then, too."

"Nah, I don't recall. I was grieving deep for that one."

"Yessir, your grandpap was a good one. He thought ahead

for things like this. I got 'em myself in my home. See, your grandpa and my pa helped build each other's homes."

"I still miss him. But I'm also happy they's both up there together now, having a grand old-time square dancing in the clouds."

"I'm certain they are."

Mr. True turned as he heard The Missus riding up in her buggy with Micah pulling the mule along.

"Excuse me," said Mr. True as he walked back into the parlor room and over to the open casket.

Micah helped The Missus down and took her chair out of the back of the wagon before walking toward the home. Mr. True stood at the casket and was adjusting Mrs. Josephine's collar just as they entered the room. The Missus could see his peripheral glances to her as she surveyed the room for a place to set her chair down. She needed to do her weeping and be on display as much as the casket was—it was important she be clearly seen. She nodded to a spot close to the left side of the casket but slightly askew to the chairs set out for the mourners.

Micah set the chair down, turning and nodding to Mr. True after he did. She sat down and turned her head away, but her eyes stayed on him under the veil. His eye continued to land on her as he dusted a dustless casket with his handkerchief. Mr. True looked down at Mrs. Josephine, nodding to her before turning and leaving.

Did he just thank her for something? she thought.

Mr. True then walked about the room, covering the mirrors with black linen and closing the drapes, something The Missus thought he should have done long before she arrived. With the house becoming dark, he then went about lighting each of the many candles the family had placed around the room.

At the other remembrances they worked together, he usually finished with all those chores prior to her arrival. It was important to do so, as they were widely-held superstitions. The Missus also abided by these details, although she thought most of them absurd. If seeing oneself in a mirror or having sunlight touch one's face at a funeral meant they'd be death's next victim. If this was actually true, she'd have died long ago. She wondered if Mr. True also believed in these foolish things or just abided by them like she did.

Finishing his duties, he walked to the corner of the room to survey his work before walking out the door.

"Come here, boy."

The Missus could hear him just outside.

"Hey, boy, what's your name?"

She could hear him pat a panting dog.

"Good, boy. Good boy. Let me see that."

What she heard pleased her, but the veil hid her smile.

"Abel, Abel, this your hound? What's his name?"

"Tanner," she heard Able say.

"Tanner's gotta bad tooth. Ya gotta pull it. It's bothering him."

The Missus felt a giggle coming on, but mourners started filtering in. She sucked it up and tried to concentrate on Mrs. Tait, but thoughts of Mr. True were difficult to detach from her mind.

The Missus had never wanted to weep. Her mother and grandmother took pride in being a Fenn weeper, but she never saw why. When she was young, her mother would force her to practice weeping, like forcing a child to do their dreaded homework. She thought weeping was a self-exiling existence, like joining a convent for life. As a child, she continually sought out friends, to little success. Later, she had minimal contact with boys outside of her relatives. Mr. True provided the first decent conversation from any man that wasn't family.

The Missus was twenty-five years old and wasn't married, never had been, and her mother had given her a Christian name at birth: Charlotte. Of course, only her family called her by that name. She possessed a long black mane with slate-gray eyes—a witch-like combination, some of the local folk whispered. Due to her profession, however, there were very few suitors for her. Weepers were never invited to socials, and the festivities at any funeral she attended typically ended as soon as she arrived. It was for that reason that she arrived at the specific time and place she was asked to arrive.

Those in the death business were an undesired necessity. They would be called upon for a family's sad times but never called upon for anything else. A weeper was a profession for outcasts, and they had no dowry to speak of. But the Fenn women did have one thing going for them, and it was a big thing: their beauty. However, their beauty rarely could be seen. Weepers always came to funerals wearing the same dark clothes and dark veil.

The Missus believed she was prettier than most. When she would go to town, she'd be unveiled and wearing her regular clothes. Men in town would notice her as she walked about, and it made her feel beautiful and unique. She thought some of them were very handsome, but none ever approached her or spoke to her. Her mother and grandmother had both found someone. They'd fallen in love. Hadn't they? How did men approach them? Why would a married man like Mr. True be interested in her? Maybe that was all there was, an interest. To act on it was another matter entirely. The Missus wondered about Mr. True, what his home looked like, and how many animals he had. She also wondered about his wife.

Late in the evening, after everyone else had gone home, The Missus and Micah were escorted out by Abel. The Missus climbed up onto the buggy and lying on her seat were two black gloves—the same gloves handed out to the mourners as gifts from the family. Had her mother ever received a gift from the warner?

"HOW LONG HAVE the Trues been warning?" The Missus asked her mother. She didn't care about the answer. It was just a segue into other questions she really wanted to ask. Issie was her mother's name, short for Isadora. She had retired as a weeper after twenty years. Now she tended to the farm and took care of her house and her own mother.

"Trues have been warning for longer than I can remember. Long as we've been weeping, I 'spect."

"Did you work with old Mr. True?" It was another answer she didn't care about.

"Yes. Both. Worked with the boy just the last eight to ten years or so. Grandma worked with old, old True."

"Is it a big family? They all still married?"

"The True before this new one is still married, I think. Don't rightly know about the young one. Oh! Yes, that boy is married. Archer, I believe his name is."

"He ain't young, Momma. He's thirty-five if a day."

"Young to me. Anyway, he came around once to fix the chickens when they got the fowl pox."

"Fix the chickens?"

"They say he's got a gift with the creatures. Knows how to fix 'em up. Everyone up here now is using him for their sickly creatures. It puts some extra coin in his pocket. Funny thing about that boy's wife; the day of their wedding was the first day they'd met. Turns out her father and old Mr. True made a gentleman's wager that set those two together," said Issie with a laugh. "Poker game, I believe."

"They abided by it?"

"Course they did. They do as they're told."

"I wouldn't."

Issie let out a big sigh. "Well, they heed their parents. Now from what I'm told, she come from wealthy folk that got more than they can say grace over. She grew up having everything done for her. I also heard she could start a fight in an empty house, and the True boy surely wasn't used to having a woman tell him what to do. He loaded the wrong wagon with that one, he did." Issie burst into a laugh.

"They have any children?"

"I don't remember. Why are you so interested in them?"

"Curious is all. The warner ever leave warning gloves for ya?"

Issie's eyes opened. "Oh, now. Did he give you a pair?"

"Yessum. Left 'em on my buggy seat."

Concern appeared on Issie's face. "You watch yourself, Charlotte. He might be wanting to hitch ya without churchin' ya."

CHAPTER 3

Mr. True

Those who seek me with all their heart shall find me where they least expect

EVERY JUNE, IN this part of the Alleghenies, the fog tended to settle in early mornings and burn off by about one o'clock. It was very annoying weather for most, as one would dress for the cold in the mornings but would end up too warm in the hot afternoons. Today was one of those cold mornings. Mr. True sat on the edge of the road waiting for The Missus. As his horse's warm breath billowed from its nostrils, Mr. True drew in the dirt with a twig.

It had been three weeks since he'd seen her last, and three weeks of living with the constant thought of her. There were only two roads The Missus could take to get to the O'Flannerys' home, and he was hoping this was the road Micah had chosen to take her down. After wiping out his fifteenth or sixteenth time of spelling M, I, S, S, U, S in the dirt, he heard the distant creaking of buggy wheels intermingled with a mule clip-clopping. Mr. True stood up and climbed the small embankment for a better view. The mule appeared over the rise in the distance with Micah pulling it along.

Mr. True made a clicking noise with his tongue, and his

horse slowly trotted over to him. He mounted it, straightened his jacket, adjusted the streamers coming off his stovepipe hat, and waited for the buggy.

"Fine morning to you, Missus."

"And to you, Mr. True, although it is a bit damp."

"Should warm up a bit later on."

Mr. True turned his horse and followed alongside the buggy. From the corner of his eye, he could see that she was wearing the black gloves he left for her at the last wake.

"Know anything about Mr. O'Flannery?" he asked.

"I do," she said. "I believe I know a bit about him. What would you like to know?"

"Oh nothin'," he said, flustered. "Of course, you'd know. I know you ask the family and alls. What I meant to say is: you heard anything of interest about him?"

"Seemed like a likable fella. Four children, three boys, one girl. One boy died at the age of eight. He was married at seventeen to his wife, Annabel. His kin came from Northern Maine. His grandpa was a congressman…"

"How'd you know all them things?"

She looked to the sky and rolled her eyes. "Cause all us weepers do our learning before, you know that. Talk to the kin or any ol' person that'll tell us something. We read anything they got that tells us something. Ponder on any rendering or daguerreotype…"

"You do all that? I mean, I knew you talked to the kin…"

"Every soul. I pretty much know their whole life story before the remembrance. When you see me sitting there, I'm pondering on it, that's for sure. Weeping for those that don't wanna." The Missus turned to the trees with a smirk.

"I'd rather be doing other things; you can believe that." Micah quickly turned to her with a disappointed expression.

"You don't like weepin'?" asked Mr. True.

"She likes it fine," said Micah, turning back to the road.

"Hush, Micah. I can have my own thoughts on the matter." The Missus turned back to Mr. True. "Would you want a stranger weepin' on ya? Someone ya don't know? I wouldn't."

"It gives ya a living. Puts food on your table."

"Certainly, it does. And I do what I do for my kin, cause it's what I'm supposed to do, so I do it," she said as she bobbed her head like an angry child.

"Well, I'll be. A weeper who don't like weepin'."

Micah stopped the mule and glared up to Mr. True on his horse.

"If ya please pardon my words, sah. But it'd be a might kind if ya don't be telling none of what she say to anybody now…"

"Now you hush up, Micah," she interrupted.

Mr. True's surprised expression didn't stop Micah. "I'm trying my best to teach the youngin'."

Micah pulled the mule on. Mr. True raised a brow, not sure how to respond, if at all. His eyes went to the trees, seeing a bit of blue sky peeking through the fog.

"Well, what I meant to say about O'Flannery was if you'd heard, ya know, that he killed his self and all?"

She turned away. "Those matters don't concern me; they concern you and the preacher."

He turned to her, making sure he hadn't offended, but the veil made his efforts futile. "No ma'am, it don't concern me neither. Don't bother me none. I just bury 'em where they tells me to bury 'em. But I did speak to the preacher on behalf of the family…"

"Who's that? Pastor Trillbee? Met him when I spoke to the family."

"Yessum. Well, the pastor said the family told him that it was a hunting accident, and Mr. O'Flannery still hunted birds in the off-season, and that's why he brought out his scattergun to the shed behind their house. Then the pastor told 'em true that O'Flannery done himself in, that's for sure. It wasn't pheasant, turkey, or even grouse season, says the pastor. Now, I go on saying that I still bring out my scattergun every now and then during the off-season."

"What did he say?"

"He looked at me like I was two sandwiches short of a picnic, he did. Then he said their story was as crooked as a dog's hind leg and that he won't be taken for a fool. O'Flannery is a sinner and won't be buried in his cemetery."

"I personally been weeping for a few little ones born and died out of wedlock and buried up there. I'm sure you can find a spot, Mr. True."

"Already did. The old picket fence fell down on one side. Just gonna bury him there. The family is gonna kindly fix the fence right after burying him; the preacher won't even know about it."

A giggle came from the veil. "Very good, Mr. True."

Tall pines trees shaded the moss and fern covered headstones. Ten people stood about the freshly dug grave as Mr. True and The Missus arrived. Trillbee's sermon about the sin of suicide must have had an effect on those who considered attending.

The O'Flannerys used Mr. True's services to acquire a

preacher from another town, one who did not know the circumstances of the death. He walked over to greet the pastor as Micah brought over The Missus' handmade wicker chair and placed it in a spot some distance away from the other mourners. He went to go back to retrieve her. He had seen the chair up close once; unique engravings of flying angels carved by a loving hand covered the back. Micah helped her down from the buggy. *Almost like a princess or a queen,* he thought.

Mr. True sat upon a boulder when most of his work was done. The stone was cool, and he rubbed his hands against it. He looked over to The Missus sitting in her chair; she was motionless except for the slight bobbing of her head and light heaving of her chest.

After the funeral was over, Mr. True gave his condolences to all the mourners as they left and watched them drive off down the dirt road in their carriages and wagons. All that was left was himself, The Missus, Micah, and the gravedigger. She sat quietly in her chair, her veiled head moving about, hands on her lap. Watching her reminded him of a bored child in Sunday school. Mr. True took a step towards her, and then another and another until he was a few feet from her, but Micah appeared from behind a tree and moved quick as spit to cut him off. "May I help you, sah?" Micah asked.

Mr. True was a bit startled. "I'm just going over to speak to The Missus."

"She ain't quite ready fo' that, sah," replied Micah with his deep voice. "She's still gotsta finish up." Mr. True studied the massive man before nodding and returned to his boulder.

It was closing upon an hour of sitting on the stone before The Missus motioned for Micah. Micah went to her and helped her rise. Mr. True saw her whisper in his ear; Micah's head turned toward him. She went to her buggy, and Micah walked to him.

"It be time to eat some lunch now, sah. We have nuff for ya if ya wish."

Mr. True typically would have left the funeral at the same time as the other mourners, and he never waited around for The Missus to leave. He had always thought that she just waited until everyone else left to leave herself. He walked over to her as she gathered things from the buggy.

"We have some apples and potato pancakes," she said. "What do you say we eat over there in that clearing? It is the only place with a few solid rays of sunshine."

"Fine by me," Mr. True said.

Micah laid out a large blanket, and The Missus brought over the basket of food and sat down. "We should have enough for all of us. We all might have to be eating a little less as I was just thinking about Micah and me when I packed it."

It was then that, out of the corner of his eye, he saw her take off her veil. The feeling was similar to the first time a boy spies a woman's breast, and it had the same reward. She turned her face to him and smiled. Her slate-gray eyes riveted him, and her hair was as dark and shiny as a crow's wing.

She looked away. "You ain't never seen me with my veil off, have you?"

"No, I ain't," he said as he studied her. She pulled the crust off her bread with her delicate fingers. "And it's a shame for me I haven't," he caught himself saying. Her eyes darted to him, then away. He feared he might have embarrassed her until he spied the small grin on her lips.

The breeze blew wisps of her hair across her forehead as they ate their meal. A few dark clouds passed by, taking with them the few beams of sunshine that had been peeking through the last of the fog.

The Missus glanced over to him. "Take off your hat." His hand whipped it off as fast as he'd swat a mosquito. Her lips curled to a smile as his black bangs flopped down in front of his eyes. He wiped them back self-consciously and smoothed his greasy straight hair. He hadn't washed it for a week and a half.

"You got black hair like your pa did," she said.

"You knew my Pa?"

"I was just a girl when I met him. Or should I say saw him. That hat of yours is hard to forget. It must be nice to be a warner. You get to travel a bit, see a lot of country. I'd sure like to be doing that. I'd like to see a lot more country, meet new people."

"It's agreeable. Besides warning, I do some animal doctoring, and that gets me around a bit."

"Yes, you helped us out with…"

"The fowl pox. I remember. It's them mosquitos they get it from."

"You like doing that? Doctoring animals?"

"I do. Did it since a boy."

Her eyes smiled at him. "A grown man helping the suffering of creatures."

"Sure, I do. But the creatures is valuable too. If ya got sickness running through fifteen head of cattle, that'll cost ya a fortune."

"I suppose. I just thought it was nice that ya ease their suffering," she said as she popped a cherry in her mouth and yanked at the stem.

"What about you? Why don't ya like weepin'?"

"I'm supposed to like it; I'm a Fenn." Her eyes turned to the sky.

"But ya don't?"

"My Momma, she talks about it all the time with my grandma. They'd say things like it'd take 'em three of four days to recover from a remembrance. That don't happen to me."

"Recover?"

"Yes. Well, ya see, we do all that studying on the person's life and all. By the time they do all that and the weepin' at the remembrance, they come home and feel like one of their own kin is gone. It takes 'em three or four days to see it ain't. That ain't me."

"They truly do feel that strongly? I never knew."

"Oh, yes. My momma told me it'd be her aim to not only weep for the dead but to make the kin feel poorly for not weepin'."

"But ya don't feel like your momma does?"

"I try, but… I don't know if I got the same blood as them. Someday, I just want to get on out of here. The only people I get to speakin' to are my family and Micah over there." She nodded at Micah, who was walking over. Mr. True followed her eyes to Micah, staring at him as he approached. It forced Mr. True to look away.

"It's about time to get on outta here," said Micah. "Feels like it gonna rain."

"Rain? It's gonna be hot today." Just as Mr. True said that a drop of rain fell on his nose. The Missus rose from the blanket with Mr. True. "They's large drops at that."

The rain began pelting her face and soaking her hair. "I love the rain. Each drop is a little kiss from our Lord, and look at how it makes the grass shine where the sunlight hits it," she said as they walked to her buggy.

"Mighty kind of ya to invite me for supper—I mean lunch, Missus."

She stopped as her eyes met his. "My pleasure, Mr. True."

They loaded up and started down the road with Mr. True on his horse, riding next to them. The large drops soon turned to deafening sheets. All three were drenched but remained stoic as if it were a blue-sky day. Reaching the crossroads, Mr. True turned his wet face to them and stopped.

"My way is this aways!" Mr. True yelled over the rain as he took off his hat. It pelted his greasy hair.

The Missus lingered in silence, appearing as comfortable in the rain as in the sun. Her grey eyes pierced him as a polite smile curled on her lips.

"Please give my regards to your wife." His left eye twitched, and he looked to the ground as Micah pulled away. Mr. True couldn't veer his gaze from the spot she had just been. The rain was now so loud he couldn't hear the buggy, and it had only gone twenty feet from him. After a few moments, his horse shifted on the muddy road. He tilted his head back and opened his mouth to the rain, swallowing as his eyes followed the muddy buggy tracks down the road. The buggy was a small dot in the distance by then. When it was entirely out of sight, he put his hat back on and turned his horse to follow wherever the tracks would lead him.

THE TRACKS WERE barely visible by the time Mr. True reached the Fenn farm. Daylight had faded, and the rain had slowed to a sprinkle as he dismounted his horse and tied it to a tree. The Fenns lived in a five-room log home located on a lonely, wooded forty acres. There were three other smaller cabins located on the property, all occupied and vacated at some time or another as the family grew and shrank through the years.

He slowly approached, looking for lights in the windows. Stopping behind a tree, he surveyed the buildings in front of him. Although Mr. True shivered with cold and fear, he blessed the weather that kept the dogs in the barn and out of the rain. There was also no moonlight to give him away. His heartbeat pounded in his ears; his legs moved without his permission toward the main house. He carefully avoided the other cabins, although he could see no light coming from them.

What am I thinking?

As he climbed the two steps to the front door, he could see light coming from under it. Something in the house was calling him like a siren's song. He stood before the old wood door, both drenched to the bone and sweating more than a whore in church.

He had been with other women before. He'd regularly stop into houses of ill repute and ante up for a lady of the evening, but he always paid for their services. He had never been with someone he had known personally, nor had ever desired to. With the others, he was simply ridding himself of a sinful desire, even convincing himself it was a form of absolution. He hadn't cared for any of those women, just used them.

But he wanted more from The Missus. This was not ridding himself of sin, but rather just the opposite.

His shaking hand reached for the doorknob.

Should I try the back door?

Before he knew it, he was in and shutting the door behind him. He stood there, frozen like a drowned cat, directly in front of Grandma Fenn. Her head was back, mouth open, snoring.

As quietly as he could, he tiptoed past her into the small hallway. He stopped at the first door on the left and opened it, stepping inside. His leg hit the bed, and he bent down to view the face, sleeping in the darkened room. A lucky guess—it was The Missus. Mr. True backed up from the bed. His heart raced, blood turning to fire. The reality of the situation now dawned on him.

What in the Holy Ghost am I doing here?

He turned to leave, then turned back to her. His pupils grew so wide open a rat could crawl in. They absorbed every speck of light the room had. He turned to leave again, then again back to her. The siren's song was screaming in his ears.

His wet clothes dropped to the ground in wet plops. Sitting on the edge of the bed, his boots, then pants came off. Gently he lifted the blankets and crawled into the bed next to her.

CHAPTER 4
The Missus

He lies here finding sanctuary by
the whispering shady trees

THE MISSUS FACED away as she felt him crawl in; the scent of pine sap told her who it was. Her eyes were wide, and her mouth open in shock. She feigned sleep, trying not to move, but her chest rocked with the pounding of her heart. She waited, but nothing happened. She wanted to turn and see.

Her mind raced. *Is he still back there?*

She moved her hand behind her and touched skin.

This is wrong. This is so wrong!

He was lying on his back, arms to his side. Only the back of her slender fingers moved against it, then slid up his side and down again. She yanked her hand back when she felt him flip to his side behind her.

She let out a gasp when his fingers took their turn, reaching around and taking hold of her breast. He kneaded it through her nightshirt. She closed her eyes, her breathing growing deeper, drawing in his scent. Goosebumps covered her skin as her morals became an unimportant shadow, pushed to the far corner of her mind. This moment was the only thing that mattered.

His hands went to her nightshirt buttons. From the top down, one by one, they revealed her skin to his calloused fingers until they introduced themselves between her legs. The Missus rolled to her back. He was staring into her eyes. Even in the dark, she saw his pupils as large as a cat's, ready to pounce—and he did just that.

His movements grew faster and faster until he promptly stopped with a gasp. He lifted away from her, looking down upon her and almost completely through her. His eyes were like a demon with black doll's eyes as wide as a full moon.

Is that still him?

He slowly rolled off and stared at the ceiling next to her. After a muted moment, Mr. True threw his legs out of bed and began putting on his wet clothes. Without one word, he left, shutting the door behind him. She heard him run off through the wet mud.

Rising, The Missus put her bedclothes back on and turned up her lantern. She uncovered the bed sheets for the bloodstain she knew would be there. She took the cloth and ripped it in half, throwing the good side in the corner of the room. The soiled side was brought into the living room and tossed into the fire.

The "poof" and "hiss" from the fire woke Grandma Fenn. "I told you never to be waking me up. Now I'll never get back to sleep!" Grandma said. The Missus stood there with a smirk, watching her grandma's head as it fell back against the rocking chair. Her mouth dropped open, and the snoring bellowed out again.

HER FOOT TAPPED nervously on the buggy's floorboards. The Missus and Micah were on their way to a funeral where she knew she'd see him. It had only been four days since that night. *How would he act, how would I? Maybe he'd attempt a secret kiss or a subtle touch on the back of my neck. If I can hide from Micah, maybe he'll follow.*

Arriving before most of the mourners, she saw him and began to shiver. Mr. True walked up to her, his hand up in a 'hello.' "Morning to ya, Missus." And he walked off.

What? Mr. True acted no differently than he ever did. It was like it had never happened.

She sat in her chair near the coffin and pretended to weep, but she was really thinking about him. He was finished with her. He used her. She had let herself be used, and it hurt. Tears began to form under the veil, where she wanted them to stay. She thanked them for showing up in her time of need, and they came willingly like good friends. Her sobs joined in, a little louder than usual, as she cried for more than just the deceased.

The memory of that night haunted her, rolling around her mind, not allowing her sleep—at least until he crawled through her window a week later. It surprised her that neither Micah, nor the dogs, nor her mother or grandmother, had caught him sneaking in. He pulled himself up and in, but tripped on the ledge, falling to the floor. Rising, their eyes locked on each other. She had thought she would make him pay for the pain of the last few days, and never see him again. That thought was tossed as quickly as he tossed his shirt.

She lifted her chin. "This is the last time you come here. Is that understood?"

He turned and sat on the bed, pulling off his boot. "Don't know if I can abide by that, Missus. I'm so fixed on ya." His back was sinewy muscle divided by the vertebrae of his bony spine. "You is all I think about. I can't relieve my mind from ya."

If he had turned around, he would have seen her blushed cheeks and knowing grin. That was why she wanted him. It was his intense desire for her that she craved. As an untouchable weeper, she had always wanted attention from men. Mr. True was the only one that had acted on it. Her hand reached out to him, and she ran her fingers down the bumps on his back.

"No. I meant this is the last time you come here. We gotta meet somewheres else. The lake."

He pulled off his second boot and nodded his head. "Every other Tuesday good with you?"

She pulled up her nightshirt. *Every day would be best for me*, she thought.

THE BOULDER WAS twenty feet high and forty across of smooth granite. The side facing the lake was cleaved off like half a loaf of bread. The Missus stood atop the boulder, peering down at Mr. True who was swimming naked in the clear emerald water.

"Jump in." Mr. True's voice echoed up the rock face. Without hesitation, The Missus dropped all her clothes and jumped in, feet first. She broke the surface with a gasp from the frigid water. "You'll get used to it," said Mr. True.

"It gets colder every time we come."

"Snowpack runoff, I'm sure."

The pair swam and dove in the water so deep they could never touch the rock-covered bottom. They eventually got out and took the path back to the top. Both lay on their backs, naked on the sun-warmed stone.

"Ya never talk to me when we're at remembrances," she said.

"Sure I do."

"I mean, ya never talk to me about us." Mr. True rolled to his stomach, putting his chin on his hands.

She tilted her head to him and shaded her eyes from the sun. "Well?"

"Well, what?"

"Why don't ya talk to me about us?"

"There's folks around. How am…"

"We have lunch together. We're alone then."

"Missus, I don't know what ya want me to say."

She studied his face for the answer he hid. For the three months they had been coming to the lake, she had hoped he would broach the subject of their union. "Charlotte. My name's Charlotte. Other folk call me The Missus. I need you to call me Charlotte."

His eyes stared into hers before a grin popped up, and he broke into song, "*Young Charlotte lived by the mountainside, In a lonely, dreary spot; No other dwelling for three miles round, Except her father's cot…*"

She smirked. "Please stop."

"*…Her hair was black as raven's wings, Her skin was lily fair, And her teeth were like the pearls of white, None with her compared.*"

She sat up, pulling her knees to her chest. His bangs, still wet, draped across one eye. She moved them to the side. "Why am I allowing a married man into my bed?" She knew he would never respond to the question in which she already held the answer: He had become her opium. On days like this, where they made love, swam, played in the lake, and baked their naked bodies in the warm sun. She would breathe him in, filling her lungs with him. Letting her euphoric mind go to places where city women existed, women with regular lives that had tea with friends, went wedding dress shopping, wore jewelry, and had family gatherings in the park. She could see their children, their home, their new life. Daniel, Claire, and Augustus; those would be their children's names.

He smiled up at her as she rolled his body to his back and climbed on top of him. She wanted to make love again and inhale him deeper than she ever had before.

AUTUMN TREES ENCIRCLED the lake all the way up to its edge on the far side. Gnarled roots larger than a man's arm submerged into its waters like water moccasins. The trees dropped their patchwork quilts of brightly hued leaves on the water's surface. They floated towards the center like little sailboats.

She stood on their boulder, watching the trout swim around and into the rock-formed caves below, occasionally attacking an intruding fallen leaf. She still felt nauseous from the walk to the lake and had to stop to vomit on the way. Whether it was from her pregnancy or the thought of having to tell him, she didn't know.

She turned to the woods behind her for any sign of him. He was late again. Her vanity created an addiction to him, and her addiction had created the life now growing inside her—the life that would destroy her life. Becoming pregnant had never crossed her mind.

A foolish notion that children only came with family; that getting hitched made them. I'm dumb as dirt!

He rode up on his black-stained horse with a pleased smile. It was a shame her words would wipe it off his face.

"*Her hair was black as raven's wings, Her skin was lily fair,*" he sang. His smile fell as he read her sadness. "What happened?" he asked as he put his hands on her slumped shoulders. His brow furrowed. "What is…" She moved in quick and kissed him on the lips. As she did it, she realized it was her first kiss. She had never kissed him before. His eyes opened wide in shock.

"I'm a married man," he said indignantly.

A puff of air came from her mouth, halfway between a laugh and a cough. Her eyes widened and flamed, almost turning him to ash. "What, in heaven's name, are you coming to me for then?" She pushed him back and turned back to the lake. "I ain't bleedin' no more, Mr. True."

Mr. True went entirely still, and his gaze drifted off to an unknown place.

She spun back to him. "Mr. True?

He absently dusted his jacket off.

"Mr. True?"

"How did it…"

"Oh, please, do not. You put a child in me."

Mr. True went to his knees. "What are ya going do?"

She laughed. "What are we gonna do, Mr. True?"

He walked to the edge of the boulder and watched the

trout. "I mean, there's this Injun woman. They say she makes up this concoction..."

"I won't be doing that."

"Well, then, I'm the wicked one. I'm the evil one. I'll just say I forced myself upon ya. And it'd be the truth. You never invited me in."

"They'll hang ya."

"Surely. They'll hang me, and that would be the end of it."

"I'm thinking, it'd be better if you used your head to think instead of putting a rope over it!"

"At least I'll die with a crooked smile to match my crooked neck."

"You're acting the fool, now, Mr. True."

He plopped on his rear; legs splayed open like a dropped rag doll. "No, I mean it. I think I'm in love with ya, Missus." She turned to him with disbelief. "It was worth it. If I get hanged, it don't matter. It was worth it."

"I'm real happy it was worth it for ya, Mr. True, but ya see, you're gonna be hanged, and I'm gonna have a child without a daddy." She knew she would be bearing a bastard child, and the community would shun her. She'd never work another funeral again. Her family would be scorned as well. They'd never hire a Fenn to weep again. No one would hire a whore with a bastard child. As for Mr. True, if his wife didn't shoot him right off, she was sure Mrs. True would simply divorce him as a philanderer. Just like her, he'd never get hired again, and he'd completely disgrace his family and all the warners before him.

"I'll think about what to do," said Mr. True as he walked back to his horse.

"They tried all within their power..."

Mr. True turned back to her. "What?"

"The song. The song you sing, Young Charlotte: *They tried all within their power. Her life for to restore, but Charlotte was a frozen corpse, and is never to speak more,*" she said with her arms crossed. "Charlotte dies at the end of the song."

"YOU WITH CHILD?" asked Micah as they were driving home from a remembrance.

She took a deep breath. "How'd ya know?"

He looked off to the woods away from her and shook his head. "Guard dogs? Them damn dogs ain't worth nothin'," he said to himself. He turned back to the road. "Ain't too difficult. Other's be seeing it soon too, I reckon."

"How do I tell my momma?"

"The warner's a married man, Missus. Your momma gonna be concerned."

Her head swiveled to him, eyes wide. "How'd you know it was him?"

"Who else it be? C'ept for a spirit."

She turned to her feet, tapping the buggy's floorboards. "I don't know what to do."

"You gonna have to stop weepin'; let your momma do it. I wouldn't be telling the warner, neither."

"Don't tell him? It's his child."

"What's he gonna do fo' ya? He's a married man. That'll cause more problems than ya got already."

"Too late. I already told him." The Missus turned to his

unblinking profile. Sweat gave his strong face a beautiful sheen. "You think less of me now, Micah?"

His gaze didn't change. "Life is a mystery. Who really knows right and wrong? I don't. Preacher says he do, but who he? I'll never think less of you, Missus. That never be me. Nope, I never think less of you."

The Missus turned away, hiding her tears. "Mr. True. He said he'd think on it and he hasn't said nothing. He didn't even bid me mornin' when I saw him."

"I'm sorry, Missus. I 'spect it may be time to tell your momma."

Micah was right. The problem won't go away like a cold or the flu. The baby was coming, and there was nothing she could do to stop it. It had to be dealt with, and the time was swiftly coming that she would have to tell her mother and grandmother. If suicide would stop them from facing dishonor, she would surely choose that option, but in this case, it wouldn't help anything.

It was after supper, and both her mother and grandmother were in front of the fire. Her mother was knitting a sweater, and her grandmother was darning a hem. She walked out to the parlor room and stood close to the fire. Her mother's eyes darted to her and then back to her work. An icy guilt covered her skin so cold that if someone touched her, they would stick. She moved closer to the fire, wanting to throw herself into it, burn off her skin, and rid herself of the shame. She had practiced it in shameful prayers to God every night, begging for redemption, but He didn't listen. God must have been a man.

She stared into the flames of the fire as it turned her grey eyes orange. "I'm with child." Both stopped their work, their eyes darting to her.

"What you say?" asked Grandma Fenn as she squinted her cataracted eyes for a better look.

Issie's eyes went back to her knitting as if she'd just been told the weather. "She said she's with child," said her mother, slip, next stitch purlwise. "Who's the daddy?"

The Missus had misjudged their reaction. The ranting and beating she expected wasn't happening.

When Issie was a young woman, she was known for having a pretty poor temper, but as age set in, she realized that many arguments were just not worth the effort. After losing her father young and then her husband (Charlotte's father), after only six years of marriage, she saw far past the trivial.

"I'd rather not say," The Missus said.

"No, suppose you don't have to tell me…"

"You better well tell her," said Grandma, shocked by the insolence. "Your ma should be beating the tar out of ya." Grandma began to cry. "Oh, my, my heart…"

Issie threw her knitting into her lap. "Now look what ya did. Couldn't you just have told *me* and waited 'til she fell asleep?" Issie shook her head.

"She'd find out soon enough," said The Missus defiantly.

"I's gotta get to bed. I heard enough," said Grandma as she started to get up. Issie rose to help her out of her chair and then to bed. After a moment, her mother came back and again sat down.

"Was it Micah?"

"Course, it wasn't Micah, Momma!"

"Well, who was it then? He's one of the few men you have the chance to see."

"Mr. True," said The Missus.

Issie cocked her head, her mouth agape. "The warner?"

The Missus nodded affirmatively. "I'm sorry, Momma."

"Don't tell me he's one of the married ones."

The Missus nodded sheepishly.

"Oh, that's right fine! Right fine! Good work, Charlotte!" Her mother stood up and started angrily pacing. "Which True boy is this? Is this that Archer fella?"

"Yes."

"How old is that boy?"

"I ain't sure."

"You were sure enough to let him put his little thing in ya! Damn, Charlotte!" Her pacing was now so heavy it was practically making marks on the wood plank floor. "Of course, his wife doesn't know about this?"

"No, she doesn't," said The Missus.

Tired of pacing, Issie sat and stared into the flames. "I'll think about what to do."

The Missus frowned. "That's just what he said."

CHAPTER 5
The Missus

Neither above you, Nor beneath you,
Always with you.

THREE WEEKS LATER, it was pouring rain again. It was six in the evening, and all three Fenn women were reading or sewing when there was a knock on the door. Issie opened the door. Standing outside was a woman, soaked to the core.

"You the old Missus?" the woman asked with a grimace that couldn't be pulled apart with two horses.

"Old?" replied Issie.

"The *retired* Missus," the woman said, shaking her head.

"I am."

"I have an important matter to speak to you about."

"Come in, then." The woman entered, leaving puddles of rainwater wherever she moved. "Stand next to the fire, or you'll catch your death," said Issie. "What can we do for you? I ain't The Missus no more, my daughter is."

The woman turned and glared at the "young" Missus seated next to her. "I am aware of that, and that's why I came. Your daughter here is carrying my husband's child."

Their attention, like the wood in the fireplace, cracked like a whip. Some of the rain dripping off Mrs. True's dress drained off into the fire, making it hiss into snakelike wisps of steam.

"I know about the child," said Issie as she sat in her rocker, ashamed. The Missus said nothing.

"I have a plan that will save us all a great deal of dishonor," Mrs. True said with a very restrained attitude. "You do understand the heaps of shame this will bring to both of our families?"

"I do, and I…"

"I will take the child. The child will be mine."

A puff of air from The Missus' nose came out like dragon fire.

"But how will that solve anything?" asked Issie.

"The child is half my husband's."

The Missus turned to her mother for support, but Issie would not return her gaze. The Missus burst into tears and stood, fists at her sides. She slammed her foot on the plank floor. "It may be half his child, but it's all your grandchild, Mother!"

Issie exhaled painfully and turned back to Mrs. True. "Listen, I can see how you'd be angry."

"No, I'm sure you can't," said Mrs. True flashing a momentary sarcastic smile.

Micah burst through the door with wild eyes. His head darted to each woman. "I heard yelling."

"It's just us, Micah. It's fine," said Issie.

"It ain't fine, Micah! This demon wants to take my child!" said The Missus with her finger pointed at Mrs. True. Micah walked over to The Missus and put his arm around her shoulders.

"Now, no one ain't doing nothing of the sort," said Micah.

"I'm afraid your nigger is speakin' out of place," said Mrs. True to Issie.

"Now, now. Let's take a step back here. My daughter can retire and raise the child here. No one sees us, No will know. I will be weeping from now on."

"You know this community. They will find out. It will be best for your daughter as well as us to hand the child over."

"Over my grave, you will," said The Missus.

Issie's head drooped. She rocked slightly in her chair as she leaned forward in it.

"Who told you?" Issie asked solemnly.

"My simple-minded husband came home drunk and said it in a stupor."

The Missus again slammed her foot down. "That no-account, snot-slinging…" Micah's massive arm pulled The Missus closer to him.

"Close to what I said," said Mrs. True. "It was just a day after I gave him my wonderful news," she said sarcastically.

"Your news?" asked Issie.

"Yes, I am with child as well. That is why my plan will work. We will raise them as twins, and that is what we will tell everyone. No one will be the wiser, and we will avoid the shame. I don't wish any disgrace to come upon my family, and I'm sure you don't either."

"I suppose," said Issie quietly.

"It will work like this: You will keep your daughter here

and out of sight. After she gives birth, you will bring the child to our home, and I will take it. Do we have a bargain?"

"You are speaking about my grandchild," pleaded Issie.

Mrs. True smiled with feigned sympathy, and she slowly shook her head. "If you choose otherwise, I will leave my husband and tell everyone about him and the whore as I go." The words were a warning shot fired at Issie's feet. Her brows raised. She wanted to put her hands up in surrender.

"Nooooo!" The Missus screamed, her knees buckling as Micah held her sobbing body. The fireplace hissed like a den of snakes from the rivulets of water flowing into it. Mrs. True bent low and leaned in, eye level with Issie. "I will ask again. Do we have a bargain?" Her words were quiet and piercing as snake's hiss.

Issie's head drooped lower. She couldn't look her in the eyes. "We have a deal."

THE MISSUS WAS in her fifth month and had started to show. She no longer ventured out anywhere near people. Micah now took Issie to the funerals, just like he used to before she retired. There was no difference between the two; they did things the same and even wore the same dress. It was just the voice that revealed them, as Mr. True had said.

The Missus walked the edge of the lake until she ended at their boulder with its emerald water below. She climbed down to a stone just off the surface. She pulled up her skirts and dangled her legs off, soaking her swollen feet in its cold waters. Her hand went to her stomach, and she thought about the life growing inside her, wondering if it was a boy or a girl, and what he or she would look like. It was going to be a girl, she thought. She'd do this every day, talk to her stomach and tell it whatever her mind came across that day. Yesterday it was her family history and things she did as a little girl, and the day before it was her favorite flowers and favorite colors. Today she thought about Mr. True.

"Your daddy rode up to me on his black horse. He was very handsome, as much as I'm sure you will be pretty. Or handsome if you is a boy, but I'm guessing you're not. Your daddy caused all this. He's the reason you won't be with your momma." Her eyes narrowed, and she looked away to the trees. "He's a fool," she said to herself before catching it. "Oh! I didn't mean that. Well, yes, he is a fool, but he ain't so bad neither. I'm sure you'll be happy with him."

The Missus pushed the water with her feet, then moved them in opposing circles. "He thought a kiss meant he was cheating. Damn fool. But I guess thinking you'd only come if your daddy and I were married ain't too far from that. Your momma's a fool too."

Just as yesterday and all the days before, she came home with tears streaming down her face. That night, like most, she fell asleep dreaming that she could keep the baby and how Mr. True would join her. They would marry, work together, and have more children.

The rooster would wake her each day to the nightmare. In her daydreams, she never expected Mr. True to divorce his wife, and she certainly never wished ill upon Mrs. True. But in her dreams, if Mr. True were to become a widower somehow suddenly, that would have been the perfect story.

The Missus had to come up with a different plan. She could just leave and move to a different town, but with no money and no family, she'd be living on the streets. She'd be a vagrant and her child, a bastard. She knew how to do nothing else except weep for a living and, most importantly, she could never disgrace her mother, her grandmother, or her family name. She had already done enough of that.

The Missus dreaded the day of the baby's birth. She hoped it would be painful. A pain so intense she would never want to see the reason for the pain. A pain so fervent she wouldn't be able to hold the child to her breast afterward. Someone would have to do that for her. When the time finally arrived, labor lasted twenty-seven hours and six minutes.

The Missus had one demand concerning her firstborn, and that was his or her first name. She demanded this of her mother, and her mother had made that a deal-breaker with Mrs. True. Since she had been a young girl, she had always wanted to name her firstborn Augustus, if a boy, or Augustine, if it was a girl. She believed it to be a noble name and one of stature. Her mother had told her stories of the Roman kings called emperors and of one named Augustus.

Augustus was born with black hair and blue eyes—a resemblance to Mr. True. The Missus smiled at his cute, wrinkled, and crying face. Issie saw Charlotte smiling at the baby and called for the wet nurse who wrapped him in a blanket and took him away. The screaming was louder than the birthing.

For four days, The Missus lay in bed. On the fifth day, she walked out on the porch and sat in the rocker, talking to herself. Her mother joined her on the porch but didn't say anything. They just sat there together, and Issie listened to her whispered rantings. Most were Bible passages, and sometimes an "Augustus" in there.

The cat came up and rubbed against The Missus' leg. She bent to pet it and scratch its back. The cat's name was Paley, an orange tabby. Paley was a stealthy mouse catcher, able to sneak up on the smartest of rats. It was like a ghost, disappearing in a flash and reappearing with a rat. It had earned Issie's respect, allowing it to sleep indoors in the winter or during rain. The Missus scratched Paley behind the ears before he perked up, spotting something under Micah's cabin and ran off, disappearing under it. A few moments later, the only thing to reappear was his glowing eyes. The Missus watched while she came up with her plan; like Paley, she would become a ghost.

Mr. True did live a day's ride away, but that wasn't all that far, she thought. Mr. True used to ride to her home regularly; she could just do the same. Her mother was now weeping again and would take Micah with her, providing the perfect opportunity. Those would be the days she'd escape to the True farm and see Augustus without anyone knowing or seeing. She'd visit her Augustus as a ghost.

THREE WEEKS LATER, her boots crunched the soft carpeting of pine needles as she approached the True farm. It was about four hundred yards away. She wanted to get closer, but she had reached the edge of the tree line. Finding it had been difficult; she had gotten lost twice on the journey. It was God's will because the second time had led her to a hill just above the farm. It had a perfect view of the back of their home and their fields, but no one could see her from this vantage point.

The Missus unloaded her mule, hobbled it, and sat down with her back against a tree to wait. Mrs. True had given birth to her baby boy two weeks before Augustus. She had overheard the wet nurse telling her mother about it, and that they had named him Jefferson. The journey to their home had been long, and after an hour, she fell asleep against a tree.

The caw of a crow woke her. She rubbed her eyes and looked out to the farm, not sure how long she'd been sleeping. Mr. True was walking through the cornfields with Augustus and Jefferson each comfortably tucked into the corners of his elbows, lying on his forearms and heads against his chest. Hearing something, she squinted as she tried to make out what he was saying. He spoke to them as he showed the babies corn, grass, insects, chickens. He was teaching them about the earth.

"That's a beautiful thing there, Mr. True," she said to herself.

From this distance, The Missus couldn't see who was who. She wanted to know which one was her son. The Missus rose and took the mule to scout the farm from within the tree line.

There was a light warm breeze blowing as she meandered through the ash tree forest. Their white-bark trunks grew closer and closer until they became so dense that their boughs whipped her as she passed. She scolded herself under her breath for not having worn riding pants as she ducked, lifted her legs, and twisted about to avoid them. The Missus should have stopped herself, but the mule stopped for her instead, refusing to move. The only way out was the way they came. She dismounted, deciding to lead the mule through the thicket on foot. She turned to him with a frown. The mule's name was Franklin, and he had been born into her family five years back. Franklin returned her frown with one of his own. He never liked to back up, and The Missus knew it. She stroked his face.

"You're gonna have to back up, Franklin. I'm sorry. Blame me, but you're gonna have to." No movement. She frowned again at him. Her impatience was growing when he hee-hawed so loudly, Franklin's spit sprayed over her face. She shook her head, surprised. Franklin never hee-hawed. From the reflection in Franklin's eye, she saw movement and whipped around to see Mr. True standing ten feet away. She jumped with a gasp. He had a shovel in his hands and sweat on his brow.

He nodded. "Missus," he said as if he'd been expecting her. He calmly put both hands on top of the wooden shovel handle as if to rest.

"Mr. True." She gathered herself, dropped Franklin's reins, and walked closer to him. He stabbed at the earth with his shovel and avoided looking her in the eyes.

"Was that you at the last two remembrances?" he asked.

"No. It was my momma. I'll be taking over on the next one."

"Oh, that explains it."

"Explains it?"

"I tried to approach you, or who I thought was you and, well…"

"What?"

"Well, she said that if I ever such as speak half a word or came to within ten feet of ya that you would, or I mean she, would cast a hex so that my… Well, I wasn't sure no woman could say such a thing."

"Spit it out, Mr. True."

"Hex my pecker to fall off is what you, I mean, she, said. And I was thinking, you might be thinking all this is was my fault…" The Missus' eyes narrowed. "And I mean it is my fault, by no means…"

"Mr. True, I want to ask you a favor."

Mr. True stopped, looking her in the eyes, then away. "Ya ain't gonna try to steal your boy back, are ya Missus?"

"No, I won't, Mr. True," she said as she averted her gaze self-consciously. "I just…" She paused and turned back to his eyes. "I just want to see him occasionally. I want to visit and see my little boy every now and then. I want to touch my little Augustus."

"Missus, I don't believe my wife—"

"Mrs. True will not know I'm here."

Mr. True studied her, looked to his feet, then back to her face. "Ya mean, more than just today?"

"Yes, he's my baby. I want to see him become a boy and then a man," she said. "I want to see him grow." Mr. True turned his attention to the fields, thinking. "I didn't mean to scare ya. I ain't here to steal him back."

Mr. True looked around in thought, nodding his head. "Suppose I could do that," he said as he stabbed the shovel into the soft dirt. "You won't be lettin' my wife see ya?"

"No, I won't. I'll be discreet." The Missus smiled. "How is my little one?"

Mr. True turned to her with a proud expression. "He's right fine. Seems like a right strong little one. They both are. Both he and Jefferson, my other boy. Both real strong little boys."

Her mouth began to quiver. A tear ran down her cheek, but she kept her smile.

"Missus, I can be letting ya touch Augustus, but he'll be getting older and getting to talking and all, if ya know what I'm saying." Kindness appeared in Mr. True's eyes. She could see he was trying to make things right. "I mean, he's a baby now and all, and that's all fine, but…"

"I understand, Mr. True," she said. "It'd just be till he starts talkin' and all." A huge lump formed in her throat. She held it back.

She watched his eyes roam her face and follow the path of the tear down her cheek. "I'm pleased that wasn't you that wanted to hex me, Missus. You have no idea how sorry I…"

"Can you retrieve my boy now?" she interrupted. He could see her pain through those grey eyes staring back at him. He nodded and walked away, dragging the shovel behind him.

Later that afternoon, Mr. True brought little Augustus out to the woods, handed him to her, and sat some distance away, resting his back against a tree. The Missus held him in her arms as he cooed and played with her fingers. His eyes looked up at her with a curious expression, almost like he recognized her. She brought him up to her nose, nuzzling him as she inhaled his powdery baby scent. Little hands went to grasp her hair and cheek. She laughed as Augustus smiled and cooed. Tiny drops of love from a mother's eyes ran down her cheek, reaching his little hand. The hand moved across, wiping them off. Charlotte took his wet palm and brought it to her lips.

You know who I am, don't you?

AUGUSTUS WAS FOURTEEN months old and starting to walk. Mr. True brought him out to the treeline by holding his hand. Augustus wobbled towards her, then collapsed into a sitting position. With the pull of his father's hand, he was up and wobbling toward her again. The Missus sat on Franklin, waiting to greet her boy with her smile. Mr. True lifted him and handed him to her. She sat him in front of her, both sharing the saddle.

A shiver went down her spine as she felt the ridges of Mr. True's fingerprint touch a hole in her stocking, her only exposed skin, and stir around in the small hole.

"I want to see you again, Missus. I need to."

An empty silence fell as she regarded his face.

He hasn't shaved for three days, but he still smells of pine sap. She breathed it in through her nose. *I love that smell.*

"A week from tomorrow, I'll stop over on my way to town. But for now, I want to be with my boy." His finger continued its small circular motions on the tiny bit of her skin. When he pulled it away, his touch left her skin as painfully as plucking a brow hair.

A WEEK FROM tomorrow came as slow as a week from next year for Mr. True. He held his excitement a secret, but his heart raced with the thought of seeing her again. He walked into the trees, and there she was. No veil, no black dress. The Missus was wearing a flower-print dress and was seated on a red and white blanket. He approached her; his pace slowed. The elements around her seemed to disappear. She became the only object within the space, the only thing he could see. Like a lighthouse to a mariner, her smile brought him closer and closer still. He sat next to her and felt her hand take his for the first time in two years. She interlaced her fingers between his, their hands fitting together like two pieces of a puzzle. A warmth came over him, and he exhaled apprehension and inhaled anticipation.

He turned to her beautiful, slate-grey eyes. His lips moved to hers as an apology for his foolish behavior that first time she kissed him. Her lips responded with the acceptance of it. She laid back on the blanket, and they made love, surrounded by the sound of the wind in the trees around them.

A week later, she approached after a remembrance. "I'll be waiting at our place tomorrow."

Without a smile, he nodded.

At eighteen months, her little walker became a little talker. Mr. True waited for her there in their spot. After this visit, he would have to tell her it must be the final time. Augustus was speaking in complete sentences, and when he said "Momma," he'd point to the treeline instead of Mrs. True.

But The Missus never showed up that day and never returned. The pang of missing her crossed with the relief of not having to tell her it would have been the last time she would be allowed to touch her son again.

IT HAD BEEN six months since he'd seen her last. Mr. True waited for the next remembrance to approach her. Micah had made his regular walk back to retrieve the chair, and Mr. True walked around to the other side of her buggy, placing his hand on her ankle.

"Missus, I hadn't seen you in a bit—"

"And you ain't never gonna see me again." The seething voice was not The Missus. His hand immediately retreated, and he looked to her veiled head. "You ever touch me or in any way conversate with me, I'll scream and let all know what demon resides inside you, Mr. True." Fear threw him back and away from the older voice, almost falling off-balance. He continued to back away, checking his surroundings as if he'd seen a ghost and wasn't sure if more were around. Micah approached, staring him down.

Mr. True turned and shuffled his feet through the dirt, not finding the strength to lift them. Shaken, confused, and frightened, he wobbled back to his wagon, like Augustus did the last time he had seen his mother.

CHAPTER 6
Augustus

I am gone into the fields to take what this sweet hour yields

"CAW, CAW," THE crow cried out.

Augustus looked up as it flew low and fast, swiping by him. The blackest of birds flew to its murder. Silhouettes cut out of the morning sky above the woods to the east.

At six years old, he had chores to do each day, but today he had managed to finish them early. Tired of waiting for his brother, he found himself walking off the farm towards them. Their distinctive caws called him like the pipe of the Pied Piper. Through the brush and over streams, he walked, tripping several times as he was looking up instead of where he was stepping. He finally came upon an open field a few miles from his home. Hundreds of crows were flying overhead, calling out to each other as they flew in great circles above him. Augustus squinted to see them better. His eyesight had grown worse over the last two years. Running across the field, he kicked something. Looking down, he saw that it was a dead crow. He kneeled and touched it. Its head feathers mirrored the long crepe streamers of his father's tall hat, and its tail feathers echoed his long black coat. His father had told him that black was the most powerful of all the colors, unseen to ghosts and evil spirits.

The crow's warmth revealed it had not been gone long. When he felt it, the flying crows around him cawed even louder.

Standing, he looked out across the field. There were dead crows everywhere, all in various stages of decomposition. Dozens of them. Was this the special place they would come to die? Was this the place for crows like the famous elephant graveyard his sister Emilia had read about to him? He sat under a tree, waiting for one to drop out of the sky like a pinecone. He hoped one would plop down right there in front of him, but after twenty minutes, nothing happened. The flock began to fly off, leaving three in the branches above him, discussing the strange human sitting beneath them. They kept watch on him with their black, licorice-drop eyes. They seemed to look directly at him, even through him, no matter in what direction the bird stood. The three were hopping from branch to branch for a better view of their intruder. Augustus turned to the one making an unusual clucking sound—a unique sound no other bird he knew about made. He knew it was their secret way of speaking to each other.

"D-D-Did you finish your mourning?" stuttered Augustus to the clucking crow. The crow replied with his cluck. "You n-n-need to bury your k-k-kin. You forgot that p-p-p-part," he said as he rose. "I'll b-b-be your gravedigger," he called back to the crow as he ran off home.

Augustus ran to the cornfields where his brother Jefferson was working, yanking corn from the stalks and tossing them into baskets.

Augustus came running up through the corn stalks and

past Jefferson. "J-J-Jefferson, get a sh-sh-shovel," stuttered Augustus. "I gotta sh-show ya something."

"I gotta finish up my chores and then we's gotta go out with Pa," Jefferson said as he continued yanking the corn.

"Where we gotta go?"

"I don't know. Doing stuff for Pa is all I know."

"We g-g-gotta dress up?"

"Yep," said Jefferson.

Augustus ran into the chaos of their house. Mr. True walked around half-dressed, long johns on the bottom as he buttoned his black dress shirt on top.

"Where you been all morning?" asked Mr. True, not needing an answer.

"Where's Jefferson? He coming?" asked Mrs. True as she served eggs and hash to his eight-year-old sister Glory. Augustus nodded on the way to his room.

"I laid out your clothes on your bed, Augustus," said Emilia, the eldest of the siblings. Augustus also nodded to her as he passed her. At twelve years old, Emilia was their mother's biggest helper.

Augustus ran into the short hallway and to the room he shared with Jefferson. Their room was more like a half-room, only as wide as a chicken coop with just enough room for two cots, only a foot of space between them. Before Jefferson was born, Mrs. True used it as a pantry.

Augustus stopped, wide-eyed. Laying there on his bed was the most incredibly handsome suit and hat he could ever imagine. Today would be the first day he and his brother would work alongside their father as beadles.

"What do you think?" asked Emilia as she leaned in the

doorway. Augustus turned to her with a smile a mile wide. "That's what I thought."

Glory came running over and peered around Emilia's back. "Let me see." Emilia moved for her, and she came in and walked up to one of the two long curved brass rods leaning against the wall. She slid her fingers across the smooth surface until she came to the bell at the end. Her index finger flicked it. "Ting."

"They sc-sc-scare away evil sp-sp-spirts," said Augustus, as if they were magic.

"I know," said Glory with a smirk.

"They're also supposed to request prayers from the mourners," added Emilia.

Jefferson ran in behind him. "No girls in our room!"

"Augustus let us in," said Glory.

"Well, get out, we gotta get dressed."

Glory stuck out her tongue as she walked out. Emilia crossed her arms. "You should be a little more generous. You all get to go out with Pa. We don't; we have to go to market with Ma."

"Beadling is work. Pa said he'd pay us," said Jefferson.

"H-h-he did?!" asked Augustus.

"He's lying, Aug. Pa ain't gonna pay you," said Emilia with a frown. "Don't put on the jacket 'till after breakfast." Emilia turned and left them in the room.

Their black suits lay next to tall stovepipe hats suited for their size. Crepe streamers draped from them, just like their father's. Jefferson put on his hat and took up his beadle bell rod. He put it between his legs and held it like his penis. "I'm a warner. Pisssss."

Augustus shook his head with disgust. "That ain't n-n-n-no warner."

Jefferson jingled the bell on the end. "Look it, look it, I'm tinkling, I'm tinkling!"

"I'm telling pa!" said Glory, spying from the hallway.

Jefferson ignored her as she ran off. "Put your hat on, Aug!" An excited smile returned to Augustus' face as he took it up. "Pa says now that we're old enough, we can work at any remembrance and they'll pay us for it."

Augustus set the tall hat on his head like a crown. "How do I l-l-l-look?"

"Like a king, Aug."

"That's w-w-what I thought."

CHAPTER 7
Mr. True

Sleep, holy spirit, blessed soul,
While the stars burn, the moons increase,
And the great ages onward roll.

Mrs. Schafer's home was a small log cabin, built on a hill that allowed it to have a root cellar below that one could walk straight into from the back. Above the root cellar was a deck with a view of the Lebanon Valley in the distance. She grew turnips, tomatoes, and beans in the vegetable garden on one side with animal pens on the other that held chickens and hogs. Mrs. Schafer sat in a rocking chair on the porch. She stood as they approached.

"I've been expected you was coming up shortly, Mr. True," shouted Mrs. Schafer, as loud as any woman could have yelled at age sixty-six. She relit her pipe as Mr. True pulled up in his wagon. Jefferson and Augustus rode in the back and remained there as Mr. True solemnly climbed down and walked to her.

"Yes, I'm afraid Mr. Shore's time came. Good Lord has seen to it," Mr. True replied.

"Good Lord, should'a seen to it a long time ago in my estimation," said Mrs. Schafer as she looked up to the small patch of blue between the oaks and pines. "No offense," she said to the sky.

Mrs. Schafer looked to Mr. True, then around him to his two boys in the wagon. Augustus and Jefferson were watching Mrs. Schafer's dog as he dug at a chipmunk's hole, attempting to catch prey that had already vanished through an exit hole several feet away.

"Yes, well, the Shore family would ask the honor of your attendance at the remembrance of Mr. Shore." Mr. True liked to use fancier words like 'attendance' instead of 'come to' or 'being at,' especially during times when he was doing his warning work, believing the words gave him the respectability of a judge. "They'd like you to have this."

Mr. True pulled something wrapped in a handkerchief from his front pocket. Holding it in his left hand, he unveiled it like a gold bar or precious jewel by delicately pulling down each corner of the handkerchief until it revealed a cookie-like pastry with the initials "DS" inscribed on it: the deceased's, Daniel Shore, initials. He stuck it out for her to take.

"Dead cakes. I hate dead cakes. When the elder Shore passed years back, they gave out cotton gloves. Gloves soft as a baby's behind. Don't this Shore want no one at his remembrance?"

"As I understand, they may have a few rings to pass out at the gravesite. Made of ivory, I'm told," Mr. True replied.

"Ivory? What, they sell the cow for that?"

"Can't say, ma'am."

Mrs. Schafer again looked past him, craning her neck to see his boys. "How's those boys of yours doin'?"

"Doin' dandy, ma'am. Doin' dandy."

"Do as they're told, do they?"

"Most of the time."

"They sure do look all fancied up in those warning duds."

"We'll be heading over to a remembrance after this. Adda Fischer? Know them?

"Know of 'em, but never met 'em. I heard she passed, though."

"You hear about her sermon?"

"Nope. Was it special or something?"

"It was cause she preached it!"

"How's that?"

"Yeah, well, Miss Adda was only forty-six. Two weeks back, she asks me to come on up and see her. I thought it was gonna be for one of her kin. I show up, and there's all her kin. I'm thinking it's a hoedown or something. Adda tells us she had a premonition of her death. Came to her in the night, and she wrote her own sermon, and she wanted to preach it herself. We all sat down, and she preached it. Preached it good, if I might say so. Two days ago, she died."

"Ha! I'll be."

"God's truth."

"Mm, I 'spect so."

Mrs. Schafer carefully searched Mr. True's face. Mr. True shifted uncomfortably.

"My boy would be about your age right now if he were alive." A nearby bird whistled, and she caught herself. "Where are my manners? Would you and the boys like to come in for a spell, Mr. True?"

"Well, actually ma'am—"

"You still doing that animal doctoring?" she interrupted.

"Ma'am."

"I've this pig; his ear got torn half off by the other'n. Every time they wrastle 'bout, it starts bleedin' again."

"I could take a gander if ya like, ma'am."

"He's round back in the pen."

"No problem, ma'am." He turned to the boys. "Augustus! Jefferson! Bring my doctorin' bag 'round back."

The boys jumped down and walked around back with their father and Mrs. Schafer. They came up to the pen where a pig with a torn ear was wallowing around with three other pigs. Mr. True didn't stand too close to the railing as he didn't want to get his suit dirty.

"I could sew it back on there, ma'am, but the truth be, that with the smell of blood, the other'n are just gonna rip it off again, so ya gotta let him stay somewheres else or in the house with ya a while 'til it heals."

"Lord, no! Ain't no mud creature gonna stank up my kitchen!"

"You could tie him to a tree, but most likely, he'll get all coiled up and start squealing a might, or a bear'll get him."

Augustus pulled on his father's pant leg. "W-We could bring him home, and I c-could sew it, Pa," said Augustus shyly.

Mr. True looked up to Mrs. Schafer. "Like the boy said, I could bring him home with me for a couple days if ya wish. I'll be obliged to ya for fifty cents and bring him back when it's all healed up. I'll fatten him up a bit, too."

"That'd be 'ceptable."

Mr. True pointed to the pig. "Round him up, boys. But don't get those duds dirty." He looked back again to Mrs. Schafer, who had a faraway smile as she watched the young boys as if remembering something from her past.

"Ya ain't truly gonna be letting the youngin' sew it on there, are ya?"

"Nah. But he'll be helping, that's for sure," lied Mr. True. Even at six, Augustus had the same gift with animals, he did. Sewing a torn ear would be no problem for him.

"The boy gonna be taking on the trade?"

"Yessum. I'm 'specting God gave him the gift with the creatures. He's learning the ways mighty quick. Well, we should be off to be inviting some other folk."

"Suppose you should. Good day to ya, Mr. True. Say hello to Mrs. True."

"I'll do that."

The boys led the pig with a rope, just as they would a dog. Leading him to the wagon, they put out enough of a lead to follow safely behind. Its ear was still trickling blood. Mrs. Schafer puffed on her pipe, walked to her porch, and sat in her rocker. Folding her arms across her chest, she blew out a flour sack sized cloud of smoke as Mr. True slapped the reins.

CHAPTER 8
Augustus

I love thee to the level of every day's
Most quiet need, by sun and candlelight.

THE SUNLIGHT FILTERED through the canopy of trees to the dirt road below. Mr. True's wagon clicked and clacked over the bumpy terrain. Augustus and Jefferson rode in the back with Mrs. Fischer's casket between them on their way to her gravesite. For most, he would use his wagon to take the casket from the home to the graveyard, but for wealthier clients, he would lease a beautiful enclosed two or four horse-pulled hearse for the occasion, all depending on the finances of the family.

The dark maple coffin lay heavy upon the back of the wagon. This was an expensive one, handcrafted, stained, and varnished to satin-smooth perfection. Both Jefferson and Augustus ran the backs of their hands over the coffin's cool surface.

"Smooth as a perfect pane of glass," said Jefferson.

"Shame it's going in the ground." Augustus smiled and nodded agreement.

The bumpy road made Jefferson's teeth chatter, and he

combined it with humming. Augustus laughed and joined him. They were accustomed to the ride and sat on the Indian-made blankets, not only to soften the ride but also to keep their beadle clothes from getting dirty.

Augustus looked at his father, who was driving the wagon. His long, black crepe streamers coming off his hat floated with the wind. He wanted to grab them like a bird in the air, but he knew his father would be furious if he did. It made him giggle. The wagon's wheels clattered a similar rhythm to the birds chirping until they came to a rise in the road. Down the road was a small graveyard with people milling about.

"Boys, it's time," said Mr. True.

The boys climbed down. Augustus fixed his suit and put on his tall beaver-skin hat. He was excited to look like his father and work with him. It made him feel important. All Jefferson told him was that it was a might better than doing chores or schoolwork with Ma.

They took their beadle bells and began walking in front of the wagon, jingling them. Augustus couldn't help turning to Jefferson with his big grin.

"Stop smiling, Aug. It's a remembrance," whispered Jefferson.

"No talking," said Mr. True.

Augustus snapped to a solemn expression as the mourners below took notice, their heads turning to the direction of the tinkling bells. Hats came off as they approached.

"Boys, soon as you hit that second tree, stop," said Mr. True quietly. The boys did, and the wagon came to a stop. Mr. True made a motion with his head, and several of the mourners helped unload the casket from the wagon, carrying it to the side of the grave. Mr. True climbed off the wagon and stood next to it.

"Boys, put your bells back and wait over yonder." Mr. True motioned for them to sit on some large boulders. Augustus and Jefferson sat watching the mourners pace about, talk to each other, and fidget with their Sunday-best clothes.

A young lady about their age held the hand of her mother. She wore a dark blue dress with a white flower sewn at the beltline. She had blond curls, and Augustus thought she was beautiful.

"You ever seen her before?"

Jefferson looked over to them. "The one in the blue dress? No. Must be a towny," said Jefferson as he picked up an acorn and threw it at Augustus, hitting him in the head.

Augustus turned to see Jefferson's grin just as he flicked another. Augustus looked down, finding one. The battle was on. Acorns and giggles were flying everywhere. Augustus jumped up to search for more with Jefferson following. They walked on top of the boulders, each one larger than the next. Both were pocketing acorn ammunition until they were a good distance away from the funeral.

A noise raised their heads. A buggy was coming down the road with a huge black man leading the way. Sitting in it like a dark queen was a veiled woman in a black dress. It was hard to take their eyes off her. They watched for a moment before running back to their pa.

"Pa, Pa, the weeper's coming up," said Augustus as Jefferson held back, not caring as much. The mood of the gathering seemed to turn somber as Micah helped her down. He went around to the back of the buggy, took out her chair, and brought it to a spot near the graveside. Coming back to her, he took her arm and walked her to the chair, gently sitting her in it like a princess. Like he had done a hundred times before, Micah walked around her chair and stood about five feet behind, like a captain of the guard.

"Augustus, go pay the weeper her due." Mr. True placed two silver coins into Augustus' tiny hand.

Turning, Augustus cautiously approached her, each step he took slower than the other. He had seen her several times before at ceremonies they attended, but each time she became more puzzling to him. Augustus felt drawn to the dark lady like a magnet. He couldn't stop but couldn't turn away, either. The coins in his hand were wet from sweat. When he came within four feet of her, Micah stepped in front of him, blocking his path. The enormous man loomed above him. Augustus looked up to Micah's face.

"Need something, son?" Augustus' coin-filled fist rose. Micah put out his massive hand palm up, and the coins fell into it, clinking against each other. Micah nodded and smiled, showing his white-white teeth in contrast to his dark skin. The smile from the normally stoic man surprised Augustus. It was a happy smile, like a child has when finished with school for the summer. Augustus turned and walked back to Jefferson.

The ceremony was a standard one. Jefferson and Augustus politely stood among the mourners while their father stood away from the gathering.

He must be making sure things went smoothly, Augustus thought.

His father always said it that way, "…making sure it went smoothly." Augustus observed the faces around him. Solemn, contemplative, crying. All were different but expected expressions. The girl in blue was crying too. She wasn't as pretty when she cried. He spotted Jefferson standing on the other side of the crowd. He had a mischievous grin as he looked back at him.

Why? What's he doing?

The sermon ended, and the gathering moved to the gravesite. The cloistered woman was sat there, her body twitching and trembling, her hand continually bringing the handkerchief under her veil.

"Boy, you got to move," interjected one of the pallbearers.

Six men were taking the coffin to lower it into the grave. Augustus' body moved, but his eyes didn't. "She's looking at me," he whispered.

Mr. True

Mr. True watched her too, sitting there, cloistered all in black. Mr. True remembered Charlotte's shape but couldn't be reasonably sure it was her, *his* Missus, the one he longed for, even after four years. He hadn't seen nor heard from her since Augustus began to speak, but he had seen the weeper at countless funerals since. He always hoped for some sort of sign to indicate it was her.

Whenever a weeper was going to work a remembrance he was at, Mr. True always made sure Augustus would be there too. In case it was her, she could see her son.

Why wouldn't you want to speak to me? Did I do something? Your momma put the fear of God into ya?

Mr. True's eyes searched for confirmation when his brow narrowed, seeing Augustus approach her a second time. He'd already paid her.

What are you doing, Augustus?

Micah moved to block him, but a gesture of her hand

motioned him away. Mr. True knew it was the only way she could see her son up close. Augustus stood in front of her for a few moments before Mr. True saw Jefferson walk a slow but steady pace up to them, ducking low behind Augustus' back, attempting to hide from the weeper. He slipped his hand up, taking Augustus' other hand, turned, and pulled him to Mr. True.

"The weeper made him cry," said Jefferson.

"What she say to ya, boy?"

Augustus remained silent and wiped his tears with his coat sleeve.

"Hmm, alright. Go on and sit in the wagon."

Mr. True waited till after the mourners had gone. He watched as Micah helped her up into the buggy. She swiftly climbed in with youthful movements.

Hmm, it's possible.

If it was her, he wanted to talk to her, hear her voice. His mind zig-zagged with apprehension and desire. Mr. True waited for Micah to retrieve her chair before approaching.

"Did the boy pay your man?" It was a shame those had to be the first words he'd spoken to her in four years, but it had to be something neutral just in case it wasn't her. Her veiled head turned to him with no response.

"Just making sure you got paid is all."

"You saw that he did," she said.

It was her, Charlotte, his Missus. Mr. True's head jerked, and his heart raced. "Why haven't ya spoke to me all these times? Has it been you?"

The veil was a cold wall between them without a response.

"Did I do something wrong? Are ya angry with me?"

She sat still as a statue. Mr. True could see Micah returning from the corner of his eye.

"What'd you say to the boy?" Again, no response from the veil. "You musta said something. I saw him crying."

"'They that sow in tears shall reap in joy.' Psalm 126, Mr. True," floated from the veil, like a subtle breeze. Micah came back with the chair, and the veil turned away. It took ten minutes for his small hope of reconciliation to vanish with her down the road.

CHAPTER 9
Augustus

Sing a song of joy and bless on earth our peaceful days

SEVEN YEARS LATER, not much had changed with the boys except their height. Jefferson and Augustus were thirteen and now only six inches shorter than their father. They walked in front of the wagon, tinkling their bells as they approached the Presbyterian church and graveyard.

"Your girlfriend is gonna be there," said Jefferson as he looked over to Augustus.

The True's homeschooled with two other families near them, the Jennsens and the Van De Bergs. The Jennsen family had four girls: Elizabeth—eight, Beatrice—thirteen, Francis—fifteen, and Betsy—seventeen.

"Ain't my g-g-girlfriend," replied Augustus with a frown. Jefferson was speaking about Beatrice, who had a not-so-secret crush on Augustus. Beatrice was nice and pretty, but Augustus had grown up with her, and she was like a sister to him. It was Betsy who interested him. She had grown into a beautiful woman within the last few years. Before his eyes, she blossomed into a fine feminine form with the most graceful curves God would, or even should, provide mankind. He believed if your eyes landed upon a form with curvier gracefulness than her, you'd be stricken dead upon sight. Every glimpse of her sent an exciting rush through him, enough to make him break a sweat. She was now seventeen and four years older than him, but Augustus had it all planned out to ask for her hand on his seventeenth birthday. She'd be only twenty-one, and the thought of twenty-one and seventeen wasn't such a big difference compared to sixteen and twenty. Augustus saw her walking into the church with her sisters. "She is a m-m-might pretty."

"Betsy? Mm-mm, she sure is. Who wouldn't like that?" Jefferson said, his eyes going wide. "I'm gonna tell her," said Jefferson with an evil grin.

"You d-d-do and I'll, I'll t-t-tell Beatrice you like her."

"Settle down, boy. I ain't gonna do it," Jefferson said.

"Boys shush up and do your job," said Mr. True from behind the wagon.

The funeral was for Eileen Van De Berg, the grandmother of their other homeschooled friend, Joshua. The wagon pulled up near the grave. Pallbearers walked over and took the casket out of the wagon, laying it next to the gravesite. There were about fifty mourners that day milling about, including his mother and Emelia. Glory must have been in the church where the rest of the children would be. Augustus caught the eye of Joshua, who was standing next to his parents, eyes red with tears. Augustus solemnly nodded to him as they laid down their bell rods into the back of the wagon.

"Come on, let's go," said Jefferson. The boys walked toward the church. Augustus was hoping Betsy would be impressed by his beadle clothing.

Near the casket was the weeper, seated and waiting. Her

head was aimed in Augustus' direction as it always seemed to be. The weeper was at most of the remembrances he went to, and he always felt her staring at him. Today, as he and Jefferson walked past her, her head followed him as usual.

Augustus and Jefferson walked into the church. Children were scattered about in groups.

"Let's pretend my baby doll died," said a six-year-old girl next to him in the back pew. She and several of the young girls were playing "funeral," a common playacting game.

"Who can I be?" asked another girl.

"You can be the sister of the dead baby."

"I'll be the weeper," said Glory as she walked over with Beatrice. Glory was now fifteen and usually watched over the younger children. Glory smiled at Jefferson. "Jefferson can be the warner."

"I ain't playing," said Jefferson, walking away.

"What about you, Aug?" asked Beatrice with a teasing grin.

"Uh, uh, no." Augustus stammered and walked to the front of the church and up to Jefferson.

"Betsy ain't here. Must be outside."

"We sh-sh-should be out theres, t-t-too. Getting too old to be with the little ones."

Augustus laid down on a pew and waited for the funeral to end. After an hour, everyone started packing up to go. Augustus put on his stovepipe hat and walked outside to look for Betsy and found her walking up to Jefferson.

"You look very handsome in that suit, Jefferson," she said.

Augustus frowned and turned his back. Ten feet in front of him stood the weeper. He couldn't see her face, but he knew she was staring straight at him. She held her hands together at waist level and made a slight "come here" gesture with one.

Augustus took a step toward her, but Jefferson grabbed him from behind.

"Time to go, Augy," Jefferson said. "You get to say hello to Betsy?"

"No, b-b-but I saw you d-d-did."

"Nah, she just was telling me she was leaving." Jefferson pulled Augustus by the jacket toward their wagon, leaving the weeper, her hand still outstretched to him.

CHAPTER 10
Mr. True

Gone. And the light of all our life gone with her

"There's a man in front of our place, Pa," said Jefferson. His hand sheltered his eyes from the sun. The boys and their father were back from warning work and returning a blue tick hound dog to its owner.

"Ah, yeah?" said Mr. True, looking up ahead.

"Looks like a giant blue jay to me," said Augustus.

Jefferson turned to him like he ate a worm. "Your eyes getting worse and worse."

The blue jay turned out to be a soldier in a crisp blue uniform outfitted with gold buttons, gold epaulets and finished with a golden braided rope dangling from one shoulder. But most impressive of all were his shiny black boots; they had no mud on them. No one from around these parts had boots without some mud.

He must shine them every day, thought Mr. True.

The soldier stood by their porch, speaking to their mother as he held the reins of his horse.

His father wore a concerned expression upon seeing him standing there with Mrs. True.

The wagon stopped, and the two boys jumped off.

"Unhitch the horse," was the only thing their father said as he dismounted and walked toward the man.

"Reginald, good to see you," said Mr. True as he approached with an outstretched hand.

"Archer. How you been?"

Mr. True's chin dropped as he saw the gold epaulets. "My oh, my, do these gold things on your shoulders mean you got promoted again?"

"Colonel now."

Mr. True patted his shoulder. "Local boy done good. Real good, Reginald."

"He surely has," added Mrs. True. "Let's hope our Jefferson can rise as high."

"If I can do it, anyone can do it, Mrs. True." The colonel looked at the wagon. "Out warnin', I see."

"Yes, yes," Mr. True replied with a smile that hinted at pride.

"And who was the unfortunate soul today?"

"Ah, poor Mrs. Van De Berg from up in Lockstead."

"The grandmother, I hope," replied the colonel as he patted the horse next to him. "My mare healed up well. Did a good job with her, you did."

"Augustus worked with her every morn."

"Jefferson was too busy with schoolwork," interrupted Mrs. True. "He's such a smart boy. Don't have time to work with the animals." Mr. True gave her a side-eye glance meaner than a diamondback.

"So, did we come to a decision?" asked the colonel with a hopeful smile.

Mr. True folded his arms. "Augustus will be well taken care of?"

"Course, he will, won't he Colonel?" asked Mrs. True.

"Of course, of course."

"And he'll see his brother?" asked Mr. True.

"They'll be right down the hall from each other."

Mr. True turned to the boys who were pulling the horse into the corral and gawking back at the colonel. Mr. True gave them the "get on outta here" head nod.

"We'll do it," he said as if recalling a sad memory while he watched the boys walk back into the barn.

"He's got the gift too, eh?" the colonel asked, smiling.

Mr. True turned back to the colonel. "Pardon?"

"Your Augustus. He's got the gift with animals too?"

"He does."

"We'd love to have you stay for supper, Colonel," asked Mrs. True with a hopeful expression. A few months back, she had nearly jumped off her chair with excitement when Mr. True told her of his tending to the colonel's horse.

"Wish I could, wish I could, but gotta get back. But thank you for the kind invitation, Mrs. True."

She didn't reveal her disappointment. "The invitation is always open, Colonel, for both you and your missus," she said.

Inside the barn, Augustus and Jefferson removed the tack from the horse and locked the gate. Jefferson grabbed the satchel with the remnants of their lunch from the wagon as he eyed the three curiously.

"Pa got something going," he said.

"What is it?" asked Augustus.

"Well, we done with the horse. Ain't got nowheres else to go but in, right?" said Jefferson.

"That's the way I see it," replied his brother. "Try listening while we pass on by."

The boys, eyes to the ground, walked toward the trio. As they were about to pass, the colonel stopped Augustus.

"And are you Jefferson?" the colonel asked.

"H-he's Jefferson," stuttered Augustus, pointing to his brother.

"Oh. Well then, how are *you,* Jefferson?" Jefferson looked up at the magnificent man, mouth agape. "Quiet one, aren't you? Very good. Seen and not heard. Very good."

Augustus grabbed Jefferson by the shirt sleeve, pulling him out of his stare and into the house. The adult trio laughed politely and continued their discussion. Both the boys immediately went to the window and peeked out at the strange man in uniform.

"He knew your name," Augustus whispered.

"I know. What are they saying?" The conversation appeared to be finishing, goodbyes were said, and Mrs. True turned to come in.

"She's comin'." The boys jumped down and grabbed dinnerware, setting the table for supper.

"Good Lord, please bless this supper table and all those sittin' at it with all your grace. Please bless all the sick and lame creatures out in the barn. Amen." Mr. True always said grace the same way every night.

It was his own superstition that forced him to say it no other way, without one word changed or out of place. This happened a few years back when Emilia was given the opportunity to say grace.

"Papa, can I say grace tonight?" Emilia had asked.

Mr. True had just sat down at the table. He cocked his head and considered her. "I tell you what. If you listen to me good tonight and practice it up in the morn, you can say it tomorrow eve. But, mind ya, I want to hear it three times perfect before supper. If it's three times just right, you can do it for supper."

All the next day, Emilia had rehearsed as she did her chores. Close to suppertime, she approached her father in the barn.

"I've been hearing ya practice. Go on, let's hear it," said Mr. True as he hammered a nail into a stall post.

Emilia began and finished all three without one word out of place. "Well, that's right fine. Right fine, indeed."

Emilia's eyes lit up. "So, I can say it at supper?"

"Why, yes, you may."

That evening the family had held hands together in prayer before Emilia: "Good Lord, please bless this supper and all those sittin' at it with all your

grace—"

"Stop, stop," he had said. "Supper table, supper *table*."

"Oh, yes, Papa, sorry. Good Lord, please bless this supper *table*..." She had smiled at her father. "And all those sittin' at it with all your grace. Please bless all the sick creatures out in—"

"And lame, sick and *lame*!" he had shouted. "Oh, forget it. Now I've got to do it three times!" Three times was necessary, not to appease God, but rather to avoid bad luck.

Mrs. True had stiffened. "I believe the Lord understands the notion, Archer," Mrs. True had said, rolling her eyes.

Mr. True did say it three times himself, one right after the other, and afterward, everyone at the supper table dished out their food but waited until Mr. True had taken his first bite before they took their own.

"Well, boys, your father has something he'd like to say—"

"I said I was gonna tell them both in my own good time, woman!" Mr. True yelled as he slammed his fist on the table.

"You don't have to raise your voice to me, Mr. True," Mrs. True replied, insulted.

"Glory eat them 'taters. You'll be hungry in the morn if ya don't," Mrs. True said. She wouldn't look Mr. True in the eye, and the children wouldn't look up from their plates. "My pa didn't know what he was gettin' me into when he married me off to you, Mr. True."

Mr. True shoveled the food in faster. "He was gettin' you the hell outta his house is what he was doin'," he muttered.

"How dare you curse in this house!"

Mr. True ripped his food apart with his teeth.

"Jefferson can grow up to be a gentleman. Can't be learnin' *that* in this God-forsaken country," she said.

Mr. True's head swiveled about the room, attempting to calm himself. He ate two more bites and forced a smile as he turned to Jefferson. "How would you like to be wearing a fancy uniform like the colonel? The man you saw out there today."

Jefferson looked up at him, eyes growing big. Augy smiled ear to ear. "Why, that uniform was the fanciest clothes I ever did see," said Jefferson, beaming.

"It certainly was. So, this Colonel Litton, the man you seen here today in that uniform, can get you boys into the soldier'n school he works at in exchange for us fixin' his horse up. Now, your ma thinks it'd be good for ya, make ya a gentleman—"

"We's gonna be soldiers?!" Jefferson interrupted.

Mrs. True shot out, "No, just you. Augustus ain't suited to be a gentleman like—"

"I ain't going nowhere without Augy."

Mr. True's eyebrows narrowed. "You back-talkin' your mother, Son?"

"I'm trying not to, but we's twins. I ain't leavin' him. He ain't leavin' me."

Mrs. True shook her finger at Jefferson. "You'll be doin' as you're told!"

"What your ma meant to say was, yes, Augustus will be going too." Jefferson turned to Augustus, both with brows high and mouths agape, beaming with excitement. Mrs. True opened her mouth to speak, but Mr. True's glare silenced her.

THE DOOR TO the boy's room creaked as Mr. True opened it. He pulled up his suspenders as he entered. It was dark, and he leaned in to open the window. Outside, the air was still, quiet and cool. Mr. True squinted at the orange of dawn's light shining in.

Both Jefferson and Augustus were sleeping in the same bed, barely fitting. Augustus must have crawled into Jefferson's bed during the night. It reminded him of when they were young and how they would spoon each other like napping puppies as they slept. It appeared that sometimes they still did.

"Boys, time to get up," he said in a soft tone. The boys slowly sat up and rubbed their eyes awake. They looked at each other.

"Augy, again?" asked Jefferson.

Augustus shrugged his shoulders. Jefferson turned to his father.

"Get dressed. Today's the day."

Later that morning, Glory sat next to Mr. True as he drove the wagon. He turned to her excited face smiling up at him. She was the spitting image of Mrs. True in her younger years. Jefferson and Augustus rode in their usual spots in the rear, both laughing and talking about past adventures.

The train bell clanged as they arrived at the busy train station. Mr. True finished tying up the horse, and they all walked onto the train platform. Glory bounced with giddy excitement as she looked at all the people dressed in their finest attire for their travels. Ladies in colorful bell dresses stood out from the men's dark suits like flowers in a sea of grass. Steam billowed out from underneath the train like a panting dragon.

"It looks so much bigger than I thought it would," said Glory, amazed by the size of the train. "And the steam and all the noises. Can I touch it, Pa?"

"Course ya can." Glory squeezed between the travelers and bags to get to the train. She turned back, craning her neck to see her father through the crowd as she touched it, looking for his approval. He nodded and smiled back, giving it to her.

"Do you have the train tickets I gave you?" asked Mr. True.

"Yes, Pa."

"You have the envelope I gave you?"

"Yes, Pa."

"Give that to the people at the school."

Jefferson grew impatient. "We know, Pa."

"Well, you better get on," said Mr. True.

Glory came back over as Jefferson picked up his satchel. "I'm going to make you proud, Papa," said Augustus.

His father looked down at him thoughtfully. "I hope you do, son."

"Both of us are," added Jefferson.

"Make me proud, boys," said Mr. True. "Now go on, get on that train."

They stepped up into the train, disappearing within it and reappearing at a window. Augustus stuck out his arm, waving.

"We gonna be soldiers!" yelled Jefferson.

Mr. True waved back. "I wish that was true, boy," he said to himself.

"What, Pa? You say something?" asked Glory.

"Ah, nothing. Let's get on home."

They turned and walked to their wagon. "You gonna miss 'em, Pa?"

"I believe so. I believe so."

THE BOYS HAD been gone for over three and a half months. The horse and wagon were ready to go outside of the True farmhouse. Mr. True came out with energy in his step, jumped up, and took the reins. Mrs. True came out behind him.

"Two cakes of soap as well," she said.

"Mmm-hmm," he murmured before heading off. The road grew thick with trees the farther away from the farm he went. It was only about a four-hour ride into town.

Not too far and just far enough, he thought.

About a hundred yards in front of him was a clearing. He saw something he couldn't make out, something substantial in the road. His brow furrowed, and he squinted; it was a buggy and mule. It was The Missus.

Her buggy was across the road, blocking it with no room to pass. She had been waiting for him. She dressed in her dark weeping clothes; her face veiled. He stopped his wagon in front of her, and she lifted the veil. It was Charlotte. He had known that he would have to answer to her sometime.

"Charlotte," he said sheepishly.

"You can call me The Missus." The words flew at him like heavy daggers, slamming into the spinning wood wheel he was tied to.

She waited for him to repeat it. "Missus."

"Where'd he go, Mr. True?"

"Off to a school, Missus. With Jefferson, off for some schoolin'."

"What school, Mr. True?"

"Soldier school. Military. Some highfalutin school."

"Why did you let that happen, Mr. True?"

"It'll be good for the boy, Missus. Make him a gentleman."

"Where is this place?" she demanded.

"Clarksburg, Virginia."

"Clarksburg, Virginia," she repeated with an irritated tone. "Micah." From the tree line, Micah walked out, took the mule's bit, and turned the buggy away down the road.

"You're not going after him, are ya?!" he called out.

Her buggy creaked down the road, her back to him. Guilt came to him, an emotion he rarely felt. He knew she was often there, up in the tree line or bushes, watching her boy. And now she couldn't.

"Good to see you, Missus," he said to himself as he watched her frame shrink smaller and smaller down the road ahead. A long while passed before he moved on. He could feel her anger leaving a trail behind her a mile long.

CHAPTER 11
Augustus

You are a song in our hearts forever

"ONE OF YOU, Jefferson True?" the young academy cadet asked.

Augustus turned around first. He and Jefferson had been waiting at the train station for over an hour. Neither of them had heard the boy approach.

"H-h-he is," Augustus stuttered while tipping his head toward Jefferson.

The cadet's grey uniform trimmed in red with perfect pleats and creases impressed Augustus. Even his boots were spit-polished to perfection.

The cadet kept his gaze on Augustus. "Who are you then?"

"He's my brother, Augustus True, sir," Jefferson countered.

"You don't have to call me 'sir.' I'm only a plebe. I was told I was only picking one up."

"No, sir, two," Jefferson said confidently.

The cadet shrugged. "Where's your bags?"

"Right here," said Jefferson as he picked up his satchel.

"Okay, then, let's go." The boy turned quick on his heels

as if he'd practiced the move a hundred times before. His gait was graceful and machinelike at the same time. Augustus and Jefferson followed him through the small lobby, through the double doors to the front of the station, where the city swallowed them up like a whale. This was no town; this was a city.

"Pardon, but what is a plebe?" asked Jefferson.

"It's what you are or will be. It's the lowest of the low, a first-year, a novice.

"I'd s-s-say it was next to a king if it comes with that f-f-fancy uniform," said Augustus.

They walked on a concrete sidewalk, something they had never dreamed of doing and continued into the depths of the city. Augustus looked for the other side of the town like it would end with an open field and a lonely road, but the buildings just kept going. He could hardly decide what to look at: the cadet he so admired in front of him, with his smart gait and crisp uniform, or the tall buildings made of stone and concrete around him. Many streets were cobblestone, and all of them were busy with carriages and wagons and people walking everywhere. The city even had a distinct, indescribable odor.

After twenty minutes of walking, they came upon a tall and long wall half-covered with vines. On the other side of the street were two-story shops and office buildings. This street wasn't as busy as the other streets. Further along down the wall was a high gate. The gate must have been at least sixteen feet with two letters spelled out in iron on each of the two doors: *W* and *H*. Another cadet, dressed in the same fashion as their guide, was standing behind the small door to the left of the main gate.

"Cadet Krieker to escort these gentlemen to Mr. Hall."

The cadet standing by the door opened the gate and said nothing. Cadet Krieker entered, and the boys followed. Jefferson turned back to Augustus.

"Gentlemen," he repeated the cadet's word to Augustus with a huge grin.

There were many more buildings in the compound, all made of brick, and the beautifully landscaped grounds had paved walkways. Over the large stone entryway of what seemed to be the largest building in the compound were the words *Wadleigh-Holmes.* There were cadets everywhere, walking, reading, milling about, laughing, playing ball on the grass. In the distance, there were some cadets marching and singing songs as they did. Augustus' mouth was wide open; this was paradise.

Silently, he had made his plan on the train, and now, he could see that it would come true. He would become a cadet, graduate with honors, join the army, and become a great leader, just like the colonel who had visited their house. His father and mother would be proud of him. They would welcome him home and show him off to their neighbors and relatives, just like his parents had viewed the colonel. He had seen in their eyes how they revered that man, and he wanted them to see him in the same way. It was his deepest and most secret wish. Thinking about his parents now made him miss them, and his goal seemed painfully far in the future.

"Oh, yes, Jefferson True. I remember. Colonel Litten's agreement," said Mr. Hall as he sat behind his file covered desk.

His tone made it apparent he didn't think much of Colonel

Litten. Mr. Hall's office within the department of admissions was crammed with overstuffed filing cabinets, stacks of files, and papers scattered everywhere.

"Did your parents send a letter with you?" Mr. Hall wore small round reading glasses sitting upon a sharp, thin nose. He peered down through the glasses as he fingered through the file on his desk.

"Yessir," Jefferson said, handing him the envelope.

"Freshmen started four weeks ago; I don't know how you're going to catch up."

"I thought we were gonna train to be soldiers."

Mr. Hall looked up from the file over his metal-rimmed glasses. "This is an academy, son. Education is its highest priority." He pushed up his glasses and returned to the file.

"We's smart, and we can handle hard work."

Mr. Hall stopped searching again, and his head popped up with a confused expression. He pushed the hair out of his eyes. "You keep saying we?"

"Yes, me and him." Jefferson used his thumb to indicate himself and his brother.

Mr. Hall frowned and leaned back in his chair. He slowly removed his glasses. "Weren't you told only one of you is enrolled?"

"Enrolled?"

"Enrolled. Attending classes. 'Be a soldier.'"

"One? No, we both are."

Mr. Hall exhaled and leaned back further in his chair. He observed them over the bridge of his sharp nose and steepled his fingers. "Hmm, I see. So, which one of you is Jefferson?"

"I am."

"Looks like you're the favored child." Mr. Hall leaned forward, pulling the letter from the envelope, and hanging it out in front of them to see. "Your brother here, Augustus, is it?" He asked, turning to and squinting at Augustus. Augustus nodded in the affirmative.

"I'm afraid, son, you've been bonded to the school."

"B-b-bonded?"

"Bonded, indentured? You know what that means?" Augustus shook his head. "It means your father agreed to pay a debt by bonding you into service. My grandfather was bonded to pay for his passage to this country years back. Indentured servitude, it's called. I'm sorry to say, Jefferson here will indeed be a cadet, but you, my boy, you will be working here. You are a bonded boy now. It's in payment for your brother attending this school."

Jefferson shook his head "No, that can't be. We're both gonna be soldiers."

Augustus felt sick to his stomach. "Ind-d-dentured?"

"Indentured servitude, yes. You'll be working in the laundry or the kitchen. Whoever needs you."

Jefferson shook his head. "Working? Our pa wouldn't do that."

"I'm afraid he did. And Colonel Litten agreed to it," he said, holding the agreement out to them again. "His signature is right here. Archer True. That your daddy?"

The shoulders of the boys slumped with their expressions. They turned to each for answers neither could provide.

"How long does he have to do that?" asked Jefferson.

"Every year you attend the academy. It's in payment for your education. This academy is not inexpensive." Mr. Hall put his glasses back on, and his eyes returned to the file. "Listen, it's not so bad. He'll be well treated. We do have other bonded boys here, although I've never had a situation where one brother is a cadet, and the other gets bonded. That's a first."

His eyes filled with tears, but Augustus willed them from falling. He wouldn't look up from his lap, and his hands started shaking. "My p-p-pa s-s-sold me. He sold me."

Jefferson could almost see the hurtful words float out from his brother's mouth and drop like stones, crashing to the floor below. His mind tried to wriggle out an answer. "Is there any way he could work to be a cadet? Work twice as hard?"

Mr. Hall continued digging through the file and signing documents. "I'll tell you that compared to most young boys in this country, your brother will be very well taken care of. Three good meals a day, a roof over his head, comfortable bed. That's a lot more than what others get."

The room grew quiet as they ran out of questions. Jefferson put his hand on Augustus' shoulder. "At least we'll be together."

"I WAS ONLY told one. I wasn't told no two," said Darius Borrelli, the head chef of the Wadleigh-Holmes kitchen, as the boys stood before him. Darius was plump, as would be expected of a head chef, and he had a thick Italian accent that many found hard to understand. His chef's hat covered his dark hair, and big, bushy eyebrows loomed above his large nose.

All three boys simply stared at Mr. Borelli. Cadet Krieker, who had escorted them from the train station, was still acting as their guide to show them around the school. Seeing neither of the boys speak up, he tapped Augustus' shoulder.

"Oh, no, sir. I believe only this one is here for the job," said Krieker.

Darius put his fists on his hips. "No matter. I don't got no work now. Go see Chin. Maybe he be needing somebody."

"Thank you, Mr. Borrelli." The cadet spun on his heels and exited as quickly as a rabbit. The boys ran to catch up.

The laundry smelled of steam, sweat, and soap. Chinese men of all ages were hustling about with clothes, uniforms, and bedding. The head of the crew, Chin, a short-statured, fifty-eight-year-old Chinese man stood before Augustus, Jefferson, and Krieker.

"This boy here has been bonded to work here," said Krieker. Chin looked the two boys up and down. "You say the commandant want this?"

"It was Mr. Hall."

"I want to know if the commandant want this. Not Mr. Hall. You see, the commandant higher than Mr. Hall," Chin said sarcastically. Krieker rolled his eyes. "I have a few more nephews that need jobs."

"Mr. Hall got the go-ahead from the colonel," Darius lied.

"Where does he sleep?" asked Darius.

"You don't have a bed for him? Put him with your other fellas," replied Darius.

Chin looked to Augustus. "No more beds."

Jefferson jumped in. "My brother and I stay together. He can stay with me, can't he?"

Cadet Krieker shook his head. "They won't allow that."

Chin bit his lower lip as he looked Augustus over. "You can sleep in laundry hamper. *Dirty* laundry hamper."

CHAPTER 12
Augustus

Do not mourn me, Or think of me with tear filled eyes, Instead speak of me with laughter, As if I were beside you.

THE WADLEIGH-HOLMES MILITARY Academy, founded in 1781, was situated on twenty acres of land, with four two-story dorm buildings, a cafeteria, a laundry, and facility maintenance building. The three-story administration building housed most of the faculty on the two floors above, but the largest buildings were the classrooms: two of them, three stories each. The parade grounds grew more dirt than grass. It was used for sports and athletics, firearms training, and marching practice. When it rained, the grounds would become so muddy one could swim in it, but they'd still make the cadets march. Two-hundred yards from the parade grounds were the barn, horse stalls, armory, and indoor athletics.

It was lunchtime, the only time Jefferson could see Augustus during the day. They were sitting next to a friend, Cadet Orsen, on a low wall outside the dorm building. Cadets were busily walking around them, to and from buildings.

"You should just run off. If it were me, that's what I'd do," said Cadet Orsen.

"We could run off, Aug. If ya wants to."

Jefferson and Orsen wore their Wadleigh-Holmes perfectly pleated grey uniforms and caps with polished black boots. However, Augustus wore the clothes he came in, with a white full-length apron.

"Where w-w-would we g-go? We g-g-got sent by Pa. We can't g-g-go home."

"I don't know. We could just head out west. Live as mountain men or gunslingers."

Augustus rolled his eyes. "You'll b-b-be the gentleman from this. A-a-a-at least one of us will."

They all looked out to the manicured lawn in front of Administration. Two cadets were replacing the guards at gates in strict military fashion. To guard the gates was a privilege, and guards got to miss a class.

"We should steal a uniform," said Jefferson. "Get you a uniform and hide you around the school."

"It couldn't work," said Orsen. "They do regular dorm inspections, and they never tell you when. It'd be impossible. And then your dorm mates would get in trouble. It won't work."

"He's right. Just g-g-get me a book or two. S-s-something I c-c-can read now and again."

"I can do that. I'm always in the library," said Orsen. "Story or fact book?"

"F-f-fact book. Thanks, Orsen."

Orsen smiled. "You fellas are my people. Us Pennsylvania folk stick together."

The school bell rang twice. "I gotta be d-delivering the laundry," Augustus said, rising.

Jefferson's eyes followed Augustus. "Don't you worry, Aug. I'll keep working on it."

ON EACH FLOOR of the dorm buildings, there were forty-one rooms: twenty on each side of a long hallway with a staircase at one end and a large living quarter at the other. The living quarters housed either a commissioned officer or a professor and their family. The officers were all previous U.S. military officers, either honorably discharged or retired. They would teach military tactics and strategy, and the professors would teach the common subjects.

Every day, Augustus delivered the laundry while the cadets were in class, placing it neatly on their beds. Today was an unusual day as all the students were performing a group marching exercise, but many were returning during the time Augustus was making his rounds.

"Chinamen are getting younger and younger around here," said Cadet Ruggles.

David Ruggles, a short, stout boy from Maryland, was sort of a bully leader among the sophomores. The other cadets in the room laughed.

Another boy spoke up. "He works here. He's a slave." The group laughed again.

David walked up to Augustus, placing his foot under the wheel of his cart. "What's your name, laundry slave?"

"Augustus."

"Augustus, *sir*," David repeated.

Although David was two years older, they were about the

same height. His eyes were intense, as if they held bottled-up anger.

"Augustus… s-sir."

Augustus realized he might have been in a dangerous spot. He had never felt intimidated before, never gotten into a fight. He wasn't sure if he should run, stay, or scream for help.

"Well, Augustus, we'll call you 'Little Chinee,' if that's right fine with you."

His crew of cadets laughed again.

Augustus decided to take the brave road and hold his ground. "My name is Augustus True," he said confidently.

David's crew raised their eyebrows and smiled as they looked over to David for his reaction.

"That's… 'My name is Augustus True, *sir*,'" David said as he brought his face close enough for Augustus to smell his breath; it smelled of cauliflower. Augustus pushed past David's foot, continuing down the hallway. David turned to him with arms folded.

"I haven't finished with you, Little Chinee!" he called out as his crew fell about in laughter.

Professor Goodwin stood in the doorway of his apartment at the end of the hallway. He had been watching the interchange between David and Augustus, making sure nothing got out of control.

"Augustus! Come on down here," said the professor as he waved him over.

He was thirty—young for a professor of history. He lived at the school with his wife and two-year-old baby daughter. Goodwin had also been teased for a stutter when he was a child. Augustus wheeled his cart up to him at the end of the hall. "Come in." The professor's apartment was nothing like the dorm rooms. Its two-bedroom space was far more extensive than the True farmhouse. "How are you today, Augustus?"

"Right fine, sir," Augustus said as he placed the professor's laundry on his sofa.

"Getting along with the boys, are ya?" The professor stared at them down the hall until they all retreated into their dorm room. He closed his door.

"Mostly. That was nothing. It don't bother me none. Mostly the boys treat me kindly. I'm trying to remember all the names as I make deliveries. Just gotta put the names with the faces."

"Do you deliver the commandant's laundry?" the professor asked as he stroked his beard.

"No, sir. Mr. Chin delivers his personal."

"You're lucky there. He's as nutty as a pecan pie. Can I get you some water?"

"Thank you, but no, I'm fine. You meanin' the commandant is soft in the head?"

"That's my meaning, but don't say I ever told you. I'm just giving you the warning in case you go up there."

"Thank you for that, sir."

Augustus had seen the commandant on several occasions but had never been close enough to hear him. He'd overheard rumors about him here and there, but they were mostly about his war exploits. Most considered him a hero.

"YEAH, WE HEARD that boy saying something about us during lunch," said Mickey with a thick Irish accent.

Augustus had just told the two dishwashers, Mickey and Ian, what had happened to him with David Ruggles.

"But he wouldn't say it to our faces," said Ian. Mickey and Ian were Irish immigrant brothers. They had only been in the country for fourteen months. Both were "bound-boys" to the academy, indentured like Augustus, but their contracts only had eight months left.

Augustus and Jefferson were eating lunch in the kitchen with them, something they'd do every day as they'd get an extra dessert in the process. Augustus returned the favor by helping the brothers bring the stacks of dirty dishes to the large sink in the kitchen. The academy trained the cadets to stack up to ten dirty dishes, then start another stack. Augustus prided himself on getting the stack of ten to the sink before the cadets stacked the next ten.

"That boy has no idea what we can do to his food," said Ian, picking up a dead roach from behind the oven.

Jefferson's face looked as if he was the one that ate it. "You would do that, would you?" Augustus went out for another stack of dishes.

"Say something about my brother, and you'll pay for it," said Ian.

"You two are the same, aren't ya?" asked Mickey.

"Course we are," said Jefferson.

"Brothers stick together, thick as thieves, we are," said Ian.

Augustus brought in another stack of dishes.

"Yesterday, y-y-you told me about the sc-sc-scholarship. What is it?" Augustus set the stack down next to Mickey.

"Wadleigh-Holmes gives out ten full scholarships per year to boys," said Ian.

"You got to do well on a set of tests," added Mickey.

Jefferson finished his dessert. "Why don't you all try it?"

"Mickey ain't smart enough for that test," said Ian; he got elbowed in the ribs by Mickey.

"Ian ain't smart enough. Plus, we do not want any part of this school," said Mickey.

"We're heading west to San Francisco," added Ian.

Jefferson turned to Augustus. "You should take it, Aug. That's the way in."

CHAPTER 13
Augustus

And life is all the sweeter that he lived

THE CLOUDS WERE pink and orange in the warm evening sky as Augustus walked the parade grounds. He tossed a baseball high into the air and caught it again. Every day after finishing work, he could do whatever he wanted on the grounds: play ball, run around, eat from the kitchen. He had the Academy to himself.

He wasn't a cadet and wasn't subject to their curfews. The cadets jealously watched him walk the fields from their dorm windows, most making indecent gestures to him. Augustus' eyesight had never been good, and in the last few years, it had continued to get worse. Squinting helped.

Augustus walked to Jefferson's window; luckily, on the first floor. "I've been waving at you for the last half hour."

"I c-c-couldn't see ya."

"You're turnin' blind as a bat."

Cadet Scott, one of Jefferson's three dormmates, studied on his bunk. "Can y'all shut it? I got studies to finish."

Jefferson ignored him but spoke lower. "Look into that scholarship yet?"

"Not yet, but I will," said Augustus, turning to the pink sky. "I d-don't mind it here, Jeff. It's a might easier here than back at home. Do a fine job here, and you never get punished or have to sleep in the privy."

"But you ain't what you should be doing, which is wearing a uniform. And you could do it too. You're the smart one."

"I'd ask you to put that in writing," said Augustus, "but I'm sure the spelling would be wrong. I'm headed to the stables."

Jefferson laughed as Augustus walked away toward the stables.

Most evenings, he ended up at the stables. It was his favorite place at the academy, and the smell of horses was his favorite scent.

Originally built as a warehouse, the ceiling of the stables was twenty-five feet high. It held thirty horses and had old oak-plank walls with a mural painted across all four sides. The mural, painted by the cadets, was a farm landscape with horses, grasslands, and a river. It gave the place more the appearance of a church than a stable.

Only senior cadets were assigned to care for the horses, tending to their needs. Most of these boys would go on to become cavalry officers upon graduation. After getting to know Augustus, they began to rely upon him for his horse knowledge. Also, the older classmen never teased him about his stutter or his poor eyesight.

"Augustus, you come here every day?" asked Cadet Major Felts.

"I do. Just to check on the horses for a bit."

"I heard you helped out Andrew with his gelding. You know about horses?"

"My pa taught me about 'em."

"That's good," said Felts as he turned to the stall across from him and called out, "Will! You were saying what about your horse?"

Augustus turned to Will in the next stall. "Yes, his right hoof smells bad," said Will.

Augustus walked over to the adjacent stall. "It's thrush," he said immediately.

"How in tarnation you know that just by looking at him? Ya ain't even seen his hoof."

Augustus pointed to the floor of the stall. "It's 'cause your stall ain't c-c-clean." Felts walked over behind Augustus.

"C-c-clean?" mimicked Will.

"Hey! I ain't having none of that. This boy is trying to help you, Will."

"Fine, fine. So, boy, why do you know it's thrush?" Will asked.

"You got a wet stall floor. It's the w-w-wet that'll cause it. Ya gotta clean it up. Make a n-n-new hay floor and keep that hoof dry as it can be."

Cadet Captain Erwin approached from the other end of the barn.

"He's right. Wet causes thrush. Augustus knows what he's talking about," said Erwin.

"You're welcome in here any time, Augustus," said Will from his stall. "You ain't no cadet here?"

"I want to be, b-b-but I just work here. In the laundry."

Will rose and put his arms across the top of his stall. "Really? Well, thank you for pressing my pants, Augustus, but I'm thinking you should be teaching the animal husbandry class, not Professor Crowder."

AUGUSTUS PLACED HIS boots in the laundry cart and left his socks on. He had run with the cart in front, sliding across the smooth, wooden floors from one room to the next, making laundry deliveries down the long hallway. The students were all in class, and the halls were empty—just the way he liked it. Hearing noises from a room, he peeked into it, seeing Jefferson tied to a chair. "J-J-Jefferson?"

"Run, Aug! It's a trap!"

Before he could grasp the situation, six cadets leaped out from behind the door and grabbed him. He found himself tied up in a chair along with his brother. David Ruggles was seated on the bottom bunk, snapping the air with the scissors in his hand.

"They ain't crying like you did, Joe," said David.

"I only cried because you cut my head," said Joe as he rubbed his head. His crew laughed.

"Why ain't ya crying, Little Chinee?"

Augustus didn't respond.

"We don't never cry," said Jefferson.

"So little Chinee, if ya ain't gonna cry, maybe you can just s-s-stutter some more." The group laughed.

"He's only stuttering cause he can't decide which word to call you. There's so many to choose from," said Jefferson.

"Oh? Is he gonna stutter out the word? I'm curious about the word you'll call me after I do this," said David as he walked towards them with the scissors.

"Don't cut the plebe," said one of the crew. "You'll be the one in trouble."

David stopped in front of Jefferson and smiled at him. "Your lucky day, plebe. But not your brother's."

David snipped away Augustus' hair. Every lock of it was cut away, getting a laugh from the cadets until most of it fell on the floor.

"Untie them."

As one, the room turned to the door where Hollis Fletcher stood, the colonel of cadets and highest-ranking cadet at the academy. All froze to immediate attention.

"What is this?" asked Hollis as he entered the room.

"Sir! He is not a cadet. He works here," said David.

Hollis pointed to Jefferson. "This one doesn't."

"Sir, we weren't going to do anything to him, sir."

Hollis cocked his head and walked over to within an inch of David's face. "Only seniors get to torment the plebes. You know this."

"But we're…"

"But what?"

"But we're…"

"But what. I didn't hear a 'sir' in there!"

"Sir, forgive me, sir."

"And there are no buts! What is your name, yearling?"

"Sir, Ruggles, David, sir!"

"Give me those scissors and get out."

They all clicked their heels and left, leaving Hollis, Augustus, and Jefferson alone in the room. Hollis had the stature and class of American royalty. All the cadets treated him like a great leader, but not because of his stunning uniform with its gold epaulets and gold-braided rope, or because of his flawlessly oiled and combed blond hair. It was the way he carried himself, his sense of honor, and how he treated everyone with respect.

"I can't bring them up on charges; most likely nothing would be done, and it would just make me look like a snitch," he said as he untied them. "And you, plebe, why are you tied up?"

"He's my brother. They used me to lure him in."

Hollis finished untying them and looked over Augustus' crazy haircut.

"Turn around and let me fix this," he said as he started snipping away. "Brothers? One a cadet, and one works here?"

"Long s-s-story."

Hollis finished cutting and looked it over. "Looks a might decent. For not going to barbering school, it ain't bad."

CHAPTER 14
Augustus

There is rest in Heaven

IT HAD BEEN four months at the Academy. Augustus would fall asleep every night on the dirty bedsheet pile, sinking in and pulling the sheets over him like he used to do in a haystack. It was large and soft and more comfortable than the cadet beds. Every morning, Chin would come into the laundry with his tea and kick the pile to wake Augustus. Chin was good to Augustus and had a soft side and a sense of humor. Augustus worked hard for him and was a big part of keeping Chin's laundry in good order.

"Augy." Chin kicked the pile. "Time to wake up." Chin stood over him, calmly sipping from his second cup of tea. Augustus knew his daily routine; Chin didn't speak until after he had had at least two cups. He'd walk the grounds with the first cup and then walk the laundry with the second to make sure everything was in its place, all prepared for the day.

Augustus breathed in the sweet, sharp smell of it as he sat up and stretched.

"New day. Go get breakfast," said Chin.

The cafeteria was mostly empty, with only kitchen staff

there to prepare the morning meal. Chef Borrelli supervised as he drank his coffee. Augustus sat with Mickey and Ian, eating at one of the tables in the large room. Cadet Lieutenant Frederick Shelby ran in from the back. "Mr. Borrelli!" he yelled from across the cafeteria. "I need some chicken broth in a large bowl!"

Darius was calm as he regarded the cadet and took another sip. "No cadets allowed in here until seven-thirty. Go."

"The commandant sent me! He needs it, or… I mean… his horse needs it… or… I shall say the commandant requested it for his horse."

Darius laughed before taking another sip and merely smiling at Frederick.

"It needs it frightfully quick!" Frederick's panic was growing.

"Is the horse so high and mighty that he can't ask for it himself?" asked Darius, looking for a laugh from his assistants.

Augustus rose. Mickey and Ian both looked to Augustus curiously.

"This is no laughing matter, sir. I'll need it in quick time."

Darius, seeing the substantial concern in the cadet, relented. He looked back to his staff. "Make the horse up some chicken broth."

Augustus walked quickly out the door, ducking and twisting through the crowd of staff and cadets coming in for breakfast. He proceeded through the cafeteria and out onto the parade grounds. Several platoons of cadets were up early, practicing assembly and marching. Augustus ran through them, ducking and jiving to the barn.

Augustus entered and ran in and down the long dirt path in the center, looking over each gate as he went. Reaching stall thirteen, he stopped, seeing no horse. Augustus pushed open the stall gate. The horse was rolling on its side, rising and repeating the movement. In the corner sat the commandant, on the floor, and his back against the wall. From his left pant leg came a wooden limb, and his right hand held a bottle of whiskey.

He had been the commandant of the school for twenty-two of his sixty-four years; General Schaffer had a gray beard and wore the air of distinction and class. He had been born to a wealthy military family, upholding the tradition of generations of military men. But, at this moment, the commandant was not very presentable. Although he was usually smartly dressed, his uniform was disheveled when Augustus saw him. An empty bottle of whiskey laid near him in addition to the half-full one in his hand. He had been up all night with his sick horse. The commandant turned to Augustus as he approached the horse.

"She's gonna die, Mr. Frog," he slurred and took another swig from his bottle. Augustus continued to touch the horse's belly. "She's been with me for fifteen years now. This damn Academy killed her like it's killing me. It's poisoned her. Poison, poison…" The commandant stared into the sad eyes of his horse. "The things that matter most… Never neglect the things that matter most… Never neglect the things that matter most, Mr. Frog." The commandant looked about the stall. "Where is that, Mr. Squirrel?" The commandant turned back to Augustus. "What do you want? Have you come for her hand in marriage, Mr. Frog? Mr. Frog, did you hear me? Are you here for her hand in marriage?"

Augustus turned to the commandant. "I-I know a little 'b-b-bout the creatures, sir."

"What do you know? How to ride 'em? Can't you see this animal is sick, boy?"

"Sh-sh-she's been not drinking?"

"Suppose."

"Ya s-s-see her looking b-b-back at her stomach a lot? She knows there's s-s-something wrong with it."

The commandant nodded.

"She also been rolling on the g-g-ground," added Augustus, not as a question.

"She has," the commandant confirmed.

Augustus pushed on the horse's belly just as Frederick came in with the chicken broth. Several other cadets followed him, including Will, Erwin, Felts, and David Ruggles, who happened to see the commotion and followed them in. Frederick placed the bowl in front of the horse.

"Ah, Mr. Squirrel, just in time for our game of chess." The cadets, initially confused, quickly recognized that the commandant was drunk.

"The broth won't work, sir."

"Whoa, whoa! Do you know what you're doing, boy? This is my animal here."

"She gonna die in a might painful way if ya don't go in and get the problem, sir."

"And you believe the problem is what, Mr. Frog?"

"It's colic, but it's bad colic, stuck colic.

"The boy's been right on a bunch of issues, Commandant."

"Oh, has he?" said the commandant before taking another swig. The commandant relented, looking up to Frederick. "Select a few of these knights of the round table to help this boy here."

Frederick looked around at the cadets and raised his eyebrows as if to say, *You heard him.*

Augustus took a piece of chicken fat from the bowl of broth and rubbed it all over his arm.

"Can y'all get it to lay on down again? Then just lay on its belly and k-keep it from g-getting up?"

The cadets forced the horse down by using its bridle and then lay across its belly, preventing it from rising. Augustus then lay down as well, but behind the horse, and slid his hand and his arm up the horse's rectum. The horse shifted its weight, but Augustus continued up to his shoulder.

"You're a better man than me, Augustus," Will said as he lay next to him on top of the horse.

"Is that completely necessary, lad?" the commandant interjected with a squeamish expression. Augustus pulled out his arm.

"My arm ain't long enough, sir, I'll be needin' s-s-someone with a longer one."

The commandant scanned his knights. "Him." He pointed to the short boy, David Ruggles. "Take your coat off, son." With a fearful expression, David did as he was instructed.

Augustus pointed to the part of the belly where he believed the blockage was. "There's a blockage right here," he said, rubbing the area.

Augustus took some more broth fat in his hand, walked up to David, and rubbed it on his arm. Their eyes locked.

"It feels like a b-b-blockage just before the l-l-last turn of the g-g-gut." Augustus turned to the commandant. "If it was farther up, your horse would be g-g-good as d-d-dead."

Augustus took David and helped him lie down behind the horse's hindquarters. The horse's tail whipped David in the face.

"Start pushing your arm slowly in," Augustus instructed.

David obeyed, but as he did, his mouth opened in disgust. "Push it slowly up there… Okay, b-b-better be twisting your arm to face up b-b-bout now."

As he did this, the horse began to rise, throwing the other boys off it as it did. David's face turned white. Augustus tried to calm the horse, but it continued to stand.

"Whoa, whoa!" David stood straight up behind the unsettled horse, his arm up and inside, all the way to his shoulder. David's eyes were wide as saucers until a smile came to his face. "I got some! But some broke off."

"Don't pull your arm out! G-g-go back and g-g-get some more."

Augustus read David's face as he felt something, then something more until he took hold of it, his eyes going wide. The horse flinched and moved about, pushing David around. Cadets surrounded the horse and began petting to calm her down.

"Just b-b-be calm and keep p-p-pulling." Again, a smile came to David's face as his arm retracted.

"It's coming. It's coming!" David exclaimed. His arm came out, pulling with it a cannonball-sized clump of hay, feed, and manure. David stood there, smiling from ear to ear like he'd pulled out a plum. The commandant stood up.

"Bravo, boy! Bravo!" Everyone became ecstatic with yells and cheers until a rumbling came from the horse's stomach. Its tail rose, and the entirety of its intestine flowed like a firehose all over David. His smile disappeared.

It was between classes, and the cadets crowded the parade grounds, walking to their next class. Cadets came running out of the stables ahead of David, avoiding him as they laughed hysterically, creating a scene on the parade grounds. The laughter continued for at least a full two minutes until the commandant appeared with Augustus at his side.

"What rank are you, son?" asked the commandant to Augustus as they proceeded toward the administration building. The commandant placed his hand on Augustus' shoulder.

"I'm not a-a-a student here, s-s-sir. I work in the laundry."

"Your talents have to be respected. I will have to promote you. I think I'll make you my attaché. The commandant's special attaché. Yes, that sounds about right."

Augustus stood with one of the high-ranking senior cadets in front of Chin.

"Mr. True will need a uniform cut to fit him. The commandant would like it to look like his, with the exception of rank insignia," said the cadet.

Chin nodded and unexpectedly smiled at the cadet. Additional work was not something Augustus knew Chin to take kindly to without argument.

"No problem. Have it done by tomorrow." Chin turned to Augustus. "You did good for the commandant, very good."

"Thank y-y-you, Mr. Chin." Augustus pulled the corners of a sheet that he had tossed his few belongings into together and slung it over his shoulder. The cadet motioned with his head for Augustus to follow him.

Augustus nodded a thank you to Chin, who smiled back at him.

"You come visit Chin. I miss you down here. You done very good, boy!" Augustus heard Chin yell after him.

The cadet took Augustus up the three flights of steps to where Hollis, the colonel of cadets, stood. Hollis jerked his head in surprise. "You?" he said with a perfectly white smile. "How's that hair?"

Augustus smiled back. "F-F-Fine, thank you."

Hollis nodded for the escorting cadet to leave.

"So, you're the mysterious Special Attaché, Mr. True. I've heard a lot about you from the commandant. He's excited about you. Let's go, specialist. I'll be showing you to your quarters."

"Specialist?"

"Yes, it's short for Special Attaché. It's what people will call you from now on."

Augustus had to keep up with his quick gait down the richly-appointed hallway. Unpleasant smelling whale oil lamps illuminated the beautiful wallpaper. The carpet was red with a squiggly design on it.

Hollis stopped in front of a door and turned to Augustus with flair before swinging it open. With a graceful gesture from his hand, Hollis motioned for Augustus to enter before him.

The room was far more magnificent than the hallway. There were couches, chairs, a fireplace with a carved stone hearth, wallpaper with the most beautiful design on it, and gold-leaf accents that seemed to be on everything. The walls were covered with taxidermy, including animal heads, birds in flight, and fish. In a far alcove was a massive standing black bear next to a dark-stained oak desk. In front of the giant windows overlooking the front of the school was a dining table that could seat twelve or maybe more. Augustus couldn't stop looking around with his mouth open.

Hollis smiled at his wonder.

"Follow me," Hollis said as he went down a short hall that had four more doors. He opened one and made the same graceful gesture with his hand again, motioning Augustus to enter. Hollis stood at the doorway. The room was as well-appointed as the rest of the place, with a substantial carved oak bed, a chest of drawers, bed stands, and some furniture pieces Augustus did not recognize or know how to use.

"Where do I sleep?"

"In here. These are your quarters now."

"W-w-where do I-I-I sleep in this room?"

Hollis was perplexed. "Why, in that bed, of course."

"With n-no one else?"

Hollis studied Augustus. The expression on the cadet colonel softened. "Specialist True, what is your Christian name?"

"Augustus, sir."

"You see, that's just it, Augustus. You don't have to call me 'sir' anymore."

"But y-y-you're the colonel of cadets."

"But the commandant has made you the commandant's special attaché. For whatever reason, the commandant has told me specifically that you now have the utmost authority—the authority of a colonel like me. Do you understand this?"

"No," said Augustus.

Hollis smiled and nodded. "Well, I tell you what. I'll make a deal with you that if you work with me and not against me, I'll teach you everything you need to know. Deal?"

"I-I-I wouldn't w-w-work against you."

Hollis stuck out his hand. "Then it's a deal."

A BLUE AND gold tablecloth covered the giant, stained, oak dining table. He had never seen one so large. He sat in the middle of it, waiting for the commandant. He ran his hand under the tablecloth, feeling the polished wood as he often did to countless coffins in the back of his father's wagon. He pulled out his hand as he heard the thump of the commandant's wooden leg approaching. The commandant entered the room in a clean and pressed uniform, hair combed, beard trimmed, and no longer slurring his words as he had earlier in the day.

"Where's your birthplace, Mr. True?"

"P-Pennsylvania, s-sir."

"First thing you'll have to do is lose that stutter if you're gonna be any sort of an officer."

Dinner was brought in by a servant—one plate of fried potatoes. The commandant didn't move, so neither did Augustus. The servant went out and came in again with another plate and then another until there were five plates before him, far more food than they could eat. The commandant reached for a plate.

"Feel free, Mr. True."

Augustus nodded and then looked around the room as he ate. He fixed his gaze on a portrait of a mother and child.

"My wife and son."

"Excuse me, sir?"

"You're looking at my wife and son. The portrait."

"I ain't ever seen one done so nice as that."

"They are living in Maine now if you're wondering. Most people do." An irritation seemed to be growing in the commandant. "A boy should be living with his father, don't you think?" The commandant speared his ham with his fork. Seething, he said, "If you're thinking she is most likely very content without me, I believe she will concur with you on that matter." The servant refilled the commandant's wine glass. "If you're also thinking she couldn't bear to live with me…" he said, cocking his head and sweetening his tone. "…you'd also be correct."

Augustus nervously looked to his plate and took another bite, not wanting to look the commandant in the eyes. When he looked back up, the commandant was studying the chandelier. "I fought valiantly in the war of 1812, and if there were a war today, I'd fight just as valiantly." The commandant's face was turning red with restrained anger building. "I was loved by my men, but—" A loud fart stopped him. "Shoot the rooster! I used to be able to hold those!" he yelled with more anger than embarrassment. "Even my body is defying me!"

Immediately rising, the commandant knocked over his chair. The servant came over and stopped, not sure what to do. The commandant threw his napkin on the table and walked toward the hallway. "Good night, Mr. True," he said as he stomped off.

Augustus took another bite before the servant moved to clean the dishes away.

THE COLONEL OF cadet's uniform was unbuttoned, and his belt not buckled as he rapidly walked down the hallway of the administration building. A cadet came toward him from the opposite direction.

"They found him. He's in the laundry," said the cadet calmly. Hollis tucked in his shirt and continued in that direction. The cadet following.

Cadet Captain Eddleston, the best friend of Hollis, stood outside the laundry, waiting for Hollis's arrival. Augustus, sleepy from just waking up, sat on the pile of dirty laundry. Chin stood at the far corner of the room and walked closer upon seeing Hollis enter.

"He slept here last night," said Eddleston. All four people looked down at Augustus, who returned their gaze with confusion.

"Augustus, the commandant asked where you were. Is this where you were all night?" asked Hollis. Augustus nodded. "Why didn't you sleep in your bed?"

"I don't know how I got here. I had a dream about my brother…"

"Who's your brother?"

Chin stepped up. "He a cadet. He always here. They tight. Tight like brothers."

"Such a strange dream. I kept saying 'two halves make a whole.'"

THE BOYS SAT alone in the two chairs in front of the commandant's desk. These were the chairs that many boys before them had sat in and told they could no longer attend the school due to some infraction of the Academy's code of conduct. Augustus was worried he'd done something wrong. He turned to Jefferson next to him. Jefferson didn't look concerned; instead, he was in awe of the commandant's office and the taxidermy animals.

The commandant entered from the far side of the dining room with the colonel of cadets following behind.

"I understand the problem. Family is family. Your brother may stay with you in your room," said the commandant as he stroked his gray beard.

Hollis's brows raised.

"Thank you kindly, sir," said Jefferson promptly.

Augustus' eyes narrowed as he resisted the tears trying to fill them. "You treatin' us like family, you are. That's a b-b-blessing of k-kindness."

The commandant stood a moment before his eyes went to his wife and son's portrait, then back to Augustus. The commandant turned away to the window.

"Ahem, Mr. True, your uniform is ready. Please put it on and follow me during parade in the morning." Augustus rose, stepped back, and came to attention.

"Yes, sir!"

It was a sunny, but sharply chilly morning with the wind whipping about, biting ears, noses, and cheeks. Augustus didn't feel the stinging cold on his face. Pride warmed him as he wore his awe-inspiring uniform and stood next to the commandant. It had a dark blue short jacket with tails, with one row of brass buttons down the middle, big, gold-trimmed cuffs, high collared neck, gold, fringe draping epaulets, and a gold braided rope, called an aiguillette, slung across the chest. The pants were white, close-fit pants that dove into shiny, knee-high black boots. The cap was called a *shako* but nicknamed a tombstone for its high extension in front. It had black plumage coming from the side, but the commandant replaced the original gold-eagle emblem on the front with the school emblem. The cadets wore a *shako* as well, but theirs had a red braided rope high on the left side and slung down, around, and back, and red plumage on the right side with a brass school emblem badge on the front.

The cadets had assembled on the parade field as they did for every Monday morning roll call and inspection. The grounds of the academy were strangely silent for such a large assembly of young men. The only sounds were the wind and the snapping of the Virginia state and American flags. The moment the commandant and Augustus stepped from the administration building onto the field, Augustus could sense the awe and shock from the cadets as they approached.

Hollis called out, "Inspection arms!"

Immediately, the cadets brought their rifles up and in front of them for inspection. Stepping quickly, the commandant and Augustus stopped beside Hollis, who stood before the assembly. Augustus, not knowing what to expect, mimicked the commandant. Hollis stood stone stiff, at attention, eyes front, and toward the assembly.

"At ease and relax, Colonel. How are you this morning?" asked the commandant as he put on his wool gloves. The statue became Hollis again.

"Sir, wonderful, sir, on this fine morning. Shall I address?"

"Colonel, you may address," replied the commandant.

"Yes, sir," said Hollis as he turned to the assembly. "Carry on!" he yelled out to Captain Eddleston, who then repeated it to the assembly.

The first platoon leader called out, "Roll call! Call out!"

Each platoon successively repeated it. As the assembly continued its Monday drills, the commandant walked amongst the rows of cadets, inspecting them. Augustus, his chin high, followed with Hollis. When the commandant found something he didn't like, such as a button unbuttoned, he'd point it out to Hollis, who wrote it in a book with the cadet's name. Augustus curiously watched Hollis take notes and listened to the mistakes pointed out by the commandant. Hollis glanced down and winked at him.

After inspecting six rows of cadets from the different platoons, the commandant walked away from the assembly. "Very good, Colonel. Carry on."

Hollis came to immediate attention and saluted the commandant.

"Sir!" he snapped sharply. Hollis returned to the assembly but not before a smile and a nod to Augustus.

Captain Eddleston called out, "Present, arms!" Immediately, the assembly brought their rifles down in front and moved their right foot further to the side as Augustus and the commandant walked off. Augustus could not help but look behind him, amazed at the precision of the cadets.

"Shall we inspect the livestock, son?"

Augustus nodded. "Yes, s-sir."

The pig pen had both indoor and outdoor pens that held twenty or so, Augustus estimated. One larger pig was moving other pigs away from a sow.

"Hmm, see this specimen right there?" said the commandant, pointing.

"Yessum… Y-yes, sir," corrected Augustus.

"What it appears to be doing is a bit more intriguing than what I'm used to seeing. It is apparently moving the other males away from that sow. Fascinating. That's strategic maneuvering," he said, pleased. "Bravo, Mr. Pig! Bravo!"

A cadet came to the pen, putting an apron over his uniform. He picked up the feed pail when the commandant noticed him. "Young man, young man!" The cadet ran over. "Oh, Corporal, please remove this pig from the others and place him in separate facilities. I'd like to make him my pet."

The corporal looked confused.

"Separate facilities? I don't know…" said the corporal as he saw the commandant's expression turn to irritation. "Yes, sir. Right away, sir."

"Good lad. Carry on." The commandant turned for the stables.

Augustus followed but turned back to the confused corporal, shaking his head and mouthing the word "*What?*"

Augustus sped up to walk alongside the commandant. The commandant kept up a strong pace despite his wooden leg, enough that Augustus found it challenging to keep pace with him.

Augustus glanced over to him. The sun wrapped a halo around the commandant's head, darkening his bearded face. The surrounding light blinded Augustus to a squint, but not before he caught a revealing glimpse of the commandant's fake smile. He hid his sorrow behind it, like a weeper behind her veil. The light was too much, and he threw his eyes back to the ground and to the commandant's wooden leg. In his fake smile, Augustus saw the portrait in his dining room and saw that the commandant had lost something far more painful than a limb in battle; for whatever reason, he had lost his family. Sorrow and regret; they emanated from him. Augustus could smell it on his skin like liquor on a drunk.

There was a time Augustus saw an old Susquehannock Indian at a remembrance, working as the sin eater. The Indian sat with the dead man laid out in front of him. The dead man had confessed all his sins to his wife before his death and had told her if she didn't get him a sin eater he'd be going south instead of north.

Augustus watched the old Susquehannock as the widow passed a plate of food over her husband's body to him. The plate absorbed all her husband's sins as it went. The old Susquehannock set it down and ate it all with his fingers, licking the grease from each one. After he finished, the same sad smile rose to the Indian's lips, and sorrow filled his eyes.

After the ceremony, Augustus overheard him speak to his father. He was the last of his kind. Most of his tribe had been devastated by smallpox before he had been born. Even more of the tribe, including his parents, were murdered by settlers after. Augustus watched as he walked off. All the mourners turned their backs to the "sin-filled" Susquehannock, shunned like a leper.

The commandant reminded Augustus of something the old Susquehannock had told his father before he walked off: *love and sorrow were the sun and moon of the soul. Whenever love tired and went to bed over the horizon, sorrow swooped in and took its place.* In the commandant, love had tired.

As they walked toward the stables, Augustus looked down at his perfectly-shined boot and his wooden leg. He skipped a step to be in perfect stride with the commandant.

CHAPTER 15
Charlotte

Just whisper my name in your heart
and I will be there

CHARLOTTE PEERED THROUGH the iron gate of the Academy. It was the city version of watching him through the bushes at the True farm. The cadet in the booth at the side of the gate curiously watched her with a side-eye glance.

"Ma'am, may I help you?" he finally asked.

"Just looking," said Charlotte.

Augustus had been gone four months, but from what it looked like, he wasn't doing too badly. It was easy for Charlotte to distinguish him from the rest there on the parade grounds. He was the one walking next to the big man with medals on his chest and epaulets on his shoulders. The other boys all saluted Augustus and the big man.

"Looks like you've done very well for yourself, Augustus," she said softly.

"What, Momma?" asked eleven-year-old Little Miss. She was also peering in the gates next to her mother.

"Just talking to myself."

"Why did we come here, and how long we gonna stay?"

Charlotte turned and walked up to Micah who was standing next to their carriage, Little Miss following.

"Why I don't know. I think city life will be much better for ya, and you can get some good schoolin' here."

"Now, Micah, I'm making a new start now and don't want to be called The Missus. I want to be called by my Christian name, Charlotte."

Micah rolled his eyes. "I can't be abiding by that, Missus. It's in my blood."

"Well, then, tell anyone who asks about me."

"Yessum," said Micah with another unseen eye roll.

Charlotte glanced about, looking at her surroundings. Across the street were shops and offices. In a window of a gunsmithing shop was a little sign that said For Rent.

"Good a place as any," said Charlotte. She crossed the street and went inside as Micah and Little Miss watched.

Inside were several guns mounted on the walls and a long, wide counter that divided the store. Two men were seated at tables on the other side of the counter, both working on guns.

"Can I help you, ma'am?" The shopkeeper rose and approached the counter. He was a good looking, middle-aged man with salt and pepper hair. He wore a leather smock covering a brown suit.

"I'd like to inquire about that 'For Rent' sign in your window."

"Excellent. It's the room upstairs, outside entrance, good solid bed, nightstand, large closet. No meals. I'm a widower and don't know much about cooking. Rent's four-fifty a month."

"Overlook the Academy grounds?"

"It does," he replied. "Will it be for you and your husband?"

"I'm a widow," she lied. "It'll be for my eleven-year-old daughter and myself, but I'll also be needing a place for my boy outside." Charlotte nodded in the direction of Micah through the windows.

"He can sleep with my two in the shed around back."

"He'll be needing a solid bed," she replied.

"They sleep on straw back there. It's plenty comfortable."

"No. He's been with my family for years now, and we treat him rightly so."

"I guess I can find one somewhere, but I'll have to charge ya an extra two bits for it."

"That won't be a problem," said Charlotte as she turned away from the man and looked toward Micah for a moment.

"The name is Eldridge Greenwood, ma'am. Welcome."

She turned back to him, her chin up in a regal manner. "Pleased to meet ya, Mr. Greenwood. I'm Charlotte."

CHARLOTTE AND LITTLE Miss entered their new surroundings with Micah carrying their bags behind them. The room was twelve-by-fourteen, and it was as Mr. Greenwood had described. Charlotte went to the window.

"Momma, where will I be sleeping?"

"Why, next to me on the bed there."

Micah set the bags down as Charlotte searched the Academy grounds. She set up a chair in front of it as Little Miss tested the mattress.

"Whatcha see?"

"Oh, nothin'. Just seeing."

"I'll be off to see to my sleepin' place, Missus." With no response from her, Micah exited the room, leaving her still staring out the window. After a few moments, she walked to her bag and brought it to the table. Inside she pulled a small music box and brought it to the windowsill. She wound it, and it began to play "Amazing Grace."

"I love that song," said Little Miss.

The next day, Little Miss and Micah were waiting for Charlotte just outside of the gates of the Academy. As Charlotte exited the gates, the two cadet guards clicked their heels to attention. She walked from the gate, made a right turn, and passed by Micah and her daughter without saying a word. They followed her from about five feet behind.

"I be thinkin' we don't need no money anyways, Missus," said Micah.

"We don't have any money? What are we doing here?" said Little Miss.

"We have some, but it won't last. Besides, I think it's apparent that I was hoping to get a position there for more than just the money." Micah knew what she meant. Little Miss did not.

"I believe you should be weepin'," Micah said with disdain. Charlotte rolled her eyes. "Your ma's ma and them befo' her was alls weepers. There ain't no weepers up theres now. A town needs a weeper."

"I'm sure my mother took over the duty, Micah. This is where we live now, and this town don't use no weepers."

"This ain't no town. This is a city. It ain't never heard of no weepers."

Charlotte stopped and turned to him with a determined expression. "I told you, you could stay, or you could go. You can still go on back home if ya wish."

"If Micah goes, I go," added Little Miss.

Micah turned his face away from her glare, looking down the street. "You knows I won't be leavin' either of you," he said.

"I know you won't be leaving us, Micah," said Little Miss.

Charlotte turned back around, and they all continued down the street. "Alls I'm saying is you have the opportunity if ya wish. Now, let's see about that school for Little Miss."

After enrolling Little Miss in school, the trio walked back. Next door to the gunsmithing shop was the Bourbon Street Diner. They didn't serve bourbon, and there was no Bourbon street in Clarksburg, Virginia. Charlotte, followed by Micah and Little Miss, crossed the street and walked to it.

She stopped and turned to him. "I'll have something sent out here for you."

Charlotte took the hand of Little Miss and entered, leaving Micah waiting out front.

The interior of the diner sported wooden tables covered with yellow checkered tablecloths and wood spindle-back chairs. Charlotte noticed a door that she assumed led to the kitchen.

They took a seat at the first table. Only one other table was taken, and Mr. Greenwood sat there eating his lunch. He didn't seem to notice her enter. A lanky man came from the kitchen doorway. He looked like he'd seen about forty winters and, upon seeing her, walked over.

"Ma'am?"

"Potato pancakes, a tomato, and some greens for us, please.

Also, the same for my boy just outside the door. Add a bowl of grits and a glass of milk as well. Thank you."

The man nodded and walked off. Charlotte turned to find Greenwood staring at her. "Good day, Mr. Greenwood."

"Missus, how are you this day?" he asked in a pleased-to-see-her tone.

"Just fine, thank you."

"Don't often see you out. How's the room? Everything to your satisfaction?"

"Quite, quite."

"I think it's a fine room," said Little Miss.

"Pleased to hear it."

"But I'd rather be home," said Little Miss under her breath. Charlotte watched Greenwood for a bit before a marvelous thought came to her.

"Mr. Greenwood, you wouldn't happen to be in need of some home cooking and a little cleaning around your place, would you?"

Greenwood turned to her. "You offering?"

"Indeed."

"I was under the assumption that you were a woman of means."

"Well, I am not destitute, I'll tell you that," she replied with a bit of indignation.

Greenwood put up his palms to her. "In no way did I…"

"I just need a little extra to get me by."

"Please, Charlotte, I did not mean to offend in any way. In fact, I'd love a woman's home-cooked meal."

"Actually, it'd be from my boy, Micah. He's a right fine cook and does a right fine job of cleaning too."

Greenwood sat back from his meal and considered it as he wiped his mouth with his napkin. "Why don't you sell him to me? I'd pay a fair price."

"He's not for sale. As I said, he's been in my family since his birth."

Greenwood nodded. "I suppose it'd save me money coming to this place. Alright, I'll try him out. How about in return for free room and board?"

She considered his offer. It would allow her to save what money she did have.

The lanky man came out with two plates, setting them on the table. "Don't be forgetting my boy outside," she reminded him.

"Got it ready in the back."

She turned back to Greenwood. "Fair enough."

CHAPTER 16
Augustus

Loved with such love, and with such sorrow mourned

THE SOAP NEXT to the washbasin was a pink, round ball shaped like a rose. So beautiful, it amazed Augustus as it rolled around in his hands. *Rich man's soap.* He felt a twinge of guilt for using it just to wash up for dinner.

Jefferson's finger poked Augustus in the back as he dried his hands with the floral towel. Augustus turned to wide eyes and a giddy smile.

"Aug! There's talk! There's big talk!" he whispered excitedly.

"About what?"

"You! About you, my brother!"

"What about m-me?"

"Some people be sayin' you got might. Like officer might, Aug!"

"Officer might?"

"Like 'colonel of cadets' might. Don't ya see, Aug? You can order people around. Tell 'em what to do. Some people are scared of that, Aug. Some people like David Ruggles and all those fools messing with you."

"Yeah?" asked Augustus with a mischievous grin.

"Oh, yeah." Jefferson smiled.

Augustus tested it out the next day at Monday morning parade inspection. Instead of following the commandant and Hollis as he did before, he walked down a different row to make his own inspections. Stopping before a cadet, he first turned back to the commandant for his approval. The commandant peered around a cadet to nod his approval. Hollis winked. Augustus turned back to the cadet before him. "Run and g-g-get a note pad and writing d-d-device."

"Yes, sir!" the boy called out before running for the building.

Augustus continued down the row. "There's a scuff on your sh-sh-shoe. T-t-tuck your shirt in tighter. Did you l-l-look me in the eyes?! Eyes front!"

Jefferson was right. They were all treating him with respect—even fear.

The cadet returned with the notepad and began taking demerit notes from Augustus for any infraction he saw fit.

Parade inspection became a favorite time for Augustus, and he could be with his two favorite people outside of his brother: Hollis and the commandant. Best of all, he doled out demerits like dead cakes at a funeral. And he did this without Jefferson, who had to be with his platoon, at attention, waiting to be inspected himself.

"Augy, this couldn't be better," said Jefferson as they were both walking across the parade ground to their next class. "We are the men we always wanted to be." Two cadets passing them saluted Augustus. "See that? You're being saluted! Saluted by officers," Jefferson said with a huge smile.

"Hollis doesn't have to salute me," Augustus replied.

"Hollis? Fine then, one officer out of the whole damn school. I still gotta salute."

"I still gotta return the salute, so what's the d-d-difference?"

"Are you soft? There's a big difference," said Jefferson.

"Maybe we c-c-can ask the commandant if you could be promoted too."

"Nah, I'm fine, Aug. Real fine. This whole set of circumstances just fell upon us. Plus, the commandant has taken a fancy to you. He thinks of you as his kin or something since his ain't here and alls." Before entering the building, two more cadets saluted Augustus. Jefferson laughed and jabbed him in the side with his elbow.

CAPTAIN EDDELSTON ESCORTED Augustus and Jefferson down the dorm hallway. With the pace Eddleston was walking, it must have been important. He stopped them before a dorm room, turned to them with a grin, and gracefully gestured with his hand to the doorway. Augustus and Jefferson cautiously peered around the doorway. Six senior classmen had David Ruggles tied to a chair with Hollis seated behind him with a smile.

"Attention on deck!" called out Hollis. All the seniors except Hollis came to attention. "Good morning, Special Attaché," said Hollis, laughing.

"Hollis, what's going on?" Augustus walked into the room, Jefferson following.

"As you were," said Augustus to the seniors. They all stood at ease.

"What we have here is a bit of cold revenge," said Hollis.

He put out the scissors to Augustus. David's eyes following them. Sweat began to form on David's forehead. Augustus hefted the scissors in his hand as he studied David's face. He took up a few strands of his hair, clipped just the tip, and sprinkled it on David's nose.

"You have t-two and a half years with me here. I won't hear of you m-m-messing with nobody, will I?"

"No, sir!"

"G-glad to hear it." Augustus turned and quickly exited the room.

"Attention!" All stood at attention as Augustus left.

David blew a sigh of relief.

"Untie this lucky chap," said Hollis as he followed Augustus out.

"Specialist!" Hollis called to him down the hallway. Augustus and Jefferson stopped and turned to Hollis, waiting for him.

"Excuse us, plebe. I'd like a word with the special attaché," he said to Jefferson without looking at him.

"Sir!" said Jefferson, leaving.

Hollis smiled at Augustus. "Augustus, I like you. We're friends…"

Augustus recognized his concern. "Did I d-d-do something wrong?"

"Well, the first thing I want to say is the way you handled that back there was outstanding. You showed restraint. Restraint and honor are two attributes of a fine officer. You know that your appointment to special attaché was highly irregular, right?" Augustus looked confused. "What I mean is, there is no rank called 'special attaché,' the commandant just made that up. I mean, in this school it has power, but in the real army, it doesn't exist. And your appointment has never happened at this school in the past—"

"But we just learned about b-battlefield promotions," Augustus replied.

"But this is no battlefield. What I'm trying to say is, senior classmen twice your size are saluting you and such. There's talk about that. Now, I like you, and I'm fine with it and all, 'cause this is my last year at Wadleigh-Holmes. But there's a bunch of cadets that aren't. I'm just letting you know. What you did back in that room was just what I would expect a great leader to do. I've learned you earn respect by giving respect, and you don't misuse power. Do you understand?"

"I do."

"Secondly, do you notice how I call you Augustus here, but in public, like the room back there, I call you special attaché? Well, I'd appreciate it if you could call me 'Hollis' in private places like this with no one around, but out there, with cadets, I'd appreciate it if you could call me 'Colonel.' It gives me a bit more respect, and I believe I have earned it after all these years here.

"You certainly have, sir. I'll ab-absolutely oblige ya."

"Fine, fine. And thank you, Augustus. Now, I believe I am detecting a might less of that stutter. You been practicing, or…" Hollis said with a growing smile, "it just might be this newfound confidence coming on."

Augustus had felt it too. "You might just be right, Colonel."

CHAPTER 17
Charlotte

We shall meet beyond the river

THE KITCHEN OF the gunsmithing shop had smelled like gun cleaning oil before the meal Micah had just prepared. Now it smelled delicious. Charlotte and Little Miss sat at the kitchen with Greenwood. Micah cleared their plates and took them outside to be cleaned.

Greenwood patted his stomach. "Fine meal, Missus. Your boy did a right fine meal."

"He always has." Charlotte looked about the room. "So, tell me, Mr. Greenwood, was your pa a gunsmith?"

"No, my pa was a teacher at the Academy across the street. I apprenticed with the gunsmith that lived here in this very shop when I was nine years old. I just continued on and bought the shop from his widow when he passed. Good old fella. Daniels was his name." The memory drew a pleasant smile.

Micah came back in and picked up the empty pot of stew. Greenwood turned to Charlotte.

"Charlotte, what about you? Why are you here? Why this town? I see you always walking by the school, looking in the gate. School interest you?"

Micah stopped at the door, back facing them, waiting for the answer. Charlotte smiled and looked into Greenwood's eyes, saying nothing.

"You're a mysterious one," he said with a grin. "I like that."

ON HER WAY to school, every day, Little Miss would cross the street to talk to the cadet guards at the gate. She asked them all kinds of questions and learned a lot. To be a guard, you had to be a second-year cadet, fifteen at least. Little Miss wasn't shy about speaking to the older boys, and they had to be pleasant to the eleven-year-old; it was their job to be sociable with all passersby.

"The academy is having their graduation festivities on Saturday. We can watch from the window," Little Miss told her mother.

Charlotte turned to her. "Really? Why don't we watch from inside?"

"Only families of the cadets invited is what they told me and some army folk. I asked if I could come, and they said no."

Charlotte grew a mischievous grin. Nothing was going to stop her. "I think we can find a way."

CHAPTER 18
Augustus

I'll see you on the other side of the stars

"GRADUATION IS COMING up, boys. Two weeks away, did you invite your family?" asked the commandant as he put his napkin on the table. Seven months at the Academy, and their first year was about to end. After the ceremony, cadets would be dismissed for their two-and-a-half-month summer.

"I did, sir. I wrote them," said Jefferson. Augustus kept his mouth shut. The plate in front of him was picked up by the dining servant, as was Jefferson's.

The commandant lit his pipe, puffing it twice. "They respond?"

"Yes, sir. They'll be here."

"I hope they don't come," said Augustus. "And I ain't going home for summer."

"Pa already bought you a ticket."

"He ain't my pa anymore." Augustus had told the commandant about being indentured to the school by his parents and how he never wanted to see them again. There was a relief on the commandant's face after he said it. Augustus turned to the commandant. "You've been more of a father to me than anyone could hope for."

A puff of smoke floated to the ceiling. "Very kind of you to say, Augustus, but I believe if your parents want to take you home, they will."

"I won't see them. And they won't see me."

The commandant took four puffs on his pipe. The smoke hid a pleased smile.

"DANG. IT. ALL!" said Jefferson, his mouth open as he gawked at the finest parade-dress uniform he'd ever seen.

Augustus strode around the parlor room in it. Jefferson looked at himself in the mirror. He wore the typical Wadleigh-Holmes first-year parade dress uniform, a grey coat with seven rows of brass buttons across the jacket, and three columns going down it. The two side columns were decorative. There was a white saber belt at the waist, which would later hold a sword for upperclassmen. He wore grey pants with a red stripe, called a blood stripe down the side of the leg, and a shako cap.

The difference between Augustus' regular uniform and his parade dress was a red sash around his waist, draping down the left leg, a sword at his hip, and the most magnificent tall bicorne black hat—the kind that was fan-shaped and went front to back with gold embroidery along the edges and a black plume rising on the left side. At fourteen, he looked like Napoleon.

"Jefferson, time to go join your class, boy," said the commandant.

"Sir!" said Jefferson. He turned to Augustus. "See you out there, general."

Jefferson skipped out of the room. The commandant walked to the window; the families were arriving and walking about the grounds.

"Looks like they are seating everyone. Shall we reconnoiter, son?"

Augustus put on his bicorne hat. "We shall."

With all the visitors and families seated on the parade field, the ceremony began with the freshman class performing marching drills before lining up and sitting at the back of the audience. Mr. and Mrs. True sat at the end of a row. She wore her best dress: a floral-patterned blue bell. Spotting Jefferson, she pointed him out to her husband.

"There he is. There's Jefferson."

All the cadets were 'eyes front' as they marched by and were not allowed to look at their parents until they filed into their seats. The Trues turned around to see Jefferson waving at them. She smiled, waving back.

"Don't he look like a gentleman? Done him good already."

The next two classes did the same as the first. The seniors went last and sat in a square of seats to the left of the stage. After the last senior sat, the commandant came out from the administration building with Augustus following in all his regalia.

The mouths of the True parents fell open.

"What in the heavens? Would you looky there," said Mr. True quietly as if he'd seen a cow fly.

Augustus took a seat on stage to the right. Military staff and professors came next and sat next to him. The commandant went to the podium and began his speech. The Trues, confused and amazed, heard none of it.

The seniors copied the West Point tradition of throwing their hats into the air, concluding the ceremonies. The Trues met Jefferson in the middle of the parade grounds with the other families.

"Well, boy, look at you! You are a sight!" said Mr. True. Mrs. True swept him up in an embrace, knocking his hat to the ground. "You made us so proud! So proud!"

"Looking like quite the gentleman, Jefferson," said Mr. True as he handed his hat back to him.

"Thanks, Pa."

Mr. True turned about. "Now, where is your brother, and what in the world…?"

"He's probably got duties to perform."

"But, about that uniform he wore?"

"It's a long story."

"Well, you can tell us on the way home," said Mrs. True. "You go on now and get him. Our train tickets are for the four o'clock train."

Jefferson put on his hat and took off his smile. "Well, that's the thing… My bag is ready to go over there in the dorm building, but Augustus don't want to come."

"Don't want to come where?" asked Mr. True.

"Don't want to come home. He ain't coming home, he said."

"What? He can't stay here. School's done for summer."

"Not for him. He's staying with the commandant."

Mrs. True's head jerked back. "Staying with the commandant? Who's that?"

"He's that bearded man with the long-winded speech. He's the commander of the school."

Mr. True stood a moment with a confused expression before turning to the administration building and back to Jefferson. "Nah, this can't be. Let's see to it. Show me where this commandant is." The crowd was slowly thinning. "This bird don't fly. Show me to that man."

"Check your pocket watch, Archer. It's the four o'clock train."

Mr. True pulled out his brass watch with a hunting dog leaping after a bird etched on it. "Three ten."

"Hurry on up then. We ain't got much time," said Mrs. True.

Twenty minutes later, Jefferson and Mr. True returned to Mrs. True on the steps of the administration building without Augustus. "Can't find him, neither of them. Asked all around. No one knows nothing."

"Well, we're gonna miss our train if we don't get moving," said Mrs. True.

"No. Now, you two, go on," he said, looking about. "I'll find him. If I miss the train, I'll just get another. You gotta get on back to the girls. I'll get to the marrow of the bone around here. This dog don't hunt."

They went in opposite directions: Jefferson and his mother to the train station and Mr. True to the administration building. Augustus walked through the doorway and stopped before his father. The commandant stood next to him. "Good day, Mr. True," said Augustus.

Mr. True smiled, eyes wide. "Augustus! Ha! Well, look at you, boy!" he said, glancing at the commandant who stood next to him, arms behind his back, and smiling pleasantly. "And callin' me, Mr. True. Ha! You know I like to be called 'pa'."

Mr. True's eyes darted back and forth between Augustus and the silent commandant.

"Funny, the only person I call 'pa' now is him," said Augustus, motioning with his shoulder to the commandant next to him. Mr. True's expression grew concerned.

The smiles continued to beam at Mr. True eerily. He glanced back and forth, uneasy.

"Now, whatcha mean there, boy? I am your pa."

"You ain't. You sold me."

Mr. True cocked his head. "Now, don't be saying that."

"You made me a bound boy, didn't you?"

"Now then, a little work don't hurt nobody. Now it's time we better be getting' on. Get your stuff and…"

"Good to see you, Mr. True," said Augustus before turning his back to him and walking off with the commandant.

CHAPTER 19
Charlotte

I love thee to the depth and breadth and height my soul can reach

CHARLOTTE SAT IN the chair, watching the parents and cadets mill about after the ceremony. She and Little Miss had left early to avoid seeing the Trues if they had been there.

She couldn't stop thinking of the moment Augustus came out on the stage with the commandant. Her jaw dropped. He didn't march with his class; he led it.

She turned to a knock on her door.

"It'd be me, Missus," said Micah.

"Come in, Micah."

Micah shut the door behind him as Charlotte turned to him. He looked to the bed and saw the sleeping Little Miss before he slowly raised his arm and pointed out the window. She pulled back the drape. Across the street was Mr. True, looking up and directly at her.

She turned back to Micah. "Tell him I'll be down in a moment, then come back up to watch Little Miss."

Micah walked out the door, shutting it behind him.

THE PARK IN town was like a little bit of the country in the center of the city. It had long, wide greenbelts of lawn, just the right number of trees for shade, and many wandering paths to stroll on. Mr. True and Charlotte sat on one of the several benches scattered along the pathways.

"I told you it'd be good for him and make him a gentleman. Hope that pleases you."

"I am pleased." Mr. True nervously shifted on the bench and played with his hat. "How'd you find me?" asked Charlotte.

"I saw your boy walking down the street. I just followed him."

"What is the point here, Mr. True? Why did you want to see me?"

"I know you was angry at me for sending him away and all, but you can see he's doing right fine. There's nothing to worry about. He's well taken care of, gonna be a gentleman."

"Have I not said I'm pleased? But if ya recall, I wouldn't even be here in this town if ya hadn't went out jugging and jawing to your wife about our child in the first place. Remember that, Mr. True."

"Yessum, well, no. Truth be, I don't remember."

"And so?"

"And so, I believe I'd like you to come back… to come back home."

Charlotte's eye's beamed with her smile. "Well, now, I'll certainly have to think on that proposal, it was so convincin'. Shall I come to your home, Mr. True? Ain't that sweet. Mrs. True fine with that?"

"You know what I'm saying," he said in an irritated tone. "I want you to be coming back. I need you. I need you back."

She searched his face for some evidence of intelligence. His logic was skewed, but it was true that Augustus was doing very well at the Academy. His decision to send him luckily ended up being a good one, but Charlotte had lost the girl she had been. She was someone different now, a determined woman with a goal, and one that didn't need a man to mess it all up like Mr. True had done more than once.

"I'm not that girl anymore, Mr. True."

Mr. True took her hand. She noticed him trying to look into her eyes, but she wouldn't give him the chance. His thumb began rubbing her hand. She remembered him doing that in their past.

A smile returned to her face. Maybe today, just for this time, she would allow herself to be there again as it was in years past. She would be that foolish girl that didn't know what the future held. She would throw herself into the moment, let it take her, and do what it may.

After he leaves, I will forget him and all this and return to the woman I should be, the woman that allowed my child to slip from my grasp.

"Your ma's the only weeper up theres now. She's too old to be doing this. People be asking for you," said Mr. True. When she didn't react, he continued. "She's gotta take care of the farm."

"She's got help for the farm."

"She's still got to manage it, take care of—"

Charlotte turned to him, interrupting, "You only want me for weeping?" She laughed. "You know I won't be leaving my boy."

Mr. True's expression softened. He took her other hand

as drops of rain started to fall. They ran off to find shelter underneath a tree. From there, Mr. True scanned the area and spotted a walking bridge. Pulling her hand, they ran under it. Other couples were also there, hiding from the rain.

Mr. True pushed Charlotte against the side of the cold brick bridge. Placing his hand behind her neck, he kissed her. Charlotte let it happen. With no warning, Mr. True stopped kissing her, turned on his heels, and vanished through the now crowded under-bridge. Awkwardly left there alone, she looked around at the other couples, some with children.

Charlotte thought about Little Miss, the daughter he didn't know he had. Mr. True had failed her, but she was also wrong by keeping that secret. She had hidden Little Miss from him all those years after she resumed her weeping duties from her mother. It was his fault she had lost Augustus by confessing to his wife. She couldn't risk that happening again.

She thought back to the time when she had told her mother of the second pregnancy. "May God forgive my soul for all the curse words I may use!" Issie said as she slammed her fist onto her rocking chair's armrest. "Can't you keep them legs closed for goodness sakes?" Charlotte had stood by the fire, avoiding Issie's flaring eyes. "Who is it this time?"

"You know who it is, Momma."

"Why, no, I do not! With your conduct, it could be anybody! We are Fenn women, and never have I ever heard of this behavior from any of our kin. You are a disgrace to our good name!" Charlotte had collapsed to the floor, crying. "I'll now have to go back to weeping *again*. What you need is a chastity belt."

"You tell that fella?" chimed in Grandma Fenn.

"No."

"You ain't gonna be telling, see? I ain't havin' another Fenn baby taken away, so's ya ain't gonna be telling," insisted Grandma. "I'm too old to be going through this again."

Eight months later, Little Miss was born. Issie had named her Melody Ann, after her aunt, but Micah had started calling her Little Miss, and it had stuck.

Little Miss had black hair, but what was especially striking about her was that she had one green eye and one brown. As she grew into a little girl, Little Miss became Micah's best friend. He loved that child like she was his own. And even though Micah never smiled, he was always smiling inside for her.

When Little Miss was four years old, he began to play weeping games with her while teaching her the trade at the same time. Charlotte could see Micah was taking on the role of father for her little girl. She decided back then that Little Miss' real father must never know about her.

As quickly as Mr. True had left, he came running back, only to grab her hand and pull her outside into the rain. They ran along the pathway some distance until he found the gardening shed that he'd already broken into. He pulled her in and shut the door.

Breathing heavy and drenched from the rain, the two stared at each other. His hand reached around her waist, pulling her in close as he kissed her. Her hand went to the back of his wet hair, sinking her fingers into it. His hand went to her breast before moving to the buttons on the back of her dress.

Both naked, they laid on the pile of wet clothes and made love. It was different than any other time with him. He was gentle but passionate. His touch spoke to her more than his words could. It told her that he desperately needed her in his life. But she wouldn't go back and the decision not to tell him solidified in her thoughts.

THE RAIN HAD stopped, and Mr. True and Charlotte walked back to the gunsmith shop. Their clothes were soaked and uncomfortable. Charlotte stopped and turned to him. "You got to go on."

"Why?"

"Because we ain't married and it looks funny, Mr. True. I am a lady."

They both looked to the Academy walls. "Can I come callin' later?"

"Don't you gotta get back?"

"I gotta train ticket for tomorrow."

"That'd be fine, I 'spect. Where are you sleeping?"

"In the train station. I've got to be leaving in the morn." He took her hand.

"Not here, Archer!" she said in a harsh tone as she yanked her hand away. "I'll see you this eve, I 'spect. Good eve."

As Mr. True watched her enter, Mr. Greenwood was watching from inside the shop as he worked on a rifle. Charlotte walked around to the back entrance. Greenwood appeared from his shop rear door. "Evening, Missus."

"Evening, Mr. Greenwood." She climbed her steps.

"I saw that young man; do I know him? Is he from around here?"

Charlotte stopped, a bit frightened and irritated. He might

have seen something from the window. "He's not from around here. He's my brother."

"How nice. I'd like to meet him sometime."

It was just about time for supper when Greenwood and his two apprentices were finishing up work for the day. Darrel, fifteen and a son of a friend of Greenwood's, was a beginner apprentice but very bright and knowledgeable about hunting and guns. The other was Hartford, an older man of forty-two, but who looked more like sixty with his long gray beard. The shop door opened and in walked Mr. True.

"We're closing up now," said Greenwood as he concentrated on his work. Hartford rose. "Something I can help you with?"

"I come callin' for Charlotte."

Greenwood stopped, looked up from his work. "Ah, yes, the young man I saw with her this afternoon."

"Yes, I was."

"Callin', you say? I had the impression you were her brother."

Mr. True, being a quick thinker, understood immediately. "Yes. I am her brother. The name is Fenn, Archer Fenn, sir." Mr. True stuck out his hand, and Greenwood cautiously took it.

"Eldridge Greenwood." He looked Mr. True over. "But you said callin'."

"Where I'm from, we say that about seeing anyone: friend, kin, or sweetheart. Makes no difference. 'Cept don't no fella say it to another fella. There'd be a problem there." Mr. True chuckled.

"Callin'? Ain't you a wit," Charlotte came in from the rear door. "The boy's just pulling on your coat chain, Mr.

Greenwood. He's a thoughtful one. He knows I never get any gentlemen callers. Always trying to brighten my spirits or tease, this one is."

Greenwood's attention was drawn to Charlotte. She stepped through their work desks and out the counter flap. She wore a beautiful blue dress with a paisley pattern, her hair up in an attractive bun.

"My brother is passing though and will have to leave in the morning—"

"So, I thought it might be nice to take my sister for a meal," Mr. True interrupted.

"Yes, forgive me for missing our supper this eve, Mr. Greenwood."

"No, no thought at all, Missus. Enjoy your time with your kin."

THE NEXT DAY stole the sunshine from the past four days combined. Mr. Greenwood was up on the roof, supervising two slaves as they were replacing old wood shingles. "Put a little more tar under those. Don't want no leaking."

"Yessum, sah."

Hearing giggling, Mr. Greenwood looked over the edge of the roof to the rear and saw Charlotte hanging wet laundry on the line. She then giggled again and ran to the other side of the sheet. It was Mr. True. He was chasing her around it. Mr. True stopped and pulled down the sheet, revealing her behind it, giggling. Mr. True pulled a small white flower from his jacket pocket and handed it to her. She put it to her nose like a smitten lover. Greenwood's expression changed from curiosity to suspicion.

The next day, Mr. True was gone without saying goodbye. The white flower was his last gesture and his last word. Typically, Micah would be following behind, but this morning Charlotte went out for a walk alone, hoping Mr. True would pop out from behind a tree or a building, but nothing came. Stopping in front of the gunsmith shop, her eyes lingered on the Academy. "What are you doing now, Augustus?" she said to herself.

CHAPTER 20
Charlotte

Though lovers be lost love shall not
and death shall have no dominion

SHE WENT UPSTAIRS to her room and opened the door. Six vases of fresh flowers had been placed in various spots in her room. It must be his last effort to get her to come home. She beamed as she came downstairs. Maybe he hadn't left town. Mr. Greenwood was working on a rifle as she approached.

"Mr. Greenwood, you let my brother enter my room?"

"No, ma'am," he said with a huge grin.

She shook her head. "How'd the flowers…" His smile gave her the answer.

The morning after, Little Miss went one way to school, and Charlotte went the other with Micah following behind. "He's a decent man," said Charlotte.

"No man's good enough for The Missus."

"We are running out of money, Micah. It is a decent proposal."

"We's gots enough to eat and drink. We's gots a place to sleep."

"Look at this dress, Micah. I've darned it so many times there's more my thread than the fabric itself. I must look like a wandering vagabond."

"I think ya looks pretty."

"You be needing new clothes yourself, Micah. He ain't gonna buy them for you. Matter of fact, he wants to buy *you*." She pointed at Micah. "Truth be, you'd just like to be back home fishin' is alls."

"Yessum. You be speakin' the gospel theres, I s'pose."

They continued alongside the Academy wall sidewalk before crossing the street to the Bourbon Street Diner. Micah stopped outside as Charlotte went in. He peered through the window as she walked up to Greenwood. He rose from his seat and removed his napkin. They spoke, he smiled and nodded, and then he took her hand to his lips and kissed it. The deal was done. That was that.

CHARLOTTE HAD NEVER experienced placing small things of beauty about a home. It was a peculiar thing that the placing of vases, paintings, rugs, and candles into a home could be so enjoyable. Her family home had always been just like it was for years and years. She had never had a say in its decoration. Greenwood's home was behind the shop, but Charlotte made her old room, with the view of the Academy, her hobby room.

Of course, the shop below was Greenwood's territory, and the business was starting to boom. Talk about a possible war between the states made his gun sales soar. Greenwood bought a new building at the edge of town for the manufacturing of his new rifle, a new design he had been working on for the last six years. Although the original gunsmith shop across from the Academy still handled the repairs and sales of existing guns for the community, Greenwood was there less and at the new building more.

It had been four months since their simple courthouse wedding ceremony, with Little Miss acting as the ring bearer, flower girl, and maid of honor.

Charlotte smiled as she sat on the bed, looking through a box of family photos and renderings she had found under the bed. Greenwood recognized the box she was looking through.

"What are you doing there?"

"These your family?" she replied as he sat next to her.

"Those are my parents. And that one is my brother. He's passed on now. I believe everyone photographed there has passed on except for me."

"No other family?"

"I believe I have some down Louisiana way. Never met 'em, though."

Charlotte gazed at the photograph in her hand.

"It's almost like I knew 'em. Makes me feel like I know 'em better. Know you better. Eldridge, I got something to tell you," she said as she took his hand in hers and moved it across her belly. His expression was that of a little boy on Christmas morning.

"You trickin' me?"

"You're gonna be a father, Eldridge."

Charlotte had married Greenwood just two weeks after having laid again with Mr. True. Her pregnancy was in question. However, no one would know but her.

"HE'S GOT EYES just like you, Eldridge," said Charlotte as she looked down at the new baby in her arms.

"Momma, can I hold him?" Little Miss asked.

"After a few days, my love. A baby needs to be held by their mother just after coming into the world."

Greenwood bent closer to the baby's face. "You know what your name is? It's Henry. Henry Eldridge Greenwood."

The name had been decided several days before, mostly by Greenwood. He had chosen Henry if it turned out to be a boy. It was the name of his boyhood boss and previous owner of the gunsmith shop. If it was a girl, Charlotte had chosen Lisette.

Charlotte no longer concerned herself with the question of paternity. Luckily, there were signs that both men could be the father, but neither would think otherwise. As months went on, secretly, she became convinced Henry was Mr. True's. She came to that conclusion not by the way he looked, but rather from his tiny mannerisms: the way he smiled, or the way he crinkled his nose when angry. Mannerisms she remembered from Mr. True.

"ONLY YOUR MOTHER and I were invited to go tonight," said Greenwood. Disappointed, Little Miss leaned on her arms over the shop counter, watching Greenwood work on the other side of it. "You need to watch Little Henry for us."

Several local business owners had been invited to have dinner with the commandant of the Academy as a gesture of goodwill in the neighborhood, but also because the Academy wanted no opposition to building a third dorm.

Charlotte appeared bored with the idea of dinner at the Academy. In reality, her mind flew about like a distracted butterfly in anticipation of it. She had even bought a new dress. This was her opportunity to see Augustus up close, and she would make the most of it. He was now fifteen, and although she saw him occasionally, she was hoping to speak to him and hear his voice.

Cadets escorted the business owners and their wives from the gates to the commandant's private quarters. Candles lit the pathway, and the cadets dressed in their parade finest.

A cadet had her hand tucked under his arm as Greenwood followed behind. She saw him there, dressed in his parade dress uniform, standing in the receiving line next to the commandant. She would be able to speak to him.

"God's glory," she said under her breath.

"Ma'am?" asked the cadet.

"Oh, nothing."

"Well, here is where I leave you. Have a delightful evening."

"Thank you, son," said Greenwood, taking over for him. "You feeling all right, my dear?"

"I'm fine, Eldridge, just excited to see all this."

They went along the line, shaking hands and meeting the other staff officers and professors. Then came to Jefferson, standing next to Augustus. They met, shook hands, and moved on.

He has grown into a fine young man, she thought.

"It's so fine to meet you. I am Augustus True, the special attaché to the commandant."

Greenwood smiled and shook his hand.

"A pleasure, young sir. I'd like you to meet my wife, Charlotte." The smile on Charlotte's face couldn't be wider.

"A pleasure, ma'am. I hope you enjoy yourselves this evening."

She hadn't been this close to him since the time he was six and had peeked under her veil. His face and body were larger, but she could still see his baby face behind the one he now wore. His eyes shone like smooth river stones.

"What a fine example of a gentleman you are, Augustus," said Charlotte.

"He is a fine boy," chimed in the commandant as he shook Greenwood's hand.

Charlotte could not take her eyes off Augustus. "Do you enjoy life at the Academy, Augustus?"

"I do, ma'am."

Greenwood pulled her a bit to meet the commandant and keep the line moving. "I'd like you to meet my wife, Charlotte."

"It is my pleasure, ma'am. I'm sure we'll have more time during dinner."

"Indeed," said Eldridge as he took Charlotte's arm and exited the receiving line.

Seating arrangements sat Charlotte away from Augustus, who, with Jefferson, were the only two cadets at the table. Everyone stated their names and explained their respective business. Then the commandant spoke about the new dorm: how it would not impact their business and how, instead, it would increase it.

During dinner, Charlotte made idle conversation with those around her but always listened for anything Augustus would say. She overheard him laugh, which made her smile. After dinner, the commandant thanked everyone for coming. Charlotte headed for Augustus, who was standing next to Jefferson.

"You two must be special, being the only two young men at the commandant's supper table."

"We live with the commandant, ma'am," said Jefferson.

Charlotte was surprised. "Is he your father?"

"He's l-l-like a father to me," Augustus said, revealing he still had an occasional stutter.

"I suppose you need a father, Augustus," she said as she revealed a small smile. Augustus cocked his head, slightly confused. "I mean, being away from home and all."

"Nice meeting you, boys," said Greenwood as he walked up, took her arm, and pulled her away.

Although the encounter was short, it left Charlotte with such a happy feeling and sense that her boy was becoming a perfect picture of a gentleman.

A FEW WEEKS after that euphoric night, the sunshine in her life clouded over. Charlotte walked into Henry's room. The nine-month-old was face down in his crib. When she grabbed him, his face was blue. Her scream shook the house. Micah, making breakfast, dropped everything and came running into the room. "Henry!" screamed Charlotte. Micah took Henry from her and slapped his back.

"What in…!" cried out Greenwood as he rushed in and took the baby from Micah. "Run for the doctor!"

Micah was already running for the door. Charlotte fell to a heap on the floor as Little Miss came running in.

"What happened?!" Little Miss saw Henry, limp, in his father's arms. Tears were flowing down Greenwood's cheeks.

A sense of calm came over the thirteen-year-old. "I believe I should hold him."

Greenwood handed Henry's body to Little Miss and went to hold his wife. No tears came to her eyes as she rocked her little brother in her arms and sang a quiet lullaby to him. When she finished, she looked at both of them. "He's with your kin now, no worrying."

A few moments later, Micah rushed in with the doctor. Little Miss sat calmly in the corner of the room, holding her brother's body. She was humming a lullaby as the doctor walked over to her. Little Miss looked up to him.

"Nothing you can do. He's with the Lord now."

The doctor wore a worried expression. "And how are you doing, Little Miss?" he asked.

Micah walked closer with a tear of pride instead of sadness on his cheek.

"Little Miss be fine. Just doin' what she posed to do. She's weepin'. She's a weeper."

THE FUNERAL WAS extensive. Most of the town knew the Greenwoods and came to pay respects.

"There ain't no weepers down heres, Little Miss. Yous gotta do it for your brother," said Micah.

"I already planned on it, Micah."

Little Miss wore all black with a black veil as weepers do. Charlotte knew the other mourners would find a child wearing black with a black veil strange, but she knew why Little Miss was doing it. Charlotte felt hollow, her mind in a deep dark well. The only light came from her pride in her little girl.

On the way to the cemetery, the procession passed the Academy. All of the young cadets were out, standing in their finest, at attention. Senior cadets held their swords upright at their waist, tips against their foreheads. And there he was, standing at attention, next to the commandant. The thought suddenly came to her. *It is his brother he is paying respects to.*

"AND HOW'S THE Little Miss this mornin'?" Micah boomed as he approached. Little Miss, now fourteen, was planting flowers in the side yard with her mother.

"Right fine, thank you. Would you like to help? Momma, will it be fine if Micah helps us plant?"

"It'd be fine," replied Charlotte.

"I got a letter for ya, Missus," said Micah as he pulled something out of his back pocket and handed it to her.

"From Eldridge? How long is that man gonna be gone for?"

Eldridge Greenwood had been gone for four weeks already and continued to send letters telling Charlotte he would be even longer. The business was keeping him busy, and he had several buyers in Virginia, but she knew it was also a way to cope with the loss of his son.

Charlotte wiped her hands on her apron and took the letter. "Where'd you get this? There ain't no address or anything on the envelope."

Micah knelt and began digging with Little Miss. "A man knocked on the door, handed it to me." Charlotte opened the letter.

My Dear Sweet Charlotte,

Over two years ago, I left my heart with you there. Every day gone by, I hoped I would see you again. Mrs. True passed on last year. After my year of mourning, I was intent on asking for your hand, my darling, but woe, I have taken ill. My daughters, Glory, and Emilia, take care of me now, and I love them for it, but my love for you will never wane. Oh, my darling, my heart painfully yearns to see you one last time. I am certain my time is short. Will you grant me this final wish of the heart?

Yours truly,

Archer True

All those years ago, Mr. True had allowed her to see her Augustus when he was a baby. Charlotte looked over at Little Miss, who was more playing in the dirt than planting.

Should I return the favor and tell a dying man about the daughter he never knew about? she thought.

"I just had an idea! Why don't we pack up some clothes and go for a little holiday to the old homestead?"

Little Miss perked up and looked to her mother. "Truly, Momma? Truly?"

Micah said nothing. His disappointment revealed that he knew who had sent the letter.

"Yes, truly. A holiday we shall have!"

CHAPTER 21
Charlotte

All that we were to each other that we still are

THEY PAID A carriage driver two dollars to take them from the train station up to the True farm, a four-hour trip. Two hours into it, the trees slowly grew denser until they covered up the sky. The sounds of the birds here were distinctive and reminded Charlotte of earlier days.

Up ahead was the True farm. Her heart quickened, and she turned to Little Miss. "Now, I'll be needing to speak with this gentleman alone for a bit. Then you can come on in with me, all right?"

"Yes, Momma."

Charlotte got out as Emilia and Glory came outside, curious to see the new visitors they had. They were both young ladies now, Glory seventeen and Emilia twenty-one. Little Miss, Micah, and the carriage driver got off as well to stretch their legs. Charlotte approached the girls.

"Hello. I am The Missus. I have come to visit with your father. Heard he'd taken ill." Their eyes opened almost as wide as their mouths.

"Our pleasure, Missus," said Glory.

"We've heard so much about you over the years, Missus," said Emilia. "Please come in."

"Let me make sure Pa is prepared to see guests. I'll be a quick minute," Glory said as she walked to her father's bedroom.

Emilia and Charlotte entered the living room; Charlotte had never been inside the True home. The furnishings were used and worn, far different than the lifestyle she now had but quite a bit better than her family had at the Fenn farm, as she recollected.

"Please have a seat until Glory returns. She'll show you in. Would you like me to invite…" she gestured outside, "is that your daughter out there?"

"I'd like a bit of time alone with Mr. True. There's a little matter of business we have to discuss; I'm sure you understand."

"Why, of course I do! You're the weeper. But I'll bring out something for them all while you're in there."

Glory came out. "His face surely did brighten when I told him you came to visit. Please come in. He's pleased as punch."

Mr. True had his coat on and nice pants but was lying awkwardly in bed, propped up with a pillow.

Glory must have got him dressed right quick, she thought.

He appeared weak and was sitting up at a strange angle. It was a sad sight to see him this way. "Archer," she said as she approached.

Mr. True seemed to be trying to say something but couldn't. Charlotte pulled up a chair and leaned in to hear him.

"Hello, Missus," he slurred.

It didn't sound like the man she knew. Lying there, he seemed as vulnerable as a baby. The whole right side of his body didn't seem to be able to move. His right eye drooped, and the right side of his mouth sagged, giving him the crooked smile he had told her he'd one day die with.

She looked back to make sure the door was closed before putting her hand on his face. He smiled.

"It's been a good while, hasn't it, Archer? A good while. What happened to us was unfortunate. Our little Augustus is almost a man now. He's sixteen. I celebrate his birthday every year without him knowing."

Mr. True tried to speak again. She moved her hand to his and leaned in again to hear. "I love you, Missus. You know I always loved you."

"I know, Archer, I know," she whispered back.

"You are my heart."

Tears came to her eyes as she sat back up, wiping them away. He half-smiled.

"You weepin'?"

Charlotte laughed. "Suppose I am."

Charlotte looked to the door and stood. She leaned down and kissed him on the forehead.

"Archer, I have someone I want you to meet. Someone you should meet. It's your daughter. We had a daughter from those times outside your farm. That's why I couldn't see you no more." His face lit up again. "Of course, don't be sayin' nothin', all right? I told her that her real father passed on. Now, you just hold on a moment."

Charlotte went to the door and peered into the living room. Glory and Emilia were sitting with Little Miss as she drank a glass of water.

"Little Miss, would you come in? I'd like you to meet someone special."

Little Miss put down her glass and came in as Glory and Emilia smiled on. Charlotte took her hand and closed the door behind them.

Mr. True smiled his crooked smile as she led Little Miss to his side. "Little Miss, this here is Archer True. He's a warner around these parts, and we worked quite a bit together. Didn't we, Mr. True?" He nodded slowly.

"It's a pleasure to make your acquaintance, Mr. True."

Mr. True slowly raised his left hand—the only arm that could still move—and held it out for her to shake. He held it, not letting go. Faint words came from his mouth, and Little Miss leaned in to listen before turning back to her mother.

"He said 'as beautiful as your mother.'"

Charlotte smiled.

"Go on now and keep those girls company. I gotta speak to Mr. True a bit more."

Little Miss turned back to Mr. True. "Nice to make your acquaintance, Mr. True."

Ten minutes later, Charlotte came out of the room and found them all talking and giggling.

"So Little Miss tells us she'll be the next weeper," said Emilia.

"Taking over for her momma?" Glory asked.

"She did? Well, that's the way it's been done, just like in your family," said Charlotte, smiling.

"Yessum. We have Jefferson and Augustus whenever they come back to us from school," said Glory.

"Yes, you do. Well, when it's your pa's time, send for me. I'm sure he'll be wanting a weeper."

"He's already told it to me personal," said Emilia. But

Charlotte knew she wouldn't be the one doing the weeping for Mr. True. She would have to go back to Virginia, and it would take too long to fetch her after his passing and before the ceremony. But with being veiled, the family wouldn't know it wasn't her, just like Archer hadn't known the first few times when she had started weeping.

Little Miss stood up. "Thank you for the water and the pie."

"You're very welcome, Little Miss," replied Glory. The girls showed them out and waved them goodbye as they headed to the Fenn farm.

Charlotte was hesitant about visiting the family farm. She had left without a word and never written since; she had no idea how anyone would react to her return. The carriage driver let them off, was given his due, and headed off down the mountain.

She stood there, praying that things would not go badly. The sad homestead looked the same. A woman she didn't recognize was sweeping the porch of the main house. She saw Thane, one of their longtime family freedmen and his wife Easter bringing in the harvest from the fields. "Would y'all mind if I have a private word with my momma? I'll let ya know when to come on over."

"Yessum, Missus." Micah took Little Miss in the direction of Thane and Easter working in the fields.

"They don't want me to hear something," Little Miss said.

"S'pose so," replied Micah.

Charlotte walked up to the sweeping woman, giving her a curious stare. "Hello, I'm Charlotte Fenn."

The woman propped the broom against the wall. "Well,

I'll be. Issie! Issie! Are you sleepin'? You should come on out here."

A moment later, her mother, now in her sixties, came hobbling out with a cane. "Who is it?"

"It's me, Momma. Charlotte," she said as she approached.

"Well, look what the cat dragged in, it is you," said Issie. "Where'd you run off to?"

"I ran off to…" Charlotte looked cautiously about, walked closer, and lowered her voice. "I ran off to find my son."

"The sun?"

"My son, Momma. My little boy. Mr. True's and my little boy. Augustus."

"The one before that one?" She pointed to Little Miss. "I figured it was something like that." Issie nodded. "Coulda let us know something, what happened to you and all. Could'a wrote. Ya took away our Little Miss. I'm sure that was the reason Grandma passed on. From a broken heart, it was. And I had to take to weeping again when you left. Lucky for me, Janey came around."

"Hello," interrupted the sweeping woman. "I took over two years ago. Still doing it. I don't mind. I like doing it. Times are getting fewer and fewer, though. I'm your cousin, Janey."

"Yes, we met when we were little. I remember."

"Well, come on in. I'm sure you'll want to be fed," said Issie. She pointed to Little Miss, now some distance away with Micah and Thane. "That one sure has grown up. You took her away from me, my granddaughter. Never gonna live that one down."

"I'm sorry, Momma."

"You ever find your little boy?" asked Issie.

"I did, and I moved in right across from where he lives."

ISSIE, JANEY, AND Charlotte sat at the dining table. "I'm married now to a man named Eldridge Greenwood. He's a good man. Treats me kindly."

"Don't know nothin' 'bout your past?" Issie asked.

"Course not," Charlotte said with a frown.

Their attention turned to the door as Micah could be heard guffawing outside with Thane. Just before they knocked, the laughing stopped except for a small chuckle from Little Miss.

"Come in." Thane held the doorway open, hat in his hand, as Micah and Little Miss entered. Little Miss walked over to Issie, wrapping an arm around her. "Now, who's this?" Issie asked with a smile.

"You remember me, Grandma," said Little Miss with a grin.

"Course I remember you. Micah still call you Little Miss?"

"Everyone calls me that."

Issie turned to Micah. "Micah, it's been a while. Watching out for my girl, are ya?"

Micah smiled. "Missus, it be real good to see you. You look like you're doing right fine."

"I think I'm the oldest woman up in these parts now. Sixty-two years old. You look right fine yourself, Micah. It's good to see you. We missed you around these parts." Charlotte shook her head in disbelief. Her mother could be incredibly inviting if she wanted to be. "And apparently Thane missed you most of all."

"Yessum, we getting along 'bout old times. I'll be getting back to it. Y'all have a nice supper," said Micah.

Issie turned to Little Miss, now sitting in her lap. "I sorely missed you, child. That was a pain I don't believe I deserved, but you's here now. And my have you grown over the years."

Little Miss smiled. "Three years, grandma."

"You turned into a beauty!"

"I was already a beauty, Grandma."

Issie slapped her knee, laughing. "Ah, ha! Ain't that the truth." She said, turning to Janey. "Wasn't she, Janey?"

"Why she surely is a beauty, but I ain't never seen her before."

Issie remembered, looking to the ceiling. "Oh, yes, you weren't here when Charlotte broke our hearts."

AFTER SUPPER, THEY sat in front of the fire like they used to in days gone passed. "Any other boys stayin' on here, Momma?"

"Why, you in heat again?"

Every jaw in the room dropped.

"Issie!" said Janey in shock.

Charlotte gritted her teeth, knowing she'd have to deal with this all night.

"Thane's about it now. Taylor passed on 'bout a year ago."

Janey rolled her eyes, wanting to change the subject. "What about this fella you ended up marrying? What's his trade?" Janey wore a curious smile.

"He's a rifle maker."

"Mmm-hmm," grunted Issie. She was looking at Little Miss. "And what about you? What do you do? You go to school, you a rifle maker, or are you a weeper?"

Little Miss smiled and said, "I believe I'll be all three."

"Mmm-hmm," Issie grunted again. "So, you all stayin'?"

Charlotte shook her head. "No, we'll be moving on in the morning. This is just a visiting stop. Just want to see how you all were doing."

Issie grunted again, suspicious. "Just visiting us, or visiting any other'n?"

"We visited with Mr. True earlier today," said Little Miss, not understanding the implications.

Charlotte looked to the ground with flushed cheeks.

"Mmm-hmm. Thought as much," Issie said as she frowned at her daughter.

"He'll be passing on right soon," said Charlotte.

"Momma!" implored Little Miss. "Shouldn't be saying that!"

"Well, it's the truth, and we might as well say it," she said as she turned to Janey. "You'll be called to do the weepin'."

Issie's eyes opened. "We weren't called when his wife passed on. Wonder why that was?" The words flew at Charlotte like sarcastic daggers.

She could not wait to leave. She wasn't the same person she was three years ago, and the Fenn farm wasn't her home anymore.

CHAPTER 22
Jefferson

O may I join the choir invisible
Of those immortal dead who live again
In minds made better by their presence.

AT THEIR SECOND-YEAR graduation ceremony, Augustus did the same thing and avoided them, but Mrs. True wouldn't let Mr. True waste his train ticket by searching for him. The year after that, they just mailed Jefferson the ticket. Jefferson returned to school for his third year with the news that their mother had passed away from pneumonia. A few months after that, Jefferson received a letter that their father had taken ill. Emilia, now twenty-four, would be coming this year to their senior class graduation and taking them home.

"Four years, four years, yes, well I'll be. Eighteen and now you've grown into fine young men, headed off to West Point, my alma mater. And Jefferson, you ended up a cadet Major! I never thought you'd graduate," said the commandant as he and Jefferson walked the hall of the administration building. Augustus walked out in front of them from an adjoining room.

"Where you off to?" asked Jefferson.

Augustus turned. "To meet with the council organizing the

graduation ceremony for the year," said Augustus. Four years at the academy had left him without a stutter.

"Just where I'm headed," said the commandant.

"I'll see you both at dinner," replied Jefferson as he continued down the hallway and into a meeting room. Six cadets sat on the desks, all with solemn faces, including a junior officer named Abbott. "What? Somebody kill your dog? It looks like you all lost your best friend."

"Jefferson, we have a serious dilemma here. Norman has an unsolvable problem with Harlan James," said Abbott.

"Harlan outranks Norman. Where's the problem? Norman's gotta stick it in his shoe and walk with it."

"Not that easy, it seems. It began with Harlan's disapproval of the election of President Lincoln, then took a different direction with Harlan decrying Maryland and Norman condemning South Carolina. Then it all ended with insulting each other's families."

Jefferson shook his head. "We graduate in two weeks, boys! Who cares? They ain't never gonna see each other again," said Jefferson.

"It's not that easy, you see. It seems… unsolvable."

"If it's that big, bring it up at tribunal, but it's gonna be hard this close to graduation," said Jefferson.

Jefferson looked at all the boy's stoic expressions. He smiled. "Why all the glum faces? Hell, then, have them fight it out then. I'll put money on Harlan. Who'll take that bet?"

"Quite, quite," said Abbott. "But you see, they have both chosen to 'fight it out,' as it were, with weapons."

"Weapons? Who's got weapons? And what kind?"

"Yes. And there's the problem. We need a key to the armory."

“Only four people have keys to the armory,” said Jefferson shaking his head. “And none of them are gonna give them to you.”

“Well, we need to borrow one,” said Abbott, his eyes unwavering from Jefferson.

“I don’t have one.”

“But, the commandant does.”

Jefferson pondered it for a moment before cracking a smile. “Those two boys don’t have the gumption to fight a duel. Sure, I’ll call their bluff. Sounds like a right good time to me! I’ll still put money on Harlan. There ain’t no way Norman’s gonna even show up.”

“Precisely,” said Abbott.

Augustus

A cadet popped his head in the door to the graduation meeting.

“Sir, excuse the interruption, sir, but may I speak to the special attaché? Privately?”

Augustus raised his brow and rose. “Excuse me, gentlemen.” He walked outside, and the cadet leaned in.

“There’s trouble. Harlan and Norman are going to duel in the stables,” he whispered. “Your brother’s there.”

“When?”

“Right now.”

His face lost color, and Augustus took off for the stables in a run. As he crossed the parade grounds, he heard it: *crack,*

crack. A sound that someone else might have taken for lumber falling or a hammer driving a nail. But Augustus knew it for what it was: two quick gunshots. He ran in and saw the carnage. Harlan was down with multiple boys surrounding him.

"He's dead."

"What the hell did we do, boys?" Jefferson asked in horror.

Augustus ran up, pushing aside the circle of cadets. Harlan lay, clearly dead, eyes still open as if he were watching the pigeons in the rafters.

Augustus looked to Jefferson, who met his glare with pleading eyes. The fury within Augustus erupted; he jumped across the body and slammed his fist into Jefferson's face, knocking him to the ground.

"You damn well should have known better!" Augustus screamed. Jefferson slowly got up, wiping the blood from his face. Augustus turned to Abbott. "I'd expect this from *you*."

"It was Harlan and Norman's idea, not mine," said Abbott coldly.

"I'm sure you helped it along," Augustus said.

"Along with your brother," he replied.

Augustus was just about to tear Abbott apart when a cadet screamed out, "Norman!"

The attention of the group turned to the boy at the other end of the stables. Norman still stood there in the spot where he had shot and killed Harlan James. The pistol shook in his hand as he reloaded the single-shot weapon.

"Norman! What are you doing?!"

Augustus parted the circle of boys and slowly walked toward him. "Norman, drop the pistol." Norman cocked the loaded pistol. "Stop it, Norman. It's all over now."

The pistol rose, aiming at Augustus' head. It violently shook in his hand.

Augustus slowed but continued toward Norman with short strides. His eyes were glazed and vacant, with nobody seeing through them. They were filled with tears, but not enough to drop as he changed the aim of the pistol from Augustus' head to his and pulled the trigger.

It was a different sound than the two small cracks he had heard from the parade grounds. This time the sound threw him to the ground like a poltergeist. The only thing he could hear was sharp, painful ringing. Augustus sat up, mouth agape.

Norman's body was thrown in the same direction the bullet went as it passed through his head and out the other side. Blood and pieces of his brain splattered across the horse stall. Horses jumped and bucked with fear.

The boys, including Augustus, were frozen in disbelief at what they had just witnessed. After what seemed like hours, but was probably seconds, a few boys ran over to Norman's body, and some ran out of the stables in fear.

Jefferson was left standing over Harlan, the boy's eyes still watching the pigeons. A few minutes ago, he had been a young man that loved dogs and sunny days. Without a soul, his eyes looked like dead fisheyes. His skin paled, and his lips were blue; his body was a shell of bone, skin, and sunken muscle. The true Harlan was gone.

Jefferson bent down to the dead boy and pushed Harlan's jaw to close his open mouth and closed his eyelids for his final rest. His hand continued to the pair of spectacles laying a few inches from his head, thrown off when his head hit the ground. Jefferson placed them gently in his upper jacket pocket.

JEFFERSON AND AUGUSTUS sat alone at the dinner table, their plates of food uneaten in front of them. The commandant solemnly entered the room and sat at the head of the table.

"You, Augustus, have been exonerated from what I've heard. Jefferson, on the other hand, I'm deeply disappointed. This error will undoubtedly have an effect on my continuing command at the Academy, and possibly my pension at retirement. I'm not sure what kind of punishment I shall inflict on you, if at all." They sat in silence before the commandant continued. "As for this evening, I do not wish to see either of you at my table. You are dismissed."

The bedroom was as solemn as the dinner table. Jefferson lay on the bed, arm over his eyes with Augustus lying next to him on his side, facing the wall. He rose under the weight of a thousand pounds and shuffled to the dresser where his bicorne hat rested. In front of it were Harlan's spectacles, a solitary tombstone in a city park.

"I can't believe you'd take those specs!" whispered Augustus as loudly as he could without the commandant hearing.

"I took them for you, you bastard!"

"I'm the bastard? This whole thing is your fault!"

The room quieted. Jefferson looked away, not knowing how to respond. He rubbed his sore jaw; Jefferson didn't remember being punched. After Harlan was killed, everything blurred. He remembered the other cadets becoming frantic around him, but his ears rang so loud in his head he could not hear their faded pleas and frightened screams. Jefferson had found the spectacles in his pocket—he didn't remember how they got there. It was like Harlan had given them to him as a parting gift.

"I'm truly sorry, Aug. They told me they was using deadly weapons. I thought it'd be swords, and someone would get cut, and it'd all be over. I just got caught up in all the glory and excitement."

"Glory?"

"I was thinking nobody would get killed."

Augustus sat on the bed. He ran his fingers through his hair. "You've wrecked everything."

Jefferson teared up and wiped his eyes with his shirt sleeve. "Them's specs, you might as well use them."

"What am I gonna do with them?" he asked.

"You're half-blind, Aug, and you know it. You've been saluting the plebes."

Augustus knew this to be true. His eyesight was getting worse. He walked over to the dresser and picked them up. "They's dead man's specs."

"Harlan won't be needing them any longer, and I'm sure he'd want you to have them. Try 'em on."

Augustus put them on and opened his eyes. The world was amazingly different. "Damn! Yous right, Jeff. I can see everything much clearer."

"Told ya."

Augustus looked into the mirror and smiled at himself. "Yeah, but people would be sayin' I was wearing dead man specs…"

"Don't give a hoot what they be sayin'. They's alls be wishing they was you anyhow."

THE MEN FROM the Academy's board of directors had been in there all day the day before, and they were back in there again on Sunday. Around campus, cadets enjoyed the day, caught up on homework, or did chores. Augustus, Jefferson, and the current colonel of cadets, Jerome Guthrie, all sat somberly on the cadet dormitory's steps, awaiting any word on the board's decision. "Here they come," said Jerome after seeing the men exit the building.

"Hold on, now. They might be going back to the stables."

"No, they're leaving. Let's go."

"No, let's give the commandant a rest. I'm sure they've put him through it," Augustus said as he continued to flick dust off his shoes.

"It's time enough," said Jefferson as he headed off.

Jerome glanced back at Augustus before following. Augustus stood, and reluctantly followed.

The trio entered the apartment and stopped in their tracks. The commandant stood on top of his desk, calmly making a noose from a rope thrown over a beam above him.

"Oh, hello, boys. No worry here. Just tidying up some things. Mr. Guthrie, how are you doing?"

"Uh, fine, sir?"

Augustus walked toward the commandant. The commandant put his palm up to him.

"No, no! No further, Augustus. This is something I must do. My command here is over."

"But you are retiring anyway, sir!" Augustus pleaded.

"I'm going to get some help," Jerome said.

"Don't do that, Mr. Guthrie! That is a direct order!"

"But, sir, please…"

"You do that, and I'll do it this minute!"

All four at a stalemate, Augustus moved forward one step. The commandant placed the noose around his neck.

"Let's rush him," Augustus said.

"No, you don't," said the commandant as he tightened the noose.

The boys rushed in at the moment the commandant jumped. The commandant choked as the boys grabbed his waist.

"Jerome, go get help," said Augustus struggling.

Jerome ran from the room just as the rope broke, sending the three to the ground. The commandant gasped and pulled the tightened noose off as Augustus and Jefferson caught their breath.

"You're bleeding, my boy," said the commandant, pointing to a small cut on Jefferson's forehead.

Jerome burst into the room with three other boys.

"It's all right, boys; the trouble's over. Trouble's over," said Jefferson.

Jerome bent over, hands on his knees to catch his breath. The cadets he brought stood there, mouths agape, trying to figure the situation all out.

"Did you hear him?! Get the hell on out of here!" Augustus said, motioning with his hand.

"No foul language there, Augustus," the commandant said. "As he said, boys, everything's fine now. Be off with you."

Jefferson stood and walked over to close the apartment

door. Augustus helped the commandant to his feet, then asked, "Why?"

"Honor, my boy. Honor," he replied. "Jefferson, can you fetch me a glass of water?"

"Sir," said Jefferson, turning to go.

The commandant walked to the window behind his desk, looking out to the school below. "I'm losing my command, Augustus. They are not allowing me to retire. They are firing me."

"That's not the end of the world. I would go with you wherever you went. To hell with this school!"

"No, you boys already have admission to the Military Academy. I've seen to that."

"To hell with the Military Academy! Family is what's most important."

Jefferson walked back into the room. "Water for you, sir."

Augustus turned to his brother. "Give it to me. I'll take it. Jefferson, can you excuse us?"

"No!" exclaimed Jefferson, dropping the glass. His eyes glued to the window behind Augustus.

Augustus turned to an empty window and froze. His head tilted to the side like someone was showing him a magic trick he couldn't figure out.

Did he disappear? Was he hiding behind his desk? Did he run past them so fast he missed seeing him?

Augustus walked up to the window, not allowing his ears to hear the screaming that came in from below it. He looked down to the body three stories below. His adopted father was gone and with him, his love. As told by the old Susquehannock, the love had tired and went to bed over the horizon, but his sorrow now swooped in and took its place in Augustus.

AUGUSTUS WAS IN a daze as he sat before the new interim commandant, General Farland. The general sat at the commandant's desk like it was his. Augustus wanted to rip him out of it.

"General Schaffer was crazier than a nearsighted chicken. Why in the heck he ever gave you that nonexistent attaché rank I'll never know. And the records show that you were supposedly indentured to the academy. No information about how you got to be a cadet and no tuition payments from either of you." The general looked at them for answers.

Augustus eyed the servitude contract sitting in front of Farlan as they both sat closed-lipped. Farland sat back in his chair and interlaced his fingers.

"This Academy has built a solid reputation stronger than the foundation of this very building. All these cadets come from prestigious families or are the sons of brave men who have fought in wars. No deranged fool is going to make a mockery of that honorable history."

"Are you going to let us graduate? It's only two weeks away," asked Jefferson.

"Now, would that be fair to the rest of the paying cadets?" He leaned across the desk. "Unless you can pay for back tuition, you won't be graduating."

"Can we stay until graduation? Our parents aren't coming till then."

"I suppose. But not here. I live here now. You can find a dorm bed until your parents get ya."

Augustus also interlaced his fingers and pushed back in his chair. "You ever fight in a war, General?"

"I was never provided the opportunity. Why do you ask?"

Augustus stood and leaned over the desk closer to him. "Cause that nearsighted chicken surely did. The war of 1812." Augustus swiped the indentured servitude contract off the desk. "You can take this academy and shove it up your ass."

The general's eyes bulged. "I beg your…"

"Shut your mouth, you old shit pile," added Augustus as he walked out.

Jefferson watched Augustus with wide eyes then stood. "We'll see ourselves out." He followed Augustus, but stopped, turning back to the general. "My brother's right. You are an old shit pile."

CHAPTER 23
Charlotte

*At the going down of the sun and in the morning,
we will remember him*

THERE WAS BIG talk in the streets about war, and Virginia was at the center of it. Mr. Greenwood's business continued to grow, as did their wealth. Little Miss and Charlotte came up to their home with shopping bags in their hands, and Micah came out to help carry them in.

"I should'a gone with you, Missus, helped you carry all these."

"No, that's fine, Micah, thank you, though," said Charlotte.

"There's something been going on over theres at the school, Missus."

"What's happening?"

"Now, it ain't who you be thinkin' 'bout, but two boys got killed there's what I heard."

"Killed? That's just awful, ain't it, Momma?"

"Who was it, Micah?" Charlotte asked.

"No ones I ever heard of, Missus."

"Those boys shouldn't be playing with guns," said Little Miss.

"No ma'am, Little Miss. Guns ain't no good."

Mr. Greenwood came from the house and up to the trio. He had been back from Petersburg, Virginia, for a week. "Doing some shopping?"

"Did you hear two boys got killed?" asked Charlotte.

"Two young boys had a duel is what I heard. Terrible. Now, would you two excuse us? I need to conversate with my wife." He looked to Charlotte, and she could see it was important.

"Yes, sah," said Micah as they both went into the

house.

Greenwood smiled at Charlotte. "I got some good news for you. We just received another very large contract from the State of Virginia for our new rifle," Greenwood said with a grin ear to ear.

"There's more to it than that," Charlotte said knowingly.

His grin disappeared. "Yes. We're moving to Petersburg. Opening a big new factory down there."

"Moving the company? Or moving us?"

"Both."

"I don't want to move," she said flatly.

"We're gonna be wealthy, Charlotte, very wealthy. Gonna buy a big house…"

"Buy it here; I don't want to move."

Greenwood faced her again. "I'm surprised by your reaction. I'd think you'd be happy—"

"I'm not."

"Little Miss will be raised in the lap of luxury, placed in the finest schools," he pleaded.

"I like this city, Eldridge. I will not move!"

Greenwood's anger grew. He began pacing. "Listen, I have been privy to information that will affect us all and that I haven't disclosed to you, but I will now. There will be war, and if Lincoln is elected, there is no doubt there will be war, we need to be on the right side of history; we need to leave now. I've arranged it."

"I will not move!"

"I will not have my wife contradicting me. I know best, and we will be moving."

She paced the porch looking to the Academy. Greenwood watched her with his arms crossed. "Alright, but I'm sending Little Miss back to my mother. I don't want her seeing any part of this war."

"That sounds prudent. Send her on tomorrow's train."

LITTLE MISS AND Micah had just returned from one of their walks when Charlotte called them over. "There's talk of war, and we've decided to send you to live with your grandmother."

Little Miss looked surprised. "When?"

"Tomorrow."

"I guess that's better than a poke in the eye. It woulda been nice if someone told me about it."

"Don't ya get all snappy with me, Miss," said Charlotte.

"Don't get me wrong, momma, I'm pleased as punch to be going. It'd just be nice if I had a few days to get myself ready.

"For what, Little Miss?"

"Settling things at my school, for one." Little Miss took Micah's arm and snuggled into him. "Can Micah come with me?"

Charlotte's brow raised. She hid the pain that surfaced when Little Miss mentioned Micah before her. Maybe she should have paid more attention to her Little Miss. "No. I'm sorry."

"Well, then, I would've liked to have said goodbye proper."

"I ain't leaving ya here, Little Miss," said Micah as he pounded his chest with the side of his fist.

Little Miss's arms wrapped around his like an anaconda.

"I'll pack your things. Why don't you and Micah go see your schoolteacher? Say your goodbyes as ya do."

Charlotte turned and walked back into the house. Little Miss let go of Micah and faced him. "I'm pleased to leave. Ya know I've always wanted to go back to the old ways like ya taught me. But it's you I'll miss. Ya know that now, don't ya?"

"Course ya will, but you'll be doing God's work on up theres. Weepin' like a Fenn." He grew a smile. "You ain't Little Miss no mo'. You The Missus now. You The Missus." Micah's smile beamed with pride.

Little Miss left the next day, and Micah dropped her off at the train station. "I'll write to you. Don't be shy about asking my momma to read them to ya, Okay?"

"I'll treat 'em like a box of treasures, and your momma has the key."

Little Miss stopped before climbing aboard the train. "I know you'd come with me if ya could."

Micah nodded. "Yessum. You knows my place is with your ma."

"Your promise to grandma, I know."

"My oath."

"An oath is the same as a promise, old man."

"Don't ya be callin' me old man, now. Now, get on in that train." He moved his hand like a fly swatter. "Ya don't want an old man weepin' now," he said as he turned away and walked off, leaving Little Miss on the first step of the train.

Two days later, Micah helped Charlotte and Greenwood fill three wagons with furniture, shop equipment, and belongings. Leading them all would be a single, mule-drawn buggy that would carry Charlotte with Micah driving. Greenwood would take another wagon, and Darrel would drive the third.

Darrel and Hartford loaded the last of the wagons with the remaining furniture. In all the confusion, no one noticed Charlotte's music box had fallen into the bush below.

Suddenly, cadets poured out of the Academy's gates in full dress uniforms, some running toward them, stopping and turning around.

Charlotte looked back at Greenwood as he came out with a chair to load up. She smiled. "Is this for us?"

Greenwood walked up to her with a confused expression.

"No."

Cadets lined both sides of the street and stood at attention. The sidewalks started to crowd behind the cadets. Charlotte tapped the shoulder of one cadet directly in front of her, curious.

"Excuse me, young sir. What is this all about?"

"The funeral for our commandant, ma'am."

Charlotte followed their eyes down the street. The procession was proceeding towards them, coming from the Presbyterian church on the way to the cemetery. The sidewalk became crowded with people stepping out from their homes and businesses to take off their hats and pay their respects.

Walking mourners preceded the family coaches. The etched glass windows of the enclosed funeral carriage displayed the commandant, surrounded by flowers inside. The carriage, with its silver and gold trimmings, was pulled by two black horses wearing wrapped-leather prongs with two black ostrich feathers coming out of the top.

Following the commandant was his estranged wife, sitting aside her grown daughter and a few distant family members.

Augustus and Jefferson walked behind the carriage, their heads down. Seeing them, Charlotte's heartbeat quickened. As he neared, she realized the irony that she stood in the same spot he had for her son Henry's procession. Augustus lifted his head as he passed and looked at her. Charlotte smiled, hoping to lift his spirits, but he simply looked down, not seeming to notice. Now, she wished she hadn't seen him.

He had become the full-grown gentleman she had always imagined he would. He would be graduating from the Academy soon, his life would be set, and he no longer needed her to watch over him. It was now time to let go of her little boy.

After the funeral procession had gone down the road, Greenwood kindly let a few moments pass before telling everyone to mount up. He locked the door to the shop, and they were off and on their way to Petersburg, Virginia.

CHAPTER 24
Augustus

Our lives are poorer without you

THEY WERE ALLOWED to stay three days after the funeral. As they had no other clothes, Jefferson and Augustus were allowed to take their uniforms except for any school insignia. They walked through the administration building that had been their home for the last four years. Walking out the doors, they were greeted by two columns of cadets, creating a pathway for them to walk through. The brothers stopped and smiled at their friends and compatriots. The cadets clicked their heels and stood at attention as they passed.

"Keep your head up, boys."

"It happens to the best of 'em."

"We're here for you, fellas."

The columns went all the way to the gates. As soon as they walked through them, the gates closed, and the columns fell apart. All the cadets ran to the gates, crowding them to see what the brothers would do next.

They walked to the curb and sat in front of the school.

"We got two weeks till Emilia gets here. Where are we gonna sleep?" said Jefferson.

"We'll be fine."

"You shouldn't have said those things to the shit pile."

"What's done is done." Augustus looked across the street to all the storefronts. In the gunsmith shop window was a "For Lease" sign. "Looky there. In the gunsmith shop."

Jefferson's head went up. "God works in mysterious ways," said Jefferson as he jumped up and walked across the street, peering in. "It's empty!" Jefferson tried the door, then ran around back. A minute later, Jefferson opened the door from the inside. "We got a place to stay." The cadets at the gates cheered as Jefferson came through the door and walked back over.

"But we still ain't got no money. No clothes but these uniforms. No money to buy food."

Augustus rose and walked up to the cadets at the gates. "You can get us some food, right, boys?"

The cadets let loose a raucous uproar of, "Hell yes."

Augustus started to cross the street. "And can ya deliver it to our new home over here?" he asked, pointing.

The cadets hooted and hollered again. Augustus walked up to the shop. On either side of the door were shrubs, a bit overgrown. Looking into one, he spotted something and pulled out a dusty wooden box. He wiped it off with his shirt sleeve. It was made of maple and varnished to perfection. Inside it was a brass disk with holes and a mechanical arm on top.

Jefferson stopped behind him. "What is that?"

Augustus rubbed his thumb across it. "I don't rightly know."

"Well, we got three weeks to figure it out."

THE HARDWOOD FLOOR of the gunsmith shop became their home. The cadets would sneak food to them, and they found blankets behind a house down the road. As the days went on, fewer and fewer cadets brought food; their popularity was diminishing. Jefferson went on longer and longer walks looking for supplies. Augustus stayed around the shop, investigating all the small things left behind: nails, screwdrivers, tiny pieces of metal, a bowl.

Jefferson wound the crank on the small box Augustus had found as the last light of another evening faded. Augustus traced a finger over his father's signature on the servitude contract.

"Why are you doing that?"

"Nothing. Just fiddling."

"Why'd ya take it?"

Augustus smiled. "Don't want to be sold again, I guess." His finger went back to tracing.

"You can't be." Jefferson's finger moved a lever on the box, and it came to life. Tinkling music echoed from the box while both stopped to listen.

"Amazing Grace," said Augustus. "How'd ya do it?"

"Wind it and move this lever." Jefferson shut the music off. "Why'd ya really take it?"

Augustus' eyes darted to his brother's. "'Cause I'm gonna show him that I know what he done."

Augustus was sleeping on the floor when the front door of the shop burst open. Jefferson came flying through.

"War, Aug, war!!"

"You're supposed to come through the back door!"

"Didn't ya hear me? I said war!"

"What?"

"Fort Sumter was attacked by South Carolina troops! The war is on, Aug! Lincoln won't stand for this!"

A rumbling sound came in from the street. Jefferson stopped, then moved to the window. The cadets across the street were hooting and hollering.

"The boys have heard, too! Let's go, Aug. Let's go!" he shouted as he ran out the front door to the gates.

Augustus sat up and rubbed his face awake. He glanced down to the servitude contract. Anger grew in him just looking at it. He picked it up, folded it, and slid it between the cracks of the floorboards. It disappeared below. He rose and walked outside to join Jefferson.

Jefferson ran along the gates to the academy. "I'm joining, boys! Who's with me?"

Some of the cadets had climbed the walls and yelled down at him. "I'm in!"

"I'm with you, Jefferson!"

"Let's go!"

They continued to shout until the commandant pushed his way through them and motioned them back from the gates.

"Move back! Move back! Get down from there! You there, get down! The audacity! Behave as the Wadleigh-Holmes cadets you are! None of you are joining anything! You are Wadleigh-Holmes cadets and will graduate as such! Then you'll be fit to serve as the officers you were born to be, not as lowly recruits!" He pointed to Jefferson on the other side of the gates. "That is a poor example of a drummer boy, let alone a private!"

A huge smile grew on Jefferson. "Yes, but this drummer boy'll be doing what y'all be reading about!" The cadets burst into laughter, infuriating the commandant.

"What side, Jefferson?" cried out a cadet.

"Hmm, whatever side gives me a gun first, I suppose." The crowd of cadets exploded in laughter.

"Fight for the Union. I don't want to be fighting against you," said one.

"Yeah, fight for the Union, I want to be fighting against you!" said another. More laughter, then the crowd settled.

"Good luck and Godspeed, Jefferson," came another voice.

Jefferson ran back to Augustus, still laughing.

"You don't know what side?" asked Augustus.

"Just foolin'. We's Pennsylvanian boys. We should be fightin' side by side with Pennsylvanian boys, of course."

Augustus stood and walked to the window. The streets were becoming crowded with revelers. "I ain't a Pennsylvania boy, Jeff. I ain't going back to Pennsylvania. You know that, right?"

"What do ya mean?"

"You really thought I was waiting around for…"

"Well, what were you doing then?"

"I was passing time. Just passing time, thinking."

"Well then, what was the ending to all that thinking?"

"I ain't no Pennsylvania boy. That ain't my home since they sold me to the academy. It may be yours, but it ain't mine. I'm signing up right here, right on down the street. I'm a Virginia boy now," he said with determination. "You can stay around for Emilia, but I ain't. I'm going now."

"THE BLOODY SEVENTH?" Jefferson read the sign above the Union army recruiter's desk sitting out front the Davy's Mercantile in Tyler county. A Union sergeant stood next to a corporal seated at the desk.

"That's right. The Seventh Virginian is called the bloody seventh," said the sergeant.

"Have you fought in any battles yet?" asked Augustus.

"We have not. But we plan to be bloody. Join up, and you can get bloody with us," said the sergeant as he turned to the line of young men forming. "Step on up and sign up with the bloody seventh Virginian!"

Augustus put his hand on Jefferson's shoulder. "Do you want to get bloody?"

"No. I want to make the Rebels bloody."

"Listen boys, sign up or get out of the way," said the sergeant.

Jefferson signed first, then Augustus. It led them to a month of training before they were called to action. Colonel Joseph Snider, the leader of the seventh, rode his horse back and forth, speaking to the men as they approached their first skirmish.

"The sheriff here in Tyler County has decided to lend his sympathies to the Rebels. Now, I will tell you that we West Virginians have no patience for such ne'er-do-wells. Especially in our own county. We shall go in and oust the scallywag directly! Tonight I will share a glass of my finest Virginian whiskey to the man who shoots this son-of-a-bitch sheriff in the ass!"

The sheriff had twenty friends and family all armed and waiting for the army to come into town. The bloody seventh came walking down the main road, wearing smiles like they were out for a bird hunt. Their smiles were greeted with the worried faces of the townspeople.

Bam!

A bullet whizzed by from down the street.

"Take cover!" shouted the colonel.

The men ran for the buildings on the far side of the street.

"Now, you boys get on outta here!" shouted the sheriff from the other side. "This is our town! No one's gotta get hurt!"

Colonel Snider dismounted his horse between buildings. "Now sheriff, you know we can't be doing that!" he said as he motioned for a group of men, including Augustus and Jefferson, to move around the back of the building to get closer. As soon and they did, wood and glass were splintering and smashing around them. Smiles turned to fear as they hit the floor.

"These ain't no rocks they're throwing!" shouted one man.

"Fire!" shouted the colonel. The overwhelming numbers of the seventh opened up on the other side of the street, little iron balls destroying everything in their path. Lying in the dirt next to a building, Augustus turned to Jefferson with eyes as big as tea saucers and shook his head. Jefferson nodded agreement.

Four hours later, Jefferson claimed it was his bullet that

killed the sheriff, although most of the regiment claimed that too. Before the sheriff of Tyler County, the war was like a hunting trip with food around the campfire, laughing with friends, drinking whiskey, and hunting down pesky Rebs. But now, the campfire gatherings had a more serious tone, and when they went up against Confederate General Stonewall Jackson, it got even more serious. After the battle, Augustus, Jefferson, and six of their comrades stood above four of the bodies from their regiment. Four, that had just been drinking and laughing with them the other evening. Ten others from their brigade were also lost.

Augustus, however, had proved himself in the fight, not by shooting Rebs, but by saving five lives of his troops. The animal doctoring he had learned from his father paid off. His colonel promoted him to corporal.

"Damn, Aug, you're moving on up. Corporal in a month," said Jefferson.

The sun had just come up, and they sat outside their tent, drinking the swill the army called coffee.

"Saving lives pays off more than killing," said Augustus.

"Your brother's jealous of you, Aug," said Tommy, a private.

"I ain't jealous of him. The extra two dollars a month wouldn't be so bad. Privates do most of the killing. The higher the rank you are, the worse of a shot you are." Jefferson stood and tossed his cup of swill. "Martha Sue over here," he said as he walked to his rifle stacked with others in a pyramid, "had already proven that."

"Martha Sue! Whew! Wee! He even named it!" said Tommy.

"Damn right, I named it. This here Austrian-made,

handcrafted, Lorenz rifles' my sweetheart. I love her so." The men fell about the place in knee-slapping laughter.

"I hear him at night," said Augustus. "He whispers sweet nothings into its barrel." The men howled, laughing so loud that others walked over to the commotion.

Jefferson took up his rifle, caressing it like a lover and placing it against his cheek. "Oh, my darling Martha Sue, you are so beautiful, and I know you love me. Will you please…" he switched his sweet tone to an angry one, "kill that Reb bastard over yonder!" The men laughed so hard that they couldn't catch their breath and were wiping their eyes.

The colonel walked over. "What did Private True do now?"

"Colonel, you need to muster this man out. He sweet-talks his rifle and named it Martha Sue!"

The colonel laughed along with them. "Well, that boy can add a hole to the ear of a running squirrel at seventy yards. If I were you, I'd sweet-talk my rifle too." The ruckus took ten minutes to subside.

Four months later, Augustus sat with his brother among the rest of the regiments, their backs against a fence. Augustus still hadn't made his mark with his rifle. He shot it occasionally but mostly carried it slung behind his back as he pulled out the wounded and treated them himself. With every officer he saved, his rank grew: corporal to sergeant, to first sergeant, to sergeant major. Saving officers was good business, but it was purely coincidental.

Their Colonel, Joseph Snider, rode up and down the line, shouting instructions and orders for the attack they were preparing for. They were about to attack a position they called the sunken road at Antietam.

"Sergeant Major, I'd prefer you stay to the rear of the

action. I'd like to circumvent you getting shot. Let the men bring the wounded to you, and you can take it from there. Is that understood?"

"Yes, sir," said Augustus.

"Ain't no glory in doctorin'," said Jefferson.

The Rebels, commanded by General D.H. Hill, had a strong defensive position, atop a sloping elevation, in a sunken road worn down by wagon traffic. They had built up logs from fences as cover and repelled the first attack commanded by Brigadier General Max Weber. The second attack, commanded by Colonel Dwight Morris, was also cut down by heavy rifle fire but managed to beat back the Rebel counterattack. The Bloody Seventh Virginian was about to be the third.

Augustus stood, looking through the field glasses to the enemy positions. "Hey, brother, what's it look like?"

"Don't look good. Two other brigades couldn't handle it. Hope we can."

"Those were all new troops, not battle-ready like us. Don't you worry."

Augustus turned to him. "Keep your noggin down."

A few minutes later, the bugler called his tune, and the seventh went in charging and firing as all hell broke loose. Augustus ran up with them, diving behind a wagon to look for the wounded. With no wounded coming, he ran up further towards the chaos and grabbed the first soldier he came across. As he dragged the man back, he saw two more go down. Pulling the man into a shallow ravine, he pulled off his satchel and stopped the bleeding.

"I'll be back. Gotta get some more fellas." Running forward again, he checked pulses until he found one alive. He took him under the arms and pulled him back to the same spot as bullets whizzed by. The men began to fall in clumps, fighting in close combat, sometimes merely feet away. Augustus started taking two at a time, pulling them backward by whatever limb he could grab first.

Colonel Snider rode up, sword in the air. His horse reared up before Augustus. "Sergeant Major True! Get out of the foray! You're too—"

The blast of smoke, air, and debris sent Augustus flying backward. After several minutes, he awoke and sat up with his legs spread out in a "v" like a child playing with marbles. His face was black, and he couldn't see anything. An extremely high-pitched ringing blasted his ears. He saw only red and realized he was lucky enough to still be wearing his spectacles. Removing them, he reached for his coat to wipe them off but found it wet. He looked down at himself; his uniform was blood-soaked. Pulling a rag from his medical satchel, he wiped the specs clean. Putting them on, he saw the chaos.

Smoke was everywhere, with soldiers running through it this way and that. Strangely, they were running at quarter speed. He couldn't understand that. He also couldn't hear them when they seemed to be yelling. To his left, he saw the colonel's horse, only its torso, the head, and neck were gone. The colonel's hand peeked out from the other side. Augustus crawled around the horse to him. The colonel blinked at Augustus and said something he couldn't hear. The horse's torso had fallen on top of the colonel's legs, trapping him.

Augustus pushed him to a sitting position and sat directly behind him, legs around him, and braced against the horse. As he started pulling, the colonel's head flopped to the side, either out cold or dead. Augustus didn't care; he kept pulling, and the colonel's leg slowly came free. From what he could see, it appeared severely fractured. Augustus stood and dragged him a hundred yards to the rear as bullets flew by them.

Bloodied men inundated the triage tent. Finding an open table, he dragged the colonel to it. He turned to an orderly who looked Augustus up and down and mouthed the words, "Are you okay?"

"Help me get him up," said Augustus. They picked the colonel up and plopped him onto the table. A bone jutted out of his pant leg. Augustus cut away the pants from the wounded leg, tied up a tourniquet, grabbed a saw, cutting the leg off. He finished sewing him up, wiped his face, and headed back for more. By the end of the day, his men had lost the battle, but he'd saved twenty-one lives.

For the next four days, Augustus watched the colonel grow feverish, vomit and convulse to the point orderlies would have to hold him down. On the fifth morning, his fever broke, and he woke up.

An orderly tapped Augustus on the shoulder. "He asked for you." Augustus' hearing by then had recovered except for the ringing.

"True. What am I gonna do with you?" The colonel's voice was weak. Before Augustus could answer, the colonel continued. "Heard my horse is dead."

"A cannonball killed it. And it almost killed both of us, too. I'm sorry I had to take your leg, but you would have bled to death. I had to."

"Oh, no. I figured. You did a right fine job, True. Right fine," the colonel said, smiling. His smile faded, and he slowly shook his head. "But before I went down, I saw you. You'd charge hell with a bucket of ice water, you would. I'm alive because of you. You not only saved me out there in the field but came in here and saved my life again."

Augustus nodded and patted the colonel's arm. "Well, let me know if there's anything I can do to make you more comfortable," said Augustus before turning to leave.

"Sergeant Major?" Augustus turned back to him. "Where'd you learn all that doctor stuff?"

"My father was a doctor." *Sort of*, he thought. "And I went to Wadleigh-Holmes Academy."

The colonel's eyes opened. "Wadleigh! I went to Wadleigh! They didn't teach that when I was a boy."

"They teach it now. Well, get some rest," said Augustus turning to leave.

"Sergeant Major, I'm making you a first lieutenant." Augustus, surprised, turned again to him. "You showed bravery above and beyond. You deserve it."

"Thank you, colonel, that's an honor."

"Why, you should be anyway with a Wadleigh-Holmes education. I wasn't aware." Augustus walked away to wash up, a smile growing on his lips.

Every time I save an officer, he thought.

Once again, he was an officer like he was at the Academy. People would call him "sir" again, not that he cared about that. Save an officer, get a promotion. If the trend continued, he would be a brigadier general someday soon.

"A lieutenant?!" cried Jefferson. "By golly, now ain't you the biggest toad in the puddle!"

From then on, if Jefferson saw an officer down, he'd pick him up and drag him back. But Jefferson's fortune wasn't as good as Augustus'. Nothing came from it, and he got tired of not being rewarded for the hard work of dragging men back. He changed his tactics and went back to just shooting at Johnny Reb.

As a lieutenant with medical knowledge, everyone believed Augustus was a doctor. He just went along with it. When speaking with other educated doctors on the staff, he knew as much, if not more, than them. He also knew many techniques they didn't because he'd learned on animals. He started to tell anyone who asked that he attended Jefferson Medical College of Philadelphia. He'd heard of that one from another doctor.

Their positions in the bloody seventh divided the brothers. Still a private, Jefferson would have to camp in a different section of the base than Augustus. Augustus started to congregate with the other officers as well as other medical staff.

CHAPTER 25
Charlotte

*And if God choose, I shall
but love thee better after death*

IT WAS ONLY a three-day journey from the gunsmith shop in Clarksburg, to their new home in Petersburg as both were towns in the state of Virginia. But as West Virginia had seceded from Virginia, they had moved from a Yankee state to a Rebel state. Because of that, visiting Augustus would be very difficult.

Greenwood's company had grown from a rifle distributor to a major weapons manufacturer in just a few years, supplying the Confederate Army with a majority of their rifles. Charlotte had gone from cleaning Greenwood's home to a lady of wealth and leisure within those same years.

Entertaining became common for Charlotte, and she enjoyed the southern, high-society lifestyle. Generals and politicians frequented their dining room table, including President Jefferson Davis. They also had extended an open invitation to General Robert E. Lee, but he was a little too occupied to attend.

Their business was all Mr. Greenwood thought about, and

entertaining politicians and generals was a part of the game he had to play. He was a busy man and not around home as much as he used to be, until the day he became ill.

"I'm sorry to say he has consumption," the doctor told Charlotte. "Several colleagues of mine no longer think this is a hereditary illness, but rather a contagious one, so you should take preventative measures such as cheesecloth over his bed and plenty of fresh air in his room. Most importantly, I would recommend sending him to a sanatorium to recover."

"He will not go. His business is far too important to him," Charlotte replied.

Greenwood's health slowly worsened until he could no longer leave his bed. Charlotte began to take notes for him and have them delivered to the executives at the plant. Charlotte learned a lot about the business and began asking Greenwood to go into detail for her. Unfortunately, being a woman business owner had its own difficulties. But as she began to suggest business moves that he agreed with, he gave her more and more authority until many executives came straight to her with their questions. They would say, "If Charlotte crows, the sun is up."

A year later, Greenwood withered away. It became her intention to make his name famous through the company and through his remembrance.

"It'll be the finest remembrance this city has ever gazed upon," Charlotte said. "A four-feathered affair."

The top funeral director of the city, although an incredibly busy man with the war, agreed to make her husband's funeral his highest priority. Charlotte asked for a four-horse team, his new hearse carriage with etched glass oval windows, and a musical trio to walk in front and play somber hymns.

Charlotte wore her black mourning dress and a

wide-brimmed, black hat with an ostrich feather flopping to the right side. She sat in the adjoining room and greeted the guests as they entered.

"I'm so sorry for your loss, Mrs. Greenwood."

"He's at peace now, Charlotte."

"He was a good man."

Micah stood behind her in the room, just as he did in the old days of weeping.

As Greenwood was a Mason, the members of his Masonic Lodge had argued with Charlotte about the entire funeral. They wanted it held at their lodge, and they wanted the lodge members to precede the hearse in mourning carriages. She negotiated that all eight pallbearers would be Masons, and they could ride in the first coach with the preacher in the massive procession of sixteen mourning carriages, including the hearse. The procession through Petersburg was the most elaborate the city had ever seen.

CHAPTER 26
Augustus

*Let us cross over the river
and rest under the shade of the trees.*

THE TRIAGE TENT was twenty-by-twenty and held eight surgical beds and all the medical equipment. The canvas sides could be rolled up to allow airflow but still shade the patients from the sun or rain. Out of the four tents in their regiment, Augustus was in charge of one. Each tent had one doctor and three to five orderlies.

Augustus sat on the grass twenty yards from the triage tent. His fingers were winding the music box he had found two years ago. The cracking and booming on the battlefield had begun moments before, even though the day was sunny and beautiful. The tent was situated on a grassy knoll with towering pine trees surrounding it in a semicircle to the west. A creek was fifty feet to the east, and beyond it were more trees. A light wind blew the grass. Except for the war, it was a paradise.

"Lieutenant True!" called out Private Stanley, a soft-spoken young recruit, and one of the three orderlies that worked in Augustus' tent. "The battle has resumed. We should be receiving casualties soon."

Augustus put the music box in his lap, cleaned his spectacles with his shirt, and put them back on before he stood. He walked to the side of the knoll where he could see the battlefield in the distance. Stanley stood next to him.

"Could you get my surgical apron?"

"Yes, sir," replied Stanley, and walked off.

The battle brought in more than the tiny group of four could handle. Augustus was strapping an arm for amputation as he called out, "How many more outside?"

"You don't want to know," said the tent's second orderly, Phyllis Legrand. Phyllis was a thirty-year-old wife of a sergeant in the regiment.

"Bring 'em in. The worst first, Doris!" Augustus shouted outside.

Doris Flagler, the tent's third orderly, was a recent widow of a soldier from the bloody seventh. Having nowhere to go after her husband's death, Doris stayed on as she didn't want to leave her "boys," as she called the soldiers.

"Yes, sir!" Doris was on triage duty, prepping the patients for surgery, stopping the bleeding, and lining the wounded up in order of need. She would patch up the ones she called 'so far gone' and told them they were next for the doctor. Most of the time, they passed on while waiting. She was good at knowing survival probabilities.

Augustus performed most of the surgeries, leaving the sewing and bandaging to Phyllis, Stanley, or Doris if she wasn't on triage duty. He worked quickly, jumping from patient to patient. The more patients he tended to, the more lives he saved.

It had been five hours since the battle had ended. The birds started to chirp again. All four sides of the tent were up to let the breeze through. Augustus just finished showing Stanley the procedure to stop the internal bleeding on a dead major by using a clamp.

"How many boys we lose today?" asked Augustus.

"Thirty and counting. About eight others are on the fence," said Stanley, wiping his bloody hands on his stained apron. "You always ask how many we lost. You should ask how many we saved."

"We save more than we lose!" shouted Doris from the triage area that she had converted to the recovery area. "He always says that. I asked the same question," she said as she put a cool rag on a recovering soldier.

Phyllis walked over to them from the recovery area. She turned and pointed to a tent about a hundred feet away. A doctor was there, working on a patient outside of it.

"He's new. Think he needs help?" asked Phillis.

Augustus and Stanley turned to it. "When did he show up?" Augustus asked.

"Not sure. They set him up when we were at our thickest." Augustus finished and wiped his bloody hands on his apron as he headed toward the new doctor. The birds and the breeze welcomed him as he walked over. The doctor seemed to be still working on a patient.

"You need some help? We're done over there."

The doctor had his back to him. "Nope. Just finishing up."

"When did you arrive? It's good you're here. We surely needed the help."

The doctor set his tools down and turned to Augustus. He had a dark mottled, patchy complexion and a mustache that dropped down to his jowls. His eyes drooped as if he was tired or had been drinking all night. He wiped his bloody hands on his smock. "Not sure I was any help."

Augustus walked in. "Any help is welcome." Augustus looked down at the patient and froze. It was a wounded colonel from earlier in the day. "This man is dead."

The doctor laughed. "Very observant. Yes, he's dead. I'm preparing him to be sent on home."

"What?"

The doctor studied Augustus' face and smiled. "He's dead. All the bodies in here are dead. I'm embalming them. Have you heard of embalming?" Augustus slowly shook his head. "Oh, so this is new to you. I thought everyone's heard." Augustus shook his head again, still confused. "Well, it's been around for thousands of years. You've heard of Egyptian mummies? Well, they were embalmed all those years back." The doctor spoke quickly like he'd given the speech a thousand times. "It's a series of chemicals you insert into the body as you remove the blood. It preserves the body."

Augustus winced as his stomach turned a bit. "The army letting you do this?"

The doctor laughed. "Yes, they contracted the company I work for to do this. President Lincoln himself sanctioned it. By the way, the name's Ben Cattell, and I ain't a doctor. I just learned this trade from my brother."

Augustus smiled. "Augustus True, and I ain't a doctor either."

Ben raised a brow. "You working on live patients?"

"Long story, but I learned the trade from my father."

Ben chuckled. "Birds of a feather. Well, I would shake your hand, but I have chemicals all over them." Ben walked to a counter and took a flask in his hand. "Drink?"

"Thank you, no."

He took three gulps from it and ended with a gasp of air. "My brother embalmed the body of the President's son himself, he did. Willy Lincoln. You read about that?"

"I don't recall."

Ben went back to the body he was working on, stepped on a foot pump, and began pumping. "Well, ya pump this fluid in 'em, and it keeps them bodies far fresher, longer. I already bled this one out, but you do that first, then fill the empty veins with this here fluid. Two months from now, the body will be looking as it did on the day of death."

Augustus watched Ben as he pumped in the fluid. The skin plumped up. "All you do now is apply makeup, and he'll look alive."

"It's fascinating."

"Come on back later tonight, and we'll have a drink."

Augustus smiled, nodded, and walked back to their tent. Phyllis, Doris, and Stanley were tending to the sea of boys recovering from their wounds. Augustus walked up to Stanley and helped him move patients into the shade. After moving twenty, he stood to survey the recovering wounded. They lay on low cots and on the grass as their moans and pleas accompanied the birds. He knew he was going to lose at least twenty percent of the boys lying there.

Augustus put his hands to his mouth to shout. "Any of you boys good enough to walk off, ya should! We ain't got no chow! Raise a hand if ya need a crutch!"

Stanley walked up. "Lieutenant, you should get some rest over yonder. You look exhausted."

"You're just as exhausted as me. I'm gotta get us more orderlies. This is just too much work," said Augustus as soldiers began returning from the battlefield, many coming through their triage to check on their friends. He watched their mortified eyes as they saw the bloody floor of their surgical tent. Augustus spun around to the stack of amputated limbs. He quickly moved to the other side of his tent and dropped down the canvas side, blocking it from view until soldiers filed past on the side the pile was on. There was nothing he could do. As they passed, several started to vomit. Augustus put his hands up in the air and shouted to them. "Boys, go that way!" He pointed to the other side of the tent to stop the flow, but they were just too beat to listen. Augustus gave up and walked off to the same spot he was at before the battle overlooking the creek.

An officer on horseback rode up behind Augustus. "Hello, brother."

Augustus turned. "I'll be," Augustus said, shocked. "If they catch ya in that officer's uniform, they'll give it to ya."

Jefferson dismounted. Augustus pulled his apron off and threw it to the ground before hugging his brother.

"I needed the officer's jacket to ride this horse to you. I hadn't seen you for a while."

"Well, it's good to see you. Sit on down before someone gets a good look at you in that uniform."

The boys sat on the cool grass and looked at the creek below. The breeze tossed Augustus' hair about. Jefferson's was too greasy.

"Damn! What a fight, Brother! We gave him hell today. Hellfire, I say," said Jefferson.

Augustus laughed at his brother. "It's good to see you, Jefferson."

Jefferson smiled. "And you, Aug." Jefferson pulled out a

flask and handed it to Augustus. "Have some. Yeah, the boys I'm with do good work."

Augustus took a swig. "Ooh, fine Virginian whiskey, I see."

"None other. The sooner we get more of this, the sooner the war will be over!" Jefferson pulled an apple from his pocket. "Want it?"

"Sure, where'd you get this?"

"It was in the jacket."

Augustus laughed weakly. Jefferson tenderly put his hand on the back of Augustus' neck. "You look tired, Augustus."

"I am."

"Look at you with all this blood on ya. There's simply no fun in doctorin'. Promotion or not, ya do all this work and get no applause. You're tired 'cause there's no rush from doctorin'. Bullets whizzing by your head, cannons blasting, men screaming. Battle is beautiful."

Augustus took his hand. "I reckon I want your beautiful war to end. I miss ya, brother."

"I know, Aug. That's why I came on over."

"We should think on something to do after all this. Animal doctorin' or schoolin' for people doctoring." Augustus touched the colonel's insignia on the jacket Jefferson wore. "I should turn you in so's you won't get killed."

"I'd just die in one of our prisons."

From the tent, Stanley called out to Augustus. "Lieutenant, you're needed." Augustus waved his arm.

Both Jefferson and Augustus stood, facing each other with silent smiles.

"Well, Aug—" Jefferson's body flinched at the exact

moment a small crack came from the other side of the river. Jefferson dropped like a sack.

"Hee, hee! Gotcha Billy Yank!" came a distant voice across the river.

Several of the Union soldiers tending to the wounded ran to the knoll and began shooting at the sharpshooter.

Jefferson lay still with only the grass around him moving this way and that by the wind, gently at first, then a bit faster. Augustus slowly dropped to his knees.

"Jefferson?"

The grass blew about faster now. Arrogantly dancing around Jefferson's head as his lips lost color like it was giddy that he was dying.

Stop it! Jefferson's jaw relaxed, his mouth opened, and his last breath left his lungs. *Stop it! Stop it!* Augustus' eyes narrowed, and he clenched his teeth as he reached for the grass, taking it into his fists and ripping it up and away. *You won't be dancing now!* His fists went to the sky, releasing the grass into its eternity.

Stanley came running to Augustus.

He saw Jefferson's pale face. "We have to move him back, Lieutenant."

"Can't shoot worth a plug nickel, can ya, Yanks?!" the distant voice called out again. Another crack came from his rifle, and another soldier fell like a sack.

"See what I mean, Lieutenant? They still out there!"

Augustus only saw the bastard grass carried off to its heaven by its dance partner, the duplicitous wind. The wind returned, caressing his cheeks and tousling his hair like a lover with a knife in her stocking. He shook it way from his face and sat, pulling Jefferson's floppy limbs up onto his lap as he spoke to the wind.

"Give him back to me," he pleaded. "I won't tell anyone, just give him back to me. I know you can do that, and that's all I'll ever ask you. I'm only half of us, ya see. We're twins, and I'm only half of us. Please give him back."

"We need to move him now, Lieutenant. It's a sharpshooter," said Stanley. Tears fell from Augustus' eyes, but he didn't sob. His eyes fixed on a spot across the river.

Another shot came within inches of Augustus' leg. Stanley grabbed Jefferson under the arms and dragged him away from Augustus, leaving him sitting there, in a daze, staring at the spot.

Union soldiers began wading across the creek, seeking the lone sharpshooter. Augustus rose and walked down the hill into the river, wading across. Exhausted, he finally reached the other side and crawled out, drenched. Stumbling up a little farther, he heard a low voice.

"Ain't got no gun, Billy Yank."

The Union troops on the bank were creeping into the treeline south of Augustus. He saw a lone Rebel peeked out from a tree just in front of him. Augustus looked to the stone covered creek bank and picked up a stone. The Rebel sharpshooter was quiet enough that the Union men farther down the bank couldn't hear him. He was a small man with an ironically kind voice.

"That stone ain't gonna do no good, Yank."

Augustus rolled the smooth stone over his hand, contemplating. It was warm from the sun. At that moment, a bugle sounded from within the tree line joined by Rebel yells. A full regiment of Rebel soldiers came out running from the tree line, killing many of the unprepared Union men on the bank. The Union men from the other side returned fire as best they could without shooting their men already there. The sharpshooter came out from behind the tree with his rifle held at his waist and aimed at Augustus as he walked toward him. More Rebels poured past and around Augustus and the sharpshooter like boulders in a stream.

"You're touched in the head, ain't ya, Billy?"

Augustus took the stone and threw it at the Rebel, but the Rebel ducked, and it missed him. A smile rose to the Rebel's lips, and he continued forward until his barrel was inches from Augustus' stomach.

"Touched or not, time to quit, Yank. Ya ain't got no gun."

"You killed my brother, Johnny," said Augustus as he calmly bent down for another stone.

"You Yanks already killed two of mine, Billy." He slammed the butt of his rifle into the back of Augustus' head. He collapsed to the ground, and a sound came from beneath him: music.

"Lucky, I didn't shoot ya. Don't want your momma losing two," said the Rebel as he knelt and found the small music box peeking out from Augustus' pocket. He took it. Seeing Augustus' spectacles, the sharpshooter picked them up, carefully folded them, and placed them back into the same pocket he took the music box from.

CHAPTER 27
Charlotte

She came and went and never ceased to smile

CHARLOTTE TOOK OVER control of the business. Her sweet smile made more deals than a man's handshake, but the arrival of Union troops changed everything. They had practically surrounded the city on the eastern and southern outskirts. The Union wanted to capture the Richmond Petersburg railroad, which supplied the Confederate Army. The city's troops dug trenches and put up walls to protect it.

The rifle business lost most of its workers to protect the line, reducing its workforce to a handful. All able-bodied men were expected to fight. Most production stopped, and the buildings went silent.

The Union's huge mortar named the Dictator, threw shell after shell day and night. The city rationed food, and troops moved into the company's buildings. Her dream of growing the business in Greenwood's name was slipping away, as was her wealth. Shells slowly destroyed the buildings.

Charlotte walked the floors of the plant like a ghost in a ghost town, with Micah following, as it was in the beginning.

"I wonder how my Augustus is doing?" she said to Micah during one of their walks within the vacant plant.

"S'pose he's fightin' this war too? I believe he'd be about fightin' age nows, I s'pose," he replied.

"I believe you may be right. I hope he's on the right side of things."

The following day, Charlotte walked the bustling headquarter halls of the Army of Northern Virginia. As a major weapons manufacturer, Charlotte was a frequent sight. The commanding general, Pierre Gustave Toutant-Beauregard, was a regular guest of the Greenwoods, attending almost every party and tea social.

Charlotte walked into the records division office and up to the counter where a young corporal stood reviewing a stack of papers.

"It's certainly much more quiet in here," said Charlotte as she walked in from the crowded hallway, shutting the door behind her. "Hello, I am Charlotte—"

"Yes, ma'am, Mrs. Greenwood. I know who you are. My pleasure. I was so sorry to hear about Mr. Greenwood."

"Thank ya kindly."

"What can we do for you?"

"Well, I'd like to see the enlistment records. I'm looking for someone." The corporal waited for more. "May I see them?"

"Which regiment, brigade, or division?"

She pursed her lips. "I do not know."

His jaw dropped a bit. "Oh. You want to see *all* the enlistment records?"

"Well, yes."

The corporal's brow raised, and he stepped back to the

door just behind him. "There are over a hundred thousand of those," he said as he opened the door to the room with stacks of boxes. "And this is all. Richmond has more. Far over a million men, ma'am. Can ya narrow it down?"

"He most likely signed up in Tyler County."

"Confederate? We don't have any from Tyler. Ya think he may have gone over to Mercer county or Monroe?"

"Possible."

"Well, you might be lucky there. We have those records, but most of those boys of Tyler signed with the North."

"Would ya be so kind as to look for a man by the name of True, Augustus True?"

"Ma'am, I am sorry, but I have no one to look for ya. Me and another man are the only ones in here now, and we runnin' 'round here like chickens with their heads cut off. The rest of 'em are fightin' on the line out there."

"Would you mind if I looked for myself?"

"Why, no ma'am. You are more than welcome."

From then on, Charlotte spent every day looking through the enlistment records in hopes of finding Augustus. After a week, she brought in Micah to help.

"A, U, G, U, S. These are the letters you look for. You see how they're shaped? This first one is 'A', and it's the first letter of the alphabet."

"It looks like a haystack," said Micah.

"Yes, it does. All these letters gotta be in this order to spell his name. Ya find it, call out."

"Yes, Missus."

Charlotte had Micah search the death records—something she didn't want to do. Days went by with no sign of his name.

After they exhausted all the enlistment and death records the Petersburg war office had, she asked for the prisoner records. Micah set to task on death records published in the newspapers.

On the second day of going through the thousands of prisoner names, her finger stopped on the list: *Augustus True, no rank, Andersonville Prison, Georgia.*

General Pierre Gustave Toutant-Beauregard sat behind his desk in the busy war office.

"Our forces don't rightly have the supply train to feed our own troops, let alone the prisoners, Charlotte. I'm very sorry to hear he's there."

"I'd like him released," Charlotte demanded.

The general sat back in his chair. "He's an enemy combatant, Charlotte." The general was overly familiar with Charlotte, calling her by her Christian name instead of Mrs. Greenwood. He never allowed people to call him by his first name and requested everybody call him General or General Beauregard. Charlotte knew him to be a flirt, and that was why she wore her mourning finest, including the large-brimmed hat and makeup. That was also why she knew he would take the time to see to her now that she was a widow.

"But there is something you can do."

"No, Charlotte, I don't believe there—"

"Honor parole," she interrupted.

He frowned. "Honor parole. We used to do those with prisoner exchanges. We don't do prisoner exchanges any longer."

"I believe you can let one more go with this noble idea."

He interlaced his fingers. "Alright, I suppose I can try. So how do you know this man?"

"My son from a previous marriage. I can count on you to do it?"

"Of course I will, Charlotte," he said as he rose and reached for her hand across the desk. Charlotte gave it to him. "It will be my pleasure," he said with the kiss of her hand. Although a flirt, he was a true southern gentleman as well. "Have my secretary in the next office draw one up. I'll sign it and send it out with the next courier."

"Thank you, General." Charlotte walked to the door but stopped before it. "General, please do come by for some tea one afternoon. You just must!"

CHAPTER 28
Augustus

May the earth lie light upon thee

THE BROWN CANVAS tent flap floated and snapped in the breeze. *Crack!* The wind was picking up in the midday heat. His face had a thin crust covering it where the dust stuck to his sweat. Daytime was the only time to sleep in that place. If you closed your eyes at night, it might have been the last time. *Crack!* His eyes opened like two glossy green and white marbles set in a mud hill. He shared the tent with thirty or so flies, and the man snoring next to him, John Dark Buffalo. The tent was John's, and John allowed him to sleep there.

John was six-foot-two, two hundred pounds of lean muscle; he was a Cherokee from the 1st Regiment of Cherokee mounted volunteers. John had begun the war fighting for the Rebels, but after he learned the North was fighting to end slavery, he switched sides. His powerful physique had withered while in prison, but the gangs left him alone after his fifth snapped neck. Augustus had fixed up John's shoulder, popping it back into place, and helped him survive a fever. In return, John offered to share his tent.

Augustus ran his fingers over scar tissue on his calf, a

through-and-through gift from the guards. He reached for his homemade crutch next to him and crawled out, careful not to wake John. The blaring sun blinded him until his sight adjusted, and he could, unfortunately, see the horror of the prison life around him.

Surrounding his tent was a sea of prisoners, about forty thousand of them, enclosed in a fenced-in section of land about a mile square. No buildings, only tents, men, and filth. Down the center of the prison grounds was a swampy area covered with feces and disease. This was Andersonville Confederate prison, a hellhole for ragged, broken, and starving Union soldiers.

"Good morning to ya, Augustus. Going to try again this fine morn? Odds are now far against ya, considering your leg and all," said McCleary, an Irish immigrant corporal from the 63rd New York. Augustus stood up and propped himself up with his crutch.

"Just as good a day as any," muttered Augustus.

Heads jerked around him. McCleary's Irish accent went from jovial to worried. "For God's sake, Augustus, I was only joking. Let's not go through this again!"

Ignoring him, Augustus hobbled through the growing crowd around him as they patted him on the shoulder, goading him on and taking bets. As John's tiny tent was in the center of the prison, it took him some time to make his way through the half-mile sea of men, and as he went, the rise of excitement grew.

Augustus hobbled up to a small rope, held off the ground about two feet by sticks. This innocuous boundary was what was called the 'deadline' and beyond it was a patch of no-man's-land, twenty feet wide, separating the prisoners from the high prison walls. On top of the walls walked the armed prison guards.

The guards casually walked the top of the wall, laughing and talking. Augustus smiled up at them. One smiled back and laughed. Slowly, Augustus lifted his wounded leg toward the top of the deadline, keeping his balance with the crutch. The crowd roared but backed away from him. He looked to the guards, no movement from them; they still smiled down at him. He moved his leg over to the other side of the deadline and placed it as delicately as a ballerina onto the dirt of the no-man's-land.

Bam!

The bullet blew into his calf and out the other side. He fell on top of the deadline, half on one side, half on the other.

Bam!

Another shot hit the dirt inches from his head. The men rushed forward, grabbed him, and pulled him to the safe side of the deadline. They picked him up and brought him to a tent in the center of the camp.

His vision was blurry with pain, but the pain was something he wanted, something he needed. He could only see the brown of the tent roof, but he heard a strangely gleeful, familiar voice.

"Little Chinee? Little Chinee? Let's take a look at this. Damn, look at this. Right next to the last one. Those boys almost hit the same wound. This gonna hurt a bit, Little Chinee."

Augustus felt the sharp pain of a searing hot knife placed on top of his wound before he passed out.

AUGUSTUS WOKE SOAKED in sweat and looked around. It was not his tent.

"Why, Little Chinee, how you feeling today?"

Augustus' head was near the opening, and as he was lying on his back, he tilted his head backward to see the face behind the voice. "You recognize me, Little Chinee?"

"David?"

"Yes, True. It's me. I gave ya another haircut while you were sleepin'." Augustus put his hand to his scraggly hair. David laughed. "Nah, just foolin', but it looks like you could use one now. And that beard too."

"Got your scissors?" Augustus asked.

"Wish I did. Scissors would be mighty handy around this place."

"How long you been here?"

"Few months longer than you. I seen you when you come in but could tell ya didn't want to talk to nobody, so's I left you alone. Plus yous with that Injun."

"Who fixed my leg?"

"Oh, I did. You was lucky on that count. It went straight through, just like the other one. Cleaned it with a hot knife. Who fixed the other one?"

"Did that one myself."

"This one's right close to the other. You gonna need that crutch for the rest of your life now." David laughed again, then got serious. "Hey, Augustus, truth be told, I've been watching you for a while now. Saw you jump the deadline the first time. Couldn't step in fast enough for that one. Almost made it in time for this one." David dusted off his pants. "Listen, since you kept your head down and didn't know I was here and alls, you don't know I got a little pull around this place. I set up this barter business and got some fellas working for me. Anyway, you one of the old gang, and I don't want to see you get shot dead when you don't have to."

"What if I want to?"

David searched his face, then cracked a smile. "You one crazy sum-bitch, aren't you? What I'm saying is if you're gonna get shot at, you might as well make it for a good cause is all."

"What's this good cause?"

"Don't get me wrong, I don't want you to get shot at all, but if you're choosing to go out that way…" David looked off into the distance. "Listen, I have this job available. It's burying the dead outside the gates. You get to take 'em out and bury 'em. It's that simple. There's only a few guards out there, and if you want to make a run for it… you have the smallest chance in hell out there, but at least it's a chance."

Augustus pulled himself to a sit. He floated his fingers across the dirty bandages on his calf. "Why you doin' this?"

"You're the Little Chinee. One of the old gang, that's alls. And ya didn't cut my hair off, and ya could've. It ain't like it's a big deal. And I ain't saying to try and run; it's still suicide. It's a job, that's all. Give you sumpin' to do."

Augustus searched David's eyes. "Well, if you're sure…"

"There is just one more thing…"

Augustus smiled, "I figured."

"Well, ya see, it's that Injun of yours."

Augustus laughed. "John? He's his own man. I ain't got no control over him."

"But you got more than most. You're his friend, ain't ya? I'm just saying to ask him, that's all."

"Ask him what?"

The two men locked eyes for a moment. "To fight the Irishman."

Augustus frowned. "The Irishman?"

"Yep, the Irishman."

"From Collin's Raiders? Those fellas want him dead; you know that."

"I was told if he fights a fair fight, they'll leave him be, and this will finish it."

"They're leavin' him be now."

"But they ain't for long if he don't fight, I's told. But also…" David leaned in and looked around to see if anyone was listening. "It's the guards setting it all up. They's betting on it. One week's ration of food from the guards. They gonna fight it out by the deadline. Loser gets pushed in. That'll finish it. Guards gonna finish it for 'em.

"He won't do it."

"You just gotta ask him, and you get the job. Just gotta ask."

"Alright, I'll ask. I get the job for sure? Just for asking?"

"Sure enough. But also, when ya get the job, if you find any gold teeth that haven't already been plucked, you gonna pluck 'em and I get 'em."

Augustus reached out his hand and took David's. "Deal."

Augustus moved off toward his tent, but David called after him, "Hey, so what happened to Jefferson?"

Augustus turned back. "He's dead."

David slowly nodded. "Lost my brother, too."

"HEY, THE RAIDERS, they're coming after you," said Augustus.

John Dark Buffalo sat crossed legged in front of the tent picking his teeth with a stick.

"They always come. What news is this?"

Augustus stepped over one man sitting close by and moved a sleeping man's legs so he could sit down in front of him. "I ain't saying this to piss you off, now, ya see? I was just told..."

"Who told?"

"The guy that pulled me from the deadline last time..."

"When you tried to make stupid and go to your white father?" John laughed with the power of a bass drum. Augustus could feel each laugh in his chest.

"Yeah."

John stood. "Let's go find some water," he said, walking off.

Augustus jumped up and followed behind him as he parted the sea of men with his massive form, pushing them aside like a train's cow plow.

"You trust him?"

"I went to school with him, but no, he's slicker than a boiled onion. I think they're gonna try to kill you. He told me it's a fight to the death."

"With the Irishman?"

"With the Irishman. I'm just telling you, so you know, but I think you outta forget all about it." Augustus ducked and jived behind John, keeping as close as possible to his back, avoiding the irritated men's shouts of: "Hey!", "Watch it," and "What the?"

"You think the Irishman can kill me?" John laughed again.

"That's not the point. You shouldn't even do this at all. I'm just telling you what they said. But to answer your question, no. If you lose, it'll be the guards who kill you."

"What about the guards?"

"They's gonna push the loser into the no man's land. The guards are the ones who want you to fight the Irishman, and they're the ones that are gonna kill the loser."

A big soldier with arms the size of small powder kegs saw them coming and stood in their path.

"I thought you said the raiders?" John made a swift dodge to the left and came up with a fist to the big soldier's face, knocking him flat. He continued like it was a quick handshake.

"The raiders are the ones setting it all up with the guards and with the Irishman. The guy that saved me knows the raiders. I just said I'd ask. And I'm asking 'cause just by asking, I get a job outside the walls every day."

"Why don't I get that job for fighting?"

"Well, he didn't say that, but, yeah, I'm sure you can have it if you want. I don't care. But they were going to give the winner one week of guard food."

John stopped, and Augustus ran into his back. He turned to Augustus, who was holding his nose.

"A week? From the guards?"

"Yep, they're the ones betting on ya." John looked at the sky and nodded. Augustus saw him thinking and shook his head. "But, John, no. This is a bad idea. It's a fight to see the Great White Father."

John turned again and proceeded on. "No, you see the Great White Father. I see the Great Spirit."

"YOU'S ALWAYS TRYIN' to die too early, ain't ya, True?" A dark head peered over the edge of a mass, eight by thirty-foot grave Augustus was lying in.

Augustus smiled up at Duffy, a crisp blue sky behind him. Duffy was a thirty-year-old slave who worked at the prison. The cold, brown dirt of the freshly dug, four-foot-deep grave was a relief from the heat.

"Good Lord, don't be wantin' yers yet, True. He'll be tapping on ya shoulder when it's time. You can be sure of that. You'd better be gettin' on outta theres. The boss man be comin'."

"True, you lying down again?"

The prison guard peeked over the edge like Duffy. Two heads now with blue sky beyond.

"I should just shoot you now to get it over with. Get your ass on outta there and get back to work. You got a full load today."

Augustus climbed out. To the right of him were the large prison walls and gate. To the left was a pile of thirty dead prisoners, and all were skin and bones.

"Better be checkin' if they're dead or not. A few we brought out last night are missin'. Must have played dead and run off in the night. Been happening. Best be checkin' and makin' sure they's dead," said the Confederate guard.

"We's got more in theres, sah?" asked Duffy.

"Thirty or so coming out with the next batch, so get on it. Fill the hole up with 'em just so long as there's at least two feet a' soil over the top of 'em. Don't want no stink coming up."

Augustus hobbled over to a stack of bodies, taking the hands of one. "Duffy, can you give me a hand?" he said as he shook the dead man's hands.

Duffy walked over. "Oh, sah, now, don't be doing them things. What if that was you?" Duffy took the feet, and they pulled it free from the stack and dragged the body over, and unceremoniously tossed it in. As they did, a troop of new prisoners marched by into the prison. Augustus and Duffy ignored their shocked and disgusted expressions as they tossed in another body.

"True, you ever think yous just like me now?" asked Duffy.

"How's that, Duffy?"

"They's got the guns on you, you get the whip, they tell you where to sleep, what to do."

"That's the gospel."

"It wasn't like that before the war, was it?"

Augustus laughed. "I'm the wrong man to ask."

"Why ya say?"

"My pa sold me to work. I was a little like you."

Duffy's eyes bulged. "The Gospel?"

"The Gospel. Not for life, though. Not like you got."

"But your pa done did it. That ain't right."

"Ain't right for…" Augustus dropped the hands of a corpse and went to his knees. "Gotta catch my breath. But I was saying, ain't right for both of us."

"Don't let boss man see ya slackin'." Duffy turned around, looking for the guard. Augustus picked up the hands again. "Ya ain't had nothing to eat, has ya?"

"Nothin'. But I'll be fine."

"I'll be burying yous in a time, I believe."

"I don't want anyone else to do it."

"But you believe me, I'll be playing your hands like you did over there," said Duffy with a grin.

"Have me wave to all the boys coming in."

Duffy laughed. "Ah! True, you crazy boy. You have slaves before the war, True?"

"Never did."

"I bet you treat 'em right if you did."

Augustus nodded as they continued to toss bodies. The grave was about full, and they reached for their shovels.

"This job is not so bad, I think. You get out of prison every day. Good to get on outta theres," Duffy said as he shoveled dirt.

"Where you sleep, Duffy?"

"They keep us in a place over yonder behind the boss man's place." Duffy pointed to a small building two-hundred yards away.

"Comfortable?"

"I had betta. Hey, so's, if you's wanting to be dead so much, why don't ya just run now? He shoot ya quick as that," Duffy said with a snap of his fingers and a grin.

Augustus shoveled dirt onto the face of the body on top.

"No one will see it out here. If I die, it'll be as I'm entertaining the boys. Making the run from the deadline to the wall." Duffy looked over to him, confused for a moment before laughing.

THE NEXT DAY, Augustus came out of the gates leading the mule cart with fifteen bodies. On average, with ninety soldiers a day dying in Andersonville, it seemed like the mule cart never stopped moving. Duffy waited for him, arms on top of the shovel, chin resting on his arms. Two other slaves stood by.

"Mornin' True, sah."

Augustus nodded. "Duffy."

"Little late this morn'. Beginning to think they started feeding y'all again."

"No such luck. These was just smellin' up the place. How is your granddaughter this morning?"

"Bless my soul. She had the baby last night. Baby boy, it was."

"I'm happy for you, Duffy."

"Let's work here!" interjected the guard, irritated. "Quit ya chattering and get the dead off the cart so's they can take it back."

Augustus pulled the bodies off by their limbs. It was always easier to stack the limp bodies than the stiff ones with rigor mortis.

Two slaves led the mule cart away and back into the prison. Duffy and Augustus began digging the first of that day's massive graves.

"Water break, boss man, sah?" Duffy asked the guard. He and Augustus had just finished digging their fourth grave in the humid Georgian afternoon.

"Go ahead, boys." Augustus and Duffy dropped their shovels and walked to the bucket of water near them. They sat on the edge of a grave, feet dangling over.

"At least you get a bit more water and a piece of bread for doing this work out heres," said Duffy as he looked to the skeleton-framed dead bodies. "You don't get nothing in theres, do ya?"

"People are killing each other for scraps in there," said Augustus. "Eating rats and sometimes each other. They think what we do out here, touching the dead, it's the worst thing you can do. Truth be, it's a might better out here."

"Touching the dead ain't bad, no."

"My pa used to do it for a living," said Augustus.

"A gravedigger?"

"Nah, a warner." Seeing Duffy cock his head in confusion, Augustus went on. "A gravedigger and a preacher put together, I guess. He'd invite folk, get the preacher, set the body in the casket, make it all nice and pretty. All that."

"My, oh my. You be doing that if ya ever get outta heres?"

Augustus shook his head. "Don't know if we ever get out of here, Duffy. But I ain't got no kin to go back to anyhow."

Duffy looked to the fields. He shook his head in disbelief. "Sometime, this war be over. You can make your own kin. Have chil'en and grandchil'en like me."

"You have the people you love, Duffy. I lost mine."

"You can have more. Always have more."

CRACK! CRACK!

Augustus again woke to the snapping of the tent flap. He rolled over. John Dark Buffalo was gone. *This is the day*, he thought as he crawled out.

He picked up his crutch and made his way toward the deadline.

He could see the crowd gathered up ahead at the deadline. The wall had six guards on top of it.

"You missed it. Yer boy is dead," said a prisoner. Augustus began to push his way through the gawking crowd.

"Yer Injun, got himself killed, boy."

"Ain't got no one to protect ya nows, Pennsylvania."

"Wasn't a fair fight."

Reaching the line, John lay in the dead man's land, flat on his back with hands outstretched as if to greet his Great Spirit with an embrace.

Augustus looked both ways like he was about to cross a street and then back up to the guards, now watching him closely. Two guards atop the nearest section of the wall smiled down at him menacingly. Augustus felt no fear as he lifted one leg over the fence and then down to the dirt. He looked at the guards. Nothing.

"Hey, boys," shouted Augustus at the guards. "Ya shot me twice before both in the calf. That's why I'm hobbling around with this here crutch. I'm gonna retrieve my boy here real slow like. Now ya can let me do that, or ya can choose to shoot me. I'm asking if it's the latter, can ya make it count?"

Prisoners around him roared with amazement. Augustus placed his other leg over the deadline and onto the no-man's-land below. Now he was entirely inside it, but still, only devilish smiles came from the guards. Augustus took two steps to John's body and knelt down to it; then, the guards aimed their guns at him.

"Don't shoot him!" yelled David Ruggles as he ran up. "He's the one you're looking for! Don't shoot! He's True! Augustus True!"

One of the guards stopped his partner from firing by lifting up his rifle barrel with his own. The guard looked at Augustus and yelled to him, "Your name True?"

The crowd quieted behind Augustus as he nodded affirmatively.

"I's told you is a Yank lieutenant?" asked the guard. Augustus nodded again.

Murmurs came from the prisoners on the other side of the deadline.

"Damn, that would've been fine to kill me a Yank lieutenant. Okay, go on to the front gate."

An uproar of disappointment came from the prisoners missing out on their 'entertainment.' Augustus smiled at John's face, frozen in a permanent grin.

"Do not think of me as gone. I am still with you in each new dawn," he said as he folded John's arms across his chest.

Augustus picked up his crutch and helped himself up. He began walking toward the gate in the center of no-man's-land, probably the only prisoner to do so and live. The prisoners began to cheer him on as he smiled and laughed back at them.

Moments later, Augustus leaned on his crutch outside the door of the prison warden's office. The same guard who stopped him from being shot opened the door and then stepped out again, leaving it open.

"You can go in, Lieutenant," said the guard.

Augustus hobbled in. In front of him sat Captain Henry Wirz, staring at Augustus with a smirk that could barely be seen through his thick bushy beard and mustache. He didn't get up.

"You may sit, Lieutenant," said the captain with a thick Swiss accent, surprising Augustus. The captain motioned to the guard. "Leave us, Sergeant."

The guard saluted and left. Augustus took a seat in front of the desk.

"Officers do not belong in this shithole. Apparently, you did not have any identifying material when you were captured. You should have said something, Lieutenant." Augustus didn't reply. The captain looked him over carefully, then smiled. "Heard you tried to get yourself killed three times."

"If your boys weren't such bad shots, it've been once."

"Oh, I agree, sir. They send me children and expect me to make them behave like soldiers." The captain's right hand sat on his belly, unmoving. He patted it with his left. "A Minie ball made this one useless. Got it at while serving as aide-de-camp to General J ohnston at the Battle of Seven Pines."

"I have two in the leg. Got them both here." Augustus gestured to the prison.

"Where were you captured, Lieutenant?"

"Don't really know. Somewhere in Virginia. Spottsylvania, I believe."

The captain turned his swivel chair and faced the window. Augustus looked around, unsure why he was there.

"God's grace is on you today, Lieutenant. We are letting you go." The captain spun his chair back to Augustus' dispassionate demeanor. A smile rose on the captain's face. "You hold your excitement pretty well there."

"Why?"

"I don't know. Some higher-up half-wit writes the orders. I just abide by them." Augustus' expression changed from curiosity to surprise. "Do you remember when we did prisoner exchanges? So much easier. Why they changed that, I cannot fathom," said the captain as he held up the contract. "So, this here you will be signing is an honor parole. It is what we used when we did the exchanges. You cannot be fighting anymore, Lieutenant. Do you think you can accommodate that?"

"I'm a doctor. I never fought anyway."

"You cannot mend Yanks either. You must go home, Lieutenant, and stay out of the war. Are those terms acceptable?"

"I can abide by 'em."

The captain slid papers across the desk to Augustus. "Sign here… and sign here." The captain took something from his desk drawer. "Show me your hand and stick up your thumb."

Augustus did, not knowing why. Quick as lightning, the captain sliced across Augustus' thumb with a knife, dropped it, and quickly grabbing the base of Augustus' bloodied thumb, he slammed it onto the paper next to the signature and again for the second one. Augustus pulled it away and stuck his thumb in his mouth.

"Blood oath, sir," said the captain as he sat back in his chair and slowly shook his head in disbelief. "Like that could quell the human spirit." The captain threw Augustus a handkerchief to wrap his thumb and looked to the door. "Sergeant!" The sergeant immediately entered. "Give the lieutenant plain clothes and take his uniform. Then tell him the safe way out of town."

The captain rose, prompting Augustus to do the same. He handed one of the two signed papers to Augustus.

"Take this. It is your honor parole and reprieve letter. Keep it safe. You will need it to prove to our troops that you are not a combatant, and to your troops, you are not a deserter." The captain offered his left hand to Augustus. "As you are no longer my adversary, I shall say good luck to you, sir."

Augustus took the letter with his wrapped hand and shook with his left before leaving with the sergeant.

As he walked off, he heard Duffy calling out to him, "Go make some chil'en, True! Ya need some kin!"

CHAPTER 29
Augustus

With the sun and the skies and the birds above me

WITH HIS CRUTCH under his arm, he hobbled north in the tattered clothes of a dead Rebel. He took a trail, fifty feet off the side of the dirt road to avoid soldiers from either side. Before letting him leave the prison, the Confederate sergeant had warned him of certain dangers ahead. "Watch out for the home guard boys. They's especially ornery. They's looking for deserters, and they'll assume anyone's a deserter."

So far, he hadn't seen anybody the entire day. Once he got to West Virginia or Maryland, it should have been safe to take the roads. The honor parole letter may save him, but he wasn't sure.

Augustus had walked away from prison with two slices of bread; it was more than he'd ever gotten while inside. Even the guards hadn't had much themselves, with the way the war was going.

John Dark Buffalo wouldn't have been happy with his prize if the fight had been fair.

His clothes draped off his emaciated body like a clothesline.

Augustus was tired and weak and in no shape to hunt for the food he so desperately needed along the way. He'd have to steal or beg from strangers on his nine-hundred-mile journey to Pennsylvania. His sisters were the only family he had left, and Mr. True was probably dead by now. Wadleigh-Holmes was in West Virginia, which was on the way to Pennsylvania. He thought he might stop there or stop anywhere if he found something else along the way. Getting to Pennsylvania would take several weeks. He'd already made peace with that.

After three days of traveling, the hunger pains returned and grew into terrible, grinding aches. Augustus heard a horse approaching from the road behind him. He hid behind a tree and waited. It was a lone Rebel officer with his arm in a sling. His horse kept a slow pace, and after he passed by, Augustus kept up as best he could without being seen from the trees. The officer's head was bandaged under his hat; it bobbed with fatigue. Augustus decided to follow him like a mountain lion following his prey, waiting for the right opportunity.

Although slow, the horse's pace was faster than Augustus' hobbling with a crutch, and the officer was getting a distance ahead of him. Just before the officer left his view, Augustus saw him tip over and fall off his horse. Augustus froze, then hobbled faster up to the officer. Out of breath, Augustus came to about a hundred feet from the officer when he began to rise, wobble and dust himself off. The officer had a pistol at his hip. If Augustus were to rush him, it'd be doubtful he'd make it halfway to him. The officer took the reins and walked over to the opposite side of the road. He looked carefully down both directions of the road before pulling off his suspenders, dropping his trousers and squatting. It was the perfect opportunity. Augustus used the horse as cover as he crossed the road. The officer's back was to him when he grabbed the horse's bridle, pulling the officer off balance onto his back.

With his trousers down, he went for his gun but couldn't find it. Augustus used the moment to use the horse as cover and hobble away. As he got his good foot in a stirrup, he heard the clicks of an empty gun. Augustus pulled himself onto the saddle and looked back at the sad Rebel officer, pants down, head bandaged, arm in a sling, on his back, and firing an empty gun. When their eyes met, the officer gritted his teeth and threw the gun in his direction, but it only flew five feet before skidding to the ground. Augustus smiled and tipped an invisible hat to him before turning the horse and heading off.

That night, Augustus headed into the woods and found a valley of tall grass. Settling for the night, he found one piece of hardtack in a saddlebag which he almost swallowed in one bite. He tied the horse up and slept well.

In the morning, Augustus' eyes opened to white clouds floating in the sea of blue. Surrounded by a wall of tall green grass, his body lay in it like a dead man in a green upholstered coffin with its lid open. From a distance came a far away voice carrying a song. It was a female voice singing *Wade in the Water*, a tune he recognized. A young negro girl's head appeared over the edge of his grass coffin. She looked about sixteen. The sight reminded him of looking up at Duffy from the bottom of the graves.

"That your horse over yonder?"

"Yessum."

"You from around here?"

"Nah. Far from here. Pennsylvania."

"You a Yankee?"

"I suppose."

"S'pose? Shouldn't ya knows?"

The girl picked at the grass, ripping at it. She looked at him with a sideways glance, then looked to the distance like it held promise. She'd occasionally turn for his reaction.

"I was a Yankee," said Augustus as he pointed to a pair of scissors in her pocket. "Can I use those?"

"Ain't gonna stick me with 'em, are ya?"

"Promise." He took them and began cutting off his beard as she watched.

"You been traveling like me. Your beard is ragged, and those shoes are gonna last as long as a June bug in a chicken coop."

"Nah. Been traveling only a few days. I was in a Reb prison."

"You escape like me? I's run off from Alabama. I brought them scissors to protect myself. They done good two times."

Without a mirror, he was missing sections of hair.

"You won't be putting your hands on me or nothing if I help you there with that cuttin', will ya? You ain't doing a good job."

He smiled up at her, flipped the scissors in his hand, handle out. She took them. Kneeling, she cut his beard closer.

"Your state a good state?" she asked.

"I know it's a might better than the state you come from."

The beard came off, and then some of his hair. The scissors were too dull to shave him, but he felt better when she finished.

"Lucky you got that horse. You steal him?"

"Off a Rebel."

"Was he dead?"

"Relieving himself."

She laughed. "And you relieved him of his horse."

"That I did."

She sat in front of him, cross-legged, and eyed him cautiously. "You take me along? I ain't knowed where to go."

He studied her. She had a small nose surrounded by a myriad of freckles and a mole on the left side of her upper lip that was king of them.

"Just walking? Don't know where to go?" asked Augustus.

"I made it this far outta some folks kindnesses. They tells me I got the gift of seein'. Seein' who ya really is inside. The bad or the good."

"If you're going my way, you can tag along."

"That'll be fine," she said with a smile.

She pulled out a gold bar and two jewels in the form of a loaf of bread and two eggs. She handed it all to him. The loaf dropped to his lap as he popped the eggs in his mouth, shells and all.

"They starve you in that prison?" He nodded as he stuffed his mouth with the bread.

Her name was Abigail, and he let her ride on the back of his horse, hands gripping the saddle instead of his waist. Passing through towns, he had her walk behind him, acting like he owned her. She spoke to Augustus all day long as they rode, asking questions, and telling tales of her life as a slave.

She could talk the legs off a chair with all her tales and askin'. Can't never get a word in edgewise, he thought.

She asked about his life, the plants, the weather, even politics. Her mouth never stopped, but Augustus enjoyed it. They were now escaping their captors together, and if they reached the North, they would be free. Augustus thought her words gave her a sense of that freedom. She now was free to speak, and her voice attempted to free as many words as she could think of.

THEY HAD BEEN traveling through Georgia for the past three days. He had his honor parole, but Abigail was a runaway slave, and Georgia was a slave state.

Augustus had decided to head into the Chattahoochee forest and take the unpopulated mountain route into West Virginia. Only Atlanta stood in their way, which they had to circumvent to avoid travelers and soldiers.

The chirping of the birds welcomed them to the mountains as they rode in. After a mile past the last road, there appeared no trace of civilization. The beauty of this place silenced Abigail's words, but her mouth remained open in awe of it.

She had never been to the mountains, never seen a forest. She walked beside the horse, her feet feeling the bounce in the thick pine needle floor. Green moss-covered boulders were scattered among pines.

"Taller than the tallest of the tall," she said.

Trees were kings there. They arranged the amber rays of sunlight into shimmering patches below. The light played across her face as if it was moving water. Reaching the top of the ridgeline, the terrain leveled and rolled.

They followed a worn mountain path with no detectable sign of foot traffic. It weaved through the boulders and trees, crossing little creeks and bigger streams. They had plenty of water, but they still needed food. Augustus had risked begging for some outside the town of Athens, but that would only last another day.

The mountain evenings were a lot colder than the summer evenings down in the lowlands of Georgia. That first night was so cold that they shivered in only the clothes on their backs. He had tried to start a fire but had no luck. They both lay on a bed of pine needles and tried to cover themselves with them. Even in the dim moonlight, Abigail could see the needles covering Augustus twitching as he shook from the cold.

"You cold, ain't ya?"

"A bit. You?"

She hesitated.

"A bit."

The crickets resumed their conversations as he tried to make her face out in the darkness.

"Now, don't get in a huff or nothing, but we could sleep close, I mean with our clothes on and all. Nothing funny going on, no touching. It'll keep ya warmer is all. Don't want ya catching your death," she said. "I still got these here scissors. I'll stick ya if ya try to stick me."

Augustus laughed, "I can face away the dangerous part of me if ya wish."

He pushed away his cover of pine needles and rolled to his other side, facing away from her.

"Fine by me," she said as she slid over and pressed her body to him, awkwardly wrapping her top arm over him. He moved it to rest under his.

She felt his ribs and withered thin form. "Boy, you are as thin as a fiddle string, ain't ya? Got no meat on ya. My scissors would just hit bone."

"I suppose."

The horse shifted near them, and the moonlight glinted off its eye.

"Hey, Aug? What's your horse's name?"

"He ain't got one."

"Ain't…? Well, ya gotta name him. What if he run off?"

"I'll just call out 'Horse, horse!'" He laughed, and she slapped his chest.

"He need a name."

"You can name him."

"I can?"

"You name him."

"Daisy. It was my Momma's name, and I loved that woman.

"Daisy, it is."

Augustus began to slip off to sleep when she said, "I knew you'd be a kind one, Aug. I knowed that when I came up on yas. I woulda had my scissors out and at the ready, but I could tells ya was a kind one."

He grinned in the dark. "How could you tell?"

"It's a feeling I get from regular folk. But with you? You was different. I saw it straight out. You got kind eyes."

The morning brought them more stomach pains. Around midday, they heard water, and as they came closer, they heard a waterfall. The water fell from a height of about twenty feet into a pool of crystal-like water a hundred feet in circumference. The pool fed a stream that ran down the mountain.

"My, my, my! Ain't that the most purty thing you ever did saw? I ain't… Ahhh!" she shouted as a fish jumped a foot out of the water.

Augustus looked down; there were schools of them.

Fashioning a tree branch into a spear, he used her scissors

to sharpen a point. He removed his shirt and waded in with his pants on. Translucent skin thinly covered his skeletal form.

"Oh, pray to the Lord almighty he catch something," she muttered. As she said that, he did.

They ate the fish raw, guts, tail, and all while it was still kicking, then he went back for more. They were easy to catch in the shallows. They would have enough for days.

Rubbing stick on stick with his hands started the fire. That night, they ate their fill of fish and slept apart on either side of the fire. He watched the flames reflect off her eyes until he closed his to sleep.

After catching breakfast, he climbed into the pool with all his clothes on, then stripped. He took them to a boulder on the far edge and cleaned them as best he could by slamming them on it, dunking them, and repeating the process.

Abigail glanced down to her dress and winced. She smelled her armpit and returned with the face of a lemon eater.

"Aug, would you do that for me? I can hide behind that tree yonder and toss it to ya?"

"Come on in and do it yourself. You can wash yourself too."

"I can't swim."

He raised his arms and glanced at the waist-deep water he stood in. "It ain't deep. You don't need to swim."

"I'm too ashamed. Can't be doing that in front of no man."

"Let me finish, and I'll get out and sit yonder with my back turned to ya."

"Uh, uh. Don't want to be going in alone, neither."

He shook his head for what to do. "Come on in with your dress on, wade over here, duck down to your neck and take it off. I won't see nothing, and you can wash yourself, the dress, and your lady drawers."

She gave him a one-sided frown. "You sure I don't need to bring my scissors on out there with me?"

"I'm sure."

She waded out next to him with a side-eyed glance, uncertain. In the end, he cleaned her dress as she washed herself. She wouldn't let him near her lady drawers; she washed those herself. He took all the clothes and laid them out flat on a boulder to dry in the sun. He returned to the pool and got in.

"I can teach ya to swim. Can't drown in this water."

She was squatting low in the water up to her neck. She shrugged her shoulders.

"See, your arms move in front of ya as your legs kick behind ya. They both work at the same time. The trick is to keep calm. Grab that rock with your hands, bring your feet back and kick."

Abigail turned to him. "You be looking over yonder. Don't want to be showing my backside."

After an hour of learning to swim, Abigail looked over to their clothes.

"I'll turn all the clothes to the other side if ya promise to turn your back and don't look."

"I'll abide," he said as he turned.

The water swirled behind him, and he heard her wet feet. When he heard the wet clothes slap down on the boulder, he couldn't resist and turned. His breath left him as he watched her climb the rock. He had never seen a woman's body, only the shape it took under a dress. Abigail had more curves than a barrel of snakes. Her skin was the color of coffee with two spoons of milk, and her nipples were two shades darker. She climbed with the grace of a mountain cat. Her body undulated, bounced and jiggled deliciously. He could not look away, and he quickly prayed to God to have her not turn his direction.

She climbed to the top of the boulder and disappeared over the top of it. He swallowed hard, left the water, and climbed the boulder. Keeping low, he peered over the other side. She lay atop the warm rock, eyes closed, limbs outstretched, granting permission for the sun to caress her skin and only the sky and the birds to look upon it.

He climbed to a lower rock, smooth and warm. Laying as she did, he closed his eyes and slept.

The next day they gutted and dried as many fish as they could take with them. As they dried, they explored the area surrounding them and found a cabin about a quarter of a mile from their waterfall pool. No smoke came from the chimney, but they waited an hour watching for a sign of activity.

"Let's go," said Augustus, stepping out from behind the tree.

"Hold it there!" said a voice from behind them. Augustus felt the fool. "Turn around and drop the scissors. I know you got them."

They turned to see a woman in her seventies. She was on the plump side, but not unusually so for a woman of her age. She wore pants, a red flannel shirt, an Indian blanket coat, and an oversized, round, brown hat atop her head. Most importantly was the double-barreled scattergun in her hands.

Abigail dropped her scissors. "Can I get those back when we leave? We weren't gonna hurt ya. We didn't know anybody lived here."

"You talk a might, girl."

"She does, but she speakin' true. We weren't here to do harm."

"I know. That's what I figured. I can read people well, and I been watching y'all since yesterday. Saw y'all naked as the day God gave ya."

"Lordy!" said Abigail.

The woman jumped a bit and turned to Abigail. "Hey, it's my mountain and you on it. And I ain't the one to be concerned with. I'm an old woman, but your boy here was spying your talents a might. I seen it."

Abigail's eyes dug holes into Augustus, and she placed her hand across her chest. Augustus turned to the woman.

"That ain't kindly. Ya might as well shoot me now with all that ornery in her eyes. She didn't have to know."

"I see your point."

He turned to Abigail. "My eyes followed their own heart. Couldn't help it. First time they looked upon a woman."

"He's right. Mens are dogs, can't help it."

"Shoulda had my scissors."

"So, let me get this straight now. The way I figure it, you're a runaway, and you're a deserter."

"Close. They released me from prison on honor parole."

"Honor parole?"

"I promised not to fight no more."

"Which side were you on?"

"Drop the barrel of that gun, and I'll tell ya."

"Sorry," said the old woman as she dropped it.

"Well, my name's Augustus True, and I was a Union doctor."

Abigail's head jerked to him. "Doctor?! You never told me you was no doctor!"

"You never gave me a chance to speak a word, let alone a sentence."

"They call me Maddy. So, Yankee doctor, eh? I was just curious. I don't preach no affiliation to neither side. Both fools."

"Mind if I get my scissors? Seems I need 'em more and more," she said, glancing at Augustus. "Had to use them twice so far."

CHAPTER 30
Augustus

Safe home at last

"MY HUSBAND AND I been up heres for the last thirty years. Spent the last ten alone after his passing," said Maddy as she sat in her rocker before the fireplace.

Augustus looked around the cabin. Furs, tools, and dried meats and fish hung on the walls. "You seem to do alright here alone."

"Getting harder the older I get. Getting' fearful of breakin' something and starving to death."

Abigail sat on the rug, her eyes concentrating on a splinter in her big toe. She scooted closer to the fire for more light. "This boy almost starved to death," said Abigail.

"I can see that. Army don't feed ya too well?"

"Prison don't feed ya too well," replied Augustus.

"Mm-hmm. Mighty fine steed you got out theres. Army give ya that?"

"I named him Daisy."

Maddy looked at her with a raised brow. "Named *him* Daisy?"

"Yessum."

"Army did give me that in a ways."

"He stole him," said Abigail.

"I was close to eating him before this one came along with bread and eggs." Augustus gestured to Abigail.

"True enough. He ate them down lickity split."

"Where y'all headed?"

"I got kin in Pennsylvania. Two sisters."

"Ma and pa gone?"

"If they weren't, I wouldn't be headin' there."

"Bad people? Treat ya, unkindly?"

"Sold me as a bound boy to a military school."

Abigail turned to him. "You ain't told me that neither. You served white folk like me. A white folk serving a white folk, that's funny." Abigail's white teeth lit up her smile.

"People do odd things in odd times," said Maddy, returning her attention to the fire. "I was thinking on it, and y'all can stay on a while if ya earns your keep, I likes the company in my older years. Better not be stayin' more than a moon change, though. Georgia's home guard be passing through about then. Don't want 'em getting neither of ya."

"The horse ain't mine," said Abigail. "But if it was up to me, I'd like to stay on. It's a paradise 'round here. I can help around the place."

Maddy turned to Augustus. "I can surely fatten you up a bit. Might be good for the rest of your travels."

"Thank ya kindly. We'd be much obliged to ya."

"What's with your leg there?"

"Shot twice in the calf."

"I can help ya with that, too, I suppose."

The following four weeks were more of a holiday than work. The pain and worries of the past never crossed their minds. Augustus went hunting with Maddy. She shot a buck, and he skinned it, dressed it, and brought it back to be smoked. He repaired her roof, cleaned out her root cellar, and made her a new wheelbarrow. Abigail cleaned the cabin and tended to her garden. On their off time, all three swam naked in the waterfall pool, but Abigail made Augustus turn his back when they got in and swim without his specs on.

With Maddy's good cooking and as much fish as they could eat, after a month, Augustus had filled out again. His calf had also healed, and he no longer needed the crutch for his leg. He and Abigail decided to leave. Maddy loaded them up with food, warm clothes, and flint for starting a fire. They rode off on Daisy with Maddy waving them goodbye. Abigail waved back to her before circling her arms around Augustus' waist and laying her cheek against his back.

IT WASN'T AS he had remembered. The True farm looked weathered and small. Smoke came from the chimney, and the crops were harvested recently. He and Abigail dismounted. He walked to the door; she stayed by the horse with her scissors ready. A woman in her late twenties opened the door.

"Glory? I'm Augustus, your broth—"

Her eyes opened, and she wrapped her arms around him. "Augustus! My oh my, how you changed!"

Augustus looked her up and down in shock. "My, how *you* changed as well. You're a full-grown woman now."

"I'm a married woman now and have a daughter myself, Augustus."

"That's considerable. A might considerable." The two gazed upon each other, both with a smile that recalled the past.

"Oh! I have forgotten myself! Please, please, come on in and sit down. I'm sure you're tired."

Augustus gestured behind him. "Would you mind? We've been traveling together and…"

"Why, of course not. Have her come on in."

The living room seemed much smaller than he remembered. Augustus and Glory sat at the dining table. Abigail sat in a chair in the corner of the room, eating the buttered bread and bacon that Glory had made that morning.

"It's so good to see you. I just can't believe you are really here after all these years. We saw Jefferson those three summers, but not you, you never came. Why not? Emilia went on down for ya for that ceremony when ya finish the school… What's that called again?"

"Graduation."

"Yes, graduation. But she came home without ya and said y'all must've run off to war. Emilia and I was always talking about what you and Jefferson would be up to out there. Two fine gentlemen officers. All the boys 'round here joined up." Her face brightened. "My husband, you may know him, George Walker? You were awfully little, but we used to see him and his family in church. George is off fightin' for the Pennsylvania 123rd. Under Colonel Clark, I believe. What about you, Augustus?"

"The Seventh West Virginian."

"I always thought you boys might be fightin' side by side or somethin'."

"I'd like to meet him sometime. How is Emilia?"

Sadness came to Glory's face. "She passed on little over a year ago now. Saddest day of my life. How's Jefferson? Is he doing well? Is he comin' too?"

"Jefferson was killed in battle back in Spotsylvania."

Glory looked to the floor. "Not too many of us left, it seems."

"When did Pa pass?" Glory looked to him with confusion. "Many people come to the funeral?"

"Pa's lying in the other room."

The color drained from Augustus' face. "But he took ill just after Ma…"

"No, he's still with us. Would you like to see him? He's very ill, but…"

Augustus shook his head in disbelief and confusion.

"Oh, is there something wrong, Augustus? Was that a big shock to hear about Pa?"

He looked to the floor. "Maybe we should be going."

Glory's eyes opened wide. "Going?"

"That man wasn't so good to Augustus."

Augustus' eyes darted to Abigail. She shut her mouth.

"What's she mean?" Glory questioned with raised brows.

"She don't mean nothing."

"Your pa sold him," said Abigail from across the room. Glory turned to her. "Yessum. Sold him like a slave to the school. He told me so."

Glory's shocked expression turned back to Augustus.

"That's why I never came home, Glory. It was Pa. He and ma bonded me to school to pay for Jefferson's schoolin'. I wasn't supposed to be schooled. I was supposed to work."

"Oh, my."

"I managed to do alright, but I never wanted to see Pa again."

"I'm sorry, Augustus. I'm sorry that happened to ya. I had no idea. Pa won't even know you're here if ya want. He's doing poorly lately. He can't move half his body, and he's always getting worse. The pastor comes just about every other day now."

"What illness does he have?"

"Oh, I don't understand that doctorin' talk."

"He does. He's a doctor," said Abigail.

"Doctor?"

"Yessum. Learned it from Pa, then more in the army."

"Well, ya see there? Pa did something good for ya. Now our doctor said Pa's time will be here shortly."

"What did the doctor say it was?"

"Something with his head. Explosion in his head or something."

"Stroke."

"Yes, I believe that is it. You can see him if you like. He won't know it's you. His eyes haven't been open for some time now."

Glory rose and went to the bedroom door, and Augustus followed. She opened it. Mr. True was lying on the bed in the darkened bedroom.

"Please don't be going, Augustus. I'd be pleased as pie if you'll be stayin' here for a while? Meet my daughter Emily.

There's still a bed in your old room. Emily and I… Oh, I named her after our… Well, Emily's at school now. Since George has been gone, she and I sleep in my and Emilia's old room. It'll be like old times. Just like old times."

Abigail took the plates to the kitchen. Glory looked at Augustus but gestured toward her.

"Oh, now what about her? She with you? Is she your girl?"

"No, she's someone I met on the way here. She'd run away and needed some help. She's a good person. I'm sure if you have any need, she'd be willing to work for her keep."

"I'll be sleepin' in the barn, ma'am," said Abigail as she came back into the room.

"You will do no such thing," replied Glory. "I can make a spot for you here or over in the kitchen. We ain't got another bedroom."

"You lettin' me sleep in your home? With you all?"

"Why, yes, of course. You'll catch your death out theres."

Augustus walked outside and over to Daisy, taking up his reins. Abigail came running out after him. "Need some help?"

"Nah, just gonna set up Daisy for the night."

"I ain't got nothing to do, so…"

"Come on, then."

Augustus and Abigail brought him in. The barn was empty of animals, but sitting in the middle was a coffin up on two sawhorses. As they walked Daisy past it, Abigail ran her finger over the smooth lacquered surface, wiping a clean line in the thick dust. Augustus removed the tack from Daisy.

"Can you fill that pail with those oats over there?"

"Yessum," she said with her eyes glued to the coffin.

Augustus grabbed another pail. "I'll go get some water."

"Not without me!"

Augustus stopped and smiled at her. "Ain't nothing in that casket. I'm sure my pa built it for himself. He was in that business."

"You ain't opened it. You don't know."

"Give him his oats. We'll get water together. I should show you around the place anyway."

She hooked the pail in his stall. Daisy walked over and stuck his mouth in it. Abigail shut his gate and walked past the coffin, never taking her eyes off of it, just in case. "Can you show me the privy first."

"Course."

They explored the farm. Time had changed his thirteen-year-old memories of it.

"*Caw, Caw.*"

"There is a place I'd like to see," said Augustus.

As they walked, Augustus told her about the crow graveyard he had discovered as a boy. The field he believed it to be was grown high with tall grass, and there were a few more poplar trees and mulberry bushes. They kicked about the grass for anything black.

"Nothing dead here, Aug."

"No. Could'a been just my imagination. I had a big one back then."

Walking back, her hand swept in and took his. He turned to her, but she refused to look over to him. Down the road, a little seven-year-old girl was approaching them. Abigail dropped his hand. Augustus knew this must be Glory's daughter, Emily. She walked up, wearing a cute yellow dress, and carrying two books. They stopped and waited for her.

"You must be Emily."

"Yes. Who are you?" She tilted her head to one side and twisted her foot in the dirt.

"I'm your Uncle Augustus."

Emily's brow furrowed as she looked at them. "Who's she?"

"She's Abigail, a friend of mine."

"Nice to meet you, Miss," said Abigail dipping into the curtesy she was taught to do as a slave.

Emily's head tilted to the side, then the other side with uncertainty before demonstrating her own quick curtsey.

"Nice to meet you." They both smiled. It made her even more adorable.

"What good manners you have. Who taught you to curtsey like that?"

"Momma did."

Augustus moved next to her. "In Virginia, they curtsey like this." Augustus did his best job of a female Virginian curtsey as Emily watched.

Abigail laughed, hands covering her mouth. "My oh my."

"That's nice," said Emily as she demonstrated a professional version of it. "You staying for supper?"

"Yeah, I'll be staying for a few days."

"My papa's in the army." She ran for the house.

"So I heard!" he called after her.

From inside the house, they could hear Emily saying, "Momma, Momma, you know how they curtsey in Virginia?"

THE FOLLOWING DAY, Augustus waited for Emily in front of the schoolhouse. She was pleased to see him, taking his hand immediately. "What are you doing here?"

"Thought I'd walk you home."

"Walk me home? Why?"

"I ain't never had a niece before. Isn't this what uncles do? Walk their nieces home and teach 'em fancy curtsies?"

She giggled.

Such a special sound. An echo from childhood.

He looked down at her brown hair-covered head with two ponytails in the back. Her gait had a fun bounce with an occasional skip. She swung his arm back and forth as they walked. He'd never experienced children before, and she was so cute. He had the overwhelming desire to grit his teeth, sweep her up and squeeze her in a hug.

"You go to that school when you were a boy?"

"No. Our ma schooled us at home. Your ma didn't tell you that?"

"Yes, she did, just checking."

"Your ma was a rascal as a child as I recall. Always trying to get my brother and me in trouble."

Emily giggled again. "If the Rebs were to win, Richmond would be the new capital of the South," she said.

"Who told you that?"

"Momma."

"What if the Rebs lose?"

Emily looked at him with a quizzical face, scrunching her nose, something else he found endearing.

"You soft or somethin'? Course theys gonna lose. My daddy's fighten' 'em."

A horse and carriage sat in front of the house as they walked up. Gloria came to the porch with a man dressed in black. She saw Emily and Augustus walking up and ran out to them.

"It was fate you came yesterday. God's will it was, Augustus. Pa's dead. Must've waited for your return. Had to be that. He passed in the night. I didn't even know it. The pastor here, he found him, he saw it. I believe Pa waited for you to be here to pass on. He must'a wanted it that way."

Augustus let go of Emily's hand and walked up to Glory, confused.

"Why would he want it that way?" said Augustus with a sarcastic smile. "That man didn't care about me."

Augustus let go of Emily's hand, and she ran to Abigail, watching them from the porch step. The pastor put up his finger as if to ask a question in class. "I'm certain your father did indeed care."

You don't know nothing, pastor, he thought, but instead said, "You're right, most likely, pastor. I'll start makin' the arrangements in the 'morn." Augustus outstretched his hand to the pastor.

"Hello, Augustus," said the pastor.

"Pastor," nodded Augustus.

"Glory speaks of you often, as did Emelia. I'm sorry to hear the news about your brother. Losing so many of our good boys in these sad days. Lord saw to your timing here. Mr. True surely coulda been a big help with his own remembrance." The pastor chuckled, Augustus didn't. "But Glory could use your help with the arrangements, and I'll send by the casket maker."

"There's no need," chimed Glory. "Pa built his coffin

himself. It's in the barn; made it years back. It's a bit dusty, but I'll make it up nice."

The pastor turned to Augustus. "I should tell you… It's a bit early to be speaking about such things, but years back, your father gave me his will. I gave it to the judge."

TWO DAYS LATER, the knock on the door shook the dust off the front wall. The judge was a large man with a giant personality. He wore a black suit and owned two law books; he had read both of those books twice, thus advancing him to the standing of the judge. He was trusted as a logical and learned man in the mountain community and had solved countless disputes between neighbors.

As evening fell, the only light was from the fireplace and the candles. Glory had put Emily to bed, leaving herself, the pastor, Augustus, and Abigail sitting at the table with the judge. The judge's voice was as powerful as his knock.

"Good eve, all, on this solemn occasion," the judge said as he looked to Augustus. "Young Mr. True, I remember you as a boy." The judge shook his hand. "You and your brother were both good boys. The pastor here told me about the sacrifice your brother made for the Union. My condolences."

"Would you like to see Pa, Judge?" asked Glory.

"Uh, well, we should really be…"

The judge turned to Glory's ear-to-ear grin as if she was eager to show him a treasured heirloom. He exhaled an exasperated breath.

"Indeed, indeed," said the judge as he rose. Glory showered

light into the room with a candle. The deceased Mr. True lay on his bed wearing his best black suit.

"Looks a might peaceful." The judge turned. "Well, let's get to this. There ain't much."

Glory and the judge returned to their seats. The judge pulled the rolled piece of paper from his coat pocket and pulled out a pair of spectacles. He opened the paper.

"The homestead and its belongings all goes to Glory for taking such good care of me." He looked up from the paper to clarify. "*Of him.* I'm just reading what it says here. That's about it with that." The judge looked at Augustus. "I'm sorry, Augustus, ain't nothing in here for you."

Seated next to Augustus, Glory touched his arm. "Place is as much as yours as it is mine."

"I wasn't expecting nothing."

The judge continued. "There are some funeral arrangements here… He wants to be buried in his black, polished casket—"

"We already talked about that," Glory interrupted. "It's been gathering dust in the barn."

"And to be buried in his suit—"

"Already done that," interrupted Glory.

The judge was becoming a bit irritated. He smirked. "… with his shoes. He wants Glory to read the sermon, which he wrote down here." He pointed to the bottom of the letter. "He wants to be buried with his kin at the Green Mountain Cemetery, and he wants one of them weepers at his remembrance." The judge looked up from the will at Augustus and Glory.

"One of those women dressed in black paid to weep at the ceremony," Glory explained.

"I remember the weepers well. I was fixed on 'em. So strange. I always wanted to know what they were thinking. Does he ask for a warner?" asked Augustus.

"I'm sure he'd expect one of his boys to take that task on his passing. Family tradition and all," said the Judge.

"There's only one boy left, and I don't want that task."

"Pa quit warnin' after Ma passed. Pa invited the whole town, all the old relatives. Sold the wagon and horse so's Ma could have a right proper funeral. Nobody came. Nobody came, Augustus. We lay Ma up on a table right here in this room. Pa pulled up a chair, laid his head on Ma, and cried. Yes, Augustus, he cried. Cried for three days straight, no stoppin'."

"Ma get a weeper?"

"Pa said Ma wouldn't want a weeper. Don't know why."

"Where would we find one of these weepers?"

"The Fenn family," Glory said. "I believe they still do weepin'. It's about a day's ride away. They call her The Missus."

THE FOLLOWING DAY, Abigail and Glory polished up the casket in the barn. As Mr. True had been a warner, he had made it from the finest maple and polished it until it was smooth as glass.

"Should we bring the casket inside and put him in it there? We got those special side doors to make it wide. Special for a coffin. We did it for Ma."

"It's just the three of us. The thing is just too heavy. We'll barely get it in the wagon without Pa even in it." Augustus looked around the barn in thought. "I'll back the wagon up to it in here. We can just push it in. After that, we'll set Pa in it."

Setting Pa in the casket turned out to be the most challenging part. Abigail and Glory each took a leg, and, although he hadn't completely recovered from the malnutrition in prison, Augustus took Mr. True from under the armpits.

"Ahh!" cried out Emily as they brought his corpse through the parlor room.

"Avert your eyes, Emily!" shouted Glory as she struggled with the weight.

The girls set Pa's legs on the back of the wagon in a spread-eagle way on either side of the coffin. They took Pa's shoulders from Augustus so he could run around and jump on the wagon, then take the feet and pull him up and into the coffin. Pa's body bent backward, laying half in and half out of the casket. The girls climbed up and held his shoulders again as Augustus pulled on the feet. His corpse plopped awkwardly into the coffin.

Wincing at her father's treatment, Glory adjusted him and fixed his suit.

"I'll find some wildflowers to put in here with him. You should get on over to the Fenns. It's a full day's ride," said Glory.

"Mind if I tag along?" asked Abigail.

"Don't see why not."

The ride to the Fenn farm had them arriving late in the evening. It was dark, but Augustus could make out that there were several buildings there. He trotted Daisy toward the light coming from cracks in the wood siding of a cabin. After tying Daisy up, he and Abigail approached the door, only to be stopped by a voice.

"Can I help yous, sah?" Someone walked from the shadows. Despite the darkness, Augustus could tell it was a black man.

"I'm here to see the weeper."

"It's a might late for The Missus. Mind if ya comes back in the morn, sah?"

A voice from within the cabin called out. "Who's out there, Thane?"

The black man turned his head without his eyes leaving Augustus. "Don't rightly know."

"Augustus True, ma'am. I be needin' your services, your weepin' services for my dead pa."

The door opened to a silhouetted girl. It was difficult to make her out in this light.

"I ain't the weeper. The Missus is sleepin'. You can come back in the morn," she said, leaning against the door frame.

"I came a full day's ride. Mind if we sleep in the barn?"

"Who's that with you?"

"Name's Abigail, Ma'am," she said.

"Hmm, girl. Do I know you? You from around here?"

"No, Ma'am. I run away from down south. This here man done help me."

"Hmm, that's fine, You can sleep over in there. There's fresh hay in theres."

CHAPTER 31
Augustus

My sun sets to rise again

"You looking for me?" Augustus awoke to the woman's voice. He sat up to a blurry figure sitting cross-legged in front of him.

"Sleep fine in here? We have other cabins on the farm, but they haven't been used for some time and need a good cleanin'."

He put on his spectacles, and a nineteen-year-old Little Miss came into focus. His jaw dropped.

She laughed. "You look like you seen a ghost. Did I scare ya?"

She was beautiful. She wore a worn black dress, had black hair, and had a small birthmark on the left side of her jaw. But it was her eyes that were her most striking feature. Cavernous eyes that a man could fall in and never hit bottom; one iris ringed in dark green and growing lighter to the center, and the other one the color of a walnut trimmed in gold.

"You the weeper?"

"Mmm-hmm."

"The Missus?"

"Mmm-hmm."

"Mornin'," said Abigail, popping up from under a haystack in the corner.

Little Miss flinched in surprise. Still fuzzy from sleep, Abigail picked a piece of straw from her mouth. There was more sticking out of hair.

She noticed the weeper and spat out another piece before saying, "Oh! Sorry, Ma'am."

"Ain't nothing," said Little Miss, returning her attention to Augustus.

"My name is Augustus True, ma'am. I'll be needin'…"

"True?"

"Yes, Augustus True."

"Your daddy the warner?"

"Yes, ma'am."

"You a warner?"

"No."

"Are ya gonna be?"

"No."

She smirked. "Don't wanna be a warner, huh? So, how's your daddy now?" she asked sweetly.

"He's who I'll be needin' your services for."

Her head nodded with a frown. "I 'spected. I met your pa. Heard he took ill," she said sadly. "It'll cost ya fifty cent if ya got it. If ya don't, I won't charge ya nothing 'cause I knew your pa and all. I can start mournin' for ya the day before the funeral and for three days after that on my own. I should be needin' a rendering or a daguerreotype or anything your pa ever wrote. All that will help me."

"I ain't got fifty cent, and I ain't got no rendering or nothing. I apologize."

"Like I said, no pay's fine. But you's a warner's son, you shoulda known about the things I be needin'," she said almost teasingly as she looked him over. "Ceremony at your farm or gravesite? When you plannin'?"

"Gravesite, and soon's you able. My pa needs to be set in the ground right quick."

"Hmm, well, suppose we can take the day, and you can tell me all about your pa since you didn't bring nothing you was supposed to bring. Can ya stay another night?"

"I'll do what I have to."

"Fine then. I'll tell Thane. You need a sin eater? He'll do it for ya, no cost. He likes food."

"No ma'am. Pa didn't say nothing 'bout a sin eater."

Little Miss stood. "I never knew your daddy had a son. You in the war, Augustus True?"

"Until the war, my pa had two sons, and yes, ma'am, I was."

She turned to walk off. "Your face tells me you've traveled a difficult path."

LITTLE MISS SAT in a rocker on the porch with her aunt, Janey Fenn. They both squinted at Abigail and Augustus, walking in the distant cornfield.

"He's a handsome one. Maybe I should take the weepin' on this one," said Janey with a wink and her tongue in her cheek.

"So sweet of ya. But I'd never want ya to come out of

retirement for me, Janey." They giggled. "How long did you do the weepin' 'round here?" asked Little Miss.

"Hmm, well, I came here about a year after your momma left. Started weepin' about six or seven year ago now."

Augustus and Abigail began walking around the outlying cabins.

"Think they's together?" asked Janey.

"They weren't sleepin' close when I saw 'em."

Little Miss turned back to Janey. "Did ya like weepin' when ya did it?"

"Yessum. I was always jealous of your momma when we was little. I knew she'd be the weeper after your grandma. When I heard your momma left, believe me, I high tailed it on over here. I didn't have no man. I was free to do what I wanted."

"My grandma taught you?"

"Mm-hmm. Issie. Poor thing. She went to the Lord just a year after she stopped weepin', and I took over." Janey's brow furrowed. "I believe that was just after you and your momma came to visit that one time. Remember that?"

"Yes."

"The family's lucky I came here to take over. Issie was good stock. I loved that old gal." They both looked back out to Augustus and Abigail. "What about you? Your momma teach weepin' to ya?"

"No, Micah did."

"Shoulda known as much. Your momma didn't take to it. You seem born to it. You like doing it?"

"Mm-hmm. Especially if I get to do weepin' for warner sons like that one," said Little Miss, busting into laughter.

They saw Abigail take ahold of his hand.

"Oh, looky there. Guess she don't work for him," said Janey. They both giggled.

"I should get started on his pa, don't ya think?"

"Suppose." Janey saw Easter walking with a pail of water. "Easter, can you go tell that boy to come on over now?"

Abigail had followed Augustus up to the house. Little Miss stood on her front porch and gestured to one of the rocking chairs. "Mr. Augustus True."

Abigail was about to follow him up when Little Miss said, "Miss? I'm sorry, but this needs to be a…"

"I ain't his slave if that's what you be thinking."

Little Miss smiled at her. "That's not what I'm thinking. And this state hasn't been a slave state for many a year now. I just need to talk to your man here privately…"

"He ain't my man neither. I mean, well…" she trailed off.

"I'm saying I just need to talk private. It's about his daddy and all. You understand?"

Abigail started to turn away with a look of embarrassment. "Course. I won't bother. I'll be around." She walked off, and Little Miss took the other rocker.

"She your girl?" she said, still watching Abigail walk off.

"No."

"Well, you're her man. She's got it bad for you."

"Met about a month ago. We traveled here together from Georgia."

"She a runaway?"

"Yes."

"Poor thing. Why ain't she your girl? She's a pretty little thing."

"She's a little young."

"Sixteen, seventeen? Maybe Eighteen. They's marrying years," she said.

"I don't know. I meant… She's very sweet, but…"

Little Miss turned to him. "You're gonna break that girl's heart, Mr. Augustus True. Well, if she needs a place to stay, that's what the Fenn farm's here for, and we got plenty of empty cabins."

"I'll let her know, thank you," replied Augustus.

Little Miss changed the subject. "So, tell me about your pa."

"My pa bound me into servitude."

She grinned and faced him. "Whoa, whoa, there. You want me weeping for him, don't ya?"

"I don't know, Ma'am. I don't know what to say. He was alright up until I was about thirteen, I suppose."

"That's good then. Let's start from your earliest memory till thirteen."

Augustus began, and the conversation went into the afternoon. After Little Miss pulled out a whiskey bottle, the conversation went far into the evening. At one in the morning, Augustus stumbled into the barn.

Abigail woke up. "Ooh, ooh! You be smellin' of whiskey, Aug."

"I'm fine," he slurred.

"You sure? Better lie on down."

Augustus flopped onto the hay next to her. "Seems my pa might not be so bad if you take away the bound-servitude business."

THE FOLLOWING MORNING, Augustus and Abigail were atop Daisy, waiting for The Missus to follow him home. Thane came from the barn, pulling the mule. Thane was a skinny black man with a bad limp. He was much older than Easter, around forty-five. Thane hitched the mule up to the buggy.

The door to the main home opened, and Janey came out to the porch. "She'll be out in a moment," she called to Augustus. "Just getting prepared and all. Won't be but a moment more."

The sun was at the top of the eastern tree line by the time Little Miss finally came out of her home as The Missus, dressed in her weeping clothes, veil down, handkerchief in her hand. She stopped to let Janey check her outfit up and down, something they did for each other. Little Miss didn't say a word as she climbed into her buggy.

The way back to the True farm was as quiet as if he'd been alone. With Abigail holding his waist, Augustus rode on ahead of Little Miss to lead the way.

Little Miss didn't want to arrive at the True's late in the evening, so they stopped at a neighbor's farmhouse for the night. The Fenn weepers had a network of homes they were welcome to stay at if they were providing weeping services far from home. Augustus and Abigail held back as they didn't know the etiquette. Little Miss waited in the buggy as Thane asked the homeowner, and Thane returned.

"They're making up the room, Missus."

A few minutes later, the wife opened the door. With the flair of a queen, Little Miss was led by Thane to the bedroom where she would be undisturbed until morning. It had been the standard practice for years and years; to refuse lodging to a weeper was a bad omen on the home. Thane, Augustus, and Abigail slept outside with blankets they had brought.

The next morning, Little Miss, still veiled, left like she had never slept or used the privy. The farmer and his wife stood together as they watched her vanish down the road. The event felt strange to Augustus with no words exchanged, or "Thank you's," said. He pulled Daisy around and did it himself.

"Thank you," he said to them.

They both jerked their heads to him, startled from the broken silence. The farmer slowly nodded to him. Augustus pulled Daisy around, and they headed home.

Augustus trotted up and past the buggy, glancing over as he did. His curiosity about her was growing. Many of his young memories had to do with her and his father's profession.

Arriving at the True farm, Glory cleaned up Mr. True's bedroom in case the weeper would need a quiet place. Glory held back her secret excitement to have The Missus as a guest. The Fenn family played a significant role in mountain history and the history of the Trues in particular.

"Good morning! It's such an honor to have y'all here…"

Thane skipped up to Glory. "Uh, I'm sorry, Ma'am, but the weeper be needin' some time and a place…"

"Oh, yes! I thought ahead and cleaned up my daddy's old room. Please this way." Little Miss only nodded and said nothing as she shut the door behind herself.

Glory made the best breakfast she could with the fixings she had, but Little Miss never came out of the bedroom to eat. Thane ate two helpings and saw Glory keep looking at the uneaten plate.

"Ah, yeah, so you just put it on down there. In front of the door. She'll get it when we're gone."

Glory put it in front of the door. By the time they finished breakfast, the plate had vanished.

Everyone except Augustus and Abigail were dressed for Mr. True's funeral. They wore the only clothes they had. Augustus hitched Daisy to the wagon holding Mr. True's coffin and took the driver's seat. Abigail climbed up next to him as Emily sat in the back with the coffin. Glory came running out carrying the wooden cross that was to be the grave marker; she stopped at the wagon bench, her eyes narrowing as she looked up to Abigail.

"Oh! Sorry, Ma'am!" said Abigail. She turned and climbed to the back with Emily and the coffin.

Reaching the cemetery, Thane took out the old weeping chair and set it near the site where the grave would be dug. Augustus grabbed the shovel from the back of the wagon as Little Miss began to carry out her trade.

"I'll help ya," said Abigail, coming up to him with another shovel. "I don't mind hard work."

Seeing Abigail offer help, Thane reluctantly stepped up to help. They all took turns till they reached exhaustion.

"She tell ya I'm a sin eater?" said Thane. Augustus looked up at him from the bottom of the four feet they'd dug so far.

"She did."

"Need one?"

"My Pa didn't say nothing about it."

"Cause, if ya need one, I'd do it for nothin' if the meal's good."

Augustus looked over to the casket. "It's a little late for that, ain't it?"

Thane looked over to it. "Oh, yeah, suppose. Just gotta hankerin' for a meal, I suppose. My favorite pastime is eatin'."

He glanced at Abigail. "Well, second favorite. But sin eating is dying out. No one does it no more. A lost art, they say."

Augustus crawled out of the grave and handed the shovel to Thane, who climbed in.

"You as good as a leper when you sin eatin'. Women won't have ya. Not even the ladies of the eve…" he stopped and turned to Abigail. "Sorry, miss."

Abigail crossed her arms and rolled her eyes. "Men."

"I don't believe any dang foolishness. Gimme the food. I'll eat it. I'm lucky I got a gal at home." Thane climbed out and handed the shovel back to Augustus.

Abigail reached for it. "My turn."

Augustus jumped into the grave. "Don't want to get that dress dirty."

"I can dig that grave faster than both y'all, I reckon."

"I'm tellin' ya, I'd make like I was all sick while eatin'. Shaking and all like I had the devil himself in me. I shoulda been on stage," Thane continued.

"Ya think?" said Abigail.

"I'd make faces like…" Thane demonstrated his maniacal expressions to Abigail's disapproval.

Augustus and Thane continued to switch off until it was close to six feet. Augustus knew his father would want a proper six-footer. After it reached the last foot, Thane jumped in and winced in pain.

"Your leg hurting?" asked Abigail.

"Nah. Ain't nothin," Thane said.

"You a runaway?"

"Nah. I've been living here since befo' I knowed anything."

"I saw that limp you have. That old or new?" asked Augustus.

Thane looked at him. "It ain't nothin'."

Glory, Augustus, Thane, and Abigail clumsily lowered the heavy casket into the grave with ropes. Thane and Glory's side almost slipped, causing a near disaster. Glory read her sermon as Pa had wanted. She had practiced it four times to make sure there were no mistakes.

During the sermon, Augustus kept looking over to the weeper. She was genuinely crying under the veil, dabbing her eyes with her handkerchief and sniffling.

It's like she loved him more than kin, he thought. *How could someone feel that kind of emotion for someone they barely knew or didn't know at all?*

After the reading, Thane offered to help Augustus fill the grave.

"I got this, but you got some blood on your pant leg," Augustus noticed.

"It ain't nothin'."

Finished with the grave, Augustus hammered in the grave marker with his shovel. Abigail watched as Thane helped Little Miss into the buggy and walked over to her. A moment later, Little Miss turned Augustus.

"Mr. True! Abigail told me you're a doctor. Can you come on over here? There is something wrong with his leg."

Thane climbed up and took the reins. "It ain't nothin'."

"It is something!" she said with irritation. "You're just too stubborn."

"It ain't nothin'."

"You be letting Mr. Augustus True look at ya leg, hear me?" She turned to Augustus. "I'd be obliged to ya."

Augustus walked around and over to Thane, sitting in the buggy.

"Can I pull up your pant leg?"

"Just do it!" she demanded.

Augustus slowly lifted the pant leg. Thane winced as it slid across the moist part of the wound, revealing the deep purple gash. Augustus bent closer to it and smelled.

He winced. "How long you had this?"

"It ain't nothin'."

"It is something. Your leg—"

"Ain't no one taking my leg!"

"No one be taking your leg, Thane!" Little Miss reassured. "Can it be fixed, Mr. Augustus True?"

It was on the verge of turning gangrenous, and if this was in the army, he'd be cutting it off.

"I ain't so sure. It's serious. Should'a been taking care of it a might earlier…"

Little Miss crossed her arms and exhaled in exasperation. "Yes, but it wasn't. What do we do?"

"I'd be happy to get to workin' on it back at my place—"

"I's gotta get back to Easter! I's gotta get back to Easter! Ain't no way nobody does a thing to me without my Easter around."

"Fine, fine, Thane!" She stopped him. "Mr. Augustus True, I know it's a distance, but would you be so kind…"

"Course ma'am, with what you done for my pa and all, it's the least I can do. I just gotta get some things from my place on the way. I can start doctorin' it up on the way back to your farm."

At the True farm, Augustus grabbed a bottle of whiskey found under Mr. True's bed, a clean sheet, and a covered pail. He placed the whiskey and sheet in Little Miss' buggy and went back behind the barn with the pail.

A few minutes later, he walked up to Thane.

"Thane, would it be all right if I took the reins and you sat in back? Your leg should be layin' up."

Thane grimaced but did it.

"Abigail, can you tie the horse to the back here?"

Abigail nodded and obeyed as Augustus tore the sheet, pulled up the pant leg, and poured the whiskey on the wound. Thane gritted his teeth and winced in pain.

"Just set it up there," he said after he bandaged it up.

"Is that all you gonna do to it?" asked Little Miss.

"Just until we get to your place. I gotta see what it looks like then and what it smells like." Augustus took the reins of the buggy.

"Mind if I tag along, Aug?" asked Abigail.

"Better to help Glory around the place while I'm away. This is gonna take some doing."

He drove away with her disappointed face watching him disappear down the road.

Little Miss shifted in her seat next to him and sniffed air up. "Poor thing. You're gonna break that girl's heart."

"I don't know. She's growing on me."

CHAPTER 32
Augustus

After life's fitful fever, He sleeps well

"I KNEW IT WAS worse! I just knew it! He never tells me nothin'! He be hiding his leg from me," cried Easter. Thane lay on his bed. "I don't want him dying. Don't let him die, Missus!" she cried as Augustus unwrapped the bandages from the wound. "Oh my! Oh my!" Easter screamed.

Augustus took the pail next to him and removed the lid. Inside were approximately twenty white maggots crawling about.

"What those fo'?" Thane asked with fear in his eyes. Augustus scooped a few up with his hand and placed them one by one on the wound.

"What you doin'?" Easter asked with disgust.

"These little helpers will eat away the bad flesh. We leave them on for a few days and see what happens."

"No one takin' my leg! No one! Only got two, and that's the good one! Well, was… But I ain't gonna meet my maker skipping in on one foot!"

Augustus finished applying the maggots and wrapped it tight, keeping them in. "Dang, I can feel 'em."

"Does it hurt, baby?" asked Easter.

"No, it don't. It kinda tickles."

Augustus nodded and walked out with Little Miss.

"I ain't never seen no white man care for no colored," she said, looking into his eyes.

Her multi-colored irises captured him, and for a split minute, he lost himself there, in the maze of them.

"He's a soul like any other."

"You a religious man, Mr. Augustus True?"

Augustus looked off in the distance. "As much as anyone, I suppose. But with what I seen, I might have fallen from the flock a bit."

"I'd be thinkin' a warner's son would be baskin' in the light of the Lord."

Augustus turned back to her. "It'd be good if he basks in that light." He gestured toward Thane's leg. "It's gangrenous. I seen hundreds die from it even after they was tended to. I'll be stayin' a few days to see to it."

"I can't ask that of ya. You can just tell Easter and me how to tend to it."

"I'm sure you'd do a fine job tending to it. It's just…" he said, lowering his voice. "I mean, if it gets worse, you'll be needing me. He could die from that leg if it don't get better."

Her eyes traveled across his face. He wondered why a smile rose on her lips.

"I'm sure you got farm tending…"

"I don't. That ain't my home no more. I've only been back a few days from the war. I'm just as good here as anywheres."

"You can stay as long as you have Easter clean up that beard for ya," she said with a mischievous grin. "But I'll be obliged to ya, Mr. Augustus True. I can feed ya well, and I'll have Easter clean one of the cabins up for ya."

"You can call me just by my Christian name if you have a desire to."

"Be that familiar with a warner's son? Ain't that a written sin in the Bible?" She winked before turning away to the house.

THE CABIN WAS comfortable. It had a window on either side of the door and a window in each of the two bedrooms. The fireplace was large and would warm the place well during the cold winters. Easter had put a newly stuffed mattress on the bed and two rocking chairs in front of the fireplace.

The morning smelled of bacon and eggs. Augustus splashed his newly shaven face with water from the water basin before heading to Thane's cabin.

"Morning, sah," said Thane, pulling off his bedsheet from his leg.

The wound showed improvement from the night, but not as much as he hoped.

"How are you feeling this morning?"

"He was with fever all night, Mr. True," said Easter.

"That's to be expected as long as it don't get too hot."

"I be watching. We's got eats for ya over with The Missus. I'm supposed to tell ya."

Augustus stood up, and Thane grabbed his arm. "Hey boy, I mean Mister. I means to tell ya, I knew your pa. I mean, I really knew your pa, if ya want to know stories." Thane grinned with four teeth missing.

Easter shook her finger at Thane. "Oh, hush up, Thane! No boy wants to know them tales about their pa!" Augustus' head cocked to the side. "Stories?"

"They'll put a smile on your lips, I think."

"They ain't funny, Thane!" she said, turning to Augustus. "Never you mind. Now go on and get your eats."

After breakfast, Augustus took a long walk around the farm and through the trees. He found a stream with fish in it. Fishing reminded him of his brother. Both had been taught to fish by their father; it was one of the positive things he mentioned to Little Miss.

Coming back to the farm, he sat on the step of his little cabin. He watched Little Miss tend to the farm chores.

In the afternoon, he checked in on Thane and listened to several of his strange sin-eating tales. After Easter went out, Thane asked for a whiskey and told him stories of Mr. True's whoring and drinking days. Augustus had never laughed so hard; his stomach hurt.

Not long after the rooster crowed, Augustus sat on the steps of Little Miss' cabin, wiping up bacon fat with a small piece of bread. Easter walked toward them as Little Miss came out with a cup of coffee for him.

"Easter, I'll be needing you to take me to do some weepin' tomorrow. Thane won't be able to, and Janey will be in town."

"But, Missus, I ain't knowin' what to do. I ain't never done that before."

"I can show you what to do. You just gotta do it."

"I'm a girl, and those men don't like no girl by the graveside. Yous knows it to be true."

"You'll just put my chair close and leave. Then you go back and get it when it's time."

"I can do it for you, Missus. I seen you do it for my pa."

Little Miss turned to him. "A warner's son helpin' a weeper! That'll be!"

"It ain't nothing. I'll see to Thane first thing. If it looks good, Easter can watch over him."

"Fine, Mr. Augustus True, fine. And I'll be obliged to ya again. I think that's a perfect answer to the problem."

Thane still ran a fever the following morning, worrying Augustus that the infection was winning.

"Keep a cool rag on his forehead and change it every now and then," he told Easter. "I'm sure he'll be fine," he lied.

"Surely," said Easter. "You understand how to be gettin' to the Miller house?"

"Yes. Don't worry. We'll be back this eve."

Augustus climbed in the buggy and took the reins. Little Miss came out shortly after dressed for weeping. A snap on the reins and off they went. It was a sunny day with a few puffy clouds and a slight breeze. Augustus thought a storm might be approaching, and this buggy didn't have a roof.

"Ya ever been to Altoona?" Little Miss startled Augustus.

"I thought you weren't supposed to talk?"

"Course I can talk. I gotta tell you what to do, don't I? I still gotta do my weeping, of course. I just don't talk to no one else, and I just did some weeping before I got up in this buggy. So, you ever been to Altoona?"

"I ain't."

"It's a nice little town. A lot of decent folk. Some rich, some poor. More of a creek than a river flowing along one side. I like it. Wish we lived closer."

"Don't folk shy away from weepers?"

"I ain't never been down theres without my weepin' clothes, but I'm sure if I dressed different, no one would pay me no never mind. Well, sometimes people recognize me cause of my eyes being different shades, but when big townspeople see me most of the time, they don't know I'm the weeper."

Augustus couldn't see how anyone would pay her no nevermind. Her eyes would make any standing man sit.

"Not many folk in the larger towns know I'm the weeper. It seems that the weepin' trade is gettin' less and less. Less people carin' about their loved ones passin'. Only rich folk be paying for a proper funeral. It's a shame."

"Same thing with warning?"

"Warners are still busy, it seems. Small towns and big towns alike still be needin' a ceremony to bury their kin. Still need to bring the coffin to the cemetery. You should consider taking up your daddy's profession. It's honorable, and your pa did well with it until the later years, of course."

"I don't want to do what he did. And I'm good at doctorin'. That'll be what I do, I 'spect. There be a warner at this funeral we're going to?"

"Mm-hmm. His name is Henry. He's a good old fella. Been around as long as your pa, I believe. Not as good as your pa but has better horses. I been seeing a might more of him since your pa took ill. He told me we'll be meeting at the Nolan home, and I'll be doing my weepin' there so's you gotta put my chair in the corner behind the coffin which should be in their parlor. Then come back and help me down and walk me over to the chair. That's when you can go back and wait in the buggy. After you see all the folk leavin', come and get me and the chair. You should be seeing the hearse carriage, then three family carriages. It's a big procession. Henry wants us just behind the third family carriage, you see?"

"I do."

"We'll be doing a fancy dance around most of the roads in Altoona. I heard this family wants everyone to see. And they want everyone to see me weepin'. After we make our way through most of the town, we'll head off to the cemetery. That's when you do the same thing ya did in their house with me and the chair, see?"

"I do. Who they burying?"

"Patrick Nolan. He had a law business and was a mayor of Altoona for some time. Seems like a good fella. He has four daughters and one son. He's leavin' a widow behind as well. Leavin' her rich though, that's a good thing. Born in Philadelphia and passed at the age of fifty-one."

"You do know a lot about him."

"It's my job to know."

The ceremony at the house went just as she had indicated, and Augustus performed his duties exactly as told. All the mourners wore their finest black clothes, and the women showed off by fanning themselves with their expensive black ostrich-feathered hand fans. The men wore their stovepipe hats with streamers, just as his father had. He looked down at his clothes, the ones Maddy had given him. They were old and tattered, and he felt underdressed as he placed her chair down.

Riding through the town, people lined the streets to watch the procession. It reminded him of the commandant's funeral. None of the family seemed to be crying except the young ones. It seemed more of a show than mourning to Augustus. Little Miss was doing it for them. Maybe that's why Mr. Nolan requested a weeper in his will. He could hear her sniffles and see her wipe away tears under the veil. The eyes of the townsfolk were glued to her as she passed. Next to the horse-drawn hearse, she was the main attraction.

At the gravesite, most of the men surrounded the grave while the women hung back, as was customary. Little Miss was the only woman near the grave. Augustus stood nearby, leaning against a tree. He watched the crows dart from branch to branch as the "ashes to ashes" sermon was read. It was loud enough for the women to hear it but far shorter than the sermon read during the wake.

After everyone had left, Augustus helped Little Miss out of her chair like he said he would. She acted like an old woman as he helped her into the buggy. He retrieved the hand-carved weeping chair and they headed home.

Easter came running out from their cabin as the buggy approached.

"Sah, sah! I peeped a little on his leg. It be bleedin' a little. His fever still there."

Augustus brought a lantern close to the wound. "Bleedin' could be a good sign," Augustus said as he peeled back the bandage. White maggots crawled about the wound as Little Miss and Easter winced with disgust. "Yes, yes, this is doing better. Bleedin' means the maggots got down to good tissue. They's eatin' the dead. Little more to go."

The next morning, Thane's leg looked even better. The maggots were working well. Augustus took the pail and headed out in search of more. He almost bumped into Little Miss outside Thane's cabin. "Where you headed off to with that quick gait?"

"Headed out to get fresh maggots."

She giggled. "Fresh flowers would be so much more pleasant, but I suppose I could still give you a hand."

"I'd like the company."

They followed a little creek into the woods beyond their

farm. The smell of damp leaves and oak trees in the air. Their feet crunched the dried ones that had fallen to the leaf-covered ground as the birds rustled in nests above them. "I put out a dead rabbit over yonder the other morn."

"Is this what little boys do, Mr. Augustus True? Play with dead animals?" She giggled.

"Yessum. I did bury 'em as a boy."

"Why, I did too! Truth be, I did!"

They reached the rabbit, and he bent down and scraped the maggots into the pail.

"I suppose weeper's daughters and warner's sons must always be dealing with dead things."

"S'pose that's true." Augustus closed the lid. "Mind if we walk to the stream sos I can wash my hands?"

"Course."

He looked at the small dot of a birthmark on her jaw, perfection found in imperfections. Her eyes shone with blue hues, the envy of any summer sky.

They walked off toward the stream. He kept turning to the birthmark on her jaw. He touched the same spot on his. "That mark ya got there. Ya know that's damage from a past life?" He smiled like he didn't believe it himself.

"Course, I know. I'm a weeper. What? Ya think my husband beat me?" She laughed.

"Oh, no. Ya gotta make up a finer tale than that. Ya got it fleeing from the castle of a wicked king."

They reached the stream, and Augustus squatted to wash his hands.

"You gonna be taking my advice and be the new warner?" asked Little Miss.

"Doctorin' will bring in more money."

"Don't be sure of that. Warnin' and doctorin' go hand in hand. Ya travel about tending to people that's ill and dying. Ya gets customers while warnin' just like you'd do from doctorin'. I'd say they go together like a horse and buggy."

"I only 'member a bit about warnin'. I left for school when I was thirteen. Was there 'til the war came. Went to the war, then to the prison, then to here. That's all my life right there. My pa never taught me much about the warnin' ways 'cept for carryin' those beadle bells. Weeper's ways neither. 'Cept what I seen you done for my pa."

"Anyone up theres to teach it to ya now? Your sister Glory?"

"Suppose, she would know."

"If she don't, Janey, Thane, and I know enough between the three of us."

He wiped his hands on his pants, and they both started walking back.

"I'd be obliged to ya."

The sound of horses caught his attention. He rose to peer around a group of trees. There they were, the blue uniforms of Union troops. Augustus reached into his jacket for his honor parole letter; it wasn't there. He checked the other pocket—not there.

W*here the hell is it?*

Immediately he ducked. Little Miss saw his fear and ducked down with him.

"What's wrong?" she asked. He must have left it back at the True farm. "You a deserter, Mr. Augustus True? You ain't no deserter?"

"No, I ain't," he whispered, putting a finger to his lips and motioning for them to crawl behind a tree to their left.

He peeked again; there were only four of them, all in clean uniforms and on horseback. It was most likely the home guard searching for deserters. With their backs against the tree, they waited until the soldiers left.

"We'd better head back, Missus."

"I have to ask, I mean, you was in the war, and the war ain't over, and ya ain't missing no arms or legs…"

"I was in a Reb prison for two years. They let me go. Someone let me go; I don't know who."

"Let you go?"

"I know what it sounds like. This letter came to the prison saying to let me go. They made me sign an honor parole letter saying I'm free, but I can't fight no more. Can't be doctorin' for the army no more neither. Problem is, I musta left the letter back at Glory's. I thought I had it with me, but…"

"You should be gettin' that letter, I expect," said Little Miss. "I could change the bugs and take care of him from here on out."

"That leg's healing now. I don't think he'll lose it. But I'll come back in a few days and check on it, Missus."

Seeing the farm up ahead, she glanced over to him then back to the ground. "You don't have to call me The Missus no more, seeing you's a warner son and all."

"What would ya like?"

"You can call me the name my family calls me. You can call me Little Miss."

CHAPTER 33
Augustus

Back home with the friends I knew

AUGUSTUS REACHED HOME without any complications. Glory saw him from the garden and called Emily and Abigail out to greet him.

"How's that boy's leg go?" asked Glory.

"Still healing up. I'll head back in a few days to check it."

Abigail frowned as he dismounted. She followed him as he took Daisy into the barn.

"Gets kinda lonely 'round here when you're gone."

"Glory don't keep ya busy?"

"I ask to help, but she ain't got much. Spend half the day walking about."

"That ain't so bad."

"Can't I goes with ya when ya go, Aug? I won't be a bother." Abigail helped him remove the tack while standing on the other side of Daisy.

"I'd like that."

Augustus couldn't see the big smile on her face.

While Emily helped Glory make supper, Abigail helped

Augustus search for the letter. It was nowhere to be found in his room. Augustus walked into the kitchen.

"You seen that letter I had? It ain't in my room…"

"I'm sorry, Uncle, yes, I have it," said Emily. "It's in Momma and my room. I'll get it for ya." Emily ran to her room and returned with the letter. "You left without it. I was gonna ask Momma if we could put it up somewhere special so's everyone who comes here could see it."

Relief swept over Augustus. "Thank you for keepin' it safe, Emily. Much appreciated."

"Supper's on," said Glory as she and Abigail bought in the plates, and they all sat down for supper.

"Mind if I ask a question? Warnin'… I mean… you watch Pa do warnin'? You know what he did and all… and how he did it?"

Glory smiled. "You interested in warnin', Augustus? What about doing doctorin'?"

"Doctorin' will be my main trade, but warnin' could add to it, like Pa did."

"Well, I'll be. Another warner in the family? You'd make a fine warner, Augustus."

"But do you know anything about it? I wouldn't know what to do; I don't have Pa to show me."

"You 'member, don't ya? You was little, but you went with him everywhere. You should know much more than I do. I just 'member Pa would do whatever the family would want him to do. The main thing was inviting the folk. That's about all I can remember. I'm sure the Fenns can help you more on that account, though. They know a bit."

"Yes, she said."

Abigail pursed her lips as she glanced over to him.

"I'm sure Glory here knows more than The Missus do. Listen to all that she just told ya. The way I'm thinkin', you also knows about doctorin' folk and the creatures. People 'round here should know about that."

"But it would be nice havin' another warner in the family. Remind me of Pa," said Glory.

"Pa have any other clothes? Mine have seen their time," asked Augustus.

"Yessum, still got a coat and some boots, but they is old."

"Any warnin' clothes?" he asked.

"We buried Pa in those. I'm sorry, Augustus, that was the only pair."

"Hmm. Well, maybe I should go to Johnstown in the morning and see if I can pick something up. If I'm gonna let folk around here know I'm doctorin' or warnin' both, I gotta look the part."

"I ain't got any money, Augustus. If I did, you know I'd give it ya."

"I know you would. No, I'll see if they'll give me credit. If not, I'll ask if I can work it off in trade. Don't matter. I gotta go into town anyway with this letter. Let the home guard know or whoever's in charge on down theres. Let 'em know I ain't no deserter."

"I believe that's a sound idea. Union boys have been by this area every now and again."

"Yes, Ma'am. Got to get to them before they get to me, I say."

GLORY AND EMILY stood next to Daisy as Augustus mounted. He reached down for Abigail's hand. She put her foot in the stirrup and swung up and behind Augustus. Glory handed them both warm jackets.

"Now, it's gettin' a might cold today, so get along and wear those jackets."

"Thank you, Ma'am," said Abigail as she put hers on and reached her arms around Augustus' waist.

"Thank you for that," said Augustus. Glory raised a curious brow as she saw Abigail's arms pull tight to Augustus' back. "We'll see you late tonight, I suppose."

"If there's a storm, you can stay at the Greer's place. You remember them?" said Glory as she watched Abigail lay her cheek on his back.

"They had those two yellow dogs?"

"That's the one," confirmed Glory.

"Thank you, Glory."

Augustus rode off with Abigail clinging to him. Glory shook her head as she and Emily walked into the house.

"Something going on there," she said under her breath.

It was only early fall, but the weather had taken an unusual cold turn. Augustus put his jacket on only two hours into his ride to town. Clouds were gathering, and it felt like they were going to have an early-season snowstorm.

"I have an idea I've been thinkin' on. The cemetery was on the way, and we're gonna make a stop at my pa's grave."

"That's sweet. You're gonna forgive him?"

"As long as he forgives me."

CHAPTER 34
Augustus

Silent alone amid a Heaven of Song

DAISY TROTTED UP to the cemetery when a light snow began to fall.

Augustus put up his palm. "Snowing. Who'd have thought?"

"Yesterday caused a sweat too. This don't happen in Georgia, where I'm from. This happen much here?"

"It don't."

The cemetery shovels were still in the corner where Augustus had left them last. "Can you hobble him while I get started?" he asked, pointing to Daisy's legs as he walked off.

"Started on what? Whatcha gonna do?"

He brought the shovel over and stood above his father's recently covered grave, looking down upon it. He turned to her with a mischievous grin.

"You ain't gonna…"

The shovel stabbed the fresh soil, and he began digging. The dirt was considerably easier to remove than it had been to dig a week ago.

"Aug, you crazy? Why? Ya can't be digging up your pa."

"I need his clothes to make a living."

"I thought that's why we were going to town?" implored Abigail.

"I ain't got no money, Abigail, and the way I see it, this man owes me."

Augustus was already two feet down. He dug faster as the snow fell, working up enough of a sweat to remove his jacket.

Thud!

The shovel hit the top of the coffin. He dug around it a bit more to make a clean opening, not wanting dirt to fall in when he opened it.

"It's getting cold, Aug," she said, shivering in the jacket. "Ain't ya cold? Maybe we should start a fire."

"I ain't cold. I've been digging. We can't start a fire. Don't want folks to know we're here."

"You're sweating too. You're gonna freeze to death with that sweat. Put your jacket back on."

Augustus looked up to her. Snow was falling around her in clumps, and the evening was coming on fast. Finishing digging around the sides of the coffin, he wiped his brow, his eyes fixed on the wood. Taking a deep breath, Abigail closed her eyes as he bent to open it. There was his father, just like he was sleeping. He took the handsome stovepipe hat lying on his father's chest.

"Here, hold this."

Abigail opened her eyes to take it and gasped at seeing Mr. True. Augustus started removing the clothes until Mr. True lay naked in the coffin. Abigail put her hand up, blocking her own view of Mr. True's genitals.

"You take his underclothes too? That ain't right."

"He wasn't wearing any."

"Well, ya ain't gonna leave him like that, are ya?"

Augustus turned to her. Her eyes were closed, and her hand was up, blocking any possible view. He laughed, but it was cut short when he saw three men on horseback coming from down the road behind her.

"Abi!"

She kept her eyes shut.

"Abigail! Open your eyes!" he whispered loudly. "Men are coming!"

Her eyes opened, and she turned and peered around the tree behind her. The men were still a good distance away but headed in their direction.

"What we gonna do?" pleaded Abigail.

Augustus' head was on a swivel, looking for a place to hide. He turned to the open casket, took his father by the armpits, and stood, falling off balance against the side of the grave.

"Damn!"

"Whattya doin'?" she pleaded.

Augustus leaned Mr. True halfway out of the coffin, arms propped up against the side of the grave before crawling out.

"Why ya doin' that?"

"Take an arm," he said, ignoring her.

"He's necked!"

"Ain't got time for that. Take an arm!"

Both reached in and took an arm. Pulling, they stood up and slid Mr. True's naked body up and out of the grave and leaned him up against a tree. Besides having no clothes, Mr. True appeared to be in a peaceful rest.

"Come on," he said as he threw in the warner clothes into the coffin.

"I ain't going in there."

"Yes, you are!"

"Uh, uh."

"They gonna hang us as graverobbers."

She shook her head as she reluctantly climbed in. Augustus quickly grabbed a stick next to the grave before climbing in with her, her back to him. He closed the lid on top of the stick to allow for a bit of light and air.

"What if they see all that out there? The open grave, your daddy out there? Daisy is hobbled out there. What if they see her?"

"It's almost dark. I don't think folk would be coming to a cemetery."

Abigail frowned. "Ya think?"

"They're probably just passing by on the way to town. Quiet now."

They waited twenty minutes before Augustus pushed up the lid slowly. "They're probably gone. I'm gonna look."

Augustus slowly stood up and peered over the edge of the grave. He saw smoke from their campfire five hundred feet from the cemetery, and they all sat around it. Augustus climbed back in and closed the lid.

"They ain't gone?"

"No, they're setting up camp for the night a bit outside the cemetery. We can wait till they fall asleep and hightail it outta here."

"Leave your pa out like that? No, Aug. We gotta bury him back."

"They ain't gonna move on till morning, Abi. We'll be here all night."

"I ain't uncomfortable, and it's dark and cold out there and warm in here."

"Lot more room in here than I thought," said Augustus.

"If ya don't think about it being a casket, it ain't so bad."

"Yeah, ain't so bad to be dead."

"Mm-hmm."

"You can get some sleep. I'll also check now and again and make sure the snow don't pile on us."

The coffin deadened most sound. She took a deep breath as cold air whistled through the crack of the lid. His arm lay on her hip, and his other was up by his head for a pillow. He sniffed her hair; it smelled like lavender. Abigail laid her hand on his, resting on her hip. She shifted and pushed up against him.

"Hey, Aug?"

"Mm-hmm?"

"You awake?"

"Mm-hmm."

Augustus could only hear their heartbeats and the sound of landing snowflakes in the darkness. She interlaced her fingers between his and, with a gentle squeeze, said, "Hey Aug, I ain't got my scissors."

MORNING CAME WITH the sun and melting snow. Abigail awoke, eyes wide, to men's voices.

"Aug, Aug!" Abigail slapped his hip to wake him.

"What?"

"I can hear 'em. They's in the cemetery."

Augustus opened the lid a little more.

"This is it. Jenkins. I saw it in there before they buried him," said the man's voice.

"Start diggin' boy," said another before they heard digging. Cold air poured into the coffin and over their naked bodies as Augustus pushed open the lid. He stood and peeked over the grave's edge. Three men were taking turns digging up a grave. Augustus dropped down, closing the lid after him.

"They's grave robbers!"

"What do we do?"

"We shoulda left last night."

"Well, we didn't, so what do we do?"

"We wait. We're lucky it ain't this grave they's robbin'.

"What about Daisy—"

"Hey, there's a horse over yonder," the voice said.

"Damn!" said Augustus.

"We're necked!" she said through her teeth.

She felt around for her clothes at her feet. It had been difficult enough to remove them in the coffin. Putting them back on would be impossible.

Footsteps came closer.

"Hee! Hee! This old boy ain't gotta stitch on. He's necked."

More footsteps. "Froze stiff!" another voice said.

Abigail grabbed Augustus' hand and pulled it to her chest.

"This boy was grave robbin' for sure."

"We ain't the only ones thinkin'."

"Maybe he was after Jenkin's too and got the wrong grave."

"They's marked, no one's that much a fool."

"Cept you."

"It surely was colder than a well digger's knee last night. Storm musta caught him off guard."

"Casket been opened. He was grave robbin' for sure."

Abigail's body jerked, and she squeezed his hand harder.

"Well, this boy's failure is our success. Let's see what this old casket's gots hiding."

Abigail jerked again. "Oh, my, no!"

Augustus threw open the lid.

"Good Lazarus!" shouted one as all three jumped back in shock. Augustus jumped out, screaming like a banshee, wholly naked and running at them. The three men ran screaming from his naked body toward their horses. Augustus kicked one man in the rear, tripping him for a second before all three jumped on their horses and galloped away.

Abigail tried to hide, pushing her face and body against the cushioned side of the casket.

Augustus walked back with an ear-to-ear smile. He climbed in the grave and stood above Abigail with her head pushed into the cushioned side.

"They's gone."

She slowly pulled away and looked up to him.

"This is all your fault. We shouldn't have even come heres," she said as she slapped his shin. Her nose, with just the right number of freckles around it, sat on an angry face. He stared down at the muscle, bone, and soft skin of a beautiful woman and smiled.

"What are you smiling at?"

Augustus kneeled and closed the lid above them.

An hour later, they were both out of the coffin. Abigail was putting her boots on while Augustus was pulling his father's body back to the coffin.

"Ya ain't gonna leave your pa necked."

"I told you I need these clothes," he said.

"Give him yours then!"

"I'll only have Sunday clothes."

Abigail stared him down. "I know this man wasn't a good daddy and sold you and all, but this ain't right for any man's final rest, Aug. You should let him rest peaceably in those old clothes. You'll be makin' money soon and buy more clothes. This man can't be doin' that."

Augustus took a deep breath, took off his clothes, and replaced them with his father's warner clothes before dressing his father.

"My, oh, my, Aug. You look fine, oh, fine." Abigail gawked at him as he modeled the warner clothes for her along with the hat.

"Give me a hand with him."

Gently, they placed Mr. True back in the coffin to rest. Abigail fixed the clothes Pa now wore. Augustus filled in the grave and made everything the way it was before he had been there. He wiped the sweat from his brow as he looked at the fresh mound of dirt.

"You gonna say something?"

"It was already said."

"But you didn't say nothing."

Augustus took a breath. "You shouldn't have sold me, Pa."

"Aug!"

He smirked and turned back to the soil. "I can remember bits and pieces of the good stuff ya did. Well, anyway, it looks like I'll be taking your trade like ya wanted me to years back." Augustus leaned the shovel against the tree. "I 'member always wanting to make ya proud, Pa. I hope ya find peace in what I'm 'bout ta do."

CHAPTER 35
Glory

So loved, so special, so missed

"MY, MY, MY, don't you look just like Pa!" exclaimed Glory. "Just the spittin' image."

Glory and Emily stood in front of their house as Augustus and Abigail dismounted Daisy.

"I like the hat, Uncle Augy," said Emily.

"He cleans up real nice," said Abigail.

Glory's smile fell from her lips as Augustus walked closer. "Wait. Ain't… These are Pa's clothes! You did…" She covered her mouth in shock. "Oh my! My! My! Augustus. That was bad, real bad. I cannot believe that, that you would…"

"What, Momma?! What are you so upset about? I think he looks right fine," Emily said as everyone's smiles fell.

"I just don't know what to say," Glory said as she headed back into the house.

Abigail dropped Daisy's reins and chased after her. "I tried to tell him!"

"I think ya look right fine, Uncle Augustus."

Augustus smiled at her. "Thank you, Niece."

Augustus took the evening to explain the necessity of what he'd done to Glory, and how they fixed Mr. True up nice and returned their pa to peace. Abigail added how he even said a sermon to him afterward and asked his forgiveness, which was almost the truth.

Eventually, Glory softened to the situation, saying, "Well, I suppose."

After dinner, they sat by the fire. Glory darned a tear in some coveralls while Augustus stared into the fire.

Emily sat with Abigail on the floor. "I'll play the weeper, and you can play the warner," Emily said to Abigail.

"I used to play the weeper when I was a little one," said Glory.

"I ain't no man," replied Abigail incredulously.

"Then I'll be the warner, and you can be the weeper. My grandpa was the warner for real."

"Certainly was, and now your uncle's gonna be it," said Glory.

"I don't like no weepers neither. Can I play the dead body or a mourner," said Abigail. Augustus glanced over to Abigail, curious.

"We need a weeper," said Emily.

"Why ya don't like weepers, Abigail? They's good folk," asked Glory.

"They's ways is strange," said Abigail. Glory looked over to Abigail as she glanced over to Augustus.

Glory raised her eyebrows. "Those Fenns are good folk. Some things ya might not know is that great grandpap Davis Fenn was a shaker. He bought all the slaves he could afford and freed 'em. He wanted to be able to send 'em back home to Africa but decided to buy and free more slaves instead. They ended up living there with 'em. Helping with the weepin' or farmin'. That's why they's got all those cabins. They's still got a few of the kin from those he bought."

"Thane and Easter," said Abigail.

"I suppose. I don't know their names," said Glory.

Glory stopped sewing. "Oh! Augustus, I remembered something while you were gone. Pa has notebooks! Notebooks on what the families wanted. You can learn a lot from those, Augustus. I'm sure it's far more than I could tell you."

Glory scurried into Mr. True's room and returned with four notebooks. Augustus flipped through them.

"I also remembered a bit more about Pa," recalled Glory. "You remember him asking us to call him 'sir' all the time?"

"I don't recollect."

Glory grinned. "Yessum. We did for a time, but you started callin' him papa and when you did, whew-wee! I thought there was gonna be a whoopin'. But no, when he heard you barely making out the word with your stuttering and all, the soft spot in him grew. He tried and tried with ya. We all stood back waiting for him to whoop ya, but no. I could hardly believe pa thought it was sweet. I tried it out and he let it pass, sure enough. I told Emilia, and Emilia tried it. The same thing happened. Even with his gruff demeanor, Pa loved his children, Augustus. He wasn't so bad as ya think. He'd ask every few years or so for us to be of calling him, sir. We'd do it for a time, but then it would pass, and we'd forget. Sometimes you'd just laugh when he requested it, and he would respond with…," she lowered her voice to imitate her father. "Then call me sir in front of company."

Augustus laughed with Glory. Emily joined in. Glory turned to the notebook he held.

"Oh, yes! I also recall Papa would never work Fridays; I remember that regarding warnin' and all. Bad luck to have a remembrance on a Friday. Something about someone else in the family will pass within a year. Oh, and one last thing I remember. It's strange, but he'd keep salt in one pocket, and he'd eat it from time to time. Don't know why."

"Thank you, Glory. Good to know. Wonder if people still believe them superstitions?"

"I believe people 'round here sure do."

"Thank you for these books. Looks like they can teach me a lot."

"My pleasure."

"With all that, I don't think you need to go to that weeper's place now, do you, Aug?" asked Abigail.

Augustus closed the book and turned to Abigail. "Truth is, I was thinking on going in the morn. These books will help me, but the Fenns can show me things the books can't."

"Hmm."

Glory watched Abigail as she turned away in a pout. She turned back to her brother, her eyes narrowing on his face.

"The army give you them specs? I remember you had trouble with your eyes."

"Jefferson got 'em for me off a dead boy who didn't need 'em no more."

"Oh my. Ain't ya scared you looking through dead man's eyes now?" Glory asked.

Emily looked up from her dolls at him, the light from the fire dancing on her face. Augustus lifted his gaze from the notebooks to Emily and smiled. He shook his head.

"I'd be scared to wear 'em, wouldn't you?" Abigail asked Emily.

Emily grinned ear to ear. "No. Not if my uncle ain't scared."

Augustus stood and tucked the book under his arm. "I'll be bidding you all a good night."

As everyone said their goodnights to him, Glory dropped her sewing to her lap. "Time for you too, Emily."

"Ahhh…" She looked to Abigail for help, who shrugged her shoulders.

With Augustus and Emily in bed, Glory put away her sewing. "Abigail, mind if I have a word?"

Abigail set the dolls on the shelf and took Augustus' chair across from Glory. Glory stared at the fire and, without looking at Abigail, said, "Is something going on between you two?"

Abigail froze. "I don't know what you mean?"

"I think ya do, but I ain't accusing ya. I hope you know that. Curious is all." The logs cracking and snapping in the fireplace was the only reply. "He and I… Well, I ain't seen him since he was thirteen, over seven years back. He and I, it seems we eat sorrow by the spoonful seeing all our loved ones leave us. And he's seen a lot too, in the war and all. My husband, God save his soul; I surely do miss that man. Miss him dearly. Every day is a day that's hard to get through…" Glory gulped in air to stop from crying. "…without him."

Abigail rose and brought back a napkin for her.

"Thank you. I'm sorry," she giggled. "Just get all… I don't know." Glory looked Abigail in the eyes. "Mind you, I ain't judging. No, Ma'am. I wouldn't be judging you," she said, the tears returning. "If you want that…" she could speak no more, her finger speaking for her, pointing to his room.

She swallowed hard, pulling her spirit back by sucking in

a breath from her nose. She stood and wiped her eyes. "I'm going to bed, and don't know nothing. I'll say this one more thing. I'm a God-fearing woman, and maybe it ain't right for me, but I know God put love into us all. Love is love, and there seems to be a lot spilling out around here…," she said, again shaking her finger at the door. "I believe the bed in there will be a lot more comfortable for ya." Glory turned her back to Abigail. "Good night, Abigail."

CHAPTER 36
Augustus

How lucky I am to have something that makes saying goodbye so hard

"MORNING. I'D LIKE to introduce myself, my name is Augustus True, and I'll be the warner in these parts, taking o…"

"Archer True's boy?" asked Mr. Danson, a neighbor from the mountain community.

Augustus wore his warner clothes and stovepipe hat. "Yessum. I'll be taking over the warnin' for my pa, and I do a fine job of doctorin' up the animals. All kinds: horses, pigs, dog, chickens, whatever ya got."

"Yes, yes, you look like the spitting image of him in that suit. That his old suit?"

"It is."

"Fine, fine. Knew your Pa, but I haven't seen you in church, young man."

"In the war, I was."

"I see, I see. Well, glad to hear you're back safe."

As Augustus and Abigail made their way to the Fenn's, they

stopped at every home they could find to introduce his new warning services.

Abigail practically bounced off the saddle with excitement. "We should get paper and post bills all about saying you is the warner in these parts."

"FITS YOU RIGHT fine, it does," Little Miss said as she looked Augustus over in his new warner clothes. "Put the hat on. It's the best part." She smiled when he did. "Now ya got to get on out theres and let people know the Trues are back warnin'."

Abigail and Little Miss sat in the two rockers on her porch as Augustus stood before them, modeling his clothes. Abigail sat up straight. "Oh, no. We already been doing that. We did that all the way here, stopping at this place and that."

Augustus smiled at her. "Yessum, we did."

"You get that letter you was needin'?" asked Little Miss.

"We did," said Abigail.

"Did, indeed." He went into his jacket pocket. "It's right…"

He felt no letter in his pocket as it dawned on him; the letter was in his old clothes, the clothes his father now wore, buried six feet below the ground. His jaw dropped, and his eyes opened wide.

"What's wrong, Aug?" asked Abigail as the color rapidly drained from his face.

"You feeling badly, Mr. Augustus True?" she said as her brow furrowed.

He turned to Abigail. "We buried it with my pa."

Abigail's hands covered her mouth with a gasp.

"Ya done what?"

"That's how I got these clothes… I mean… I had to get these clothes from my pa."

Little Miss shook her head. "Ya mean you got them from your sister…"

"No. I got them from my pa," Augustus said as he looked to the ground.

"We buried your pa. You went to your farm…"

"I told him not to do it!" said Abigail.

Augustus shrugged. "These clothes were his only warnin' clothes and I…"

Little Miss' eyes went wide, and her jaw dropped before she burst out into uncontrollable laughter. "Oh! My! My, oh my! You did not! I don't…! Never have I heard…! You crazy—"

"It's no laughing matter. The letter is now buried with him," Augustus implored as she continued to hold her sides, laughing so hard. "That letter is essential."

"What do we do? What do we do?" said Abigail in a panic.

"Suppose you should forget about it now!" Little Miss now held her stomach from the pain of laughter.

"I need to get it," Augustus insisted again. "I need to go back and get it."

Little Miss calmed down and looked Augustus in the eyes. "No, you ain't! Shame on you! Digging up your pa was wrong, Mr. Augustus True. Wrong!" Little Miss scolded. "Doing it *twice* is twice as wrong! You shouldn't have done it, no how, no way. Losing that letter was God's way of teaching ya a lesson, it was!"

Augustus sat down in the rocking chair and thought about it.

"She's right, Aug. Wasn't right in the first place," said Abigail. "It was God's will, it was. He don't want you to have it."

Augustus took a deep breath. "I suppose."

Little Miss scrutinized the clothes and said, "I thought they were his. I just didn't…"

"Yeah, his only pair," replied Augustus.

"So, you get 'em for doctorin' or warnin'?"

"Both," said Abigail. "And he looks right fine in 'em for both."

Little Miss smiled at her. "Yes, he does."

"Yes, but Thane ain't the only reason we came. I'd like to take you up on that offer about learning what you know. I got these books he wrote too. They'll help with the what and how much, but all the formalities…"

"Surely. But it'll take a good time to learn all these things. You planning to stay?"

"If it wouldn't be too much trouble."

"Not at all. I got plenty of cabins."

"We only need one," said Abigail.

Little Miss raised a brow with a smile. "Oh, well then, alright."

Easter came from across the field. "Ah, Mr. True, looking fine as frog fur, ya are," she said, smiling. "Look like your daddy, you do. There's gonna be a lot of people up here's pleased as pie that you'll be tending to their departed loved ones. I'm sure of that."

"Thank you, Easter."

"Thane's doing fine. His leg is looking clean. He's walking around again."

Augustus stepped off the porch. "Let's walk over and take a look."

Augustus examined Thane's wound in the privacy of the cabin. The maggots had done their job and eaten off the dead flesh.

"Looks good, like ya said. I should stitch it. It'll just leave you with an ugly old scar."

"Already got a lot of them," said Thane.

Augustus worked to close up the gash. After he finished stitching, he poured the whiskey over it.

He looked up at Easter. "Now, remember what I said; it's whiskey only now, three times a day. But he can't be drinking it."

Easter stood and crossed her arms. "Oh, he don't like to drink that 'ole stuff anyhows, Mr. True," she said as Thane secretly winked at Augustus.

ABIGAIL SET TO the task of making the simple, single-room cabin their home. The bed was in the corner, and it had a fireplace built from large river rock, considering the size of the cabin. She cleaned it then took a rug, two rockers, a round table, and two chairs from another empty cabin. She had never had a home of her own and had never had a man of her own.

"Could we live here forever, Aug? I like it here."

"Suppose if we had money to pay The Missus. We gotta pay our way."

"You'll be warning and doctorin' soon enough. Then you'll have as much as ya want."

"We can pray on it, that's for sure."

"The Missus, she call you Mr. Augustus True, your whole name. That's strange, ain't it? I ain't never heard no one call each other by their own full name before."

"I believe it's a sign of respect."

"Hmm, I can see that." Abigail hung drapes on the first of two windows. "True."

"Hmm," said Augustus as he looked up from his notebook.

"Oh, nothing. I just said True, your last name. I like that name." Abigail walked over to fix the drapes on the second window as he returned his attention to the notebook. "Augustus, would you mind if I take that name? Mine's not really mine. They forced my daddy and momma to have their names, I ain't even gonna say it caused it's the massa's name." He looked up from his notebook again. "Would ya mind it? Mr. Augustus True?" she smiled at him teasingly.

"I wouldn't mind none."

"Abigail True. Like we're married. Abigail True. It sounds sweet, don't it?"

"Sweeter than stolen honey. Come here, Abigail True."

Abigail dropped the linen drape and went to sit on his lap. "Abigail True, I ain't never had a sweetheart before."

"I ain't neither," she said.

As much as he could, Augustus studied his father's notebooks. Mr. True had written down everything he should pay attention to for each funeral: the family, the preacher, which service, outside or inside, graveside or home wake, the number of mourners, flowers, and where he placed them, ostrich feathers, coffin makers, florists, and so on.

Every detail one could think of; there were even doodles of the weeper in her chair drawn in the margins. Most importantly, at the bottom of each journal entry was what he purchased, its cost, and, of course, what he charged and his bottom-line profit.

Every evening he and Abigail had supper with Little Miss, Thane, and Janey. Each, in turn, told him everything they knew as they ate. Sometimes the conversations would go late into the evening. That left his days open for reading the notebooks and spending time with Abigail.

After supper in the Fenn house, Thane stood up. "I'd like to do my talkin' to Mr. True in private."

"Why?" asked Easter.

"Man stuff. There's things the delicate ears of y'all shouldn't be hearing."

Augustus followed Thane out and down the road to the farm. He pulled out a whiskey bottle, took a swig, and handed it to Augustus.

"You settled on hearing what I's gotsta tell ya? It might not be to your tastes."

"If ya gonna show me more of those sin-eater faces, then no, I ain't settled."

"No, it ain't that."

"It's all the whorin' ya did before ya became a sin eater."

"Hell, no. ain't that it's about your pa."

"I'm settled." Augustus took a swig.

"You don't have much of a liking to your pa, do ya? I just get that feelin' 'bout ya."

"If he'd pass by my house, I'd tell him to just keep on going."

Thane burst into laughter and took another swig. "Well, this has to do with his business, which is whatcha wanna know. Now, I'll start by saying your daddy did a respectable job during the day, but there were times I'd find your daddy in town off whoring and drunk as a fiddler's bitch. I'd have to wait sometimes hours for him, but he'd give me a ride back home and go on and tell me all sorts of things. I got some two-bottle tales there, I 'spect. Just know he'd meet the grievin' families in the evening so's he could use it as an excuse to stay out all night whorin' and drinkin'. He also told me his secret fishin' hole was the church. Most of his work came from the congregation. That's what you should do, I 'spect. Meet up with all the preachers. Say the True's are back and all."

"Sound advice, sound advice. But that ain't all that bad. I was expecting you was gonna tell he was wilder than a peach orchard boar."

Thane took a swig from the bottle. "Nah, just needed an excuse to get out here to take a pull from my bottle."

CHAPTER 37
Augustus

Your life was a blessing, Your memory a treasure

THE CHURCH WAS one of two Presbyterian churches near them; it was also the church the True family had attended for three generations. It sat in a wide-open valley with the pastor's home next to it. All white with a blue-trimmed steeple, it had a circular patch of finely-trimmed green grass in front where the congregation would pull up their buggies and carriages each Sunday. Including that church, Augustus had mapped out five others he and Abigail were to visit and meet with the preachers that day.

Augustus and Abigail tied Daisy to one of the hitching posts and walked up just as the pastor came out of his home. Abigail shyly stood back about ten feet.

"Hey there!" Augustus waved. "Morning, Pastor."

"Morning. Can I help you? Saw you coming from far off."

"The name's True, Augustus True. I…"

"I remember you. My pa was the preacher back then. You and your brother went off to school."

"We did."

"I went over and saw your pa when he'd taken ill. A shame.

I thought he'd get better, but he never did. It was a long illness. Glory hasn't been to us in a few years."

"She'll be back now. She couldn't leave my pa."

The pastor nodded. "What about yourself? Where you been? We all need the Lord Jesus Christ."

"I was in the war, just got out. Then with my pa and all. But I was planning on coming tomorrow."

"Wonderful."

"Yep, me and her." Augustus gestured to Abigail.

"Oh, is she a family hand? We have our negro services later in the afternoon. Four o'clock."

"Well, I'd like to bring her with me…"

"Oh, no. I'm sorry, I can't oblige that. The congregation and all." Augustus dropped his chin to his chest. "I'm sorry, Mr. True. Is that a problem? How long she worked for ya?"

Pennsylvania had repealed its ban on race-mixing law back in 1780. The preacher was a good example of contrary public opinion.

"She don't work for me."

The pastor read his face and frowned. "I'm sorry, Mr. True. This may be the wrong congregation for you."

Augustus thanked him and turned to Abigail. Her back was already to him, walking over to Daisy. She had heard everything. Mounting up, she avoided eye contact.

The next church was Baptist. Abigail stayed with Daisy.

"I'm out letting folk know I'm taking over the family warning."

"Good on you, Augustus," said the pastor looking out to Abigail. "The Trues out saving niggers like the Fenns used to?"

At the fourth church, Abigail hid behind a tree before they

got there. The pastor was pleased that Augustus would continue the True tradition and told him they'd spread the word.

"He liked ya 'cause I wasn't with ya. Don't accept me here as much as in Georgia. I'm in a free state, but not truly free," she said. She wore her disappointment like a wet dress.

When a knock sounded on the door, Augustus opened it to Little Miss, all gussied up for church.

"Would you like to attend church with me this morn? It'd be good to get to know all the congregation."

Augustus looked back to Abigail sitting on the bed. She looked away before he turned back to Little Miss. "Maybe next week. I got a lot of reading to do."

"Surely," said Little Miss as she watched Abigail. "Good morning to y'all."

Augustus sat on the bed with her and put his hand on her knee. The girl that could talk the coon out of a tree was silent.

"Things ain't perfect, but we got each other. Better than where we both come from."

"That's true, Mr. True," she said with a sad smile.

"Easter and Thane do good here. I spoke to The Missus, and she'd lease this place to us after I get to working."

"Easter and Thane's the same color."

"We just gotta work around things like that."

The term "funeral" was taking the place of "remembrance." The business was changing and growing. Augustus' first was for the two-year-old daughter of a young couple from Johnstown. The little girl's grandparents, Mr. and Mrs. Fallbrook, were familiar with Mr. True.

Children and unmarried women had to be handled differently. The horse would have to be white, to demonstrate their innocence, as would the carriage and many of the associated things. Augustus needed to lease these things as he didn't own any yet. Johnstown was a larger city and still unaffected by the war. The good thing for Augustus was that the town had an undertaker who he could lease items from.

He sat at Mr. and Mrs. Fallbrook's dining table with them and the little girl's parents. The mother, Mrs. Henry Clement, was still in a state of shock and crying. She had already purchased and was wearing her bereavement dress. With a solemn expression, Augustus pulled out his notebook to write down their requests.

"We would like to add a couple of photographs as well, one with her awake and one peacefully sleeping," Mrs. Clement said as she wiped her nose with her handkerchief.

"Would you like me to pass out gifts as I make my warning rounds?"

"No, thank you, Mr. True. The photographs are more important, and we will be paying additional for the white carriage."

"Indeed," replied Augustus. After finishing up with all his questions, he closed his notebook and headed over to Parker and Sons, Undertakers.

"I remember your father, and I remember the dead cakes! They were awful. He was more traditional, your father. More influenced by the Dutch families around these parts," said Mr. Parker.

Augustus stood with him in his warehouse full of hearses, caskets, and tools of the trade.

"I wanted to become more favorable to the times. You still called a warner?"

"I am."

"Yeah, they used to call y'all *aanspreekers* if I recall. I like the term 'undertaker.' Taking people under the ground, it just sounds right. Calling the ceremony a 'remembrance' or 'funeral' is still about fifty-fifty depending on where the people come from."

"I suppose," agreed Augustus, but the truth was, he was learning the terms for the first time himself.

"Two ponies is the standard for children," he said. "I'll lease the white hearse carriage on credit. You can pay for it after you get paid."

"The family can only afford one pony."

"Well, the one can easily pull the hearse," said Mr. Parker. "The pony comes with white ostrich feathers, and the hearse has two white feathers on each corner of the roof." They walked over to it as he spoke. "Etched glass and white satin inside. Beautiful piece."

"Sure is."

"The coffin is over here. Polished white finish with gold trim. They'll love it."

It sat there, so tiny and sad. Two pallbearers could easily lift it, but according to the parents, they wanted four, all older cousins of their daughter.

"I'll take the coffin today. The deceased is laid out on her bed for now," Augustus said.

"They'll be wanting to put her in the main room, I'm sure. I'll get my sons to deliver it to them today with the flowers," Mr. Parker said as he stuck out his hand to Augustus.

"You're too kind," replied Augustus as he shook it.

Mr. Parker smiled. "You should come work for me. I need a hand. You remind me of one of my sons. Lost him in the war a year ago. At Antietam."

"I was at Antietam," replied Augustus.

"Well, I'll be! Twenty-Third Pennsylvanian?"

"No, I schooled in West Virginia. I signed up with the Seventh West Virginian. I was doctorin' for them."

"We's Pennsylvanian men," said Mr. Parker proudly. "Too bad ya weren't doctorin' for the Twenty-Third. Wish ya could have saved my boy."

"Wish I could've too. I was a might occupied for that one, I recall. Had a horse blown to bits all over me while I was trying to save a man. Almost killed me."

"Whew weee!" cried out Mr. Parker as he looked Augustus over. "Ah, hell, take the second pony on the house. It'd look so much better with two. The family will be a might pleased with it and since the child was so young and all… Yeah, take the second one on me."

"That's a might generous of ya."

"So, why ain't ya still fightin'? You wounded somewheres?"

"Got captured, sent to prison, and they gave me an honor parole. Can't fight no more."

Mr. Parker slowly nodded his head and stuck out his lower lip. "Hmm, you one of the lucky ones, I suppose."

"Well, I should be getting on." Augustus shook his hand again.

"I was serious about that job offer. I could use the help."

"Thank ya for that, but I prefer working for myself. If ya cut your own firewood, it'll warm ya twice."

"Even so, you ought to move down here. I can't handle the work now. The town's growing, and it needs either my company to grow or another company. I'd like ya to work for me, but I wouldn't mind the competition either."

"I'll think on it, thank ya," said Augustus as he turned to leave.

Mr. Parker called out after him, "So why ain't ya still doctorin' around these parts?"

"I am a bit, mostly for the animals, people here and there. Wanted to take after my pa," he lied.

Augustus walked out of the big warehouse doors. Parked directly in front of him was a wagon pulled by a mule. On the side was written "The World-Famous O. Roche Photography." A slim man with light brown hair to his shoulders climbed down. He had gray at the temples disclosing his age of forty, and a small, wiry beard on his chin. He wore a blue bow tie and, like Augustus, wore spectacles.

"Excuse me, are you the photographer?" asked Augustus.

"I am. I am." He had the strange habit of not being able to look Augustus in the eyes.

"Augustus True. I'm an undertaker," he said, sticking out his hand. The photographer stared at it but didn't move.

"I'm sorry, sir. He doesn't shake hands," said a young red-haired man, Ray, coming from the other side of the wagon. Next to him stood a brown-haired boy, Lou, in his mid-twenties. He also wore spectacles. But over strange irises that flickered rapidly, without stopping, back and forth.

"Yes, I'm sorry, I do not shake hands, shake hands. The name's Osborn Roche."

"My uncle here is world-famous. He's done portraits for Generals McClellan and Burnside and Vice President Hamlin."

"Pleasure meeting ya. I'm impressed. Are you here to see Mr. Parker?" asked Augustus.

"I am. We are old associates, associates."

"I was just speaking to him about needing a postmortem photographer. Would you be available?"

"Possibly, when is it?" asked Ray.

"It's the day after tomorrow. Saturday. Here in town."

"We were planning on heading west," said Ray.

"That's true, and we'd have to find a place to stay. It wouldn't be worth the client's money, money," said Osborn.

"I can offer ya a place to stay. Up with me. We have empty cabins, and it's only four hours from here.

Osborn put his fingeer to his lips in thought. "Hmm."

"We'll feed ya well," pleaded Augustus.

"Yes, Ray. Let's do the job, job," said Osborn.

"Alright, Mr. True. Let us take care of some business with Mr. Parker, and we'll follow you up," said Ray.

CHAPTER 38
Little Miss

My day was happy - and perchance
The coming night is full of stars

THE PHOTOGRAPHY WAGON rolled into the Fenn farm with Augustus on Daisy. Little Miss, Easter, Abigail, and Thane walked out to greet them.

Augustus dismounted and stepped up. "Missus, this here is Osborn Roche. He's a world-famous photographer and—I'm sorry, I didn't catch y'alls names," said Augustus as he gestured toward the two boys.

"Ma'am. I'm Ray," said the red haired boy.

"Lou," siad the brown.

"Good day," said Little Miss with a slight tilt of the head as she curiously eyed Lou.

The central room of the Fenn house had a kitchen counter along one wall, chairs and stool along the walls, and a dining room table in the middle, seating six. Little Miss and Easter finished bringing the food to the table.

"Please sit," said Little Miss. Thane took a seat and looked around at the others who were not moving.

"Please, guests first," added Little Miss. Thane reluctantly rose.

"No, please. Ladies, ladies first. I insist," said Osborn.

Little Miss smiled. "Delightful to have a gentleman at our table," said Little Miss. Thane rolled his eyes as Easter, Abigail, Janey, Little Miss, and Lou sat down. Thane jumped at the last seat.

"You's a girl, ain't ya?" Abigail asked Lou.

Thane's eyes grew wide. "That ain't a nice—"

"Yes. I am."

"I knew it," said Easter.

"Yes, I saw it too," said Janey.

"Why you cut your hair like that and alls?" asked Abigail.

"I worked for the army. They wouldn't let me work if they knew I was a girl."

"Men, Please, help yourself to a plate of food and take a seat. We ladies are chatting," said Little Miss. Easter turned to Thane, providing him with a disapproving look. His eyes went to the ceiling before he took his chair away to the wall.

"You fought for the army? A woman?" asked Easter.

"No. I didn't fight. I'm an embalmer."

"What's that?" asked Abigail.

"I met one while in the army," said Augustus. "They make it so a cadaver can last for a very long time and be shipped home."

"What's a cadava?" asked Easter.

"A dead body."

Lou turned to him. "You remember the man's name? The embalmer?"

"No. But he had a pockmarked face and reddish-grey hair."

Lou slowly turned to Osborn, then back to Augustus. "That was my uncle Ben."

"Yes. I believe Ben was his name."

"Where y'all from?" asked Little Miss.

"Ray and I are from Pittsburg. Lou's from Alexandria. Yes, from Alexandria," said Osborn from against the wall.

"They call you The Missus. Why?" interrupted Ray. "Is that the name you were born with?"

"No. I'm a weeper. All the women kin in my family are weepers."

"What's a weeper?" asked Ray.

"They mourn. Mourn for your family. You hire them," answered Osborn.

"Yes. That's right. I was born with the name Melody Ann, but all my kin call me by Little Miss."

"Little Miss. Mind if I call ya by it, Little Miss?" asked Ray with a gleam in his eye.

"You being too familiar, boy. Gotta show respect to the Weeper. She's called The Missus," demanded Thane.

Little Miss stared into Ray's eyes. "It's fine, Thane. He can call me that."

"So, The Missus don't mean you're married?" asked Ray.

"No, I ain't. Never have been."

Ray smiled. "Is it morning already, 'cause I think this room just got brighter."

Thane slapped his hand on his knee. "Boy, how old are you?"

"Ray, that's enough. Enough," said Osborn.

"I'm seventeen. Old enough to know a beautiful woman when I see one."

The dining table burst into laughs, gasps, Rays, and Thane's outrage.

"Alright, alright," said Little Miss.

"My apologies if my words are distasteful, Little Miss. I meant no harm by 'em," said Ray.

"I don't mind it none. And it's not often a weeper receives a compliment from a handsome young man. I'm flattered, Ray. Thank ya."

"Well, with that, we'll be saying goodnight to ya," said Osborn. "Let's go, Ray."

Little Miss put her hand on Lou's hand. "You need a place to sleep, honey?"

"That would be nice."

"Good night, Little Miss. It's been my pleasure," said Ray, walking backward out the door.

Little Miss smiled at him. "Why, thank you, Ray, and good night to you too."

Little Miss turned to Easter and Abigail. "Why don't y'all sleep over here. We'll have a girl's night."

The men gone, the five women laid out bedrolls in a circle, their heads in the center, and two candles in the middle. Little Miss brought over five small cups.

"Round two of Virginia's finest," she said as she put them down.

"Your eyes. They flutter back and forth. Is that a condition?" Easter asked Lou.

"It is. Don't know what it's called, but I've had it all my life."

"You see alright with it?"

"I do with my specs," said Lou, touching them.

"Forget about all that, Easter. I wanna know, is that red-haired boy your beau?" asked Abigail.

"He wouldn't be my beau flirting with Little Miss, would he? No, my beau is Osborn."

"Oh, dang it all," said Janey.

"What?" asked Little Miss with all the women turning to Janey.

"Oh, I was hoping he was single," said Janey, with her eyes landing on Lou.

Abigail turned to Janey. "But that fella talks strange, and there's something with his eyes too. Like he's shy or something," said Abigail. She immediately turned to Lou. "Don't mean nothin' by it…"

"It's fine. Osborn is different, but the truth is, he's the kindest, sweetest, most charming man I've ever met," said Lou, her eyes rolling to the ceiling.

The four other women joined in, hooting quietly.

"I didn't even like men before him, but he lit a candle that turned into a fire inside me," added Lou.

"Really? What did ya like…" Janey asked, clearing her throat. "…Before him?"

Lou smirked. "Nothing really. I mean, I've seen a few girls I thought were pretty."

Abigail and Easter's eyes went wide.

"Oooh, don't be thinkin' on it. It's damnation it is. Against God's law, that is." said Easter.

Lou shook her head. "No, I never meant to do anyth—"

"I seen some girls I thought were pretty too," said Janey.

"Ain't nothing to that. Like lookin' a beautiful sunset." Janey smiled at Lou.

"Well, Osborn is the only one for me now. He doesn't know it. We've only kissed once," added Lou.

"Ooooh!"

"What about Ray?" asked Janey with a sly smile and a side-eye glance to Little Miss.

"He's smart, and he was raised by Osborn, so he's kind too. He watches out for Osborn. Osborn is a talented artist in photography, and it's most of what he thinks about. Ray takes care of his peculiarities. He's a good catch," she said, looking to Little Miss.

"Ooooh!"

"We saw the county fair's in town. We were gonna go. If y'all would like to come along, you can get to know Ray a little better," said Lou.

"Ooooh!"

"That'd be fun," said Little Miss as she turned to Abigail and Easter. "Wanna go? Augustus don't have work tomorrow."

"They ain't gonna want no coloreds there, Missus," said Easter.

"I'd go if Augustus wants me to go," said Abigail.

Janey turned to Lou. "You gonna marry him?"

"Who, Ray?" said Lou. The women laughed.

"No. Your fella," asked Janey.

"Hmm, If I ever married, Osborn would be the only man I would want, but I don't know if he'll ever marry. He doesn't like to touch."

Janey perked up. "Doesn't like to touch? Not even on the pecker?"

The women burst into laughter. Lou had to wait for it to subside.

"I don't know about that one, but he's told me hugging and kissing are a big part of a marriage, and he doesn't like to touch. I told you he's peculiar."

"Never met a man that doesn't like to touch," said Abigail.

"What about y'all?" asked Lou.

"Janey and Little Miss are alone. I'm married to Thane," said Easter.

"I'm with Augustus. He's just my beau, though," said Abigail.

"How'd ya meet 'em?

Easter took a sip from the cup and returned with disgust. "Yuck. No more of that. Anyway, I've lived on this farm since a child. They say I just showed up one day. Anyway, the mens took care of me and raised me. When I got old enough, most of the mens had left or passed on. Thane was always around, and he done some sweet things to me, so I took a liking to him."

They turned to Abigail. "I found Augustus sleepin' in a big field down in Georgia. I'm a runaway, and I saw him and could see kindness in his face. He took me along with him, and it proved true. He was kind."

Another joint "Ooooh!"

"You wanna marry him?" asked Easter.

Abigail turned her eyes away from them. "I ain't sure no more. Being with a white man ain't easy," she said sadly.

"Thane and I call us married, but we weren't married in no church. There's no one up here that'd marry two coloreds. We just gave us both promises and call us married."

"There'd be no one to marry a white with a colored the same," said Abigail.

"You could just say you was married like us," said Easter.

Abigail slugged down her cup. "I suppose."

CHAPTER 39
Augustus

Speak your love still once again

THE FOLLOWING MORNING, Little Miss and the four women came out of the Fenn house to see Ray setting up his camera.

"Good morning, Ray. What's that?" asked Little Miss.

"It's a way to thank y'all for supper last night," said Ray.

"I ain't never had one done of me," said Easter.

"Me neither," said Abigail.

"My uncle is the master, but he's letting me do this one on my own," said Ray, turning to Osborn, nodding.

Ray shot the portraits of Little Miss by herself, Easter and Thane together, Augustus and Abigail together, Janey alone and one with them all including Osborn and Lou. The photographs were printed on a thin sheet of metal, coated with a dark lacquer.

"They's tintypes. All the boys get 'em in the army," said Augustus.

"Don't they have a daguerreotype shop down in Johnstown?" asked Ray.

"Not yet," said Little Miss. "Got one in Altoona, though."

"That'd be a good place to set up a shop," said Ray as he glanced over to Osborn.

"Alright, y'all ready to head out? Abigail and I will take Daisy. Osborn, maybe you can drive The Missus' buggy. Lou, Ray, and Janey can sit in the back."

Easter and Thane waved them off, and they headed down the road to the county fair.

Three hours later, carriages and buggies began to line the road up to the fair. Augustus and Abigail rode up to Little Miss' buggy.

"Y'all wouldn't mind if we go on up ahead, would ya?"

Little Miss smiled. "Not at all. We have our chaperones."

Augustus put Daisy into a trot.

"Why'd ya want to go on ahead?" asked Abigail.

"So, we can spend some time together alone." "That's sweet," she said as she peered over his shoulder and smiled. "I ain't never been to a fair."

The fairgrounds held massive circus tents, outside stages, food booths, and rows of carnival games. Stage callers with megaphones called out for the vaudevillian acts, and politicians stood on podiums.

They walked about, first stopping at the horse races.

"They's ladies! And they's wearing men's trousers! Can ya believe that?" Abigail laughed in disbelief.

They stopped at the carnival games to watch. The *ting, ting, ting* sounds echoed toward them. They walked over and watched as the rings bounced off the bottles, laughing at the misses and clapped at the successes.

She beamed at him as he took her hand and walked from stage to stage.

"Tomorrow will be my first remembrance. Gonna be making money for us," he said.

"You surely are." She smiled up at him.

"I spoke to the other undertaker there in town. Mr. Parker. He told me there's too much work for him. He wanted me to go to work for him, but said if I wouldn't, he wouldn't mind the competition."

"Oh yeah? That's good, Aug. Real good. You gonna be busy."

"Well, yeah, and I think it's time we move on down there."

Her head turned to him. "To where?"

"To Johnstown. That's where I'll be working."

"I thought we'd be here forever?"

They stopped at a stage where a man was selling a "magic elixir" and claiming it helped a deaf boy hear again. The people surrounding him were laughing.

Augustus also laughed at the outlandish claims of the man when he noticed Abigail looking at two young ladies in bell dresses who were whispering and pointing at them. He could see her amber-brown eyes filling with sadness.

"Let's look over here," he said, walking over to the sheep-shearing contest. Augustus began to see what she likely saw before him; the rolling eyes of disdain and contempt. She let go of his hand.

"Would you like a stuffed potato?"

Abigail shook off the shame and smiled at him. "Ya ain't got no money."

He grinned. "After tomorrow, I'll have some, but for now, we can always imagine it."

"Um, umm. That stuffed potato was delicious," she said as she stuck an invisible fork in her mouth.

"Mine has bacon," added Augustus.

Two teenage boys passed them. "Them two," one said as he pointed and giggled.

Augustus watched them as they passed and turned to Abigail. "What did they mean, 'them two?'"

"You know, Aug. They seein' me here with a white man. I'm just a nigga and don't belong. Get on outta here, nigga. That's what they's saying. Get on outta here."

Her face was stiff. He reached down and took her hand. "That's just gonna make it all worse. You doin' that."

"Let's find the others," said Augustus.

"No. Can we just go back home?"

"Alright. If that's what ya want."

IT WAS LATE in the afternoon when Little Miss' buggy came back from the fair. Augustus went out to greet them.

"We missed y'all out there. Ya go back early?" asked Little Miss.

"Abigail wasn't feeling all that well."

"Sorry to hear that. Gonna be over for supper?"

"I'm sure. We'll see ya in a bit," said Augustus walking back to his cabin.

Abigail was lying on the bed. He sat on it next to her.

"Little Miss is asking 'bout ya," he said. Augustus sat down at the table to pick up where he left off in his notebook.

"Oh, is that what ya callin' her now? Little Miss?"

He turned to her with curiosity. "That's her name, Abi."

Abigail unconsciously picked at the bed cover she was lying on. "Only kin call her that. You heard 'em last eve. Supposed call her The Missus. That's what ya used to call her."

"What is this, Abi?"

"This ain't gonna work with us, Aug," she said, biting her lip and holding the tears back.

"Where did this come from? What is so wrong?"

"You saw what happened today. Those boys. Everyone out there judging us."

"That ain't everywhere. We's fine here. We can just avoid certain places and—"

"Avoid? Ya mean stay hidden? Always be hiding us? Might as well be running from the massa."

"Stop this! I love you, Abi!"

"It ain't gonna matter if you do. I'm a nigga, and you're a cracka, and that's all we'll ever be. That's all the world is gonna let us be. Can't change that! Folks wanna lynch you! They'd wanna lynch me just for being together!"

"Abi, this is a free state…"

Abigail sat up in the bed, her back against the wall. "Free state? Free state! Don't matter that Pennsylvania's a free state. Folk ain't free in their minds. I'm still a nigga, and you still a cracka, and that's all we'll ever be. I be bringin' all sorts of pain to your life!"

"Ya surely bringin' pain right now, girl!"

Abigail closed her mouth and stared at him as he dressed.

"You been in piss-poor humor for days now," he said as he glanced over to her. "Now get a bit gussied up and come over for supper," he said as he walked out the door and slammed the door behind him.

Ray and Osborn were sitting outside on the porch rockers.

"I ain't late for supper, am I?" asked Augustus.

"No, not yet," said Ray. "Hey Augustus, tomorrow, do ya think it'd be alright if I asked Little Miss to go into town with me?"

Augustus sat down on the porch step. "I think it'd be fine. She don't need a chaperone." The bats were diving through the night air for insects in front of them.

"So tomorrow, I won't be helping my uncle out. Would ya mind watching him a bit—"

"I don't need a chaperone either, Ray," said Osborn.

"He doesn't need a chaperone, but sometimes he says things that people take the wrong way."

"Apparently, I don't understand most humor," added Osborn as he twisted his beard.

"And he doesn't like to shake hands—"

"I don't like to be touched," added Osborn.

Ray leaned down and tapped Augustus on the shoulder. He turned to Ray, who mouthed the words: "Watch him."

"The Missus tells me it's your first funeral tomorrow," said Osborn.

"It is, and I'd be much obliged to ya if ya could chaperone me," said Augustus. "If you won't take one, I will."

CHAPTER 40
Augustus

Good-night, sweet friend, good-night: Till life and all take flight, Never good-bye.

DRESSED IN HIS warning clothes, Augustus peered into the back of the enclosed photography wagon. There was a small bunk along one side, and on the other was a desk with cabinets all around, holding all the equipment needed for developing the photograph. Little Miss came around to him.

"Well, don't you look like a fine gentleman," she said. "Help a lady in?"

Augustus climbed in after her and looked around in awe when Ray appeared at the entrance.

"I'll ride back here. You can ride up front with my uncle," said Ray.

Augustus peeked in a few drawers. "I don't know. Can I trust you two back here?" Augustus joked.

"Go on, get on outta here," said Little Miss.

"You like it?" asked Ray.

"Impressive. I like it," said Augustus, turning and climbing out. Ray climbed in. "Missus, hit that wall there if he can't control himself. I'll toss the carpetbagger out."

Little Miss threw her handkerchief at him before he could shut the wagon door. He picked it up and brought it to his nose, smelling it. Augustus turned to see Abigail watching him. He whipped the handkerchief away from his face and waved at her. She glared at him and turned away, walking toward their cabin.

Reaching Johnstown, Osborn dropped off Little Miss and Ray before continuing to the funeral. The deceased's name was Darla, taken too early by pneumonia.

"Feel free to ask me questions; we can work together," said Osborn. They walked into the parlor room. Darla's small, white coffin sat on a table, pushed up against the far wall.

Augustus helped Osborn bring in and set up his camera. Osborn began opening all the drapes.

"Oh, I need all those closed," said Augustus.

"Yes, certainly, but after I photograph the deceased. I need light."

Osborn walked up to the coffin and removed Darla, lying her on her side on a chaise lounge. He gently put a pillow under her head.

"You see? It looks like she's having a restful sleep."

Osborn removed the lens cap. Augustus watched him mouth the numbers to ten before he put the lens cap back on. He pulled out a thin box from the camera.

"I'll be back in a moment," he said, leaving Augustus in the room with Darla "sleeping."

A strange feeling came over him as he watched Darla. He didn't know where to put his eyes. They always returned to the two-year-old on the lounge.

Augustus' eyes opened wide when he thought he saw her move. His heart was racing. Darla moved again, rolling forward. Augustus ran up to her, catching her just in time before she fell to the floor. He looked around, making sure no one was there to see the near disaster. Augustus gently placed her back into her coffin just as Osborn walked in.

"Oh, you didn't have to put her back, I need to take a few more photographs."

Osborn took Darla out again and sat her up against a pillow. Taking a stick of colored chalk from his pocket, he carefully drew eyes on her eyelids.

"Would you be so kind as to retrieve the parents?" asked Osborn.

Augustus found them sitting in the foyer and brought them to Osborn.

"Please stand on either side of her," he asked as he placed a doll in Darla's lap.

Augustus stood next to the camera.

"See now? It looks as if they are all playing with the doll," said Osborn with a pleasing smile. Mrs. Clement began to cry.

"The photograph will not turn out well if you are heaving like that, Mrs. Clement," said Osborn.

She only cried harder. Mr. Clement went around to console her.

"Would you like to take some time?" asked Augustus. Mr. Clement nodded and took his wife from the room.

"You did well there. I am not as good with niceties. Niceties and formalities are a part of your job. Now, go see if they will return."

Augustus left and returned with a frown.

"They couldn't bear it, and guests are arriving, Osborn."

"Fine, then. I'll take one without them."

Osborn took the photo and left the room again, leaving Augustus alone with Darla and her doll. Darla was staring straight at him.

Augustus began to hear Darla's grandparents outside, greeting the incoming guests. Osborn returned.

"Alright, let me help you now," said Osborn as he picked up Darla and set her gently back in her coffin.

"It used to be traditional for the family to clean up the deceased and prepare it for the coffin, but that is changing. Now I see all the undertakers do this. Have you prepared a body before?"

"No."

"With my profession, I do this myself, just as you saw me do, unless an embalmer gets to it first."

Osborn took his handkerchief, spit on it, and wiped the chalk-drawn eyes off Darla's eyelids, then adjusted her and the flowers surrounding her.

Osborn looked around the room. "We need a lower table than this. Can you look about and find one? About knee level."

Augustus returned with one. Osborn placed the coffin on top of it, stood back and surveyed his work.

"They do that so that the mourning children that come can view and kiss Darla on the cheek. Children who kiss the dead shall receive the gifts of strength and long life. We are allowing Darla to provide those gifts."

"Alright," said Augustus, nodding. "Thank ya for all this, Osborn. I'm obliged."

"My pleasure. Now, let's close all the drapes and make sure the food is properly served."

The service was ready to begin. People began entering, viewing the body, eating, drinking, and milling about. Augustus heard several conversations start and never finish as they walked in and out of the room.

The four cousins assigned to be the pallbearers ranged in age from eleven to fourteen. Osborn helped Augustus arrange them, oldest at opposite corners.

Augustus showed them how to carry the coffin as Osborn counseled them.

"And no smiling. I need to see sad, solemn faces." The four children nodded. "And you two go first out the door. You need to take the casket out of the house feet first. Feet first."

"Why feet first?" asked one.

"You don't want Darla to be calling you to follow, now do you?" asked Osborn. All four heads shook. "That's why you have to make sure it's this end out first."

The three rambunctious boys and one girl started to argue and fight with each other.

"Settle on down now. Like he said, solemn faces," reminded Augustus.

Standing close by, Augustus whispered instructions as they picked up the coffin and headed out the door through the crowd of mourners on the house steps and in the street. When they reached the little white hearse, Osborn and Augustus finished the job for them, loading it in.

After the graveside service, the family and all the mourners had left. Osborn and Augustus waited for the gravediggers to fill the grave before taking back the hearse and picking up Ray and Little Miss in town.

"You'll make a fine undertaker, Augustus," said Osborn.

"I prefer my doctorin' to it. It gives me more money, I suppose."

"Maybe, but there's not many that can do what we do. I believe you are suited for the death business."

CHAPTER 41
Augustus

To live in the hearts of those we love is not to die

"WHAT DID YA do today?" asked Augustus as Abigail sat on the bed watching him walk about in his long johns.

"I helped Easter with the wash and some of the chores."

Augustus laid out his warning clothes on the dining table and began wiping the dirt and dust off.

"Osborn, Ray, and Lou are leaving in the morning. Thane's setting up a bonfire. Are ya comin'?"

"I suppose. Can we do something tomorrow, Aug? Just you and me. Take Daisy out or somethin'."

"I have an appointment. Another job. Gotta leave early in the morn."

"In Johnstown? Maybe after we—"

"Altoona. I'll be gone for two days."

Abigail watched him as she sulked.

"You in love with The Missus."

Augustus jumped and faced her. He shook his head. "What?!"

"I seen it, Aug. I know you love me, but I seen it with yous and her."

His eyes had narrowed. "I hear you clucking, but I can't find your nest."

"Why are ya gussying up your clothes then?"

He jerked back his head. "Because they're the only clothes I own."

"It's in the eyes. I'm a woman. A woman can see these things, can feel 'em. And she's sweet on you, Aug. She's sweet on you plenty."

"That's foolishness. She's sweet on that Ray out there."

"She ain't. She's just playin' for your attention. I see it."

"You're being foolish now," he said, heading for the door. "I'm headin' over to be with our guests. You come on over when ya feel right in the head."

CHAPTER 42
Charlotte

We will be with you in spirit

SIX MONTHS OF battles around the city had left the eight bedrooms, four bathrooms, two powder rooms, parlor, kitchen, den, office, library, great room and maids' quarters empty. Most of the staff were gone or fighting. Usually, the army would need to house officers in a home of that size, but since she was Mrs. Greenwood of Greenwood Armory Manufacturing, they left her alone. It was now only herself, Micah and her two female housemaids, Elsa and Victoria, in the mansion.

Greenwood Armory had a handful of employees to build their rifles, but as the Confederate Army was not paying its bills, neither could Charlotte pay her employees. The company was bankrupt. Charlotte had hoped to use the remaining stock of rifles to settle their debts after the war, but a Union shell blew up her dream. The home and furniture, her jewelry, and personal possessions were the last bits of wealth she had left, but she couldn't find anyone to sell them to.

"Oh, ma'am! She's dead!"

"What's that?" Charlotte ran down the stairs. "She's dead?"

"A Yankee bomb got her!" Victoria is dead!" cried Elsa. "The Yankees put a bomb under our boys' lines, and it blew up!"

Charlotte had heard it earlier. It was no ordinary shell explosion. The bomb was so big that it had shaken the house violently, and four windows had cracked.

"How do you know she's dead? Did you see her?"

"No, ma'am, someone told me."

Charlotte looked around quickly. "Where is Micah?"

"He's outside. I just told him about Victoria, and he went to find out for sure."

"All right, let's just wait for confirmation. We have to be resolute. Maybe she'll come walking in that door at any moment. You don't know for sure. Did the Yankees get in?"

"No, ma'am. Our boys fought 'em back and wiped 'em out."

"Wiped 'em out?"

"Thousands dead, ma'am. Thousands."

Charlotte comforted Elsa and made some tea. Micah came back about an hour later. "Victoria is dead, Missus."

At his proclamation, Elsa ran down the hall to her room, sobbing.

"We have to leave here, Micah. We'll be dead too if we don't, and there's nothing left here for us."

"You speakin' the gospel, Missus."

Two days later, they packed up a small buggy with as much as they could carry and headed out. Elsa was invited along, but she refused; she couldn't leave her family. Charlotte told her she could stay in the mansion until she returned someday, but inside she knew she would never return.

"Where do you think you're going?" yelled a corporal with a giggle.

Charlotte and Micah had made it to the edge of Petersburg. The road leading out of the city was blocked by trenches, wagons, earth, and whatever else the troops could throw on there.

"We're leaving the city. Can you tell us the safest way?"

"Ma'am, there ain't no safe way. You'll die out there. The sharpshooters will kill ya. I'm sorry, ma'am."

"Can I speak to your sergeant?"

"He died this morning," he replied, looking around him. "But there's some lieutenant around heres, I believe. Haven't seen him in a bit." Charlotte stared at the corporal. "What? I mean, I'm telling ya the truth. If you go out theres, you die. Sos, you can't go out theres!"

Charlotte turned to Micah. "Let's go back. Take me to the war office. I'll see about this."

Entering the war office, Charlotte spotted General Beauregard surrounded by officers and walking toward them down the hall. The general stopped upon seeing her.

"Charlotte. How are you? The letter got through the lines. I'm sure they have received it by now."

"Thank you kindly, General. But I was wondering how to leave the city. We tried—"

"Charlotte, you are far safer here in the city than out there. The train is attacked daily."

"The Yankees won't let women and children out?"

"My dear Charlotte, the Yankees are not getting in. You are far safer here. Forgive me, Charlotte, but I'm a might occupied." The general walked off with his officers in tow.

Charlotte came out of the war office and up to Micah, waiting at the buggy. "He said the same thing as the corporal. Let's go back to the house. We are stuck here for now."

Coming back to the house, Elsa wasn't there. Charlotte helped Micah unpack the buggy and put things back. After they finished, she didn't know what to do.

They both sat in chairs in the parlor room, silent. Micah heard something in the kitchen, probably Elsa coming home. Laughter and voices were approaching. It was Elsa with a young boy, a teenaged girl, and an older woman. She had brought her family to the house and froze upon seeing Charlotte.

"Ma'am! I thought you'd gone…"

"There is no way out of the city. We had to come back."

"I'm so sorry about this. This is my son and daughter, and my mother here."

"Hello, ma'am," said her mother.

"I'll take them right back to their place, and as soon as I get back, I'll make you up some tea," she scrambled.

"Elsa, it's fine. They can all stay. You can all stay here. It's a big lonely house now, and we all need family."

CHAPTER 43
Augustus

Softly at night, the stars are shining on you

AUGUSTUS HAD RETURNED to the Fenn's. Easter was rubbing clothes on the washboard out front when he trotted up on Daisy. Her eyebrows drew together, and she backed away from her wash and him as if she feared him. The house behind her, she yelled back to it.

"Little Miss! I needs ya! Mr. True is back!"

"You look like you seen a ghost, Easter. What's wrong?" said Augustus, dismounting. Little Miss came out.

"Augustus. Get another funeral?"

"I did."

"Did ya ask if they need a weeper?"

Augustus tied Daisy to the porch rail.

"'Course I did. I'm sorry, though. They didn't know what a weeper was."

Easter stood with arms crossed, watching them. "Who snapped her garter?" said Augustus.

"There's something we gotta tell ya," said Little Miss.

"Go on and tell him, Missus," said Easter.

Thane walked over as Augustus looked around the farm. “Where’s Abigail?”

“Well, that’s what I got to tell ya. Abigail left,” replied Little Miss.

“She don’t want to be with ya no more, Mr. True,” said Easter.

Augustus shook confusion out of his head. “Left? Where’d she go?”

He stared into Little Miss’ eyes.

“She went west. Off with Osborn and Ray just after ya left. She ain’t comin’ back.”

“But why? did she say—”

“It’s ‘cause your color, Mr. True,” said Easter. “She tells me ya ain’t gonna have a good life with her. Ain’t gonna be like it should. Folk won’t be liking ya, won’t be giving ya work.”

“It could get ya lynched. I heard it happenin’” said Thane.

“I’m sorry, Augustus,” said Little Miss. “I’m sorry ya had to come home to this.”

“They say what towns they’d be passing through?” asked Augustus.

“It’d be a mistake ta go on after her, Mr. True,” said Thane.

“Thane’s right,” said Easter. “Me and her talked on it a bit, and that girl can talk. She’s settled on it, Mr. True. Settled as mountain stone.”

Augustus turned to each of them before untying Daisy. Little Miss stopped his hand with hers.

“It’s late. If ya go, go in the mornin’. We ain’t stoppin’ ya. We got pork stew for supper. You picked the right eve to stay.”

Little Miss’ brown and green eyes stared into his, holding him there more than her hand did.

CHAPTER 44
Charlotte

I'm the guiding light in your dreams
and I'll be travelling by your side

WINTER STRETCHED ON slowly, and as the new year approached, the house felt more like a prison than a home. Everyone worked together to get provisions. Elsa and Micah were always out searching for food because almost all of the butcher shops were closed. Micah found one with meat for sale at five dollars a pound. Charlotte did have a store of jarred and pickled fruits and vegetables in the cellar, but that was running low.

Then the day came when the cannons stopped pounding, and the gunfire silenced. A few hours later, unarmed Rebel troops marched down the street with Union troops pointing guns at them.

Before the war, Petersburg had gas-fueled streetlights, brick sidewalks, a municipal water system, four volunteer fire companies, over a hundred and fifty grocers, two daily newspapers, four banks, and four savings-and-loans. Now that the war was over, it was a wasteland.

Union troops were all over the city. Charlotte didn't know

what she should do. Stay indoors? Try to leave now? She was the wife of a Confederate armory supplier. Would she be detained? A knock on the door preceded the crack of it being kicked in.

What was the point of the knock?

"Who the hell is in here?" yelled the Union sergeant.

Charlotte came down the stairs with the flair of southern class. "May I be of help, Sergeant?"

"Any Rebs in here?" he asked as he walked in like he owned the place. "Nobody's gonna get hurt or nothin'."

"No, just women and children and one manservant."

"Wells, it don't matter none anyways, you gotta get on out of here. We're taking this place."

"Where do we go?" she asked.

"I don't care, just get on up on outta here. That's all I care."

Elsa's family gathered with Micah and Charlotte out by the buggy house. Micah was hitching the horse up while Charlotte stood near Elsa.

"You may come with us, Elsa. We can take turns sitting in the buggy. It is a good while away…"

"No, ma'am. We need to stay here. My husband wouldn't know where to find us after the war is over. But thank you, and God bless you. You are so kind. It was a pleasure to work in your home."

"Now, wait a spell!" yelled someone down the pathway. A Union captain came walking toward them with three soldiers by his side. "You can't take that horse, nor that buggy."

"But, I have nowhere—" Charlotte pleaded.

"Ma'am, I don't care. This is all Union property now. The only thing you'll be taking is the clothes on your back, and mind ya, you are lucky to have those. Now you best be getting out of here before my boys get ahold of your fine southern bourbon tonight, I'll tell ya that," said the captain with his fists on his hips.

"But, Captain—"

"Git!"

"Come along, Micah." Charlotte started walking, Micah following.

They walked down one road, then another, past Union troops, past Confederate prisoners, past stacks of dead, past cannons, all the way out to the fields beyond the city where they could see other refugees like themselves, fleeing. The troops didn't seem to care and let them pass like ghosts. It seemed like they were all just happy it was over.

Charlotte was thankful they didn't arrest her. Now that they could safely leave the city, they could go back to the old farm. The problem was that they had no food or water and had three hundred fifty miles of road ahead of them.

There were hundreds of refugees marching out of town, most without a destination. Micah and Charlotte joined in with them.

"Where are y'all headed?" Charlotte asked a woman walking next to her.

"We don't rightly know yet, just away from here. What about you all?"

"We're headed back to our old home in Pennsylvania."

"I hear that all the railroads are blown up so you can't be catchin' a freight."

"You gotta watch out in a lot of these towns," cried out one man. "The soldiers will get you. Yanks or Rebs, it don't matter. I guess if ya get north of the Mason-Dixon Line, it'll be a might safer for you. You're lucky you have this boy with you, but as soon as you get past north of that line, he'll be a free man, so you better think about that one."

Charlotte smiled up at Micah. "Yeah, don't want to free this one. I think he'd be a might dangerous if he were free."

"You got any food or water?" a skinny man of about forty asked Charlotte.

"Just like you, we don't."

"Well, there's water up yonder at the creek. You got anything to carry it?"

"We got out with just our clothes."

"Here, I got a pot!" cried out a woman who overheard their conversation. "You can have it. I got two." Micah took it from her as she narrowed her eyes at Charlotte. "Ain't you Mrs. Greenwood?"

"I am."

"My, how the mighty have fallen."

Charlotte returned her remark with a sideways glance. "I always believed it was better to have rose up and fallen than to have never rose up at all. Thank ya kindly for the pot."

The skinny man spoke out to the group, "Anybody that wants to travel with my family is welcome. There is safety in numbers."

Charlotte looked at him. He was most likely a preacher taking the job of the leader, she thought.

After reaching the creek, everyone had their fill of water and stocked up. Micah filled the pot with water and held it upright as best he could, trying not to spill what little they had.

That night they camped just off the road. Someone started

a fire with a flint, but no one had food to cook. This was only the first night of a long journey, and Charlotte was exhausted.

"I need to be off by myself," she said to Micah.

"No, Missus, I be following."

"I have to use the privy, Micah."

"I'll go with you and turn my back. That'll block others from seeing, too."

Charlotte knew he was right but dreaded it. "Yes, but you'll hear me…" She trailed off indignantly.

He turned from her. "I'll turn my ears to the trees."

After completing their first twenty miles, their clothes were filthy and reeked. They adjusted to the smell over the second twenty miles. Micah had a good pair of boots that would easily last the entire journey, but Charlotte had high-stepping, fashionable shoes that already seemed to be falling apart. She knew she would have to find another pair of shoes along the way.

The long line of refugees was growing smaller as they proceeded north. Small bands of them would peel off to look for another town or possibly to find food on their own.

After three consecutive days with no food, Charlotte saw Micah weakening. The group they were in now numbered forty-four. Large plumes of black smoke came from the north.

"I'm sure that's Sutherland's Station. I heard about the battle," someone said.

"Well, let's just go on up ahead to that rise over yonder and see what it looks like."

The group came to the top of the rise in the road. The Union troops in the distant city looked like little ants on a kicked-over hill.

"We're gonna head east. I don't want no part of that," said the skinny man as he headed in toward the trees.

Charlotte pulled Micah. "We should leave these people. We'll be better off on our own. We got to get some food in that town. We'll wait 'til nightfall." Micah agreed with a nod.

By evening there were no sounds of battle, and the Union troops had settled for the night. The night was dark with no moon; Micah and Charlotte slowly walked toward the city along the side of the road. If they heard someone coming toward them, they ducked into the tall grass. The April night breathed a bitterly-cold breeze, carrying with it the sickening smell of death.

"Can you hear that?" Charlotte whispered. Distant moans and cries came from the west. Together, they dove into the four-foot-tall grass. They crawled away from the road until her hand found the wool jacket of a soldier. She couldn't see if he was a Yank or Reb. She gasped.

"You all right, Missus?"

"I found a dead man," she whispered back as Micah crawled up next to her and began scouring the dead man. Feeling around like two blind folks, they found his canteen, then some hardtack, a hardened square of bread the army issued to them.

"Found food. It feels like a dead cake," said Micah. "Let's go on. There's gotta be others."

They crawled off, side by side, and after another fifteen feet, came across another body. They scavenged another canteen, a piece of salt pork, and a pistol.

Charlotte imagined the grass had probably hid the soldiers

from being found after the battle. Many of them had most likely been wounded slightly but died waiting for the stretcher-bearers to find them. The poor boys' deaths had saved them, and Charlotte gave thanks to the Lord in silent prayer, wishing a blessing on every poor wretch they came across.

They had collected four canteens, two pistols, and two Union army backpacks full of food before heading out of the tall grass toward the tree line. The closer to the tree line they got, the more dead horses, unexploded ordinance, destroyed wagons, and body parts they came across. She was glad the darkness veiled the filth and blood that covered her.

For the next few days, they stayed in the trees, far from the road, but always kept an eye on it. It was their only compass. They still hadn't found a stream to wash in; they looked like the walking dead and smelled like it, too. Water and food were running low—coming upon those hidden dead soldiers was a spot of good luck that hadn't been repeated.

"I see a cabin up yonder," Micah pointed. Charlotte saw it, too.

"Let's be cautious," she replied as she pulled out the Union pistol. Charlotte had never shot a pistol, and neither had Micah. The cabin was empty. The door had been kicked in, and everything was in disarray. Micah found bullet holes in the wall.

"I don't see any bloodstains; that's good," said Charlotte as she walked about. "It'll be a might warmer in here to sleep, at least."

"Can't be making a fire now, Missus. They'd see the smoke," said Micah as he looked at the fireplace.

"I know. But at least it's shelter. Haven't had that for a bit."

Charlotte curled up in the corner of the cabin, making sure no spiders were sleeping there first. Micah put his back against the wall facing the door, staying up as long as his eyes allowed him.

"Thank you, Micah."

"For what, Missus."

"You and me, we've been together for some time."

"Like I was with your momma."

"Were you as close to her as you are to me?"

"I knew you as a child, so's that makes it more of a bond, I s'pose."

"Well, I see how you are and how you watch out for me, protect me."

"It's my job, Missus. It's what I do."

"I know. I want to tell you how much I appreciate it and all."

"Mm-hmm."

"What does 'mm-hmm' mean?"

"Missus, You ain't gotta 'preciate nothing. I saw you grow up and alls. You're my kin. Kin just do. They don't get 'preciated. They just do. You? You been my momma, my sista, my friend, alls. You been it alls. You're my kin. Don't gotta 'preciate nothin'."

Charlotte wiped her tears away in the darkness.

"I've been thinking, when we get back, it's time I tell Augustus who I am. The Trues have both passed, and there would be no harm in it. I just believe he should know. And I want him to know I'm his mother, and that I was there for him, watching him all those years. He should know. Don't ya think?"

"You speaking the gospel theres."

Charlotte could only make out Micah's silhouette against the wall as her eyes closed. "I love you, Micah."

"I love you too, Missus."

"Hey Captain, there's two carpetbaggers in here!"

Rubbing the sleep from her eyes, she turned to the silhouette of a Union soldier with the morning sun coming in behind him. The captain clip-clopped his horse over to peer into the doorway.

"It's a nigger and a lady. Well, she don't look like a lady, more like a hobo."

"Get outta the doorway, Corporal, so I can take a gander." The corporal sauntered away as a few more soldiers peered in without blocking the captain's view. "Check 'em out, Corporal."

Micah woke and sat up. He knew the danger. The corporal entered with his pistol drawn and aimed at Micah.

"Don't move, nigger." He squatted down to search the belongings near Micah without taking his eyes off him. The corporal stopped, feeling something. "Captain, they's got Union-issued belongings!"

The captain motioned with his head for others to go in. Three did. They pushed Micah and Charlotte around, looking for things behind them. "They's got pistols! Union-issued pistols!" They pulled everything out in front of them.

The captain dismounted and walked in, removing his gloves. He looked down on them. He hadn't shaved for two weeks, and his dirty officer's coat was draped over his shoulders. He looked very tired of the war.

"What are you doing with these things?" asked the captain.

"We were starving and needed to eat. We took them off boys who wouldn't be needing them anymore," said Charlotte.

"You took a lot more than food it looks like to me. Those are Union Cooper pistols you got there. They are very tough to eat."

"Took 'em for protection, not to harm anyone."

The captain nodded, and he whipped his leather riding gloves in his hand. "Stealing from our dead boys, that ain't right."

"We came from Petersburg. We hadn't had any food since we left."

"Petersburg?" said the captain, understanding. "So, you're no carpetbaggers. You're southern sympathizers."

Charlotte sat silent.

The captain slapped his gloves again and turned. "Shoot the nigger. Do what you want with the woman."

"No!" cried Charlotte. "I am a Pennsyl—"

Bam! Bam!

Micah's head flew back, blood spattering against the wall. Charlotte's scream trailed off as she fainted.

Charlotte awoke the next day, bent over a broken stool. She moved off it and rested her back against the log wall. The sun came in through the open doorway, and birds were chirping. Beautifully peaceful until she moved again. Every part of her body hurt. She was naked, bruised, and bleeding. She didn't remember them shooting Micah until she looked over and saw him lying there, eyes open, as if he was surprised that he was dead.

Charlotte slowly got to her feet and searched for her clothes. They were nowhere in the cabin, so she went outside. They had tossed her underclothes around the trunk of a tree and her dress up on a branch. She reached for the dress, but it was too high. She took the broken stool and spent the remainder of her energy tossing the stool up, trying to knock it off the branch. After an hour, it finally came down.

All that day she sat with Micah reciting stories about all the good times, all the times he had known she should be doing something better, all the times she had done things he wouldn't approve of. She laughed and cried over her protector, companion, and best friend for the last time.

The afternoon sunset was coming on, and she knew she had to leave in search of food. She had nothing to bury Micah with, nothing for a proper funeral that he deserved. Taking the broken stool, she leaned it against the wall and sat. Micah would get her best weeping job ever.

The black dress and black veil made no difference. She didn't just weep for him; she wailed. An ear a half-mile away could've heard it. It was the wail of the highest pain, a pain she had never felt before, and it continued until sleep found her with her head on his leg.

In the morning, she awoke and laid Micah out peacefully on the floor of the cabin. She fixed his legs straight and crossed his arms over his chest as if he were in a coffin. She found a small, tattered, red window drape and covered his face with it. As Charlotte's shoes were missing, tossed somewhere far away, she removed Micah's big boots, setting each foot down as softly as she would a princess. Far too large for her, she found more torn drape material and stuffed it into each boot. Strapping them on, they pulled up to just below her knees. The heavy boots felt like stones were tied to her feet.

Leaving, she turned back to him at the doorway. "Greet me at the gate when it's my time. It'll be you who I want to see most."

She shuffled in Micah's big boots down the dirt road with wagon-wheel ruts carved into it. Her heart dropped and climbed with every dip and rise, on and on, until it was before her.

It changed since she was here last. The house ahead waited for her with a lantern in the window. It would be foolish to imagine that things would the same as when she was a girl. She couldn't guess who would have lived there, who was still alive, who was left.

Charlotte walked up unannounced to the Fenn farm as if she had just gone fishing. With her sunken eyes, thin hair, and ripped and torn dress, she looked far older than she had before she left.

Thane saw her first. He didn't recognize her; in fact, he wasn't sure she was human. He stared at her, fearing he was seeing a spirit.

Charlotte recognized Thane but was too exhausted to say hello or even smile at him. She continued to the main cabin. She wanted to see Little Miss. She needed to see her daughter.

CHAPTER 45
Augustus

To the world she was just a part,
To me she was the world

"YOU GO SEE President Lincoln's funeral train?" asked Mr. Becker, a beekeeper and an old friend of the True family. Augustus walked with him across his bean field toward a series of hive boxes.

"I did when it was up in Harrisburg. Needed to pay my respects," Augustus replied.

The air was cool, but the sun warm. Augustus was there to discuss the arrangements for Mr. Becker's grandchild, Ben, who had passed at the age of nine months from smallpox. The family could not figure out how Ben contracted it as no one else in the family had sickened.

"I went to the Harrisburg stop, too, with the family. He surely was a great president. Such a shame," said Mr. Becker. "Anyway, I was thinking, I am only about ten years older than you. After you left home, my family would gather with your family and your sisters on occasion. Course we'd meet up at church, too. I remember seeing you at church. You left when you were…?"

"Thirteen."

"Ah, yes."

"Yessir, that was some time ago," said Augustus.

Mr. Becker pulled a house key from his pocket. "So, this is the first time seeing this, right?"

"Yes, sir. This will be my first. I've never told the bees before."

"It's an old beekeeper tradition. We tell the bees everything: deaths, weddings, new babies. They gotta know to keep 'em happy."

There were ten beehives spaced twenty feet apart. Becker walked up to the first hive. Bees were buzzing about and didn't seem to mind him. Only a few flew out of the hive to check him out. He smiled as the bees landed on his face, happy to greet them.

Taking his house key, he leaned down to it, gently tapped it three times on the top, and whispered, "Ben is dead."

His smile eroded, and he stood. Speaking the three words out loud triggered the reality of them. His grandson was dead. Tears filled his eyes, and his jaw dropped, unable to speak.

"I understand, Mr. Becker," said Augustus as he walked to him and took the key from his hand. "I'll do the rest." Augustus handed him his handkerchief.

"Learn this all from your pa?" asked Augustus as they walked back to the Becker home

"And he learned from his and so on."

"And now I'll take the key when I do the warning for ya?"

"Yessir, and the bees will help you do your job telling others."

"I'll give ya the key back at the remembrance."

"As I said, we'll be doing it simple," said Becker. "Using your wagon will be fine. We ain't passing out no gifts. Mary will be cooking the meal; we'll take care of that."

"Need a weeper? I got one of them."

"No, don't believe so. Because Mary Beth wants a mourning doll made in Ben's likeness, and I know those aren't inexpensive."

"I understand. I'll go into Johnstown to have one made. I know of a quality dollmaker down there. I'll need a rendering or photograph of Ben."

"We don't have one. He was only with us a short time."

"Course. I'll have to bring the dollmaker on up here. He can remove or add sand to get the exact weight when he's here, and he can put all the lifelike qualities to it right there in your home. We can have it all set up right next to Ben so all the guests can see and compare. I'm sure you'll be pleased with his work."

The Becker funeral was his fortieth since he'd opened his undertaking business in Johnstown. He rented a commercial building with a small flat above it where he could store his wagon and Daisy. Augustus painted a sign above the garage of his building: AUGUSTUS TRUE, UNDERTAKER. The rural families would remember the True name, and the city families were more familiar with the term 'undertaker.'

"Say hello to Mrs. True for me," Becker said as he waved goodbye.

"Certainly will. I'll be back day after tomorrow with the dollmaker and the casket."

AUGUSTUS PULLED UP to the Fenn farmhouse and dismounted from the new wagon he'd purchased from a family in Johnstown. It wasn't an enclosed hearse, but it was clean and had the class to carry a coffin. He walked around to unhitch Daisy when he stopped, seeing Janey on the step, head in her hands. His brow pinched together; something was wrong. He stopped removing the tack from the horse and walked toward her.

"Janey? You all right?" Hearing Augustus, Thane came out of his cabin and stood on the porch, arms crossed, staring at him instead of helping him put the horse away like he always had. Instead, he stood silent with a strangely concerned expression. "What's wrong?" Then, Easter came out behind Thane, also concerned.

The hairs on the back of his neck stood up. "Is it the baby?" Panic was setting in, and he ran to the front door, past Janey with her red face.

"Better go in, Augustus," she said sadly.

Augustus approached the door. The tinkling sound of Amazing Grace was playing from the music box inside. He opened the door. Little Miss was in front of him, seated on the love seat with her head in her hands. "Is it the baby? Are you all right? What's wrong?"

She turned to him, her face wet with tears. "Oh Augustus!" she moaned as she lay on her side, revealing her five-month pregnant belly.

"Augustus," a voice calmly came from the other end of the room.

Augustus' head swiveled to Charlotte standing there, holding the music box in her hand, clothes torn and filthy. He took two steps back from the apparition.

"This music box used to be mine. Wherever did you find it?" she asked. Augustus stood, mouth agape.

She closed it and set it on the shelf. "Hello Augustus, do you recognize me?"

Augustus steadied himself. "Who are you?" His eyes searched the room for other apparitions.

"You should, Augustus! She's your mother!" cried Little Miss. Augustus turned to her and shook his head in confusion.

"She's right. I am your mother, Augustus. I am your real mother."

"My mother has passed on—"

"Mrs. True took you from me the day of your birth." Stone-cold resentment hung on her every word like a noose. Augustus slowly shook his head side to side. "Your father and I… Well… Little Miss is your sister." His head swam in a sea with no land in sight. "Jefferson was your half-brother. You were born two weeks apart, and she sold the story of you two being twins."

Augustus fell to his knees; his stomach was turning.

Charlotte gestured to Little Miss' pregnant belly. "I see that I am about five months too late to reveal this tragic news."

Augustus tilted his head to Little Miss, her head was in her wet hands, sobbing.

"The baby… our baby," he whispered.

"I know this is a shock, my darling. I don't want to hurt you. The truth be, I have been watching over you your entire life. I found you at the Academy and moved in across the street. The gunsmith's shop? Do you remember it? I was waiting for the time to tell you everything, but circumstances, unfortunately, prevented me from doing that. It was also me who released you from prison." Charlotte slowly walked over to a portrait of one of her grandfathers. She didn't remember which one. "I never could have imagined for this to happen," she said absently.

Little Miss turned to her mother. "I love him, Momma."

Charlotte turned on her heels to face him, but her finger pointed at Little Miss. "And *that* is the reason you must go, Augustus."

"What are you saying, Momma? No!" Little Miss screamed.

Augustus turned to Little Miss. "I don't care about all this. So what, it happened. God ain't gonna punish us; we didn't know. I ain't going nowhere."

"She's your *sister*, Augustus!" yelled Charlotte.

"But that's my child," he said through his teeth, staring at Charlotte and pointing to her round belly.

"No, Augustus. This is not right and can't be. You're wrong. Laying with your sister *is* an abomination against God. Don't you see? It can't stand."

"But we love—"

"Exactly, my boy. She loves you. You two love each other. With that love, do you truly believe you will not touch her again? I've done wrong myself. I know the power of love; it's too powerful for anyone. Can't you see this? You will be damned by God. I will not have both my children's souls damned by God." Charlotte exhaled long and slow as she accepted the painful necessity of her decision. "You have to be away from her. You have to leave."

All sound in the cabin floated up and away like chimney smoke. The light seeped through the floorboards like water.

Augustus shook his head, looking to the floor. "I won't… I can't."

Charlotte's expression changed from a look of sorrow to

ice-cold resolution. She stamped her foot defiantly. They both spun their heads to her direction.

"Little Miss disclosed to me that you no longer have the honor parole letter," she said with a sharp and cold tone. Augustus' brow narrowed. "I will be seeking the Yankees and telling them you are a deserter. You *will* leave this place; on your own, or in chains."

"But that is my child," he repeated quietly.

"And, unfortunately, your niece or nephew." Charlotte plunged the words into him like a Bowie knife.

Sixty seconds of silence felt like three years as each in the room considered their options.

"It is an abomination against God, Augustus," said Little Miss. "I remember you told me you're not baskin' in the light of the Lord, but I do, Augy, I do. God will punish us, or worse, our child will be punished."

He looked to her like she was someone he'd never met. "How can you agree? The child is ours! You can't take that back! We did not know!"

Charlotte walked up to him, taking his shoulders and helping him stand.

She hugged him, but he didn't respond. She put her lips to his ear, "I'm not punishing you, Augustus. I'm punishing myself. I've searched for you most of my life, and now that I've found you, I'm forced to send you away."

"But she's my family now," he pleaded.

"I'm sorry. I'm so sorry, my sweet boy," Charlotte whispered as tears again filled her eyes. "This is for the best."

His eyes grabbed hers in a chokehold before twisting away from her. He turned to Little Miss, disgusted, before running out and past Janey outside. He untied Daisy and jumped on, disappearing down the road.

The last sound he heard was Janey calling his name. "Augustus!"

THREE MONTHS PASSED; he had moved into the flat above his business.

I wonder if she had the baby yet? It must have been born by now. Was it a boy or a girl? What did it look like? What color eyes did it have, what color hair? And the name? I need that name. I need to call it something.

He decided to make the journey to the Fenn farm. He packed up Daisy and headed out. He arrived in the evening and camped in the trees, letting the horse wander out to the pasture behind him. He crept up through the bush and saw the lights of the Fenn cabins. His child was in there somewhere.

The next morning, he ate the dried bacon he had brought and waited. They were all there: Thane, Easter, Janey, Little Miss, and her mother—*his* mother—the woman who destroyed it all.

Where is my child? Many children died in childbirth or shortly after. About half his funerals so far were for children ten and under.

Wait!

Charlotte exited the house with a baby in her arms.

Oh my! There!

Charlotte began singing to the child and rocking it in her arms on the porch. The morning sun was behind her, and

Charlotte shielded the baby from the rays. Little Miss walked over, and Charlotte handed the baby to her. Little Miss sat in the porch rocking chair and put it to her breast. He could only see black hair when it cried and latched on. It was a dear little thing, brand new to life, wrapped in a purple blanket.

The sun crossed the sky and lay low in the western sky. Augustus sat there still. Even though the baby went in and out throughout the day, every glimpse was a gift. He decided then and there that he would come to the tree line of the Fenn farm once a month, every month. He would watch his son or daughter grow up from a distance.

CHAPTER 46
Augustus

In their death they are not divided

"ASHES TO ASHES, dust to dust..." Augustus had heard these words so often that he had memorized them. In fact, he had memorized all the different pastor's burial speeches.

Mourners were tossing handfuls of dirt into the grave of a forty-two-year-old woman.

"You're the undertaker?" asked a woman as she approached Augustus.

"I am."

She was a beautiful young lady with a long, regal neck, rosy cheeks, and a perfect nose that fit her face.

"Do you work for Mr. Parker?"

"No, I have my own business—"

"Oh, yes, on Mayerling? True something."

"Yes. Augustus True."

"You're new to town. I grew up with Mr. Parker's sons, Owen and Luke."

"Yes. Mr. Parker has been very good to me, helping me out even though I'm his competition."

"You were new to the business?"

"I sort of took over for my father. He was a warner. Have you heard of that?"

"Like an undertaker but in the hills."

"Yes."

"Where are you from?" she asked.

"About a four-hour ride or so. Up in the hills east from here."

"Hmm. Well, nice to meet you. Mr. True." She smiled and turned.

"May I have your name?" Augustus asked before she could leave. She turned back to him.

"I thought you'd never ask. My name is Rachel Nelson." She put out her hand. He wasn't sure if he should kiss it or shake it. He chose the latter.

"Augustus True."

AUGUSTUS WOULD PLAN his visits to the Fenn farm around any warning work he had. After two months, Augustus still couldn't guess the sex, but it surely gained weight on his or her mother's milk. Even from a distance, he could see those plump bracelets of fat folded at the wrists and ankles. The baby seemed easy to feed, opening its mouth wide when she pulled out her breast.

After staying as long as he could, he would head back down the hill to Johnstown. He still missed Little Miss, but the love was gone. It had left him the moment she sided with her mother. A local preacher had performed his marriage to Little Miss. No official paperwork had been taken to the county. In Johnstown, no one would know he'd married his sister except for one person. He stopped by Mr. Parker's business on the way home.

"Do you know Rachel Nelson?" asked Augustus.

Mr. Parker grinned. "Yes, the Nelson's have been friends of ours for years."

"Mr. Parker, I need to tell ya something. Something I need your help on."

"I thought something was weighing heavy on you, boy. Of course, Augustus. What can I help you with?"

"My wife up and left me months back—"

Mr. Parker's mouth dropped. "But with the baby? Did she ever have the baby?"

"The baby ain't mine. I heard she went west with the fella. I weren't tellin' no one 'cause it makes me look the fool."

"My boy, not a word will come from my mouth. I assure you."

"Thank ya. I'm so obliged. With that said, I met Rachel at a funeral and thought she was delightful—"

"She's quite a handful, Augustus. It'll take a certain kind of gentleman to tame that one, I'd think." He grinned. "But you know it's bad luck for a bride and groom to meet at a funeral? She too pretty to be scared off with that one?"

"I'd say so," said Augustus.

"I BELIEVE IT'S time you asked for my hand, Mr. True," said Rachel as they walked in the city park. Augustus and Rachel had been courting for five months.

"Aren't I supposed to be the one that decides that?"

"No, you are the one who is supposed to ask that. I decide it. But you have been twiddling your thumbs."

"I just wanted to be established enough that your father would allow me to—"

"He already speaks about you. He likes you. Said he sees potential and all that," she said as she stopped and turned to him. "Ask him tonight after dinner."

"Aren't I supposed to decide when to…" he teased.

"Good!" she said and continued walking. Rachel was a bold woman, and that's what Augustus loved about her. It made him laugh. She would argue with storekeepers about prices, call out rudeness in people, and voice her opinion no matter the company she kept. He loved that strength in her even more than her beauty.

The business was changing as much as it was growing, and he never had a request for a weeper. He would always offer the service in hopes of seeing and speaking to Little Miss. People would ask for new things or want their funeral done a different way, or they would see another funeral and want it that way.

He brought a pair of Union army-issue field glasses on a monthly visit to the Fenn farm and saw his baby in a little blue dress, a little girl. Easter played in the dirt with her like she was a little girl herself. The two played for hours until his little sweetheart fell asleep in Easter's arms. On every successive visit, the desire to touch her and know her name grew.

"WE WOULD LIKE a weeper at our mother's memorial," said David Baily, the son of the deceased.

Augustus' face remained solemn, but inside he was smiling. It had finally happened; a client requested a weeper.

"Not for ourselves or what people think, of course, but rather because our mother would have wanted it. She often spoke of the mystery of the weepers. She knew the Fenn women, or at least knew of them. I'm not sure. But she had seen them on many occasions and wanted to be one as a girl. It's funny. She would tell us stories," said David as they sat at his dining room table.

That day, Augustus sent a note to the Fenns by courier.

Fenn Farm,

Hills of Bakersville,

Bloomfield Township, Bedford County.

We honorably request the weeping services of The Missus at the memorial service for the passing of Mrs. Jen Baily. Service to be held next Saturday, July 2, at the home of David Baily, son of the deceased. 12 McGarry Alley, Johnstown. Mr. Baily would be pleased to meet with you this Thursday and bring photographs or answer questions at the home of Jen Baily at the family homestead in the Road 2, Hills of Susquehanna Township.

In Sincerity,

Ethan Parker, Parker and Sons Undertakers

The Baily family had moved to Johnstown, but their mother, Jen Baily, had stayed on long after Mr. Baily had passed.

AUGUSTUS DECIDED TO bring up the casket for Mrs. Baily Thursday and prepare the body.

"You just missed her, Augustus," said David. "We answered all her questions and lent her all the photographs and a diary."

"Did her voice sound young or old?" asked Augustus.

"I don't know. I'd say in the middle, in between."

In the middle didn't help him. As Little Miss was no longer pregnant, most likely, she would be the one doing the weeping. Augustus knew their mother would not be with her. It was the perfect opportunity to plead his case.

"Would you please assist me in placing your mother into the casket?"

"Certainly."

"Is she already dressed in her eternal clothes, or would you be having me dress her?"

"She is already dressed."

The Baily's had decided to place her body in the casket and left resting at her home until the day of her funeral when Augustus would retrieve it and bring the body to the Baily home in Johnstown. From there, they would follow the typical procession through the town to the local cemetery just outside of it.

On Saturday morning, Augustus drove his wagon back up to Susquehanna Township and collected the casket.

On his way back to Johnstown, his wagon was click-clacking and making his teeth chatter as it had done when he was young. It reminded him of his brother.

Jefferson is probably laughing at me right now, he thought.

The road came out from the trees and began to run alongside a large pasture to the right. The sun was beaming down. Ahead was another road intersecting with the road he was on. It also came out of the trees on the other side of a pasture. Little Miss' buggy was on it. His wagon and her buggy were on a collision course.

His wagon reached the intersection two minutes before hers. Augustus' heart raced as he waited there, almost blocking her path. She could cut the corner and move into the grass if she wanted, but that would be strange. Thane was leading the mule with an angered expression and came to a stop five feet from him.

"You should get on outta here, Mr. True," said Thane.

Augustus ignored him. "We need to talk, Little Miss."

"She ain't gonna speak to you."

"That's fine. I'll speak to her. We's going the same way, and it's a long way at that. Shall we get started?"

Thane shook his head in disgust and continued down the road. Augustus kept pace alongside their buggy. Little Miss wouldn't turn her head to him.

"Little Miss, I understand what we did was wrong, but it ain't fair to keep the child from me. I'm her father, and it's cruel. I can't understand how you can't see it ain't fair to hold a child away from her father, just as it wouldn't be if I kept her from you."

"First off, I'm The Missus, not Little Miss no longer as far as you're concerned. And second, how'd ya know she's a girl?" she asked without turning.

"What's her name? Can you tell me her name, at least?"

"One thing I know for sure is that I would never name her," she turned her veiled head to him, "Rachel."

"So, you know about Rachel? Have you been spying on me?"

"She's jealous of ya, True!" called out Thane.

"You hush up, old man!" said Little Miss to Thane. She quickly turned to Augustus. "Ain't that the pot calling the kettle black!"

"If you recall, you sent me away. You agreed with your mother—"

"*Our* mother."

"*Your* mother. And I do recall you calling our union an abomination."

"It is an abomination, and we will be punished," she said as she turned to him and flipped up her veil. "You might even be punished for suggesting it ain't, Mr. Augustus True."

"So, since you're jealous, you won't be letting me see my daughter?"

"Your daughter's name is Dierdre," she said as she rolled her eyes.

"You're acting like a child!"

"I just told you her name, didn't I?"

"You should also be letting me see her and hold her and talk to her. I'm her father!"

"That ain't gonna happen," she said.

"That ain't gonna happen," Thane repeated.

"Why?"

"'Cause she can't ever know you were her father, that's why," she said.

Augustus looked down at the ground, dumbfounded. He

turned to her. "Well, then, I won't tell her. Easy as that. Or you could just explain I'm your brother. Easy as that."

"It ain't easy as that," Thane interjected. "Her momma won't agree. She don't want you around. She don't trust that nothin's gonna happen between you two. You can see that Little Miss is still jealous," Thane said.

"Hush up, old man!" Little Miss said, embarrassed.

"I've been camping overnight in the trees by your farm so I can watch…"

"I know ya been there. I seen things ya left behind."

"Does your ma know?"

"Your ma, too, remember? And no, she does not know."

"You can bring her out to me. Take her on walks and find me. I can spend some time with her."

"I don't know…" she said as she thought about it.

Thane turned to them. "Easter can bring her out to you. It ain't good having you two alone with each other."

"Hush up, Thane!"

"You hush up, youngin'!"

The wagon and buggy rode side by side silently for a mile or more.

"Fine, Easter will bring her out for ya. How often is this gonna occur?" asked Little Miss, resigned.

"Once a month, say the fifteenth unless it's a Sunday. If so, the sixteenth."

"Fine then. But this can't be going on forever. It'll be awful strange to be bringing out a twelve-year-old girl to the tree line to see some man she has no relation to."

"You're right. I guess we can cross that bridge when we come to it."

"Fine then. So, can you now go a bit faster, so we don't have to have any further conversation?"

"Certainly. Good day, Little… I meant, Missus. I know you didn't want to see me, but for my part, it was good to see your face again." He cracked his reins and pulled ahead. He looked back. "And, thank you for this."

AT THE FUNERAL, Augustus avoided contact with her and waited in other areas of the home so they wouldn't see each other. Luckily, the fifteenth of the month came around just ten days later, and Augustus patiently waited. He had arrived the night before and had camped like always.

He wanted to have the day with his daughter or, at least as much time as they would give him. Augustus watched the family come and go to the privy and complete their morning chores. The minutes seemed like hours with no sign of Dierdre. Finally, around midmorning, Easter came from the main house carrying her. Easter sauntered around, singing to her, playing with her, dancing around. She wasn't making a beeline straight to him, as that would be too obvious. Eventually, she made her way over, and as she did, Little Miss came out and watched her enter the trees with her arms crossed.

Easter smiled on seeing Augustus.

"Hello, Mr. Augustus," she whispered loudly, not to wake the baby.

"Hello, Easter." He excitedly smiled back.

Easter lay a sleeping Dierdre into his arms. She was magic;

a beautiful little girl with tiny hands, tiny feet, and a tiny nose. Her tiny fingers curled around his finger even as she slept.

Easter sat down next to him and smiled, watching his adoration of his daughter.

Dierdre suddenly opened her eyes. She had slate-gray eyes like her grandmother. Augustus could see himself in them, the person he used to be before he tripped and fell into the sad holes of life. There in her eyes was innocence and love, given and received. He felt an emotion he'd never felt before; a warm rush of love. Love for a little person he'd just met, the second after he held her. He'd do anything for this child. Even kill to protect her.

Easter also smiled down at Dierdre in his arms. She made cooing sounds to her, before turning back to Augustus' face. Tears were rolling down his cheeks.

"Oh, my!" she cried out, flapping her hands to stop the emotion. "Oh, no, boy, don't you be doin' that now!" Tears in her eyes, she turned in different directions as if she was looking for someone to stop her tears.

"I can't help it. She is so beautiful," said Augustus.

"I ain't never seen a man cry. Oh, my, oh, my ya gotta stop! Ya gotta stop!" Tears poured down both of their cheeks. Easter pulled her apron to her face, covering it as she cried into it.

Little Miss came running over, looking behind herself as she did. "Shh! Shhh! Stop that! I can hear you from the house!" she whispered loudly into the bushes.

Hearing her mother's voice, Dierdre's eyes grew wider, and she let out a wail.

"She don't know who I am," said Augustus.

Easter wiped off her face and took her from Augustus. "She's just a youngin' now," she said, still sniffling. "She'll get used to you. Now, she'll most likely need to be fed, so's I'd better get back. She'll last longer and longer with ya as she gets older," said Easter. Augustus watched her go, filled with a new emotion, a feeling he never had before.

AUGUSTUS MARRIED RACHEL in a modest ceremony paid for by Rachel's parents. Rachel stood out from the guests like a ray of sunshine through a cloudy sky. She wore a white satin dress with lace embellishments. In his life, he had become accustomed to seeing women in all black, and he was marrying one all in white.

With every step forward for his business, Augustus would invest back into the business by purchasing something or paying off something he owed. After only nine months, he was finally able to buy an enclosed hearse on payments. It was only two years old, good as new, polished satin-black with silver decorative lines, and each corner of the roof had a sitting eagle from which the ostrich feathers would stick out.

CHAPTER 47
Charlotte

We in spirit, Still live, love and commune,
With all on Earth

"I AIN'T SEEN ANYTHING like it, Little Miss." Easter sat on the porch step next to Little Miss. It was a late summer evening with the cicadas so loud it made it difficult to hear each other's whispers.

Charlotte stood just behind the door inside, watching them through the crack. She froze as they both turned back to the door as if they'd heard something. They sat shoulder to shoulder, but she could hear every word.

Easter continued, "Seeing a daddy's love of his child. It's the most beautiful sight. And he plays with her like no one's watching, making faces, acting the fool just to make her smile. It makes me laugh. I gotta cover my mouth."

"Maybe one of these times I'll come out and see it," said Little Miss.

A cold sweat formed on Charlotte's brow as she stepped back from the door. From then on, she knew she'd keep an eye on Easter when she watched Dierdre. Dierdre was now nine months old. She'd seen Easter walk into the woods with Dierdre many times but thought nothing of it.

The day came that she saw Easter whisper something to Little Miss and take Dierdre from her. Waiting until she was entirely in the woods, Charlotte went into the tree line farther south. Walking through the thick woods, she watched Easter work her way up to Augustus.

Charlotte stopped.

Augustus was seated, holding out his arms for Dierdre. Easter handed her to him, and she watched Augustus hold his daughter and tenderly touch her. Easter walked a distance away to give him his time alone.

The painful irony of it came to her, and Charlotte's face fell faster than double-struck lighting. He was in the same position she had been. By keeping the siblings apart, she had kept Augustus from his child in the same way she had been kept from Augustus.

DIERDRE WAS TWENTY-TWO months old, and Charlotte had learned that every fifteenth of the month was when Augustus would come. On that day, she'd pay more attention but never wanted to stop Easter from bringing out Dierdre. Her only desire was to keep the siblings from getting back together.

It was on a fifteenth of the month that Charlotte awoke early in the morning to Dierdre's baby talk from the other room. She put on a jacket and opened her door to see the back of Little Miss heading out the door with Dierdre. Charlotte threw on her robe and shoes and went to the door, peeking before heading out to follow her. Charlotte walked from pine tree to pine tree until she was about forty feet away and behind some scrub brush. She peered through and could see Augustus, asleep on a bedroll.

He must have come in the night.

Little Miss sat as she always did cross-legged, holding Dierdre. Dierdre's babbling woke him.

"Morning," she said. He rubbed his eyes and put on his specs.

"Morning, Little Miss, how have you been?"

"Smartly, I suppose. Heard you're married now," she said. Charlotte could hear a hint of longing in her voice.

"I am."

"Gonna have more children?"

"I hope so."

Little Miss looked sadly into the distance.

"What about you? Have a beau?"

"You know I'm a weeper. No man wants a weeper." Dierdre stood up and wobbled over to him. "She's walking since last time. Walking all the time now."

"How's my girl?" Augustus said to Dierdre as she smiled back at her daddy.

"I'll leave you," said Little Miss, rising.

"You don't have to. You can stay."

"I want to," she said as she strolled off.

Charlotte ducked low, but Little Miss took a different direction to a spot some distance away. She watched her daughter as she took a stick and dug in the dirt with it, the way Mr. True used to. She'd lift her head occasionally to watch Augustus play and chase the new walker. Dierdre screamed and laughed so loud that Little Miss looked around in fear. Charlotte had to cover her mouth to not laugh.

After a time, Charlotte spied a tear on her daughter's cheek. It was a terrible shame the three of them couldn't be a family. Even after the two years they'd been apart, she could see that Little Miss still loved him, and now he was married to someone else. Unlike past weepers, her daughter was more like her after all; she wanted someone to share her life with.

The art of weeping was disappearing, losing favor with the people. Farming and a few livestock were the only things keeping the farm going, and it was barely going. Leaving could help her daughter start a new life.

Augustus began missing his visits to the Fenn farm. His family life in Johnstown and his business kept him so busy that when the fifteenth of the month came around, it became difficult to make his appointments.

The times he could come, Augustus would apologize for missing the previous time. He could see in Easter's face that she was disappointed. Little Miss never came out again to the woods after that one time.

Augustus thought of her often, always curious about her and what she was up to. He would watch for her as he played with Dierdre.

One time, Dierdre ran out from the tree line, hoping her father would chase her, but he stopped. Little Miss came out of her house and saw Dierdre in the pasture in front of the tree line. She walked a few feet closer. Still, about a hundred yards away, Augustus could see her squint to try to see through the trees behind Dierdre. She knew he was there, watching her. Her hand went up for a small wave to the ghost behind the trees. She turned and walked back into her home.

As his life became more complicated, his visits to the Fenns became even less frequent until they stopped altogether.

CHAPTER 48
Augustus

In my end is my beginning

AUGUSTUS TRUE UNDERTAKER became Augustus True and Son Undertakers after the Trues had their first child. Rachel knew how much Augustus' brother meant to him, so they named him Jefferson. Ten months after that, he changed the name again to True and Sons Undertakers after they had another boy whom they named Nicholas after her father.

His sons were now five and six. He and Jefferson started beadling at six. Augustus was so proud of them that he expected they would want to be a part of the family tradition.

The new practice of embalming was becoming more and more common and more requested. Augustus added the new service to the company by hiring an embalmer. His mortuary would also supply other undertakers with embalming services.

Augustus added a casket-making shop, staffed with a skilled craftsman, an additional white hearse, a white child's hearse, two white ponies, and four black horses. His original horse, Daisy, had died. It was a sad occasion because that horse had been with him for so long. Daisy even let him sleep right up against him on cold nights when he was away from his warm bed.

Mr. Parker from Parker and Sons had passed on. His one remaining son, Joshua, did not want to run the business anymore and was planning on moving west. Joshua asked Augustus if he wanted to purchase the business, and if his company would do the honor of laying his father to rest. Of course, Augustus agreed to both. He arranged the entire funeral for no charge.

Augustus and Rachel had two daughters, Wendeline and Terry Ann, four and two, respectively. Augustus now had a family of four children: two sons, and two daughters, just as his father had.

The Trues moved just outside the town to a larger house that had a barn and corral for the animals. Rachel loved the country life, as she called it, even though they were only ten minutes away from Johnstown. Rachel still had all her friends, and the Trues entertained often.

Wendeline and Terry Ann were homeschooled, but Rachel and Augustus sent their boys to boarding school. Every summer, they would come back and work with their father in his business. Nicholas liked to help the casket maker in the shop, and Jefferson liked working with his father and dealing with customers. Wendeline was especially good at putting the makeup on the deceased.

SIX YEARS HAD passed since he had seen Dierdre. She would have been eight by now, and he thought about her often. He had no way to see her except to spy from the tree line again. He decided to send a letter to Little Miss and ask her about

Dierdre, hoping she might be kind enough to reply with some details about her. Instead of using the post, he sent a private courier to deliver the letter personally. He asked the courier also to take note of the place, as he was curious about the comings and goings and who lived there. The courier returned the following day.

"That farm is empty. No one lives there no more."

"No one? Not even a freedman and his girl?"

"All the buildings are empty. Few chairs and such, but that's it."

The following week, Augustus made the trip himself. Maybe the courier went to the wrong farm, even though he had described it precisely. Although the farm was just as he had described, he walked around and checked every room and cabin.

From there, Augustus decided to ride up to his sister's place. Glory's hair had since taken on some grey.

"Heard anything about the Fenns?" he asked.

"Why you little devil! Asking 'bout your old sweetheart."

"No, just thinking on it. Needed a weeper a time back. Sent a note up to the Fenns with no reply."

"I ain't heard nothing. Not many folk asking for a weeper these days."

"True enough. Only the older folk. I think the Fenns moved on; ya sure ya ain't heard nothing?"

"Moved on?"

"Yes. The farm is vacant."

"My, my. That family has been there since before time started. I didn't hear 'bout hide nor hair of 'em leaving or thinkin' on leaving."

Augustus rode home with the feeling he'd missed something in life. He regretted not seeing her and missing his monthly visits. Now he had no idea where they could be.

IT WAS CHRISTMAS of 1887, and Augustus was forty-four years old. They had the house decorated with red ribbon and wreaths. Wendeline and Terry Ann were helping Rachel make the meal of turkey with sweet bread and cranberry sauce.

Nicholas, now nineteen, was seated by the fire with his sweetheart, Ginny. Augustus enjoyed conversations with Ginny, as she was very involved with the women's suffrage movement and could hold her own in political arguments. Jefferson, now twenty, had been at university studying mortuary science.

There was a knock on the door. "It's Jefferson!" screamed Rachel excitedly from the kitchen.

Augustus rose to answer it. "He's knocking? University life must've given him manners."

Augustus could hear giggles and laughter from the other side of the door before he opened it. Jefferson stood, smiling and laughing. He was holding the hand of a young lady with beautiful slate-gray eyes.

"Father, I'd like to introduce you to my sweetheart, Dierdre."

Please show us a kindness and leave a review
of Weeper by Greg Morgan
on Amazon.com or Goodreads.com.

Thank you for reading
Weeper, by Greg Morgan.
If you would like to know more about the
author or the next two books in the
Death Shall Have No Dominion series,
please visit greg-morgan.com